SECOND HARVEST

SECOND HARVEST

Naomi Jacob

HLS

HUTCHINSON LIBRARY SERVICES/
HURST & BLACKETT

HUTCHINSON LIBRARY SERVICES LTD
3 Fitzroy Square, London W1

London Melbourne Sydney Auckland
Wellington Johannesburg Cape Town
and agencies throughout the world

First published by Hutchinson & Co (Publishers) Ltd 1953
Hurst & Blackett edition 1968
This edition 1973

Printed in Great Britain by litho on antique wove paper
by Anchor Press, and bound by Wm. Brendon,
both of Tiptree, Essex

ISBN 0 09 115000 0

To
Elsie and Doris
Waters

With Love and Admiration
Mickie

PART ONE

CHAPTER ONE

NOT even the most uncritical person could have called the street salubrious. It was badly lit by infrequent gas lamps, the road was sadly in need of repair owing to the heavy traffic which passed over it towards the docks, by day and often by night. Only one side of the street was built on; the other side consisted of a high tarred fence which overlooked the railway line. On that fence small handbills in a greater or lesser state of decay hung or flapped in the evening breeze. The shops on the other side of the street were mean, shabby places, with poorly dressed windows displaying dingy and shop-soiled goods. There were only two well-painted establishments—the Pride of the River, a public house very smart in red and light brown paint, and a shop which had been newly painted a bright and rather offensive shade of blue.

Before this shop, which in itself was not a place of any great size or dignity, a short, stocky young man stopped and stared. His rather highly coloured face was wreathed in a wide smile, and he eyed the lettering above the shop with satisfaction. It was his own handiwork, as was the painting of the window frames and the door. He read the statement that the shop was "Towers' Universal Stores", and below in smaller letters, "Ship Chandlers".

He stared in at the window, the only window, except that of the public house, which ever seemed to be cleaned in Bank Street. It contained a wide selection of goods; there were long, lightish grey stockings hanging on a rod, several pairs of high sea-boots, some dark blue jerseys, sea-mitts, and several sail-palms. In a small glass case looking very neat and smart were deposited cap badges of the various great—and local—shipping houses: Thomas of Liverpool, Turnbulls of Bristol, Millets of Sunderland, and the Britannic Line of Cardiff. Great names these, and, in addition, Moscrops of Whitby, Pickerings of Middlesbrough, Cutlers of Hull, and Grants of Seaham Harbour.

Amos Towers' smile widened. "Gives the window a proper classy luke."

He pulled down his waistcoat, and opened the house door at the side of the shop. It opened on a long narrow passage, the floor of which was covered with very clean and shining linoleum. There was a smell of dubbin, tarred rope, oilskins and sou'-westers, to which was added a faint but definite scent of hay. This came from the mattresses, stuffed with that substance known to the sailors as "donkey's breakfasts". There was also the smell of washing soap, sheets which were still in their state of pristine purity—and full of dressing—a hint of coarse tobacco and paraffin.

Amos was familiar with the smell, he regarded it as homely, and friendly. He threw his cap, a rather loud-patterned check, on to the hall stand, and for no particular reason shouted, "Dad, Mum, Ah'm back!" then walked along the passage and opened the door of the kitchen.

There, under a flaring gas-jet which added to the heat of the room, which was already considerable, were his father and mother. She was a short, stout body, with very smooth hair, and bright eyes. Not a handsome woman by any means, but immaculate, and with an expression which was kindly and filled with welcome.

Her husband, Abel Towers, sat in the large wooden arm-chair, with the cushion of red turkey twill, smoking a short briar pipe. He wore a fringe of grey whiskers, and had removed his coat. His feet were thrust into carpet slippers rather worn down at the heels with toes embroidered with a fox's head. They had been his wife's Christmas present to him in the first year of their marriage, twenty-six years ago.

He removed his pipe, spat accurately into the fire, and said, "Aye, we heard t'door shut. How does t'shop front luke, eh?"

"Tip top! Ah'm reit pleased wi' it. Only us and the public house seemly knaw what a lick o' paint does to a place."

Mrs. Towers said, "Nay, there's nowt but a slummocky lot here and hereabouts, that I will say."

Amos winked at her, a very friendly, pleasant wink it was. "We'll show 'em, Mum, won't we?"

"Why, if God wills, my son."

She was bustling about setting the kettle on the fire, and arranging the tea things on the white cloth for a last cup of tea. She, like her husband, always wanted things "shipshape and Bristol fashion".

"Nay, let it but be a bit bread an' cheese, it's no mower bother to set it out reit nor it is to slap it on t'table all of a muck."

Her husband said, "Any pickled onions, luv? I could fancy some wi' that bit o' cheese. Noo, Amos, you're luking like a cat as 'as had a good lap at the cream. What's up?"

Amos flushed. "Nowt," he said. "Ondly, I'm courtin'."

His mother set down the teapot heavily. "Nay, tha's never!"

He nodded, still smiling. "Nay, but I am so! Started this evening."

His father knocked out the ashes of his pipe. An observant onlooker might have noticed that he was careful not to soil the milk-white hearthstone.

"Let's be hearing," he said briefly.

Still flushed, Amos told his story. He had taken a walk in the park. It was a dreary place, where old men sat spitting at nothing in particular all day long, where noisy children played, screamed, and proved themselves to be the bane of the life of the park keeper. Amos, it appeared, had gone there for a walk, and had seen a girl, a most attractive girl, some distance ahead of him. It was evident that her shoes were hurting her, for presently she sat down on one of the seats, and kicked them off.

"I could see her wriggling her toes, like it was a reit relief to be rid of them. Then suddenly up rushes one of them young limbs of Satan, and offs with them. She give a cry, and I rushed forward. I told her I'd catch him, and gie him what for."

Amos caught the boy, cuffed him soundly, and returned with the shoes.

The girl was pretty, very neatly dressed, and thanked him with evident relief.

"Four and eleven I paid for them," she confessed, "and I doot if I'll ever be able to wear the nasty things."

"If you ax me, miss," Amos said, "t'heels is far ovver high."

"An' toes is ovver narrer," she added.

"Mind you, they're bonnie shoes, but I'd rather have comfort nor elegance, if you ask me, miss."

They had talked and presently he had discovered that she worked as general servant with Mrs. Clutterbuck, wife of the jeweller and watchmaker. They were nice folks, and treated her very well. She got good wages, ate "the same as the fam'ly", had one evening out each week and every other Sunday—evening and afternoon as well.

Amos walked home with her, and discovered that she was an orphan; her mother had died when she was three and her father two years ago. She was their only child, and was twenty-three years old. Her home had been in Wensleydale, "wheer they make the grandest cheeses you ever tasted". She didn't know many people. The servant at Mrs. Jackson's, "Jackson's the butchers in Stenningly Street", had been a friend of hers, but she was walking out with a young man called Charlie Smithers, and Ellen didn't see so much of her these days.

Amos said, "Why, it lukes as if you'll have to get a young man o' your own ter walk out. wi'."

She laughed. "Nay, I'm not a great one for makin' friends. I like to keep meself to meself."

He told his father and mother that he gathered up his courage, and put a bold front on it. He asked her if he might meet her on her next Sunday out, and take her a walk. He suggested that after a walk she might care to come back to his home and take tea with his mother and father. Mary Ellen Clothier, being a North Country girl, realized that this suggestion proved that Amos was not merely "laking", not only wishing for a chance walk, and the opportunity of snatching a few kisses and having a "cuddle". It proved that he was serious, and in taking her home to his father and mother he showed that his intentions were honourable.

His father listened to his story, then said, "D'you mean ter tell me as you've really got a mind ter this young lass?"

Amos, his pleasant face shining with embarrassment and pleasure, nodded. "That's reit, Dad. T'minute I set eyes on her, summat—as you might say—clicked. There's something about her—Mary Ellen Clothier's her name—that made me feel prop'ly *good*. You'll know what I mean, Muther. Wholesome, that's what she is—wholesome."

"Why, fetch her here," his father said. "Let's have a luke at her."

His mother added, "An' don't expect me ter pervide a gert, big tea. There'll be nowt that's not just simple and homely, think on, our Amos."

"That 'ul suit me, Muther," he said, and winked at his father.

Mary Ellen was excited. She had never "walked out".

True, there had been lads in her own village who had hinted that they found her attractive, who had danced with her at the village dances, and had escorted her home to her father's cottage when the festivities ended. But as she said to herself, "That had been t'start an' finish on it." Now, this pleasant-looking young man, wearing good clothes, who had so gallantly rescued her shoes from those horrid lads, had made it quite evident that he found her very much to his liking and that he wished to see more of her. In her small, meticulously tidy attic room, she peered at her face in the small, rather spotted mirror. It wasn't a bad kind of face, she decided. Her skin was smooth and carried a pleasant colour, her hair was a light, warm brown, always very smooth and neat. She wished that she were a little taller; her father had often said that she was "nobbut a slip of a thing". She was plump, but not fat. She thought sometimes that with her brown hair and neat little figure she was rather like a partridge.

Anyway, the nice young man—his name he had told her was Amos Towers—seemed to want to see her again, and he had asked her to go to tea at his home, to meet his father and mother.

Sunday came, and Mary Ellen was conscious of a slight sense of excitement. At three o'clock she had everything "sided away", had washed and changed into her best dress, a dark blue merino with small white cuffs and collar. Her hat was dark blue too, with a nice crisp bow and two small white roses. She eyed the new shoes, debating if it was worth while to be smart at the expense of comfort. Rather regretfully, she turned from them and put on her good, well-polished but eminently sensible shoes.

As she ran down the stairs, she called, "I'm just goin', m'm."

Mrs. Clutterbuck called back, "All right, Mary Ellen, enjoy yourself."

"Thank you, m'm."

He was waiting at the end of the road. Mary Ellen walked sedately towards him, and they met and shook hands. She decided that he was even nicer than she had thought. He looked so clean and well shaved, his clothes were good, and he carried a pair of dogskin gloves in his hand. He no longer wore a cap, but a well-brushed bowler. She decided that he looked a perfect gentleman, without being in the least "dandified".

Amos said, "Why, I am glad to see you! If I may say so, you luke real nice. That dark blue suits you prop'ly well. Now, it's a tidy step to our house. Can you manage that far or shall we wait while a tram comes?"

"Nay," she said, "I'd enjoy the walk. It's kind of your muther to ask me."

He laughed. "Eh, she wants to see you. It's the first time I've ever brought a young lady home—and I'm twenty-five!"

"Don't you like young ladies?"

"I don't know about young *ladies*, I know that I like *a* young lady very much!"

As they walked, Amos explained to her about the shop, warming to his subject. He told her about his hopes and plans for its expansion. At present it was a small business, but even now he had painted it up, added new lines, and they had to go less and less frequently to buy from Harris, the big chandlers.

"You see, we don't aim—at least we've not aimed up to now—to carry expensive things, like sextants and the like. If we're asked for them, either Dad or me slips round to Harris's and gets one. I'm going to change all that, and shortly too, mind me!"

They walked through the rather dreary streets, passed the ugly Town Hall, along towards the station, where dirty children and equally dirty bits of paper whirled about in the little wind. No one could have called it a handsome town; it looked as if it had been put together in haste and carried with it a sense of impermanence. Nevertheless it was already a rich town, and it proved the truth of the Yorkshire saying, "Wheer theer's muck, theer's money."

Amos pointed out the buildings of note. "Yon's the Willingbrough Conservancy. That there's the County Club, wheer all the gentry go—I've never bin inside, but I'm told it's something worth seeing. That building there's the Cambridge Music Hall. It's a bit rough, but they get some good talent. Dan Leno once danced there. That house wi' the brass plate is where our doctor—Willis—lives. He'll never get fat on what we pay him—we're all as strong as what horses are."

She said all the right things when they reached the shop. She admired the blue paint, she stared at the goods displayed in the window, pointed to the cap badges and said they looked pretty enough to make into brooches and suchlike.

Amos opened the door, and as he hung his hat on the rack, called, "Mum, Dad, I'm back, here's Miss Clothier."

They were sitting in the front room, both looking slightly uncomfortable in their best clothes. Abel wore a tightly buttoned blue reefer coat, and had retained his collar and tie; his wife wore a dress of black alpaca, with a small black satin apron embroidered with forget-me-nots. The dress was fastened at the neck by an immense pinchbeck brooch, which had belonged to her mother.

Amos said, "Well, Mum, well, Dad, this is Miss Clothier." Then, turning to Mary Ellen, he added, "This is my Mum and Dad, two of the best ever."

Mrs. Towers said, "Pleased I'm sure. Sit down, Miss Clothier. This is only a very simple home, but there's a kind welcome for you."

Abel nodded. "We may be rough, but we're always ready to greet a pretty young lady. Our Amos hasn't given us a treat like what he's giving us today before. Not like us old sea-dogs, with a wife i' every port, eh? Slow and steady is our Amos."

Mary Ellen asked if Mr. Towers was a sea-faring gentleman. He might have answered with truth that he had never been further than Hull on a trawler, and that had caused him such sea-sickness that he had lain in the scuppers and prayed loudly and fervently for death. It was his delight to pose as a "proper old salt".

"Sea-faring?" he exclaimed. "The Seven Seas is like a buke to me! I know every inch on 'em. Steam and sail, what we call 'square-rigged' or 'windjammers'. Sail's goin' out. Soon there'll be no sailing ships left. Sad, very. Lovely things the old clippers, them what used to make the runs from China with the tea for the markets. Aye, at that time tea was six shillings a pound, but mark you, it was tea, not the blash wot we get now."

"You must have seen some strange sights, Mr. Towers."

"I b'lieve you, m'dear. I've seen sights as would curl the hair on your pretty head, so's it 'ud never lie down again. Savages—man-eaters, head-'unters, war-dances which I could never explain to you, m'dear, as what they do—them savages —isn't fit for a lady's ears—nor eyes, come to that. I like ter think as I was one o' them as planted the British flag on which the sun never sets, in parts wheer never white man 'ad trod."

Mrs. Towers interrupted him. "Well, come on and plant yourself at the table in the other room, for tea's ready. Now,

Miss Clothier, you mustn't luke for a grand set-out like what you see at Mrs. Clutterbuck's. It's all simple and homely. Now, Dad, get moving."

Mary Ellen really liked the kitchen better than the stiff and formal front room. She admired the shining grate, noticed the geraniums which stood on the window-sill, and the truly astonishing enlargement which hung over the mantelpiece. It depicted Mr. Abel Towers, wearing a peaked cap, and a tightly buttoned reefer jacket. He was leaning against what appeared to be a hanging lifebuoy, which bore the inscription, "H.M.S. *Majestic*". In the distance waves in a great state of agitation could be seen. Mr. Towers held a very large telescope under his arm, and stared fixedly in the opposite direction from the stormy seas.

She said, "Oh, Mr. Towers, was that taken when you were at sea?"

He smiled tolerantly. "No time for takin' photers aboard the old *Majestic*! The Admiral 'ud have had a fit! Certainly he'd have had me put in irons! No, that is what the French call a Sooveneer—that means a kind o' remembrance, a keepsake as you might say."

Mrs. Towers said briskly, "Siddown, Miss Clothier, please. Now, Amos, will Miss Clothier have some cold 'am, or a bit o' veal-an'-'am pie? All cooked at home, m'dear, and though I says it as shouldn't, my veal-an'-'am pies—well, taste a bit and see."

Mary Ellen was accustomed to Yorkshire teas, but she thought that she had never seen a more generous one. In addition to the cold ham, the veal-and-ham pie—how perfectly cooked, the pasty looking so glossy—there were meat patties and sausage rolls. There was a fine plum cake, some small fat rascals, an open jam tart and a plate of ginger biscuits. "It's all simple and 'omely," Mrs. Towers assured her, "but it's all wholesome, and made i' the house."

"Muther's a famous cook, Miss Clothier," Amos told her.

"Nay, I can see that, Mr. Towers. I'm reckoned not too bad myself, but I've never made a veal-and-ham pie like this. It's wunderful."

He longed to tell her that he thought her wonderful. She sat there looking so nice, eating so prettily, being so attentive when his father embarked on one of his long and completely untrue stories. It had long been agreed upon by himself and his mother that if it pleased Dad to tell "fairy tales", well, what did it matter? It pleased him, and hurt no one, so what harm was there in it? Amos watched Mary Ellen's bright, intent face as she listened to a story of how the elder Towers had been shipwrecked in mid-Atlantic, and when all hope was abandoned they managed to climb on to a great iceberg which came floating past. There they found hundreds of sea-birds' nests. The eggs saved their lives, until they were picked up by the great trans-Atlantic liner, the famous *Britannic*.

"Treated like dukes, we were. Captain couldn't do enough for us. In fact he insisted on me havin' his cabin. Like a palice it was. Made me wear his best uniform. He wore his second best all the trip."

When Amos walked home with Mary Ellen, he knew that he was in love. He found himself listening intently to her voice, thinking what a pleasant voice it was; she was so neat, her figure so trim. More, she had opinions of her own and did not hesitate to voice them. They had argued together, happily, as real friends can.

As the weeks passed his feeling for her became both clarified and stabilized; he wanted a home which she would share, he wanted to show her that he could—and would—make a success of things. Amos Towers had ambitions, plans and dreams which he intended to make realities.

It was Mary Ellen's annual holiday which made it clear to him that the time had come to speak openly to her. Mrs. Clutterbuck was a good mistress and, as such, granted her servant a whole week's holiday each year, and, in addition, paid her wages. Mary Ellen had an aunt, Mrs. Sophia Baines, who lived near Middleham. She was as excited as a child, for Mrs. Baines held a great place in her affections. She spoke to Amos of her; of the "nice tidy little house", of the garden where syringa bushes and lavender and rosemary grew. She told him of the great tabby cat, Thomas, and the little dog called Tiny.

"Eh, and the view's something luvely. You luke out of the window an' it seems as if all Yorkshire's spread in front of you. Great wide fields, with dry stone walls; little hills, rising slowly to the moors, where you can see the sheep cropping away, luking for herbage to eat. I've heard say that our Yorkshire sheep have to search for their living, in the South it's all there spread i' front of them. Farmer Haynes as lives near my

auntie says as our sheep would kill themselves in a week with
over-eating if they were set to graze on what they call—the
Downs."

Amos said, "It all sounds luvely. I'll"—he stumbled over
the words—"I'll miss you, Mary Ellen."

He saw her pleasant face flush. She said, "Why, I'd been
thinking how I'd like to show you the place. I leave on Monday
morning, and—well, why not come over on the Sunday, spend
the day, and we could both come back together—Sunday
evening? D'you think that's a good plan, Amos?"

"I think it's a grand plan, an' I think as you're the grandest
lass i' the world for having thought it all out. Will I come!
Nay, don't be daft, lass, I'll be thinking of nowt else all the
week." He caught her hand in his. They were sitting in a field
among the fresh grass, with the scent of meadowsweet round
them, and a lark singing high up in the blue. The peace of a
Sunday afternoon was everywhere.

Mary Ellen said, "I could tell when it's Sunday, even if I'd
no calendar nor nothing. There's an extra peace about Sundays.
It's not only that it's quiet—there's summat else, a kind of
holiness."

Amos nodded. "Aye, it's nice, isn't it?" Then, still holding
her hand, he said, "Luke, I'm coming next Sunday to see what
this place is like, to meet your auntie. . . . Eh, I hope she'll not
turn against me—and then when we get back, 'appen I'll ask
you to come and see something." His voice sounded almost
as if he spoke of a wonderful dream, Mary Ellen thought.
"It's a house, aye and it's mine. I've bought it. It's in Aislaby
Street, number sixteen. They're new houses; every one has a
bathroom, and a nice kitchen grate and a good copper. Both
me and Dad and Mum are tired of living i' Bank Street—
anyroad, I've ideas how to use the rooms. They're coming to
live at number twenty, Aislaby Street. They'd have room
enough for me, but I said I wanted a house of my own."

She nodded. "A house of your own, eh?"

"Aye . . . I mean a house as belongs to me. I don't want to
live there alone. What 'ud you think of coming to live there—
with me, Mary Ellen?"

She repeated, "To live theer with you——"

"That's it—Mr. and Mrs. Amos Towers. My dear, I'm
asking you if you'll marry me, I love you with my whole heart.
Until I met you, I'd no thought much for girls. I never went

walking wi' a girl until I met you. I can't give you luxury—not yet," he added with emphasis, "but I can give you comfort—and luv. What d'you say, my dear?"

She looked at his kindly, fresh-coloured face, which wore a slightly worried expression, saw his clear, steady eyes, and his firm mouth. She drew a deep breath, then said, "Nay, Amos luv—of course."

"D'you luv me, Mary Ellen?"

"I allus have done, ever since you clouted that bairn's lug for running off wi' those pinching shoes o' mine. I only thought the other night—I've never worn them again, they're just lying i' my cupboard, but it was the best value for four and eleven I'm ever likely to get."

He slipped his arm round her and drew her close. "Luke at that," he said softly. "You buy a pair of shoes, they don't fit—and it changes everything for you, for me. Nay, the ways of God are strange, eh?"

She nodded contentedly. "That's it—they're past finding out, as the Bible says."

Amos saw her off on the Monday morning. His last words to her were that he'd be at Middleham station the following Sunday morning, by the train that left at ten o'clock. He added, "And mind, I'll be fetching an engagement ring an' all. Luke, I've fetched what they call a ring card. See which size it's got to be. Aye, that's right. I'll mark it with a pencil cross, so as I'll not mix your size with the size of the other lassies I'll be offerin' rings to."

She said, "Nay, Amos, give over! What a road to talk!"

That evening he walked down to Clutterbuck's, and, scarlet in the face, asked to see some engagement rings. Clutterbuck, a mild, hard-working little man, who was already a Town Councillor and had visions of the day when he would be Mayor of his native town, bustled about making great play with the keys of his safe.

"Just in time, just in time," he assured Amos. "I was on the point of closing the—er—establishment for the night. Yes—for the night. So you are contemplating matrimony, eh? Here we are!" He laid a tray of neatly displayed rings on the counter. "It might—er—simplify matters if you gave me some —er—some indication as to the—well, the amount you wish to spend on this ring. Yes?"

"I'd like to spend five 'undred pounds. I can't. But I can

and will spend twenty. I want something nice, to suit the young lady who's going to wear it."

Twenty pounds. Clutterbuck blinked his eyes. The young man was quite decently dressed, but he had expected him to ask for something round about seven or eight pounds. Twenty pounds. He picked up the tray and put it back in the safe, saying, "Ah, something better than those—yes, quite. A trifle more—shall we say—elegant? Now, here you are, sir." Clutterbuck often said that courtesy cost nothing, and paid dividends. "There's a sweetly pretty ring. Pearls—yes, pearls."

Amos shook his head. "Nay, my muther warned me against pearls. She says they mean tears, like what emeralds mean jealousy. Now, yon's pretty. What do you call them?"

"Indeed, it is pretty. Those, sir, are turquoises, four of them as you see, each with a small diamond to make the effect more brilliant. Turquoise, diamond, turquoise, diamond. A nice setting, modern and yet elegant. The ring itself is eighteen carat gold, the best gold made."

"And the price?"

Mr. Clutterbuck, inserting a watchmaker's glass into his eye, peered at the tiny ticket. "The price is fifteen pounds and twelve shillings. Shall we say if you like—fifteen ten? The size? Oh, you have a card? Prepared I see for all eventualities, sir. Very wise, very wise. Yes, the size is correct. Allow me to place it in one of our velvet cases; very attractive it looks, very. May I wish you every happiness, and hope that —when the happy day arrives—you will give your bride a wedding ring purchased from Nathaniel Clutterbuck?"

Amos counted out the money, grinned and said, "Why, I'd not be surprised. I don't feel, however, as your good lady 'ul feel too friendly disposed towards me." He laughed at Clutterbuck's astonished face. "I reckon as I shall be taking away from her t'best worker she's ever had, or is ever likely to have, choose how. Aye, my name is Amos Towers, and this here engagement ring is for Miss Mary Ellen Clothier. I'm seeing her on Sunday. Stayin' with her auntie, she is, at Middleham."

Clutterbuck stared at him. "So you're the young man. Towers—will that be Towers the ship's chandler? It is? Well, well. Yes, we shall miss Mary Ellen, but you'll get a fine wife, Mr. Towers. I should like you to know that it is my custom— yes, custom—to present the buyer of every wedding ring with a case of very fine plated tea-spoons. In your case"—he laughed—"there will be no exception to the rule. In fact, Mrs. Clutterbuck and I shall be happy to add our small contribution to the—er—wedding gifts."

Amos pocketed the little velvet case. This was one of the Town Councillors; no wonder they talked so much and got so precious little done in the Council Chamber. Lot of windbags! Still, you never knew when a Town Councillor might come in useful in business.

"We'll be pleased to see you and your good lady at the wedding. I'm sure that I'm speaking for my young lady. Good night, and many thanks."

The little velvet case was taken out many times during the coming week. Amos liked the feel of the velvet under his fingers, liked to take out the ring, move it so that the little diamonds caught the light and seemed to wink back at him. His father and mother both admired it, and the following Sunday morning he departed for Middleham, assuring his father and mother that he wouldn't call the King his uncle nor the Queen his aunt!

His mother said, "God bless you, my dear lad. Gie her our luv."

Abel nodded. "Aye, a neatly built little craft, trim and seaworthy. I wish you both a fair wind and a flowing sea!"

Mary Ellen met him at the little station at Middleham. She thought that she had never seen a man who looked better. His clothes were lighter than those he usually wore; he had a red rose in his buttonhole, and his straw hat was encircled with a band of red-and-white ribbon. He wore a heavy gold watch-chain stretched across his waistcoat, and from it hung a very elegant tiger's claw, mounted in gold.

She felt suddenly shy. This well-dressed, elegant and delightful young man was to be her husband. During the week she had tried to tell Aunt Sophia of his charm, his cleverness and his complete integrity.

The old lady had listened, and said finally, "Nay, Mary Ellen luv, ha' done. I'll see him o' Sunday, and I'll judge for mesen, sitha. Luv sees everythink through rose-coloured glasses."

And here he was at last, holding her hand and leaning down to kiss her cheek, saying, "Eh, Mary Ellen, lass, it's bin a damned long week!"

"Bless you, it's nice to know you've missed me. What's that you're carrying, luv?"

He laughed. "I'm carrying plenty o' cargo, as Dad 'ud say. Something for you, my dear; this 'ere's a veal-and-ham pie Mum made for your auntie."

On the way home, Mary Ellen walked through the village conscious that many eyes followed them, and many voices whispered, "Sitha, yon's Clothier's lass, Mrs. Baines's niece. She's gotten herself engaged, an' b' t'luke of him, she's done well for hersen. He's a likely-luking lad."

She pointed to a neat little house situated just out of the village. "Yon's my auntie's cottage," she said.

Amos nodded. "Aye, now first, let's get our bit of business done. Come over by this gate." He set down the veal-and-ham pie with great care, then slipped his arm round her. He gave her the little blue velvet box. His heart was hammering with excitement. "Take a luke at that, luv."

She opened the box, and gave a little scream of delight. "Oh, it's luverly! I never saw anything so pretty. See the road the diamonds sparkle in the light. Amos—it's over-good for me, it's too grand."

He took the ring and slipped it on her finger. "One day," he said a trifle heavily, "you'll think nowt on this ring, not when you wear the diamond rings I'm going to see as you get— i' a few years, my dear luv."

She said, indignantly, "This will always be the most wonderful ring in the world, never mind whatever others you give me. There's only one other ring I really want from you, Amos luv. That's one with no stones in it." She flushed and smiled at him.

"It's arranged for. Me and Councillor Clutterbuck had a long confab about it. They're coming to the wedding, they're giving us a wedding present, and wi' the wedding ring we get a case of tea-spoons. So, you've not got to 'break the news' to Mrs. Clutterbuck when you get back—she knows all about it. They think a lot of you, Mary Ellen."

"Do you—think a lot of me?" she asked.

"Nay, I think of nowt else, my dear. That's the truth."

CHAPTER TWO

THE following week Amos took her to see the house. Mary Ellen was delighted. It was so new, shining and clean; everything was so conveniently placed, and the fact that it contained a bath seemed to her to put the final seal of elegance on it. The Clutterbucks had a bath, she told Amos, but it was nothing nearly so nice as this one.

"I know the chap as did all the plumbing in Aislaby Street," Amos said. "Jimmie Bannister he's called. He says that every bit of piping, all taps and so on, is the best to be found. Josiah Cummins, as built the whole road, built to sell, sitha. He's a keen chap is Cummins, and he knows as he might be able to sell rubbish, stuff held together by the paint as you might say, to some of the nobs who want to live outside the town on that new estate as they're building there, but he'd not catch working folk as know the value of every shilling with trash like what some of them new villas is. I' ten years' time I shall be able to sell this house for more'n I gave for it."

Mary Ellen said, smiling happily, "I'd never want to leave this dear little house, not was it ever so."

He put his arm round her and pulled her to him. "Aye, my lass, but you will! You're not going to spend the rest o' your life in a little house with two bedrooms and a little slip of a room. No more am I! I've got ideas, plans. Just wait while I get going, my luv."

The weeks which followed were filled with excitement. There were nights when Mary Ellen could scarcely sleep because of the thrilling things which kept happening. Aunt Sophia Baines came over from Middleham, and announced that she was taking Mary Ellen shopping. Amos was having dinner with them, it being Mary Ellen's day off, and Mrs. Clutterbuck had said generously, "Nay, I'll see to the dinner, Mary Ellen. Off you go with your auntie."

"Can I come an' all, Mrs. Baines?" Amos asked.

"Nay, that you can't," she replied. "We're buying the linen. We don't want a young chap trailing round wi' us, choose how."

"Can I meet you for tea at Longton's 'Kafe'?"

"Aye, why not? That's different. Make it half past four. We'll be reit thrang while then."

Mary Ellen almost gasped at the lavish way in which Aunt Sophia bought: sheets, including two pairs of linen sheets smooth as satin; pillow cases, small towels, bath towels, even bath mats to stand on when you finished your bath; bed covers, and an eiderdown covered in a lovely shade of blue satin on one side and blue sateen on the other; glass-cloths, dishcloths—there seemed to be no end to the things which her auntie regarded as necessities.

"Auntie," Mary Ellen said softly, "I've a bit of money put by. I don't like you spending all this on me."

"If you've a bit o' money saved, you keep it, my girl. And as for not liking—why, you mun lump it, that's all! It's my pleasure. I've no daughter to spend me brass on, and Walter Baines left me very comfortable—very comfortable. I'd not wonder if you find yourself comin' in for a tidy bit one day, and the cottage an' all."

After that brief interlude Aunt Sophia went back to her orgy of buying. Blankets, soft and fleecy. Mrs. Baines commented as she rubbed a corner between her finger and thumb, "Aye, that's a reit bit o' stoof, that is. I'll lay it's Yorkshire wool, that is."

Shining, glossy table-cloths, table napkins to match, tray-cloths, "Though I reckon there'll be plenty given you as weddin' presents. I've a goodish few at home. I'll sort them out for you. Let's have a couple o' nice duchess sets, miss, for the dressing-tables. Might as well do the thing reit while we're about it. Noo, table-cloths for the kitchen. You'll not be havin' meals i' t'best room every day."

By the time they joined Amos at Longton's "Kafe", Mary Ellen felt that not even the Queen of England possessed finer linen.

Eating a great deal of Longton's famous Dundee cake, Amos said, "Aye, and you're not done yet, my luv. Dad and Mum's meeting us at Hobhouse's at a quarter past five. They want to give you *their* wedding presents."

Mrs. Baines asked with a slightly acidulated tone, "Who said as I'd been giving our Mary Ellen her wedding present? Standing i' t'place of her poor muther, I've done nowt but pervide t'linen same as all brides' muthers does. My wedding present I'm keepin' to meself. She—aye, and you, for it's for both on you—'ul get it nearer the day."

"That's very handsomely said, Mrs. Baines," Amos assured

her, and his tone of sincerity removed the slightly disapproving expression from her kindly face. "Dad's givin' us the furniture for the front room, an' Mum's givin' us the suite for the best bedroom."

So again Mary Ellen's head whirled, and she stared at the furniture, and thought that it was the most beautiful she had ever seen.

They were married from the Willingbrough home of the late Walter Baines's widowed sister. The honeymoon—Amos could only spare three days—was to be spent at Scarborough. "The Queen of Watering Places," old Towers told them with as much pride as if he had built the town himself. It wasn't a big wedding, for the Towers had not many friends. Amos was attended by his friend, Jimmie Bannister, as best man; Mary Ellen was given away by Farmer Holme, a lifelong friend of Aunt Sophia. Councillor and Mrs. Clutterbuck graced the ceremony with their presence, and returned to the wedding breakfast. There the wedding cake, made by Aunt Sophia, and Mrs. Towers' gigantic veal-and-ham pie were much in evidence. Abel Towers made a speech which he had rehearsed for days, which was received with great applause.

"These two folks, so loved by us all—for already Mary Ellen is like what a daughter might be to me an' my wife—are setting out on a voyage which we all trust may be a long and prosperous one. True, they may run into squalls, they may be buffeted by the winds and tempests of life, but one thing I know full well—neither of them will ever be held fast in the doldrums! They may crowd on a bit o' canvas, but I'll lay it will never be too much, and they'll keep the barque to her course all the time. With their charts to show them the right road, with their compass to direct them to the safe harbour, they'll do all right. So here's to that nice little seaworthy craft—just launched, and ready to sail the Seven Seas and back again—Mary Ellen Towers, coupled with the name of the pilot she's taken aboard—my son, Amos."

Jimmie Bannister whispered to Mrs. Clutterbuck, "Not much that old sea-dog doesn't know about the sea, eh?"

She replied, "He seems a very clever old gentleman. I can see how my husband, the Councillor—a very fine speaker himself—appreciated that speech."

"Have you seen the wedding presents?"

"Indeed I have. The silver tea service from the bride's aunt is magnificent, and that canteen of cutlery—I may tell you that came from my husband's establishment. Mrs. Baines ordered it especially."

"The vases"—he pronounced the word "vazes" as is customary in Willingbrough—"are very handsome."

"Our gift, my husband the Councillor's and mine, to the happy pair." Mrs Clutterbuck was obviously gratified.

The bride and bridegroom departed for Scarborough.

The minute Mary Ellen saw the hotel she knew that she wasn't going to like it. Not that it wasn't a good hotel, it was admirable, it was too good. Their bags, which had seemed adequate and even smart, seemed to shrink before the eyes of the majestic hall porter. The corridors were too long, the carpets too thick, there were mysterious bells and switches in their room, and neither of them dared to press or move them for fear it brought an army of servants.

Amos stared round their bedroom, whistled softly, and said, "Why, it's summat like, this is, eh?"

"It's—it's over-grand, Amos luv."

"Let's have a luke at the bathroom, eh, lass?"

They entered the bathroom and stared. Today any young couple would take such a bathroom for granted, or possibly declare that it was old-fashioned. To Amos Towers and his wife it appeared immense, luxurious and a little awe-inspiring. He whistled again. "That mahogany must take a bit o' polishing. Ah, well, it's all an experience. We'll only have one honeymoon."

The three days passed slowly. They walked on the Spa—known to them as the Spaw—listened to the band, watched the pierrots, and Amos told Mary Ellen that quite probably some of those young men wearing white suits and "dunces'-caps" might one day be famous.

"Nay, I doot they're famous now," she objected. "I'll bet they get a lot of money. Mind, they're reit clever."

One night they went to the theatre, where they saw a wonderful play called *A Royal Divorce*. It was a touching and exciting play. Amos said that it fairly carried him away, and Mary Ellen shed tears over the unfortunate Josephine. The days were filled with excitement, but as Mary Ellen packed their bags she sighed with relief. She was thankful to be returning to their own home; their own life seemed to offer sufficient excitement without coming to Scarborough to look for more.

So in 16 Aislaby Street they settled down, and Mary Ellen found life very pleasant and not in the least difficult. Old Mrs. Towers always "popped in of a morning", bringing something she had cooked, a cake, a pie, a pot of jam or marmalade. They got on well together; they agreed that never was a man so hard on his socks as Amos, but that to make up for it he was as tidy a man as ever stepped.

Amos found life very good; he loved his home, revelled in the meticulous way in which it was kept; he enjoyed the good food which his wife prepared for him, and he was immersed in his plans for the store. His father was tired of business, and confined his visits to Towers' to three mornings a week. He had never been an ambitious man, and he was content to leave all improvements to his son.

"So long as you don't run us into debt, get the old ship into dangerous waters, do what you like. Mind you, I'd like to see us make profits, but so long as we dean't lose—I'll say nowt."

Amos nodded. "I'll see as we don't lose, Father. Whatever improvements we make, they mun pay their way—or I shan't mek' 'em."

The rooms which his father and mother had occupied he turned into additional storerooms. To the stock he added a number of tinned goods, small additional comforts, more things that sailor-men might need for shore wear—smart socks, ties and the like. He added paper and pens, bottles of ink, and blotting paper; for the use of such lads as might be studying seamanship, cases of dividers, compasses, protractors, and books dealing with nautical theory. He interviewed travellers, bought carefully, making limited purchases until he saw how "the stuff moved".

He came home in the evening and recounted these things to his wife, who listened and thought what a wonderful man she had married.

"My word," she said, "you've got a reit headpiece!"

He laughed. "Nay, luv, I'm only just started. Tell me that i' another five years, an' I'll show you something worth seeing."

Their first son was born fifteen months after their marriage. They were both consumed with pride, for the child was a very lovely baby. Old Mrs. Towers declared that she had never seen anything like him, and his grandfather prophesied that one day he was destined to walk the quarter-deck wearing the uniform of an Admiral of the Fleet.

"He must have a real luvely name, Amos," his mother said. "Don't think I'm unkind. I luv the name of Amos because it's yours, but I don't care a lot for Abel."

"I don't care for either on 'em if it comes to that. There's precious few Bible names as I do like." He considered. "He's a grand bairn an' he ought to have a reit good name. How about Victor? Victor Harold Towers, that sounds all right."

Mary Ellen beamed at him delightedly. "Victor Harold Towers. Oh, Amos luv, it's a noble name! That's what it is— noble."

The child grew and remained a handsome little boy. Eighteen months later his brother was born, and, although not quite such an outstandingly handsome child, was exceedingly good looking, and sound in wind and limb. He was christened—and again the choice of names was left to Amos —Wilfred Ronald Towers. Mary Ellen was delighted.

Business was good. Amos was still planning to add new lines, and had put in a new shop front; on the façade was painted "Towers' Ships Stores. The small shop with the big reputation." His father often walked down to Bank Street for the sheer pleasure of admiring the handsome front, the shining window and the glossy paint.

"Mind last time you painted it, lad," he said.

"That's right, Dad. No time to do things like that myself now. Too much work i' t'shop. Never been so busy."

When Victor was five years old the war clouds gathered in South Africa. A great wave of inflated patriotism swept over the country. True, there were a few people who doubted if— for once—Britain was completely in the right, but in general the attitude of the Boers was stigmatized as impudent and untenable. Cecil Rhodes was a national hero, "an Empire builder", at a time when the British Empire loomed large on the world's horizon. Dr. Starr Jameson was regarded as being the epitome of British pluck, and when his Raid failed, the sympathy of the public was with him.

The young German Emperor rushed in with his telegram of congratulation to President Kruger, and the whole British Empire felt its fury rise. It was said that the Prince of Wales, always a popular figure, experienced exactly the same anger as the man in the street.

Men rubbed their hands, told stories of how the Prince had always disliked his nephew, how the young German had always detested his uncle, had referred to him as "that old peacock". Old peacock indeed, to refer in such terms to the man who had made the British almost popular in France!

"Like his b—— impudence!" was the general feeling.

Who were the Boers? A handful of Dutch farmers, badly dressed, wearing outdated beards, content to be guided and governed by an old man who looked like a decayed Nonconformist preacher—Oom Paul Kruger! The whole thing was incredible; something must be done. Either the Boers "behaved themselves" or Britain would make them! Anyway, a war with that handful of peasant farmers was nothing. No one in his senses could regard it as a full-sized war. They must learn their lesson, and that lesson could—and would—be taught very quickly.

The young men of England, the Yeomanry, the volunteers, were wild to go the instant that war was declared. It was going to be a glorious adventure, "over by Christmas". Amos had his doubts. He had all the Briton's pride in the Regular Army, he believed in Roberts, Buller and Kitchener with his whole heart, but somehow—he doubted.

He wanted to do what, in his sight, was right, patriotic and decent, and yet when he heard of men rushing to enlist his heart misgave him. His father was growing old; true, his mind was as clear as ever, but apart from his three mornings a week at the store, he visited the Wellesley Arms, where his stories of the sea had become a feature of that hostelry's smoke-room. Not that Abel Towers was a hard-drinking man, but he enjoyed company, and it flattered his vanity to have someone call, "Cap'n Towers, tell us of the trip of yours round Cape Horn, that one you made in a windjammer."

Amos heard of men going "to the Front", read the progress of the war, studied the articles of a new journalist, G. W. Stevens, and felt less certain that the whole thing was going to be a "glorious picnic". There was a phrase that stuck in his mind, a phrase which Stevens had written, "and the Army Corps had not yet left England". He read the poems of Rudyard Kipling, and felt increasingly that things were not going to be too easy. Something about, "All along o' muddle, an' all along o' mess"—it didn't sound good to him. When England went to war there should be neither muddle nor mess.

Yet what was going to happen to the store if he joined the Army? Had he to go and see the structure which he had built so carefully totter and disintegrate? He was a careful and clear-thinking young man, he loved his wife, his children and his business, but he had a definite pride in his country, coupled with a rigid sense of fair play.

England, the Empire, must be defended for the good of the British people, indeed for the good of the whole world, Amos argued, and how could he stay at home, unexposed to danger, while other men fought, suffered and died? He rumpled his hair in his distress, muttering, "Nay, say what you like, it's not jannock. I'm not going to sit back and let other chaps do the work, it's not my way."

That night, when he had finished the admirable supper which Mary Ellen had cooked for him, he pushed back his chair, lit his pipe, and stared at her with his pleasant, clear eyes.

"I doubt as I shall have to join up, my luv," he said.

"Nay, they'll take the unmarried chaps first, my dear. No hurry for you, with a wife and two bairns. You're thirty past, plenty o' younger fellows nor you can be better spared."

He met her eyes very steadily. "I don't know as *anyone* can be spared," he said gravely. "We're in it up to the neck, never mind what these softies say about it being over by Christmas. Not it! Not t'Christmas after that neither. I'm no flag-wagger, Mary Ellen. I don't want to leave my home more than what the next chap does. But . . . I'm damned if I'm going to play for safety while other chaps gets killed. No, if they want me, they'll not need to come and *fetch* me. I've over-much pride to let 'em do that, choose how."

Amos went to the recruiting office the following morning. Mary Ellen watched him go, with tears streaming down her face. He looked so smart, so well set-up; he walked so briskly with his shoulders squared and his head erect. Of course they'd take him, they'd be daft if they didn't.

He returned in time for dinner, his face white with fury. He could scarcely speak, but flung down his hat on a chair and muttered, "Lot o' damned fules, that's what they are!"

"Amos luv!"—for he rarely swore, particularly as now

young Victor picked up everything and was certain to begin saying "damned fules" when the opportunity offered. "What t'ever's happened?"

He glared at her, his face suffused with rage. "They won't take me!"

"You're not ill? Oh, my dear, don't say as you're ill!"

"Ill—nothing! Seemly, I've got flat feet. Me wi' flat feet! That's the first I ever heard of it—flat feet! And I've got a hernia."

"What t'ever's a—'ernia? Is it dangerous? Oh, Amos!"

"It's what folks as talk plain call a rupture, that's what it is. I've got to go to t'doctor an' get a truss. Will I? Not me! I'm wearing no such contraption, nor belts and suchlike. Or I can have an operation. I can see myself. I've had it ever since I was a bairn, it's nothing but a little lump, it doesn't pain me, and it's never grown i' all these years." He added, still sounding like a sulky child, "What's for dinner? Hanging about i' yon recruiting office has made me sharp set."

"Steak-and-kidney pudding, an' it's just ready. Now, never mind, my dear, it's God's will, and there's no use of you upsetting yourself."

His anger flared up again. "Aye, an' when chaps say, 'Not i' uniform, not going to fight, not doing anything when your Queen and Country need you,' what am I to say? 'Sorry, chum, I've got flat feet and a hernia'! Nice that 'ul sound, eh? 'Flat feet and a bloody hernia'!"

She said sharply, as she lifted Victor into his high chair, "Luke, any more of that temper and bad language, Amos, and I walk straight out. Be'ave yourself!"

"I'm sorry, I'm upset, Mary Ellen."

"Aye, well eat your dinner and you'll feel better."

He picked up his knife and fork. "Happen I will," he said. "Happen I'll not!"

She noticed, however, that he ate with an excellent appetite and accepted a second helping.

Nothing more was said about the matter, but Mary Ellen —who adored her husband—knew that he was depressed. She knew him, as she herself said, like the palm of her own hand; she had studied his moods, knew when he was elated, when he had suffered some trifling set-back in business, and now she watched him, lynx-eyed, sensing that this depression was growing and strengthening.

He would come back from the store and sit slumped in his chair.

"Aught wrong, Amos luv?" she would ask.

"Nowt, not really. Fred Monkhouse has gone."

"Fred Monkhouse? Not dead!"

"No, dead, no!" impatiently. "Joined up. Off to train for the Army."

Mary Ellen thought long and deeply. She was a healthy young woman with a healthy appetite and sufficient energy for two. Now she studiously denied herself "second helpings", pleading the excuse, "Nay, somehow I'm not hungry these days, luv." At night she would sit, her hands lying on her lap, and sigh.

"I ought to be getting on with my mending. There's young Vic wants new stockings knitted against the Winter. Somehow, I feel that tired! It's not like me."

Amos watched her, as she had watched him, carefully, anxiously. Surely she was thinner; her cheeks were less rosy than they had been. He suggested that she took a tonic, but she shook her head.

"Nay, it's just worry, luv."

"Worry? What have you to be worried over, my dear?"

"Why, if you must know, Amos—I'm worried over you. It's the thought of that hernia of yours."

"Why, there's nowt to worry about over that!" he exclaimed. "Lots o' folks have them and never gie them another thought. Why, I thought you'd more sense, Mary Ellen, I did really."

"Happen you don't hear all I hear," she replied. Her tone was portentous and even sinister. "I heard summat this morning as flaid me, Amos luv." Under her breath, she whispered, "Dear Lord, forgive me for the lies I'm telling!"

Amos leaned back in his chair, and smiled at her. "Let's hear the latest gossip about hernias," he said. "Come on, out with it."

"In Perks this morning, two women were talking. One had a friend; seemly, her husband—this friend's husband—had a hernia. She'd begged and begged him to have it seen to—it's nothing much if it's taken in time." Her emphasis on the last words successfully removed the smile from Amos Towers' face. "He put off and off, and suddenly summat went wrong. They rushed him to the Infirmary, operated—but it was over-late."

"He died, eh?"

She nodded. "That's it. Now that put the cap on it, as you might say, Amos. You've got to have that operation, while there's time. Never mind telling me that it never bothers you. When it does start to bother you—well, it might be over-late."

"Aye," he said sobrely, "lukes as if I'd better."

He went to talk to his father, who persisted in recounting the awful operations which had taken place at sea, when there had been no surgeon on board, and the only means of rendering the patient unconscious was to make him completely drunk on rum.

"Have it done, Amos lad," he counselled, "have it done while you're in calm water, wi' everything you can want at hand. Aye, Mary Ellen's right. Into the Infirmary wi' you, lad."

It was then that his mother asserted herself. "Infirmary— nowt o' t'sort. All right for folks as haven't addled a bit of brass. We *have*. We can pay, and we ought to pay, choose how. Get yourself off to that Dr. Trevick. He's young but they say he can pretty well cut your head off and stick it back as good as ever. He's gotten a nursing home. You're our only son, you've gotten a bonnie wife and two nice bairns, and it behoves you to take care of yourself."

"It 'ul cost a mint!"

"Nay, it won't. And if it does—we'll find the brass somehow. Now, i' t'morning, think on, Amos."

Dutifully he answered, "All right, Muther. I'll see to it."

So in due course Amos Towers was admitted to Dr. Trevick's nursing home and operated on. He came round declaring that he was very hungry and was inclined to be annoyed when he was refused food and merely given a cup of weak tea.

"If my wife gave me tea like yon," he told the nurse, "I'd have something to say—nobbut blash, that's what it is, blash!"

When Mary Ellen came to see him, having left Victor and Wilfred in the charge of their doting grandmother, he was visibly excited.

"Doctor says I'm champion," he told her. "Says he's never had a healthier chap on his operating table. I was a bit dowley yesterday, but this morning I had tea and toast and a lightly boiled egg. Mind you, they don't half luke after you i' this place. I'm having some chicken for my lunch, and potatoes and veges. I was only just i' time, for the doctor's off to the Front any day now. I said as I wished I could go and all. He laughed—very pleasant, larky kind of chap he is, nowt standoffish about him. He said, 'Nay, I doubt if they'll want you, with that scar, and those flat feet of yours. You stay where you are, my lad, and be thankful not to be in it. It's not going to be a picnic, I can tell you.' So now, if anyone's got anything to say to me about my Queen and Country needing me, I've got my answer. And I'll give it to them and all."

Mary Ellen walked home, well content. Any danger was over; Amos need have no fear concerning the wretched hernia, but what mattered most in her eyes was that he "had his answer" to give anyone who dared to imply that he was shirking. She confided, under oath of secrecy, to Mrs. Towers the elder. The old woman listened and nodded.

"You were right, Mary Ellen, perfectly right. Mind you, I'm glad as our Amos has had this operation, but it 'ul stop all yon depression and bad temper. Whiles he thought as he ought to go, he were nursing a grievance. Now he's got t'doctor's word as he can't go, and they'll not want him—he'll be a different chap."

"Men is mostly thick-headed. You've got to hammer things into them before they understand. It's cost a bit. Amos 'ul have to be a bit careful of hisself for a while, but—it's money well spent."

Amos returned home, he made faces when he lowered himself into a chair. When the weather changed he put his hand to his side and said, "This weather tickles up the old scar. T'doctor told me as it might." On the whole he was very cheerful, his appetite improved every day, and Mary Ellen watched over him as she might have done over an ailing child.

He began to walk abroad every day, and came back with long stories of the smart retorts he had made to men who had asked, "When are you going to join up?" In these encounters, Amos's wit and readiness of retort had always routed his questioners, leaving them "luking very soft and silly".

In the early days of 1900 he met Dr. Trevick, who was home on leave, and asked him if there was any chance that "they" might take him for the Army.

"Mind you, I've been lucky, Doctor. I don't say as I've not made money during the war. I have, and I've made it honestly. I'm not ashamed of doing so. Ondly, now things do seem to be dragging out a bit, and——"

The doctor laughed. "You think that you might just turn the tide for us, eh? Come up in the morning. I'll run the tape over you, but candidly I don't think they'd ever pass you for active service, Towers."

The doctor shook his head. "You can risk it, see if they'll take you, but I know the medical wallah, and I assure you that I shall warn him against accepting you. Sorry, Towers, I applaud your wish to go, but you would be a liability, not an asset. That's my honest belief."

Amos sighed. In years to come it would have been pleasant to tell Victor and young Wilf how he "did a bit of soldiering", but, after all, a live dog was better than a dead lion, and he must make the best of it.

His store had prospered during the war, he had been forced to employ two assistants and a boy with a bicycle, which had a little truck attached, to deliver goods. Mind, it was a shame; poor old Josiah Harris had three sons; they had all been fine young chaps, and had gone overseas very soon after the war started. Two of them hadn't come back. They said that their loss had broken their mother's heart. The third son had been discharged after months in hospital. He had had enteric, and even now, though he was working in his father's store, he looked pale and thin, and his cough was terrible. Yet, here was Amos, better off than he had ever been, with a lovely wife and two bonnie sons—people stopped to stare at the boys when Mary Ellen took them out. Victor was so tall and straight at six years old that folks took him for eight or nine. Wilf was only four and a half but sturdy, with a mop of dark curling hair, and a tongue which "went like the clapper of a mill".

The war ended, petered out. The Boers had been clever—tricky, many people preferred to call them—and finally that indomitable little soldier, Lord Roberts, had been sent out to "clean up".

He was "Bobs" to everyone, and he set to work to rout out all the snipers, the commandos, and the elusive members of the Boer Army.

The old Queen died before the war ended. Her passing

marked the end of an era. Speculations ran rife. "What would the German Emperor do now?"

Amos said, "Do? What the devil can he do?"

Some of the "clever-clevers" wagged their heads. Charlie Masset said that there was "something called the Salic Law" which made it possible for a man to inherit through his mother.

Amos said, "Who's muther? The Kaiser's muther?"

Charlie nodded. "His mother was the eldest daughter o' the late Queen, named after 'er—Victoria. He might try it on."

"Aye, like the Boers tried it on! Where's it landed them?" Amos snapped, "Lot o' rubbish. We want no more wars. This 'un's been enough. Thousands dead, thousands ruined for life, millions o' money spent. Nay, let's leave wars alone."

He said to Mary Ellen, "Aye, it's over—bar the shouting. We've won the war."

She nodded. "Now we'll see what they do about winning the peace, for peace takes some winning same as wars do, Amos luv, think on."

"Happen," he agreed. "In fact, I seem to remember a bit of poetry I learned at school—'Peace hath her victories, no less renowned than war'—that's bearing it out, eh?"

It was early in December when he received a letter from Josiah Harris asking if he would call and see him. Amos showed it to his father, who gave it as his opinion that the breeze was freshening, though from what quarter and in what direction he couldn't rightly say.

Amos was surprised at the solid dignity of Josiah Harris's office. His own was strictly utilitarian, a very plain and highly varnished roll-topped desk, office chairs, one or two filing cabinets, and, for no particular reason, a map of the estuary of the river, and a plan of the docks—the latter very much out of date.

Here he found Harris installed in a fine swivel chair, behind a handsome, leather-topped desk. The walls were half covered with very elaborate lincrusta, the rest in expensive and rich-looking wallpaper. There were two large leather arm-chairs, and a carpet which was thick and heavy, its colours being dark blue and a fine red. There were several pictures of well-known steamers hanging on the walls, and over the mantelpiece a splendid colour print of the famous *Cutty Sark*.

Harris held out his hand. "Glad to see you, Towers. Sit

down. Let me offer you a drink—no? A cigar then—I can
recommend these. Now, I wish to talk business. To make myself
plain. This war has completely changed my life, the life of my
dear wife and the life of the only son it has pleased God to
spare to us. I will not enlarge on the whole tragedy—you
probably know it."

Amos nodded. "Aye, it was terrible. I can assure you, sir,
that the whole town sympathized with you and Mrs. Harris."

"Everyone was most kind—most kind. Now, if my remaining son, poor fellow, is to retain any semblance of health, he
must live in a warmer, more temperate climate—we had
thought of taking him a long sea voyage, and then settling
in either Bournemouth or Torquay. Perhaps you see what
this is leading to, eh?"

"Why, the business, I suppose, sir."

Harris nodded. "Exactly—the business. I can't take it
with me. . . ." He gave a wintry smile, and Amos felt a sudden
rush of personal sorrow for the man who had built up this
prosperous concern, and through the "bludgeonings of Fate"
was forced to leave it. "I don't believe in employing a manager,
and that would involve my coming up here to pay periodical
visits. I don't wish to do that. My memories of the place are
too painful—my fine lads . . . George and Francis, gone; and
Clement a shadow of his former self." The old voice shook
suddenly.

Amos said, "I do understand, sir, and I am sorry. I'll do
anything to help if I can."

Harris recovered himself. "Thank you, Towers. I doubt
if I can offer you the business—to sell it that is. Its value
would, I can state honestly, be far more than you could afford.
I have no doubt that you could raise the money, although
money is fairly tight at the moment. What I should prefer—
prefer—would be that you should run the place, use your
initiative and pay me a yearly percentage of the profits. Take
the stock—as it stands—the building—the goodwill—in fact—
take the lot! Pay me thirty per cent of the profits, a lump sum
to be agreed upon later, and at my death pay the same to my
son Clement."

CHAPTER THREE

AMOS returned that evening to Aislaby Street walking on air. Harris, the biggest, most important ship chandler in the district, had offered him his business! Somehow or other he must take advantage of the offer. This was what he had worked for, this was where he became not merely the owner of "the little store with the big reputation", put the part owner, at least, of the great firm of Harris and Son. This was where he moved from Aislaby Street to one of the splendid new villas on the outskirts of the town. His sons should go to the best school in the district. Mary Ellen should go to the best shops for her clothes. They would visit the theatre every week, and he could imagine telephoning for his stalls:

"Your usual seats, Mr. Towers?"

"That's right—my usual seats!"

As he entered, the manager, the great Harrison Blacker, would come forward, beaming. There might even come a time when Amos himself would wear a white shirt and a dinner jacket!

"Hello, Towers, how are you? Mrs. Towers, always pleasant to see you."

"Hello, Blacker. Hope it's a better show than last week."

"Tip-top show, old man. You're going to enjoy it. Meet me in the bar at the interval, won't you?"

"If it's a good show I'll stand a round; if it's a bad one—you will."

Laughter, possibly the statement that he—Amos Towers—was a caution. Mary Ellen smiling as they slipped into their seats. "You're a one, Amos, you are really. You know everyone."

"Or everyone knows me, eh?"

By the time he reached home, he had, in imagination, become a Town Councillor, was practically one of the Aldermen, and in the running for Mayor. Mary Ellen called as she always did, "That you, Amos?"

He replied, as he invariably did when business had gone well, "It's me. Who were you expecting, eh?"

The two little boys were seated at the table having their tea. Amos kissed Mary Ellen and the children. He asked if

they had been good, and listened with grave interest to Mary
Ellen recounting their behaviour for the day.

He removed his coat, hung it in the passage, and sat down,
heaving a slightly overdone sigh.

"Tired, luv?"

"No, not all that." He was debating whether to blurt it all
out, or to assume the air of a man who has faced dozens of
problems, the solution of which involved the loss or gain of
millions. He decided to be calm, slightly calculating, and
completely unmoved. "No, not all that tired. I went round
to see poor old Josiah Harris this afternoon."

Mary Ellen nodded sympathetically. "Poor man, and they
say as the only son left is a delicate, waffley kind o' lad."

"Aye, that's so. Clement's the only one left. They're
thinking of going to live in the South—Bournemouth or
Torquay."

"And what about the business, Amos?"

"Well, the business—eh?" His tone was studiously unconcerned. "Ah, the business. Well, he thinks of giving that
up, getting rid of it."

That startled her. "Never! Giving up that great business!
You never say!"

"Why, selling it, I mean. In fact, that's what he wanted to
see me about. It's on the cards as I—with Dad's help—may
take it over." He added hastily, "Nothing's settled, o' course.
I've got to talk it over with Dad. But I was Harris's first
choice as you might say."

She stared at him, and he made a great effort to sip his tea
in an unconcerned fashion, as if buying Harris's business was
nothing out of the ordinary. He watched her. Her eyes were
very bright, her lips parted. What a bonnie lass she was, and
how he'd glory in giving her all the nice things she'd love.

"Aye," he said, "I was the chap he picked on first."

At last Mary Ellen spoke. "Amos! You to run Harris's!
it's—why it's almost a shock, my dear. That great business,
all them clerks, an' vans. That great building! Nay, it seems
impossible."

He shrugged his shoulders and took a second piece of the
open tart of which he was so fond.

"It's not settled as yet. I must talk it over tonight with
Dad."

She watched him, her eyes filled with admiration. "You

take it all so calm like, as if things like that happened every day. Oh, Amos!"

That evening, when he talked with his father, Amos realized that he had allowed himself to be carried away with the unexpected grandeur of the idea of running Harris and Son. His father listened, grunted from time to time, and rubbed his chin.

When Amos ended his recital, conscious that his self-confidence was slowly diminishing, his father spat with great accuracy into the fire.

"That all?" he asked.

"That's as far as we got wi' the discussion today, Dad."

"Aye, an' a damn sight far enough, if you ask me. Thirty per cent! He's gone mad. Thirty per cent—you've got to pay him, per annum, then to pay his son, and when you're dead an' gone, Victor or Wilf 'ul have to go on paying for all evers. Nay, Josiah Harris were never be'ind t'door when cheek an' imperence weer given out, I'll say that."

"He's prepared to let us down lightly on the stock——"

"Like 'ell he is! What's he doing? Makin' a sale or makin' a investment? If it's a investment, he mun tak' risks. I don't see much risk about thirty per cent. Noa, my lad, noa, and damned well noa again. You're over-headstrong, Amos. Have you seen the stock? It's the finish o' a war. I'll lay as stock's low or lowish. What about t'goodwill? Can he guarantee that? Has he any contracts—signed, sealed and all shipshape and Bristol fashion? What about t'building—leasehold or free-hold?"

Feeling more and more like a small boy, Amos said, "Why, Dad, we didn't have time to go into all that. He just said five thousand down and thirty per cent."

Old Towers nodded. "Aye, he opened his mouth all right too. If the stock's right, goodwill and all t'rest of the items in order, we'll pay him ten thousand. Down! Aye, Muther and me can raise that, and what we're short on, Mary Ellen's aunt 'ul be glad to find. Ten per cent per annum, while the takings —net takings, sitha—is under five thousand a year. Once they're over five thousand—which will have come about owing to your work, your ability, your sense of seamanship as to how to steer the ship—that ten per cent drops to eight. That's the firm offer o' Towers—father and son. Harris can tak' it or leave it."

Amos said, "He'll leave it. I bet you a bob he'll leave it."

"And I'll bet you two bob he'll tak' it. Happen he'll hum and haw, mak' objections, raise difficulties, but—you'll see."

And see he did. The following day, he and his father went to see Josiah Harris. Old Towers was dressed in his best double-breasted jacket, his fringe of beard was thrust forward almost aggressively, and his peaked cap which carried the badge of some unknown steamship company was worn at a defiant angle. He carried his blackthorn stick with the silver band on which was engraved S.S. *Monte Video. Nil desperandum*.

Amos said as they walked from their own store to Harris's office, "Now don't be too hard, Dad. Think on the poor fellow's had a lot of trouble."

His father stared at him. "The fac' as he's had trouble won't sell an extra pair o' sea-boots, will it? 'Soft words butter no parsnips'—I'm sorry for him and his missus, but I'm here to talk business, not cry me eyes out."

When they got to Harris's store he gave his instructions to the chubby-faced office boy.

"Tell Mr. Harris as Cap'n and Mr. Amos Towers are here— by appointment."

While they waited, he straddled his legs wide, and swayed slightly as if standing on the deck of a pitching ship. He stared round him, at the desks, the great ledgers, the massive pewter inkpots, the maps which hung on the wall, and delivered his verdict.

"A well-found craft this, my boy. Trim and tidy, every-thing prop'ly stowed. Looks seaworthy."

They were taken to the handsome office, where Harris was waiting for them. Abel Towers removed his cap, and laid it on the wide mantelpiece. He caught sight of the fine picture of the *Cutty Sark* and nodded his approval.

"Brings back mem'ries," he said. "What mem'ries to be sure!"

Harris said, "You sailed in her, Captain Towers?"

"Not 'er. Sister ship. Laid alongside o' 'er, time and time again. But I've come to talk business, and if you get me started on the old days o' the tea trade and the wool trade . . . we'll be 'ere all night. Let's get crackin', Mr. Harris. Now this is, as you might say, just a kind o' clearing the decks for action, not the action itself, eh?"

Amos sat and listened. He was astonished at his father's

grasp of detail, of his knowledge, and most of all at his tenacity.
Amos had always regarded his father as being less astute than
himself; on this particular afternoon, he wondered how he
could have made such a mistake.

Harris said, "Then I take it that you dislike the payment
of five thousand, Captain Towers?"

"I do. Spoilin' the ship for a happorth of tar. I prefer to
make it ten thousand, sir."

"And the yearly percentage?"

Amos tried to listen attentively, telling himself that this,
after all, was his business as well as his father's, but the two
heavy voices running on and on, arguing quietly yet firmly,
made him feel numbed and dull. His attention wandered, try
as he would to keep it fixed on the matter in hand. From time
to time snatches of talk reached him, or a phrase came clearly
and distinctly.

"Thirty per cent is ridiculous—fer meself, I'd not trust
any investment as reckoned ter pay mor'n fifteen. . . ."

"A unique opportunity, Captain Towers. Unique opportunities are met with very, very seldom."

Again the mental fog descended, and Amos let himself
drift into the pleasant mazes of speculation. He would have
denied, and denied forcibly, that he was either romantic or
imaginative, and yet, sitting here in the well-furnished office
of Josiah Harris, he was dreaming dreams concerning the
future. If they pulled off this thing there stretched before him
years of work, hard work, even anxious work—but the work
which he loved. He had developed their own store successfully;
he had evolved various systems of book-keeping, stock-
taking; he had made careful and accurate calculations as to
how much might be put aside every year for improvements.
Each year had seen some new addition, some new venture,
some new scheme which should increase the reputation and
efficiency of their store. He weighed up everything, refusing
to allow himself to be merely attracted by some new lines
unless he could justify such a proceeding completely and
entirely.

He had seen the stock-rooms at Harris's; he had returned
to his own store suffering from an acute sense of envy. He had
seen lines displayed which were complete, a full range, for
example, of sea-boots of all prices. Here there would be no
"I'll see if we've your size i' stock. . . ." Automatically each

size *was* in stock. He had launched out into a small stock of tinned goods, but there again he had frequently to answer, "No, sorry, I've plenty of pineapple, but I'm out of tinned pears."

He had often stood at the door of his own store and watched the captains of steamers walk past—on their way to Harris's. One or two of them knew Amos, and nodded to him in a friendly fashion, even passing some flattering remark about the look of his store.

"Never behind in making improvements, eh, Towers?" Or, "Keep this place of yours fine and dandy."

He'd smile and say, "Glad you think so, Cap'n Anderson," or, "That's how I like it, sir." They were pleasant, affable, at odd times they had even come into his store, spent money, praised the goods, but—and that was what always spoilt his pleasure in those sales—they came to him because they had forgotten to buy what they wanted at Harris's, or because it was too late to go there.

"I'd never consent to thirty . . ." His father's voice cut into his thoughts, followed by the crisper tones of Harris.

"It requires thought, Captain Towers, considerable thought."

"Admitted, oh, aye, admitted. This is just a kind o' trial trip."

Mechanically Amos said, rather too loudly, as if to show that he had been following the whole argument closely, "Absolutely. We'll have to have our respective lawyers meet, eh?"

The two elder men turned and nodded. Harris said, "Oh, quite."

Amos went back to his dreams.

Imagine sitting here, at that fine, solid desk, with its polished leather top, in that impressive chair. Imagine rising to meet some important captain.

"Ah, good morning, Captain Cartwright. Hope you've had a good trip." And a few moments later, after compliments had been exchanged, "Now, Captain, what can I offer you? I've some good dry sherry. My kind friend, Captain Bartlet of the *Cleveland Lass*, never forgets to bring me a case. Just name it, Captain—sherry, whisky, brandy—decent French brandy—or Bass! It's all here."

Then, cigars lit, glasses filled, sitting there, notebook and pencil before him, flinging out hints from time to time to spur the captain's memory. Routine stuff was dealt with by the Superintendent of the Line, but there were all those additional things, the prices of which swelled the accounts so pleasantly.

Other dreams. "I've started a new venture, Captain. Yes, tailoring. Got the finest cutter north of the Humber. Polish Jew, a wizard. He made a suit for me. My wife says I've never had such a suit in my life. You've not met my wife, I think? Why not come up for a bite of dinner one evening? You, Captain Cartwright, and Captain Wilson—as you're both in port together. The Laurels in Freemoor Avenue."

At the close of a deal, offering a little present. Nothing ostentatious, a bottle of good French scent, a few pairs of gloves from Genoa, a nice Indian shawl. Nothing that could offend in any way, just a friendly bit of appreciation. He sighed; the prospect was wonderful.

"Well, I think that's as far as we can go, Captain Towers. The main thing is that there appear to be no insuperable difficulties. I see your point about the percentage, and taking into consideration the increased amount you are prepared to . . ."

Amos moved impatiently, and glanced at the clock. They had been here for nearly an hour! Talking, talking, talking. Then they'd meet again and talk some more with lawyers shoving their spoke in. He didn't care, he had made up his mind. If old Harris's demands were too stiff, if he turned obstinate—well, let him! He, Amos Towers, would take the thing on. He didn't care how hard he worked, what hours he worked, he was going to have Harris's. All right, if it was hard going for a few years, he'd face that, and so would Mary Ellen. If they couldn't move into a lovely big villa, very well, they'd stay where they were for a bit. Aislaby Street was quite comfortable.

His father was droning on about trial trips and maiden voyages, about cargo and freight, stowing this and that away, and Harris was listening and nodding. Amos shook himself fully awake and stood up. He hoped that his voice didn't shake.

"Well, Mr. Harris, we've taken up a good deal o' your time, but I think we've clarified several points." He thought, "Don't anyone ask me what they are, for I haven't an idea. I only know that I'm going to have Harris's."

Harris nodded. Old Towers said, "We certingly have cleared

the deck fer action, my boy—me and Mr. 'Arris. Now all we want is a long pull, a strong pull and a pull all together, eh?"

Harris said, "Exactly. I'll make an appointment with my solicitor and let you know. Then we'll meet and you'll bring your solicitor with you, eh?"

"Eggzacerly. Now it only remains ter say—adoo, as they say in French."

As they left the building, Towers said to his son, "I reckon as I steered a pretty straight course, eh? He 'ummed an' 'awed, but he'll take fifteen per cent all right, and on that slidin' scale as I tole you about last night. No use shouting "Ome again' before you're into port, but between you an' me, Harris's Store is in our pockets. The rest 'ul only be, as you might say, formalities."

Amos went back to Mary Ellen; he felt that he was walking on air. While exercising his Yorkshire caution, he made no rash statements, did not even speak outright about his intense desire to own Harris's, he did allow himself to talk to her about "what might happen". That evening when he kissed the little boys good night, he knew that his eyes misted over. They were going to have everything that he could give them. He stared at their two bright little faces—Victor so fair, so pink and white, Wilf, darker and rather more heavily built—and for a few seconds allowed his imagination to have full rein.

"Bless 'em, they shall have everything. Go to lovely schools, wear real tailor-made clothes, and one day both o' 'em shall marry girls as grand as the one I managed to get." He caught them into his arms, held them close, whispering, "Just wait, my little, lucky lads, just wait."

There were consultations with solicitors, meetings with Harris, but never again did Amos Towers allow himself to sink into the semi-somnolent state which had overtaken him during that first interview. At all future interviews he was, as he told Mary Ellen, "on my toes".

He insisted on taking his friend, Jimmie Bannister, over the building, and Jimmie, for his part, insisted upon various repairs, replacements and replannings.

"Nowt much," he told Amos, "but it 'ul show them as we've our eyes skinned."

It was Amos who insisted on a complete stock-taking, and who was surprised to find that Harris's fell short of his expectations. Possibly since the death of his two sons, Harris

had become disheartened, tired, disappointed, and in con-
sequence had allowed stocks to dwindle.

Amos told Mary Ellen, "Not that I care. Between you an'
me an' the gate-post, some of his lines are out of date. Good
enough, but old-fashioned. I've smarter, more up-to-date stuff
in my own place. No use carrying such a stock o' sea-mitts
that the wool's half rotted before you sell 'em. No use carrying
a great stock o' ditty-boxes. I' these days the chaps i' the
fo'castle have lockers and suchlike. Sail's goin' out. There'll be
no more six-month voyages, when they had to spread a sail
to catch a drop o' rain water, and then it was 'all hands to the
wash-day!' Think on this, luv, there wasn't a scrap of sea-
water soap i' the place!"

Before the negotiations were complete, Aunt Sophia Baines
departed this life, having contracted pneumonia, and pneumonia of the particularly deadly type indigenous to the
district. Except for a small legacy to her widowed sister-in-law
—who was well provided for—and a sum of money to buy a
memento to her friend Holme, who had come to Mary Ellen's
wedding and had given her away, she left everything to her
niece.

Mary Ellen and Amos went over to the funeral. The day
was grey and cold, and the long scarves of mist trailed across
the hills. While there was no rain, the trees in the village
churchyard dripped steadily. Friends and distant relatives
followed the coffin through the lych-gate, up the narrow
path to the old church, the men looking stiff and awkward in
their Sunday suits of black, the women with their faces buried
in black-bordered handkerchiefs. The vicar walked before
them, his surplice hanging limp and dank in the heavily
moisture-charged atmosphere.

At the grave-side the clay was heavy and unbelievably
cold. The acid tang of fading flowers and evergreens reached
Amos's nostrils as he stood, his hand under Mary Ellen's
elbow. The earth scattered on the coffin fell with a rattling
sound like distant gun-fire. Mary Ellen sobbed miserably.

Then it was over and they walked back down the village
street to the pleasant cottage where Sophia Baines had lived
her useful, bustling life. As the door was opened the sudden
rush of warm, well-heated air assailed them.

Amos thought, "This is more like it. I hope when my time
comes folks won't stand about in the damp, getting their

boots clarty while they lower what's left of me. The old lady's still a lot more *here* than she is i' that dismal churchyard."

Tea was laid in the bright, cheerful kitchen, prepared by friends of Aunt Sophia who had denied themselves the pleasure of going to the churchyard, in order that everything might be "done decently and in order".

As he carved the exquisitely cooked home-fed ham, Farmer Holme said, "Why, this is a sad day—a bit o' fat, Mrs. Huddlestone? I never thought as my kind friend, Sophia Baines, 'ud jine 'er Maker afore I did. Mrs. Wilki'son, will you take 'am or a bit o' chicken, or"—with sudden if carefully suppressed jocularity—"a bit o' both? Aye, the ways o' God are past findin' out. One thing I do know, an' it's this. My old an' trusted friend, Sophia Baines, couldn't stand folks bein' miserable. She gave perticlar instructions to Mrs. Baker an' Mrs. Fothergill as she wanted everyone to have a reit do. Mrs. Baker, Mrs. Fothergill, am I k'rect?"

"Indeed you are, Mr. Holme."

"Nothing truer, Farmer Holme."

"Then let us do our best to abide bi t'wishes of the dear departed."

After that everyone certainly brightened considerably, and although there was no undue and undignified merriment, the guests allowed themselves to smile at some of the stories of the Dales and the moors which Farmer Holme recounted.

Mrs. Baker, going to the front door, returned to announce that Lawyer Jackson had arrived, that he was being regaled with sherry and some of the excellent plum cake in the front room. As soon as was possible, he would like to read the will, to those selected to hear it.

Mary Ellen said, "Oh, Amos, come wi' me, luv. And you, Mr. Holme. And you, Aunt Willis. We'll not be a minute longer nor we can help."

The lawyer, whom Amos stigmatized as a "lah-di-dah chap", told them that the will was a simple one. Did they wish him to read it all or might he merely give them a résumé?

Farmer Holme said, "Gener'ly it's read complete like."

Amos said, "With the permission o' my wife—as next of kin—I fancy that the gist of the will is sufficient, sir."

Holme said, "As you wish, as you wish."

The smart, clean-shaven lawyer in his well-cut clothes began to give them the facts. Farmer Holme was to have ten pounds with which to buy a suitable memento. Mrs. Willis also had the same amount, to which was added a dozen silver tea-spoons, and the marble clock which she had always admired. " 'To my niece, Mary Ellen Towers,' " the lawyer read, adding, "I am reading now the exact phraseology of the will, the deceased bequeaths all monies, property, and household effects. She merely adds a wish that her lifelong friends— a list is appended—may be given some small memento each 'of a value not to exceed thirty shillings each person'."

Farmer Holme said, "An' that's t'lot, eh?"

The lawyer nodded. "A very simple, straightforward will."

"Like 'er as made it," Holme said. "An' if Mary Ellen is willin', might we ax what it's all worth?"

Mary Ellen said, "Nay, I've no objection, none."

The young lawyer allowed himself to smile. "Mr. Holme, you may remember that my father drew up and administered the will of the late Mr. Baines?"

Holmes nodded. "Aye, I mind. That surprised some on 'em, that did."

Amos felt his heart beating. They were going to hear something. That news might make all kinds of things possible, for he had complete faith in himself, and in Mary Ellen's affection for and her trust in him. He felt that Harris's was coming nearer and nearer to him!

"Mrs. Baines was a woman of considerable property," the lawyer said. "I doubt if she gave her full confidence to anyone except my father, and Mr. Holme. Her husband left her six thousand pounds, in money and property. I think that I should be safe in saying that she had, by accepting the advice of her two friends—for my father always regarded himself as her friend as well as her lawyer—and by her own astuteness, doubled that sum."

Holme chuckled. "Aye, an' mower, a goodish bit mower."

Mary Ellen caught her husband's hand. "Amos, it can't be true!"

He refused to show surprise, saying calmly, "Seemly it is, luv."

Mary Ellen remained at her aunt's cottage for three days, while old Mrs. Towers happily looked after the two boys, spending her time baking for them, making delicious sticky toffee, and doing her very best to ruin their digestions for ever.

When she returned, bringing with her more boxes and crates than Amos had believed possible, Mary Ellen confessed that she had never known that Aunt Sophia possessed so much linen, silver and old china.

"And, Amos, a gentleman came over from Scarborough, *Scarborough* mind, and asked to see such furniture as we might want to sell. I was fair moithered. I said as I couldn't decide. He said he'd leave his name and address. I went to the Vicar —oh, he was kind. He said, 'Now Mrs. Towers,' he said, 'be warned by me. I can tell you as the Squire, the Hon. Jervase Bonnington, has always had his eye—both eyes in fact,' he said, and laughed, 'on those Chippendale chairs in your aunt's front room, and a corner cupboard and a tallboy.' Seemly a tallboy's some kind o' chest o' drawers. So he got the Squire to come round. Amos!" her voice became shrill from excitement, "just think! Six dining chairs, and two carvers—two 'underd and fifty pounds. The tallboy—nay, I never thought much on it—seventy pounds, and the corner cupboard—the Squire, the Hon. Jervase, said as it went back to the Resurrection of the Monasteries. When would that be, Amos? He'll give us seventy pounds for it."

Amos, Jove-like in his calm, said, "Nigh on four hundred pounds. Now, it's none o' my business, my dear, but nigh on four hundred pounds is a lot of brass. It 'ud tak' a bit o' addling."

She chattered on excitedly. "There's that much china, real old china, there's glass and silver, and linen—Amos, enough linen to last us for years an' years. Nay, that dear Aunt Sophia, keepin' so quiet about it all. I can't get over it."

It was that evening that Amos talked to his wife as he never imagined that he could talk to any woman. He confided to her his ambitions for Harris's, told her some of his plans, and also that, while he admitted that his father was clever, that he knew precisely how many beans made five—he was old.

"No gettin' away from it, luv. He's *old*."

Amos wanted to go in with his father on equal terms. If they were to pay ten thousand, he wanted to find five of them. He couldn't do it. He had saved three thousand, but if he invested all of that sum, he had to start again from scratch. New stock was wanted, new lines added. His father, while reasonable enough about small sums, was likely to dispute the expending of large amounts. Amos wanted to be on equal terms, to be on the same level with his father, not a junior partner.

It was then that Mary Ellen proved herself. She watched him gravely, then said, her voice completely matter-of-fact, "Well, and so you can. If Aunt Sophia's left me twelve thousand, or maybe a bit more, the money's there. Take it, luv. What's mine is yours, same as what's yours is mine."

Amos watched her quizzically. "And you'd not want int'rest, nor papers and documents?"

She laughed. He thought how pretty she was, how her skin was still as fresh and firm as the day they first met. She always looked so neat and trim. Other chaps' wives might have wisps of hair hanging about. Mary Ellen never did. She was like the home she kept so beautifully for him and their children —sweet and clean. He waited for her to speak.

She smiled a pleasant, slow smile that began with her eyes and seemed slowly to descend to her lips. "Nay, our Amos, don't talk daft. If I could trust you wi' myself, if I could be happy to give you two grand little lads, as you might say—to talk a bit fancified—gie my whole life to you, hand it into your care, why, surely I'm not going to fash myself over a bit of brass. Have sense, lad."

He stood grinning like a schoolboy—only Mary Ellen, knowing him so well, realized that when he spoke his voice was not quite steady.

"You're a grand lass," he said. "Never think as I don't know that, aye, an' value it. But—you will have documents, an' you will have int'rest, an' it 'ul be t'first things as I pay, mind that. You've got to have your own banking account. If you like to come in with Harris, Son and Towers—reit, but because you're my wife, an' t'grandest wife a chap ever had, you're going to be treated like the *most* considered investor. Bless you, we're going to make a grand thing out of it all."

Finally the whole thing was settled, the transfer signed, the money paid, various alterations made, and Amos Towers surveyed his new domain. He had no illusions, the first year or two were going to be hard going. Harris had been slack of late years, he had traded on his reputation, and now although he still had a good turnover, though he was still regarded as one of the most successful chandlers in the North—Amos heard things. The Superintendent of the Forest Line had said, in company, that he disliked having to buy elsewhere, but that Franks of Hull could do better for him than Harris of Willing-brough. A big burly seaman came into Towers' Stores and asked for sea-boots.

"Sitha," he said, "when Ah paay fer sea-boots as is wood-pegged, Ah dean't want ter find as 'arf t'pegs is nobbut nails, tin tacks, or summat o' that."

Amos smiled. "You'll not find that sort here."

"I found it last trip—an' not a 'underd miles away from 'ere."

Another, a second mate, grumbled, "Wish you made uniforms, Towers. I got a uniform from Harris's—oh, very dossy it looked too. Dog's wool and okum, I tell you! First drop of wet, it shrunk so's I wasn't decent wearing it."

Again Amos smiled. "Give me time, mister. Before long I'll offer you material for uniforms as will stand wind and weather. The stuff will be all wool and a yard wide."

He heard of jerseys. "Luked all reit, but, man, fair riddled wi' moth. Might ha' bin good yince, but, man, that was a hell of a long time past."

The day came when he officially "took over". No one except himself knew the sense of trepidation which filled him. He, Amos Towers, walking into Harris and Son as owner. He wore a shirt which Mary Ellen liked particularly, and a suit which he felt was serious-looking, yet impressive.

As he left the house she put her arms round his neck and kissed him, holding him close.

"Good luck, my dear luv. You're going to make such a success."

He nodded. "Aye, with you beside me—happen I will."

She laughed. "Happen! Get along, you and your 'happens'. I tell you it's as sure as Christmas 'ul come. Now get along with you! You great booby. If they'd got half your brains they'd do. God bless you."

CHAPTER FOUR

So Amos Towers took over the running of Harris and Son.
His father had virtually announced that he was too old to take
an active part in the business, but he was sufficiently active
to come down two or three times a week and—Amos knew it
to his cost—interfere. Finally he was obliged to insist that no
order given by his father was to be put into operation without
his sanction. Nine times out of ten, if Amos vetoed any order,
the old man forgot all about it, and all was well; when he
remembered something that he had ordered, discovered that
Mr. Amos had countermanded it, then there was the devil to
pay.

He would storm into the office. "Did I tell James as I
wanted . . ." whatever the order had been. "Or did I not?"

Amos, trying to be reasonable, calm and kind, would
expostulate mildly, "Sitha, Dad, if we'd done that it would
have upset half the stock-taking. Be reasonable."

"Niver mind t'stock-taking! What am I 'ere? A' office lad,
or summat? Isn't my money i' the business? D'you think as
I've not got its interests at 'eart?"

"Nachurally, Dad. But I'm here six days out of seven. I'm
trying to run the place i' the most economical way, to gain the
best returns."

"I'm accustomed ter walk me own quarter-deck," the old
man grumbled. "I dean't care aboot takin' orders, an' when I
give orders I like to see 'em carried out. I doot as you're getting
over-big fer your boots, our Amos."

The first two years were difficult. His visions of moving
into one of the handsome new villas faded; he needed every
penny they made. He saw that if they were to remain the
first ship chandlers on the river they must be able to offer
something rather better than every other chandler in the
district.

"Aye," as he said to Mary Ellen, "an' not only i' t'district,
but over the whole North o' England. I'm not only up against
Willingbrough, nor Slumpton, nor Hellingly, I'm up against
the lot on 'em. I doubt as Harris wasn't all that overcome wi'
grief that he forgot to bowl a fast one at us. The books looked
all right, the fall could be accounted for by the war. What

didn't strike any of us—barring Harris—was that *after the war*, now—could we pull up again?

"We can, luv, and we will, but it's going to be a hard furrow to plough. I hoped to be able to tell you as we were selling this house and moving into a luvely villa, out Freemoor way." He shook his head. "I daren't do it, luv. You've got to be patient. You shall have a luvely home——"

She interrupted him. "Listen, Amos Towers, whatever are you blethering on about? I *have* got a luvely home. I've had it for best part of seven years now. If I had to stay here for the rest o' my life, I'd be content. I don't doot as the villas out Freemoor way are luvely. Well, let 'em be. We'll move when we're ready an' not a minute before!"

He sighed with happiness. "Eh, you're a bloody marvel."

She was taking the admirable steak-and-kidney pudding out of the oven. He saw her stiffen, whisk round and place the pudding on the table more forcibly than was her wont— for she was a quiet-moving woman. "Luke!" she said. "This isn't t'first time I've spoke to you about nasty talk. Worried you may be, tired you are, but—use yon word agean and you'll get the rough side o' my tongue, choose how."

Meekly he said, "I'm sorry, lass." Then by way of placating her, "That pudding lukes a bit of all right."

She replied sharply, "It's no different than what all my puddings are."

Only later when he was working at some accounts which he had brought home and lifted his head to look at her and smile, only when she saw how weary he looked, did she come over to where he sat and lay her hand on his shoulder.

"Sorry I spoke sharp, dear luv. It's only as I think that much of you, I can't bear you to say anything as is out of place."

He caught her hand and kissed it. "Bless you, you were right. It's nobbut a daft habit one gets into."

At the end of two years Amos knew that the tide was turning. His father admitted, a trifle grudgingly, that he had done a great deal to set the place to rights. He had cleared out a great deal of old stock, and when old Towers suggested that they might have a sale at the old store, to get rid of the stuff, Amos shook his head.

"I'll not sell poor stuff to anyone," he declared. "If you like to have it advertised plainly in the window that it is damaged stuff, well and good, but we're not palming off rubbish as stuff worth buying. We've got to build up confidence in us, Dad," he insisted. "That's where Harris let us down. Happen it wasn't altogether his fault, but that's what happened. It runs all through the business—superintendents, captains, officers, engineers, A.B.'s and deck-hands—they're all ready to fight shy of the place and take their custom somewhere else. We've got to get 'em back."

Amos worked; at home Mary Ellen kept a watchful eye on every penny they spent; not that the boys were ever allowed to go about looking shabby, or Amos either for that matter, but she wasted nothing, never spared herself trouble or energy to make sixpence do the work of a shilling.

Amos, she thought, looked thin and tired, and she often recalled, half regretfully, the old days when the little store had been easy to manage, and had not demanded all those mysterious things called "overheads" to keep it running.

Then one evening he came in smiling, sitting down with a sigh of content and saying, "Tide's turned, my lass. Very shortly it 'ul be running fresh and full. I had Captain Forman in this morning."

Even Mary Ellen knew who Captain Forman was—the Superintendent of the Forest Line, a tall, gaunt man who was reputed to be the keenest buyer in the shipping business, and yet who kept the crews who shipped on the Forest boats happy and content living in well-found vessels.

Later she came to know them all, these important superintendents, who held so much power and who could make or mar the firms with which they dealt. There was Mr. Thomas John Evans, a little Welshman with a dead-white face, sharp dark eyes, and hair which looked as if it had been dressed with a fine application of blacklead. The Superintendent of the Glen Line was Captain Marsh, a big, burly Yorkshireman, a yard wide, and weighing a good eighteen stone. The most important of them all was Captain Mac Muir Stevenson of the Loch Line. Tall, incredibly thin, with sandy hair and bushy, sandy eyebrows, he dressed in tweed suits which smelt of peat and heather, and his linen was always immaculate.

It was Stevenson who first talked informally to Amos. Marsh was always friendly enough, inclined to bluster, but never unreasonable; Evans grew excited and argumentative, he waved his hands—very small, neat hands they were too—

about as he talked, and his accent became more and more marked as his excitement grew. Forman was slightly aloof, reasonable, able to drive a hard bargain but unstinting in his praise for what was good.

Stevenson had been a Master Mariner himself, and in charge of many famous vessels; he was known to be clever, cautious, and yet possessing the ability to take risks if the occasion demanded it. It was said that he was as important in the firm as old Jamie MacBride or his son Thomas. He showed no inclination to begin talking of business. He settled himself comfortably, stretched out his long, tweed-clad legs, which terminated in excellent brown shoes—at a time when the majority of businessmen wore boots—accepted a cigar and a "dram", and smiled at Amos.

"Ye'll mind, Mr. Tower, my firrm dealt wi' Harris for monny a year, eh?" Amos nodded. "It grieved me, aye, I was sair grieved tae be forrced tae sever ma connection wi' that mon. Tae tell ye the plain truth, he lost grip. Then again he made a great mistake o' attempting tae mak' much o' little."

He settled himself more comfortably in his big leather arm-chair.

"Times ye can mak' mickle mair, but mind ye, the mickle must be fine quality. There's nae gold tae be fin' i' trash. Better yin order wi' a satisfied customer as a result, than three or fower an' all ready tae be dissatisfied, tae nurse a grievance against the trader.

"Furthermore," he sipped his whisky with quiet appreciation, "never overload yer ship. Harris had big ideas, his hoose was fine, his table fair groaned wi' the best, his sons—puir laddies—had nae expense spared i' their education, nae mair i' their clothes. His wife was aye elaborately dressed. Noo," with the air of a man who is preparing to sum up and come to the leisurely end of his discourse, "a' these things are good. I'm the last mon i' the world tae decry the good things o' life. But those things must be servants, not masters. Have what you wish, what you can, but never fail tae realize that many, many things can be dispensed wi', if you fin' you're overloading your ship. Once you find you've loaded her over the Plimsoll Line—jettison some o' yer cargo rather than imperil your vessel, your crew and yer ain guid standin' i' the eyes o' men. Am I making myself clear, Mr. Towers?"

Amos nodded. "Indeed, sir, yes. I can see you're right.

That's what me and my wife—I'd like you to meet her one
day—have tried to do. Come to that, it's more her doing than
mine. I was for making a move, for getting a bigger house.
She wasn't for it, not while we were prop'ly on our feet."

Stevenson nodded. "Aye, I must meet her. Mind ye,
Towers, when I refaired tae the Plimsoll Line I was not
restricting myself tae shipping alone. The Plimsoll Line is
something mair than a white mark painted on the side o' a
ship. It's a white mark painted on a man's character! One
might almaist say—painted on his soul. Only in these days,
we're maistly a wee bit shy o' mentioning our souls. We might
talk aboot our guts, our livers, and the like, but tae the
modern way o' thinking there's something a bittie uncouth
in mentioning the soul.

"Mind ye, Plimsoll fought, aye an' pretty well died, for
yon white line, invented, planned, devised for the safety o'
the men who went down tae the sea in ships and occupied their
business i' great waters. It was not for the profit, benefit or
satisfaction o' the shipowner, the shipping companies or their
shareholders. There have been men—why, let's be honest an'
call them merely politicians—who have done their best tae
tamper wi' the Plimsoll Line"—his eyes twinkled suddenly—
"an' in mair ways than merely applies tae ships!" The twinkle
was extinguished, the eyes were hard again. "It's an ill thing
tae meddle wi' what are fundamentals. Noo, Towers, ma
laddie, let's get doon tae business. Always keep the Plimsoll
Line showing between you and the salt sea."

At night Amos recounted to Mary Ellen all that Stevenson
had said. She listened, nodded and gave it as her opinion that
he was a man worth attending to.

"Come to think on it," she said, "it's sound common sense.
We'll mind our step, luv."

The captains of various ships began to call on Amos in his
comfortable office. They were kindly, warm-hearted men, with
eyes wrinkled at the corners from staring into the bad weather,
but they were clear, bright eyes, and when they offered him
their hands in greeting he felt that they offered their goodwill
at the same time.

Little Simpson, with the hard mouth and strong jaw, had
the softest heart imaginable, and if on the way to the docks
he found a stray kitten it went back, as he said, "to join the
ship as super-cargo". There was the tall, elegant Clotherly,

who was captain of one of the smart banana boats for South America, which had special compartments for the fruit, and six magnificent suites for the South American millionaires. Amos had been taken over one—the *Marcus Antonio*—and thought that he had never seen such luxury in his life. Clotherly was a strange fellow; he was said to read poetry, and to keep a Greek testament on the table beside his bunk. Once in a moment of expansion he told Amos that his uncle—"on my mother's side"—was a bishop. There were others—Harrison, Campdon, Pearson and the big, jovial Cartwright, who was every man's friend, and had not an enemy in the world.

Amos once said to Captain Harrison of the *Molly Adair* that Cartwright never seemed to be put out by anything, "always ready with a smile".

Harrison, who came from Hull, slanted a glance at him. "Aye, allus got a smile, has that 'un, but watch him when wind and tides and every other damn thing is ageanst, and see him then! He's like—like—why, he's like the b—— Rock o' Gibraltar, is that 'un."

How Amos enjoyed those afternoons and early evenings, when these men dropped in for a chat and possibly a little business at the same time. He would sit behind his desk in his neat, well-made clothes, his immaculate if inconspicuous tie, and listen as a boy might have done to their stories. With his eyes very bright and his heart beating he would watch and listen, almost breathless, as if he feared to miss a word.

Those stories might begin, "Did I ever tell you of that night in Bombay?" or, "Surely you were lying next to us, Compton, in Valparaiso when——" Harrison, leaning forward, his glass of whisky grasped in his hard, capable hand, would demand, "Cartwright, mind that time when we were apprentices in the old *Crocodile*? Round the Horn? All the sticks lifted off of her? Tell 'em, go on!" Tales of the captains under whom they had sailed, characters to whom time had lent a touch of fantasy; one who had his boots made at Peels and his clothes at Pooles, another who dosed the whole crew with Epsom salts every Sunday morning after he had read the Service.

It seemed to Amos that the air, growing thick with tobacco smoke, also became charged with a hint of salt water; he felt that if he licked his lips he would taste the tangy spray on them. These men were his heroes. These men—and there were some of them who cheerfully went out in ships which were shorthanded, undermanned, badly found, where the galley poker had to do duty as a marline spike if necessary—still were content. They laughed at the shortcomings of their ships, at the miserly habits of their owners. They all grinned and said, "I'll be glad when I can leave it all behind me and have done with the damned sea."

And Amos knew so well what they would do when it came to the time for them to retire. They would take a little house, as near to the sea as possible, they'd rig up a flagpole, and probably a telescope, and spend their days peering out to sea— with envy in their hearts for the men who were still "going down to the sea in ships".

They were kind in speaking about their ships too. Amos remembered once, when Captain Pearson had been given command of the *Eagle Glen*, Simpson saying, "The old *Eagle Glen*, what a bitch she is! Watch her, Pearson, she's a man-killer. She rolls like a sow, sticks her nose into it, and never makes any effort to ride 'em. Oh, a bitch, that one!"

Harding Cartwright leaned forward and knocked out his pipe into the big ash-tray. When Cartwright moved the others waited, because he never moved unless he was going to speak, and when he spoke—he said something.

"I never like to hear anyone talk that way about a ship," he said slowly, not as if condemning Simpson, but almost as if he excused himself for not holding the same opinion. "I know the *Eagle*, and let's admit that there's nothing of the bird about her. But—if she rolls, and she dies, if she pitches—which she does, and if she doesn't ride to them but wallows in the trough, has it never struck you that it's not her fault? The fault lies with the men who designed her, the chaps who built her, the overseers who watched the job being done. If someone —some man—hadn't scamped his work, she'd be a better ship. Taking them by and large, ships are a good deal more decent than humans."

Clotherly laughed. "You're a sentimentalist, Cartwright. I believe that to you every ship is a 'lovely ship'. I've been told that you pet them, treat them as a man might treat his mistress."

"I can't say. Never been able to afford a mistress, and shouldn't have wanted one if I could. Of course I pet them. Of course I try to keep 'em smart. They've got their pride, they like looking nice. That's one of the reasons they're called 'she'. I remember my first command. The *Water Witch*"—there was a roar of laughter. "Oh, I know what everyone called her! Old Rawlinson had her, that's right, old 'Clouting' Rawlinson. I was first mate, just got my master's ticket. He died of jaundice off Montevideo. He'd treated her hard, blackguarded her, driven her, grudged her a lick of paint, and she—well, she lived up to your variation of her name.

"My first command. I was as proud of her as a dog with two tails. You were with me, Beasley," turning to a rather younger man, "you remember."

Beasley smiled. "Captain, you were an infernal bore with your precious ship! But I admit that she made the best run of her life."

"There! I admit that I *petted* that ship, as I might have petted a lost dog with whom I wanted to make friends. I've even patted the rail and said, 'Go on, lass, you're doing fine. We'll surprise them yet.' All right, silly, sentimental, but somehow or other it paid!"

How Amos loved them all, and with what pride he'd make his small offerings. "Would you do me a favour, Captain? No, it's nothing, only scent. For Mrs. Harrison, with my compliments," or, "I expect she's got dozens better than this, but—it's just a shawl. Captain Willis brought me some back from India last trip"—he'd smile—"for my lady friends. With my best wishes."

There came a day when the auditors had been at the store, and Amos came home, his smile wider than ever.

"Mary Ellen, luv, we're flitting. Things are all right. Harris is paid. By the way, did I tell you that he's lost that last son of his, poor chap? Yes, died two days ago in Bournemouth. I ordered a wreath to be sent down from Beater's. Aye, very sad. But what I want you to do is to find a house. Now, I'm not set on one of these great big, gormless-luking villas. I'm getting a car, aye, I am. It 'ul be secondhand but it 'ul mean I can get in and out easily. I've heard of a place, it's called Nunfield Little Manor. Nobbut a bit outside the town. In another year t'trams 'ul be right up to it. Will you go and see it, luv? I stopped off at Morley's an' got an order to view. Mind, if you'd rather have something new—well, it's your house and you mun have what you fancy."

She clasped her hands. He thought that she looked like an excited girl. "An old house?" she breathed.

He nodded. "I b'lieve so. But mind you, it's in tip-top condition."

"And you promise faithful that we can afford to flit?"

"Cross my heart, m'dear."

The next day he swore that he had no time to come with her, that he was too busy, but when he returned at midday he announced in an offhand way that he had ordered Marchant's car, and was driving out with her.

Mary Ellen Towers never forgot that day. It was one of those bright days only to be found in the North Country, when the air is clear as crystal, and holds a certain astringent quality. The hills stood out with complete clarity against the horizon; they seemed, Mary Ellen thought, close enough to touch, if you stretched out your arm. She could see every detail on their sides, each bright bush, changing to scarlet in the Autumn air, each farm-house stood out distinct and sharply etched against the cold, pale sky.

They drove out of the town towards the country. Amos scarcely spoke, and she realized that he was secretly excited and absorbed. She glanced at him, saw his face in profile, grave and intent. A good face, she thought. Not handsome as both Victor and Wilfred would be handsome, his nose was too blunt, his cheek-bones too high. Yet there was about him something which was eminently satisfactory. She tried to find a word which expressed him. What did she see in his face? The word came to her—steadiness. That was Amos Towers— steady, standing firm by his beliefs and principles. He would never waver, he mapped out his course, he believed it to be the best road for him to take and—he stuck to it.

She sighed gently with a secret satisfaction. They had been married for nearly thirteen years, and she still loved him as she knew that he loved her. He had never done anything to jeopardize that love which she felt for him, never disappointed her, never made her feel that she would have wished him to be different from the man he was.

The car stopped at a six-barred white gate, and Marchant slid back the window and said, "Like me to drive in, Mr. Towers?"

"No, don't bother," Amos said, "we'll walk."

He swung open the gate; it led to a short drive, with fields on either side, and a narrow hedge of privet, carefully clipped to mark the separation. The road itself was well kept, and ran for possibly twenty-five yards towards the house.

Amos handed her out and said, "Nunfield Little Manor, m'dear."

Mary Ellen looked at the long, low, grey stone house, with its old slate roof where patches of lichen and house leek showed bright and green; two storeys, and over the front door a small porch built of stone; inside the porch were two stone seats. Set in the roof were four dormer windows, telling of spacious attics, places where all manner of things might be stored.

The two rows of windows twinkled and glanced in the thin sunshine. The whole place looked friendly, serene and permanent.

"Oh, Amos," she breathed. "Isn't it over-grand for us?"

"Nowt grand about it," he said stoutly. "It's just a good house, well built, built to last, sitha. Let's have a luke, lass.

He opened the front door, and stood swinging the massive key in his hand. A long, low hall, tiled in black and white, doors on either side—old doors with beautiful brass fittings and finger-plates; white and shining walls, a sense of space and comfort. He threw open doors and made his announcements.

"T'dining-room—nice room, eh? Good windows, good fireplace. The floors are sound as bells. Here on the other side is the drawing-room. Panelling's pretty, isn't it? I like that palish grey, but we'll change it if you like. This smaller room is called the morning-room, I reckon it's really a breakfast-room. Lukes out on to the back——"

She said very softly, "Aye—and the hills."

The staircase was wide, with low treads, and a wide hand-rail. The bedrooms enchanted her, the cupboards were spacious, the windows sufficiently large. The bathroom was more than adequate, as the kitchen had been.

Still in his role of being completely unimpressed, Amos said, "Aye, t'bathroom's not bad. Ours is better. Leads off of our bedroom. Here, luke."

The idea of having a bathroom dedicated especially to her use and her husband's had never occurred to Mary Ellen.

"Two bathrooms," she said. "And this one—just for us?"

He laughed. "Let me catch anyone else using it, an' there'll be bother. Aye, this is ours. Like to see the attics, eh?"

Attics, with sloping roofs, and dormer windows from which you could see the hills, and the moors stretching away—it seemed—to infinity.

"Nay," she said, "I can't take it all in, luv. You must keep the key and let me come here by myself. I'd like to just wander about. It's all too much."

He led the way downstairs, through the kitchen with its clean stone floor, and fine shining range with the little brass tap at the side, where water had dripped for so many years that it had worn a little hole in the stone.

Flinging open the back door, he said, "Here's the yard. Yon place there was a loose-box or carriage house or summat of the kind. It 'ul make a fine garage." He pronounced it "garidge". "There's the wash-house, coal-house, woodstore, all handy, eh?"

Mary Ellen laid her hand on his arm. "Let's go and lean over yon wall and just think for a bit, Amos."

They walked across the yard and, with the sun on their backs, leaned on the top of the wall, watching the picture which was spread before them; fields, now grey-green, bordered by dry-stone walls, and here and there well-laid hedges. Here and there a herd of red-and-white cows grazed contentedly, and a flock of sheep, cropping busily at the short turf. High overhead a kestrel flew, hovering, then suddenly darting away to be lost to sight in the pale blue sky. Hills rising gently, their sides marked here and there with great, grey boulders, relics of a time when the glaciers covered the country. There was one, Mary Ellen remembered, which was always known as the "Wild Boar", a great mass of rock, supposed by some stretch of imagination to resemble a boar. Here and there patches of heather, not quite so bright in its regal purple as it had been a month before, but still handsome and arresting, and among the heather an occasional patch of golden gorse.

Somewhere from a neighbouring farmyard a cock crowed loudly, boastfully. Mary Ellen started, and Amos turned to her, smiling.

"Well," he said, "how d'you find it all, luv?"

"Nay, I'd never want to live anywhere else so long as I live, m'dear. It's all wonderful. I'm slow, but let me have the key and I'll come and wander about here by meself. I'll get the feel of it all. I'll mak' plans, try to imagine what we'll need."

"Whatever you want," he said, "you've got to have, think on."

"Is the rent very high?" She asked the question almost timidly.

"Rent! Nay, if you like it, I'm not rentin', I'm buying."

"Amos! To be ours for ever and ever?"

"Ours, aye, while we live, an' then it 'ul go to the lads. I've a fancy to have a place of our own. There's plenty o' room, room enoof to build on, if we felt like it and need it. Room for an extra garidge, an' wi' things moving as they are, the time 'ul come when Vic and Wilf 'ul both want cars of their own. I liked it the moment I set eyes on it. Now, as it pleases you— that's settled everything." He moved a little nearer to her, and slid his hand along the top of the wall until his fingers touched hers. "Happy, my luv?"

"Happy!" She shot a glance at him so filled with delight and excitement, making her look so young and eager, that he caught his breath. It didn't seem possible that they had been married thirteen years, that they had two big sons of twelve and nearly eleven! She still looked so young; her figure was as neat and trim as it had always been, her skin clear like that of a young girl.

"Happy!" she said again. "I thought that I knew all about happiness when I got married to you. Then when Victor was born I knew that I'd never known happiness—really, completely before. It was the same when Wilf was born. To have a husband like I'd got was wonderful, to have a luvely son like our Victor was more wonderful still. And when Wilf came— well, it seemed that there was nothing left for me to wish for."

Amos stood watching her intently. "Go on," he said, "tell me some more." He was like a child, begging for a story, Mary Ellen thought.

"Why, luv, you know the rest. Taking Harris's, that was a struggle for you, but you won. It seems as if all these years my happiness had been mounting up and up, as if now it's 'pressed down and running over'. She laughed. "I'm almost 'flaid some of it might run over and get lost! And now—this! This house, this home that's going to be ours. Amos, m'dear luv. Better tak' me home again to Aislaby Street or I shall start crying an' carrying on like a silly bairn. It's all too much for me."

He came close and caught her in his arms, holding her close and kissing her flushed cheeks, murmuring, "Aye, my bonnie, bonnie girl. Tha'll never know how much I luv you, never, not if we live to be a hundred."

She struggled a little, whispering, "Amos, have done! Willie Marchant can see us, as like as not."

"Let him!" Amos cried. "Let him! Make him envious because he's not got a wife like mine to kiss. No more has anyone else, come to that. Just one more, my little luv. Bless you."

They drove home in silence, their hands clasped under the rug which Marchant laid over their knees. Mary Ellen loved the sensation of holding her husband's hand. It was so firm, so strong, there was nothing soft or flabby about it. The touch of it gave you confidence, a sense that, whatever happened, you had Amos, with his good heart, his clear brain, and his unswerving honesty behind you.

That night they told the boys. They had finished tea, and laid out their books to prepare their home-work. Amos in his chair by the fire watched them. Victor's fair head and Wilfred's dark one were bent over their books, both absorbed and intent.

He said, "You can stop work for a minute or two. I've something to tell you both." They laid down their pens and looked up expectantly.

Victor said, "Is it about the pantomime at Leeds at Christmas?"

His brother said, "No, of course it's not. Dad, can I get to the exhibition in the Town Hall? There's some marvellous new machines there. Is that what you were going to tell us—that we can go on Saturday?"

Victor added, "There's a man who makes toffee and throws it round a hook until it's quite white—it looks like silk."

"The Royal Engineers band is coming next week to play there," Wilf said. "Oh, Dad, can I be an engineer when I've finished school? Not a soldier, the other kind, that go into ships and run the engines. Can I, Dad?"

Amos watched them, listened to their excited voices, and smiled.

"Luke, I said I had something to tell you. D'you want to hear what it is, or do you both want to go on jabbering to me? Just tell me!"

Victor laughed. "No, Dad, we do want to hear. Tell us, please."

"Very well. We're moving!" He leaned back, feeling that he had dropped his bombshell.

"Oh, moving, eh?" Wilf said; his voice held disappointment.

Victor said, "Moving, Dad? Where to? Away from Willingbrough?"

"Not far. We're going to Nunfield Little Manor."

Wilfred whistled. "Whew! That's a big house, a lot bigger'n this one."

"How will we get to school, Dad? It's a long way to walk," Victor said. "Could we have bicycles?"

"You'll have bicycles all right. Most likely next year you'll go to boarding-school. A big school with lots of boys, where you'll learn to play cricket and football, and—oh, lots of things."

"Will there be an engineering shop at this school?" Wilf asked.

"Happen——"

"There's one at Sedleigh. Thomas Billet told me."

"Happen there'll be one where we're sending you both."

Victor said, "I don't want to have an engineering shop. I'm going into your business, Dad. I'm going to be a ship's chandler, and talk to captains."

"Don't you want to hear about the new house?"

They answered in chorus, readily and politely, "Yes, Dad, of course."

CHAPTER FIVE

THE years which followed seemed to Mary Ellen Towers to slip past so quickly and smoothly that she looked back on them scarcely comprehending that they were gone. So many things seemed to renew themselves for her, seemed never to grow old or stale, but always to retain their freshness and unexpectedness.

After Abel Towers died, slipping away very quietly, with much less insistence on his own importance than he had shown during the whole of his life, Amos enlarged the store. The size of it astonished her, and no matter how often she saw it, she felt that it was an almost incredible achievement. True, there were larger buildings in Willingbrough, but Towers and Sons (late Harris and Son) represented to her the realized ambition of her husband, Amos. She felt that, come what might, the big, well-designed building would remain a monument to his ability, his integrity and his energy.

She remembered so many stages of Amos's advance. How

he had realized one of his ambitions—to make uniforms on his own premises. He had come home one evening, driving his first car, a second- or even third-hand Standard, and had sat down, his face bearing that look of satisfaction which meant that he had some secret to impart, and wished to keep it until he felt that the psychological moment had arrived.

She had said nothing; she knew that these things gave him pleasure, and felt that he and Victor and Wilf were all, really, children who must be humoured.

After supper he said, "Mary Ellen, luv, who made that coat and skirt you were wearing when you came down to the store last time?"

"Made it?" she asked, for, like so many Yorkshire folk, she often answered one question by asking another. "Made it? Why, Miss Rollit. She makes all my dresses."

Amos nodded. "Aye, but coats and skirts aren't like other clothes. They need a man to cut them. Now, I'd like you to come down to the store, pick a bit of cloth as suits you, and let my tailor make it up for you."

He said "my tailor" in a manner which was studiously nonchalant. She could have laughed with pleasure at his childish "play-acting". He might have had a tailoring department for years!

She said, "So you've gotten a tailor now, have you?"

He looked up from his evening paper. Amos Towers, like other good citizens, regarded the careful reading of the Willingbrough *Daily Despatch* as part of his civic duties.

He said, "Me? Oh, aye; didn't I tell you about it?"

"Not a word!"

"Must ha' slipped my mind. Why, it was this road. I heard of a tailor, Polish Jew seemly, name of Petrovski. He worked for Bagstock's until old Bagstock died and they gave up high-class tailoring and only sold ready-mades. He thought as he'd start on his own, but he'd no capital worth speaking of, and things have been going badly with him. Came round to see me—well, to be frank, I sent for him. Shabby-luking little man, shy, had a baddish time. He looked thin as a rail. I put my ideas to him. He very near cried with joy. I told him to find a couple of other good tailors—to work under him—and a couple of girls to do the basting, button-holes and suchlike."

She beamed at him. "You think of everything!"

"Got to, in business, else the other fellow thinks first," he

laughed. "So he got cracking and brought a couple of chaps,
Poles, or Jews, or both, like himself. Schneiders he calls them—
that's the Jewish or Polish for tailor. Fitted up a nice work-
room, couple of fitting-rooms, everything—as Dad used to
say—shipshape and Bristol fashion. I said, 'Now, Mr. Peters,
for we can't call you Petrovski, it's too difficult, you're the boss
here,' I said. 'You'll do the measuring and fitting and cutting.
I understand that there is a lot in the cutting, eh? Your
first job is to get started and make yourself a nice suit, something like what the head cutter 'ud wear in a classy shop, see?
Give you my word, luv, he nearly cried. Said a whole lot in his
own lingo, and told me that never should I have a more
faithful servant. I don't believe that I will neither. He's doing
fine. Captains, officers, chief engineers, all coming wanting
stuff, and are they delighted!"

She remembered her first tailored suit. The little Jewish
tailor treated her as if she were a queen. He bowed, called her
"most gracious lady"—though he didn't speak very clearly,
kind of thick.

"At first," he told her, "the Baal-bos said, 'Peters, only
uniforms.' Yes, a'right, only uniforms. Bit later 'e say, 'Peters,
reckon we can do shure'—no, not shure—vait minute, pleese,
I recall qvickly—shore. The vord—shore, to vear ven not on
sheeps, no?"

She nodded. "That's right, Mr. Peters—shore clothes."

"Yes, yes." The little man was growing excited; he used
his hands a great deal as his excitement grew. "Emechine, if
you please, gracious lady. The Baal-bos send me off to Brad-
ford. Me—not only to be cutter, but now I am—buyer for
great Towers Stores. I vas ver' frightened. 'How much I spend,
mister sir?' I esk. He move his shoulders—like so. 'E say,
'Doan metter so much, but only the best, nossing not first
qualitee.' "

Mary Ellen listened, watched, and sympathized. She sensed
how the little man must have felt, knew how she would have
felt herself. Amos was so magnificent; how she admired his
courage, and his "only the best is good enough"!

She said, "Oh, Mr. Peters, what a terrible responsibility.
You must have felt nervous. How did you decide what to buy?"

For the first time he chuckled; she saw his keen, intelligent
eyes crinkle at the corners. " 'Ow? Leetle secret, madam.
I mak' leetle list. Names of alles captains, superintendents,

C

so on. Uniforms all blue. Oh, ver' smart, ele-gant, gentlemensly. Off the sheeps, per'aps want to have pleasant change, yes? Captain Evans only, I t'ink, like dark grey. Captain Clo'erly must be tip-top, schmart, last t'ing in newness. Captain Stevenson, alvays I vatch, ver' fine man. Best qvality tweeds. So, I buy. T'ink for younger officers, some'sing cheerful. They say 'Natty suiting.' I get—natty suiting."

"I think that you're a very clever man, Mr. Peters."

He shook his head. "Me—good craftsman. Your 'usband is clever man."

She sighed with content as she remembered it all. Now, Amos was always having to refuse orders, orders from men who had no connection with the sea. His answer, he told her, was always the same.

"Delighted, when we haven't a single order outstanding for sea-going customers."

"When is that likely to be, Towers?"

"Couldn't say, not for another three or four months."

And Amos, as he told her, would chuckle and rub his hands.

The boys had gone off to their grand boarding-school with trunks filled with well-cut clothes. Together they had gone to Redburgh. Amos had said, "Yes, go together, and they make a reduction for quantity!"

Victor, just turned twelve, was considerably taller than his younger brother. There was no question that the elder boy was almost surprisingly handsome; more than that, he had un-doubted charm. Not that he exerted it consciously, or used it to gain anything material. It was simply that his smile came easily, he talked readily, and he was interested in the people he met. Wilfred had his mind set on machinery. From a small child he had loved any toys which were clockwork; he had never wished to smash them in pieces, but spent his time examining them with concentrated attention, trying to decide in his childish mind exactly "how it worked".

At school they had both worked well, and Wilfred had been the highest in all examinations pertaining to anything mechanical or mathematical. He liked subjects which were, as he had told his headmaster, "exact". His brother, on the other hand, found that anything connected with people, the development of the inhabitants of the world, literature and the like, interested him far more than Wilf's "exact sciences".

Neither of them ever deviated from his original wishes;

Victor longed to enter his father's business; Mary Ellen thought sometimes that his wish was prompted by his love of people. In the store he would meet many new individuals daily, hear of distant lands, customs and products.

On this afternoon when Mary Ellen sat in her sunny sitting-room, raising her eyes from time to time to look out over the paved yard, bounded by its low stone wall, to the fields which lay beyond it, to the hills and moors, she told herself, as she did so often, that she had every right to "count her blessings". There had been hard years, when she and Amos first married, when she knew that he was fighting for a real foothold, when he was counting every penny, and longing for the day when he might congratulate himself that he was making real progress.

"Not," she thought, "that he ever wanted much for himself, his tastes are simple enough, but he hates failure. He's got big ideas, not because success means more money, greater comfort, but just because he wants to show that he's as good as the next chap, and happen a bit better. Now, luke at him, he's not fifty yet, and he's got the biggest business of its kind in the North. He's a Councillor, and respected too. He's got good friends, he's trusted and believed in. He's bought his own house." Her thoughts halted and she let her glance roam round the pleasant sun-lit room, with its bright curtains, and good, well-made furniture.

She had loved the Little Manor the first time Amos brought her to see it, and her love for it had grown. She had treated it as she had always tried to treat her children—denying it nothing that was for its good. She turned back to her mending, and her smile widened.

"Think of it," she mused, "there was me, servant at Clutterbuck's, doing everything, washing and all. Now, I've two servants of my own, aye and good girls they are, hard workers, and honest as the day. I treat them right because I know exactly what it's like to be a servant. As if that wasn't enough, my husband's made money, he's gotten a car and talks of getting a new one! My boys are at a big, expensive school. Vic's leaving at the end of this term to join his father. Wilf will leave next year to go to an engineering school— maybe one of those big places on the Tyne where they learn them to be engineers. Here we are in this dear safe house, comfortable as we can be, no worries except little ones that don't amount to anything, and—who is to thank for it all? That grand husband of mine!"

Amos, sitting in his office, drinking his afternoon cup of tea and nibbling a very dry and not particularly pleasant-tasting biscuit, was letting his mind run on along much the same lines.

"Forty-eight," he thought, and ran his hand lightly over his head, making a little grimace when he was conscious that the hair was thinning a little. He stood up, and shaking down his admirably cut trousers into their careful creases, he looked down, surveying his figure under the well-fitting waistcoat. There was a slight but distinct bulge. He shook his head. "Nay, I hate losing my hair and my figure," he thought, "but a chap can't have everything. I've been over-busy in the last years to think about exercise. I tried golf, but it seemed a poor way of passing the time, and I could pass time more profitably. When old Josiah Heal said to me what were my 'hobbies'—hobbies!—I told him, 'Work, Mr. Heal, the more work the happier I am.' No mistake, work pays. It's paid me a grand dividend. There were some difficult years, but we weathered 'em, though if I hadn't had that lass beside me, that lass I met only because she'd bought a pair of over-tight shoes, I doubt if I'd be where I am today."

The boys were coming home, the school had broken up earlier than usual owing to an outbreak of scarlet fever, and they wrote with enthusiasm of the debt they owed to the boys who had so thoughtfully contracted the disease. They appeared to regard them as public benefactors.

Amos read the letter and smiled. "Aye, Vic's finished with school. I had a kind of idea that I'd have liked him to go to a university, but—though mind, the lad's not done badly—he doesn't seem to be cut out for a—well, what you might call a scholastic career. Wilf's a better scholar, really, I reckon. Ah, well, I wonder what they'll finish up doing, both of them."

"Doing?" Mary Ellen asked. "Why, it's all settled. Vic 'ul come with you, and Wilf's going to Cadman and Riley's."

Her husband met her eyes squarely. "Haven't you read the papers, luv?"

"Well, I have—and I haven't. I read the births, marriages and deaths every night, but somehow I never seem to have

time to read the other part, not unless there's anything special
—like the wedding of someone we know."

He nodded and repeated, "Anything special, eh? Ah, well,
no use of meeting troubles half-way. Only things are looking
pretty bad—as if when that Archduke was shot they lit the
fire under the pot, and now it's bubbling away, and likely to
boil over any minute."

She stared at him, her pleasant, comely face losing the
colour which made her look so young, made her seem almost
pretty. Her eyes, those good, clear eyes which he loved, which
never wavered or faltered, grew wider. As she watched him,
Mary Ellen knew that there were new lines graved at the
corners of his mouth, saw too that his eyes were heavy as
if he had slept badly, or had been working too hard and too
long.

"Whatever do you mean, Amos?" she asked. "Not . . . not
war?"

"God knows," he answered heavily.

"But, my dear, what's the death of this foreign Archduke
got to do with us here in England? We didn't shoot him.
Most of us never knew that he existed at all. You can't tell
me that there'll be a war over that?"

"Any stick does to beat a dog with," he said. "When folks
get jealous-minded, when they want to pick a quarrel, they'll
find some reason for doing so, easily enough. Germany's
jealous of us——"

"But the German Emperor's our King's own cousin,
Amos!"

"Nay." He shook his head. "I can't see that making a lot
of difference."

Valiantly Mary Ellen tried to cheer him. She knew her
Amos, knew so well how he "got things on his mind", churned
them over and over, worried them as a dog might worry a
bone, and in all probability this war scare was something
which he had heard at the Conservative Club. Men were
dreadful when they got together! Talk about women! Why,
men nattered and gossiped and made mountains out of mole-
hills worse than any woman ever did. Possibly he'd got a
touch of liver, the same as he had last year. She'd see that he
took two of those little pills when he went to bed, then a good
dose of liver salts in the morning, and he'd bother less about
Archdukes and Emperors, and the rest of it. Regretfully she

wished that they were not having roast goose for dinner—they called their evening meal "dinner" now—but the boys would be back and there was nothing Amos liked better. Roast goose with all the "trimmings".

She smiled at him, though somehow her face felt strangely tight, and the smile did not come easily.

"I don't know," she said. "Blood's thicker than water, never mind whether it's Kings or who it is. And even if there was a war—which I'm sure there never will be—we've got too many clever men at the head of things—that doesn't say that whoever fights us will come *here*."

"It means that we'd have to go—there," Amos said.

"What has this all to do with the boys?" She had not wanted to ask that question, because ever since the discussion began she had been afraid of the answer. Now it had become too strong for her, and she repeated it. "What has it all to do with the boys, Amos?"

"Vic's eighteen and Wilf's only eighteen months younger, m'dear."

"You mean they'd—go for soldiers! Nay, Amos, you'd never allow them to do that, surely, not if it was ever so. Our boys go to be soldiers! Whatever next!"

"I doubt if I'd have much say in it, Mary Ellen, luv."

It was at that moment they heard the sound of the taxi driving up. Both Vic and Wilf had insisted long ago that they neither wished to be "seen off" nor met at the station on their return. Mary Ellen, much against her will, had respected their wishes.

She sprang to her feet and rushed to the front door. Emily, the maid, was there first. She was an elderly woman and her affection for the boys was almost maternal.

Luggage was being hurled out of the taxi, boxes and bags unearthed from the inner recesses, and ropes being untied with great efficiency from boxes which had overflowed, as it were, on to the roof. Victor, staggering under the weight of two immense bags, rushed towards his mother.

"Mummy, we're back. How are you, darling? You're looking lovely. Hello, Em'ly, you get younger every time I see you."

Mary Ellen flung her arms round his neck. He was so tall that she had to stand on the tips of her toes. Soldiers indeed! Not if she knew anything about it.

Wilfred deposited his load, and pushed his brother on one side.

"Go on, that's enough. Let me have a look in. Mummy dear, it's lovely to be home. Wasn't it grand about the scarlet fever? Hello, Em'ly, glad to see us?"

It was easier to put her arms round Wilf's neck, and how good it was to feel the breadth and strength of his shoulders. He'd never be as tall as his brother, but he was solid, firm, like a rock. Soldiers!

They rushed into the house, and almost knocked their father over. He looked small beside them, shorter than Victor, and far more slight than Wilfred.

He clapped them both on their backs, his smile wide, his eyes shining.

"Both of you got all kinds of horrible spots, eh? I suppose that you've got out of the term exams; couple of cunning Isaacs you are. Is your baggage up?"

"The driver and Bradshaw are seeing to it," Victor assured him. "Oh, Mummy, are we too late for tea? I'm simply famished."

"So am I! It's a rotten journey from Redburgh. We were given sandwiches. What a swizz! Nothing in them but slices of cheese."

"Taken from the mouse-traps—stale as anything. We spent *pounds* in slot machines——"

"At every station, trying to get chocolate. Beastly when you got it."

"We ate it just to stave off the gnawing pangs of hunger."

Emily came in with a tea-tray. Mary Ellen said, "Dad and I have had ours, but Em'ly thought you might be hungry."

"Hungry! That's putting it mildly, Em'ly. Famished— dying of malnutrition."

She looked at them. "'Ave you washed yer 'ands? They luke as if they could to with a wash. Filthy, they are."

Wilfred looked at his hands, good strong hands, with square palms and capable fingers. "Oh, let us off just for once, Em'ly."

Victor added, "Special occasion, Em'ly. I defy anyone to call my hands really dirty."

As his brother had done he spread out his hands for inspection, and Mary Ellen studied them as she had studied Wilf's. Longer fingers, large well-shaped nails, and slim wrists;

had she been sufficiently familiar with such words, she would have called them "expressive".

She nodded at them both. "Just this once," and then remembered that after all they were not boys any longer, they were practically men.

Victor, cramming hot tea-cake into his mouth, asked, "How's everything, Dad? Things going well? Of course they are! I'm longing to see the latest improvements."

Amos nodded. "Mustn't grumble. We're jogging along."

"May I have another cup of tea, Mummy? I say, Dad, is there going to be war? Everyone at Redburgh says there is."

"If everyone at Redburgh says there is, what's the use of asking me? Lot of clever lads at Redburgh," Amos said.

"Don't rag," Victor said gravely. "No, honestly, do you think it will fizzle out, or will the balloon go up? If it does—whew—it will be a real conflagration. Germany will fly at France, and that automatically pulls us in, doesn't it?"

Mary Ellen handed Wilfred his cup, and hoped that her hand didn't shake. She said, "Vic, dear, Germany would never fight England. Their Kaiser is King George's own cousin."

Both her sons stared at her. Then Victor said gravely, "But, Mum dear, it doesn't only rest with the Kaiser or King George."

"If our King or the German Emperor said there was to be no war—well, there'd be no war," she persisted.

"Darling, much more likely there'd be no King or no Emperor. The time's past when Kings made the wars."

"Then who does make them?" she challenged.

He shrugged his broad shoulders. "Politicians, financiers, armament makers—to name just a few."

She clicked her tongue. These lads thought they knew everything. She wished that their father would speak up and tell them not to talk so silly. If this was the kind of rubbish they were taught at school, sending them there was just a waste of good money.

With a note of asperity in her voice she asked, "Are you trying to tell me that the—well, the last word doesn't rest with the King?"

"I don't think the first or the last, Mummy."

"Then what on earth do we have a King for?" she demanded.

Victor said, speaking very gently, "Because we like Kings in this country; we believe that a limited monarchy is a good thing. We've got a first-rate King. He works as hard as anyone in England, but he is a limited monarch. Certain things are left to his advisers and ministers."

"Well, if he can't stop wars, it seems to me a waste of time having him. However, there won't be a war, and if there was one, your Dad and I should take particular care that neither of you had anything to do with it. Remember that!" She knew that her voice trembled, and felt that tears were very near.

She looked round the little group of men, the people who represented all that she held most precious in life, her eyes hostile and angry. She felt that while none of them spoke, they were in some strange way banding together against her. She remembered the Boer War, when she had watched Amos growing angry and restless, grumbling and worrying what other men would think of him for not going out to fight. Was she going to have to face the same thing again—with Victor and Wilfred?

Amos spoke at last. His voice sounded as if he were trying to placate her, soothe her as he might have tried to pacify a child.

"Well, there isn't a war yet, and so there's no need to get ourselves into a taking about—something that may never happen."

His gentle Mary Ellen almost snapped, "Why, from the way you were talking it seemed you'd all made up your minds about it!"

Victor laughed, and with the sound of his laughter the tense atmosphere seemed to Mary Ellen to grow less charged with emotion—emotion and fear. He said, "Darling Mummy, poor old Dad never said anything. Be fair."

"He seemed to be taking your side anyway."

"But we've not got a side. We only wanted to find out what Dad thought."

"Let's—in the words of the vulgar and ill-educated masses —put a sock in it," Wilfred suggested. "We'll go and get that much-needed wash, shall we?"

As Victor passed his mother's chair, he laid his hand on her shoulder, saying, "Don't worry, not on our first evening anyway."

When they came down to dinner, washed and brushed, immaculate in black jackets and striped trousers, Mary Ellen knew that her heart missed a beat. What other woman had two such sons? Small wonder that she worried!

How she loved to see them eat, enjoying her beautifully cooked food, revelling in the stuffing, the sauces, the well-prepared vegetables. Amos too, she thanked heaven, enjoyed his food, and made no bones about it either.

Later the two boys walked out into the cool, star-lit evening, and stood leaning—as their father and mother had done when first she came to see the house—on the old dry-stone wall. For a long time neither of them spoke, but stood watching the dim outlines of the hills in silence.

Wilfred broke the silence. "It's a nice spot."

His brother nodded. "Grand—it's a grand country. Worth fighting for if one had to."

"You would want to fight?"

Victor turned and smiled at him. "I shouldn't want to. I don't believe that reasonable people do want to fight. It's a senseless, extravagant way of settling a dispute. I should go, because I couldn't bear to try to stay out and let someone else run risks, face dangers, even something worse, on my behalf. You'd feel such a slug."

"I know. You're lucky, Vic. You're eighteen and four months. I'm not seventeen yet, shan't be for two months. I bet"—more cheerfully—"that I could pass for eighteen. We've both got our O.T.C. training behind us too. That might help. I simply couldn't go back to school, swotting a lot of stuff that doesn't matter a damn, while you were in uniform."

"Mother'd be frightfully against it. She was really upset tonight."

Wilfred said, "Listen. It's the idea of a war at all that upsets her. She's got guts enough for twenty. She'd only have to hear someone say that they wondered why the Towers boys weren't in uniform, and she'd rush us both round to the recruiting station within ten minutes." He laughed. "You'd see."

"I suppose so. It would be a queer business, wouldn't it, Wilf? Going overseas, somewhere, living a new kind of life, under conditions that were completely strange, having to learn to kill other men who personally had no more grudge against you than you had against them. Or knowing that one of them might quite easily put paid to your bill and finish everything. I expect you don't allow yourself to think that way in a war."

"Honestly, Vic, you think that it's coming?" There was curiosity but no particular apprehension in Wilfred's voice.

"I don't see how it can help coming. We've got Grey, he's wise, but that German fellow with his bombast and swank about God being on his side, Germany's jealousy of Russia, Austria taking a hand, and we're committed to help France—no, I don't see how it can help coming—and coming jolly soon."

"Germany's got a better army than we have, Vic."

"Bigger—we don't know that it's better, Wilf. England hasn't put up too bad a show up to now." He shivered. "It's getting chilly. Let's go in."

Mary Ellen felt that this thing called "war" was approaching nearer and nearer, gathering speed as it came, until she thought that she could actually hear it rushing towards her. The boys, who had always found so much to do when they came home, seemed now to be always at a loose end, always waiting for the latest editions, always "slipping down to the station" or to the post office, when she knew actually that they sped down to the newspaper offices to see if fresh telegrams had come through to be displayed in the windows. At home they never mentioned the political situation, and when she ventured to make some remark concerning it, she felt that she faced a conspiracy of silence.

It was Amos who broke that silence, when he sat down as if he were more than usually tired, sighed, and said, "Well, we shall know tonight. They've got until twelve o'clock. If they don't answer—that settles it."

It was almost a relief to Mary Ellen to know that by twelve o'clock the suspense would be over, and they would know the worst. She had no hope left that there would be a peaceful settlement. She had tried to resign herself to the inevitable. Again she looked at the faces of the three people she loved so dearly. Her hands were clasped tightly, the knuckles showed white. Her lips felt dry, her eyes smarted as if someone had flung dust into them.

She said, "God help us all."

Amos nodded. "Aye, we'll need it too."

They sat silent, and it was something of a relief when Victor said that they'd ride down to the newspaper office and see if any news had come through. They both stooped and kissed her before they went. She felt that she was saying "good-bye" to them, that they were already caught up in the horrible machinery of war.

She heard their voices talking excitedly as they rode down the drive, and instinctively stretched out her hand and laid it on her husband's.

"They'd not take you, would they, Amos luv?"

He shook his head. "They wouldn't last time. I doubt if they'd take me this time, not for a long while anyroad." He paused and cleared his throat harshly. "They'll take the young, unmarried chaps first, m'dear."

"Aye, young chaps—like ours."

"That's right."

She laughed shakily. "I doubt if there's much 'right' about it. You'd not try to stop them going then, Amos?"

"No, I'd not raise a finger, luv. Mind, it would almost break my heart to see 'em go, but it would be a sight harder to know that other men's sons went, and mine tried to shuffle out of it, or get themselves safe, comfortable jobs. We've bred 'em clean and decent, and I'd never want to see them aught else."

Almost indignantly she answered, "Why, neither of them could be anything but clean and decent, you know that as well as what I do. They're a long time, aren't they?"

"It seems long," he said; "it isn't really."

They sat there, Amos holding her hand, trying to comfort her by pressing it gently from time to time. There was nothing left to say, the only thing they could do now was to wait. Amos Towers knew nothing of the Sword of Damocles, but he felt conscious that he was waiting for the fall of something which would end the life he had known and force him to embark on an existence of which he knew nothing, concerning which he could only speculate vaguely.

He had worked, he had attained a certain position in his native town, through his own efforts he had built up a successful business, had been able to send his sons to a good school, given them a home which was not merely comfortable but where there was a certain amount of restrained luxury. He sighed. And now . . .

Emily came in with the hot water which Amos always drank before he went to bed, in the belief that it warded off rheumatism. Mary Ellen always drank a cup of exceedingly strong tea.

"Thank you, Emily. Don't wait up, we'll let the boys in."

Emily sniffed with a touch of ostentation. "If you don't mind, mum, Cuke an' me'd like to wait up while the young gennelmen cums back wi' whatever news there is. 'Ow much hope d'you think there is, sir?"

"None, Em'ly," Amos said, "none at all."

She squared her spare shoulders. "I wish as I could get me 'ands on that Keyser o' theirs. I'd gie him summat to remember. Upstart rubbish, upsettin' everyone like this!"

The hands of the clock had passed twelve when Mary Ellen started up, crying, "There they are! Oh, Amos, if only——" She caught her breath in a sob and he said quietly:

"Nay, luv, dean't take on, there's a good lass."

The boys came in. Victor looked white and strained. Wilfred was obviously in a state of suppressed excitement, his face was scarlet, his eyes shining.

Mary Ellen did not speak. She stood twisting her fingers, her eyes on the faces of her sons.

Amos Towers said, sharply, almost furiously, "Well? Don't stand there saying nothing! What is it?"

Victor answered, his voice quiet and controlled, "It's—war, Dad."

His mother said, "Go and tell Cook and Em'ly. They're waiting to hear."

CHAPTER SIX

THREE months later both the boys were in the Army. Victor had been given his commission on the strength of his O.T.C. training at Redburgh. Wilfred had cycled to Newcastle, where he had lied about his age, and had been accepted. He returned home, his face wreathed in smiles of satisfaction.

"They took me! Said that I was a very good specimen."

Amos said, "You know that I could tell them you lied, don't you?"

"Yes, I know that, Dad, but you won't, will you?"

"No, I shan't, because I know if I did you'd find some other recruiting office and find another mug who'd believe—or say that he believed—your lies. Anyroad, by the look of things we've sent a lad to do a man's job, and we might as well let it go at that."

"You're not angry, Dad?"

"Nay, I'm past being angry, lad."

Wilfred turned to his mother. "Mummy, say something."

She sat suddenly very erect and held out her hand. "I'm very proud of you, Wilf. You've lied, I expect that you've broken the law, but—I'm proud of you."

He sat down, he looked from one to the other, then said, "You see, I just couldn't stand old Vic being out there, and me—going back to Redburgh. It would have been too—well, too degrading. Vic and I have talked all this out. If I'm sufficiently strong, fit, well grown to be in the first fifteen—mind, Vic never got into it!—I'm all right to be where he is."

Amos said, "Well, Vic's a bowler—football's not his game."

Wilfred threw back his head and laughed. The sound startled both his father and mother. They stared at him, and he laughed again.

"What a loyal pair you are!" he said. "No one must say a word against Victor or me, never mind if it's me speaking of Vic or Vic about me!"

Amos said, "Well, and why shouldn't we be? Tell me that."

"No reason at all, only it's jolly nice."

They saw him go, both smiling. Only when he had gone did Mary Ellen remember that she ought to go through her linen cupboard and set it to rights. Amos wondered when it was ever in need of "setting to rights", but he said nothing, and showed no surprise when she came down, her eyes still red with the tears she had shed.

It seemed to her that she never decided whether the days fled past so quickly that she could not keep track of them, or if they crept past so slowly that it seemed that they would never end. Each postal delivery was something to rouse new fears in her heart; as she sorted the letters she knew that her hands shook. How she hated those field postcards, which told you so little, which merely gave you a few bare facts. As she read them, her heart flamed with indignation against a state of things which prevented boys from writing to their mothers, from telling them all those small, apparently unimportant things which meant so much.

She knitted furiously. Both Victor and Wilfred must have had sufficient woollen garments to clothe half a dozen men;

exquisitely made socks, gloves, mufflers, cardigans and woollen helmets. Nothing was too difficult, too intricate, for her to attempt and accomplish.

She read the news, scarcely understanding what it all meant; she listened to the conversation of other women when she went to the various sewing parties which had been organized. She heard about the Retreat from Mons, of the Angels which had been seen there—and accepted it as a sign that the Powers of Goodness were on the side of the British.

In 1916 Wilfred came home on embarkation leave, and talked cheerfully enough of going "over there". He was tremendously proud of his corporal's stripes and boasted that he'd be a sergeant in no time. He went, and it seemed to Mary Ellen that the last real link between herself and her sons had been severed. Now they were both in a world of which she knew nothing, of which she had no mental pictures; all she had was her imagination, trying to think what it was all like, and only succeeding in giving herself sleepless nights.

Amos was busier than he had ever been. He admitted that there were grave difficulties, difficulties which were growing more and more trying to overcome, but he shrugged his shoulders and said that obstacles were only there to be surmounted. From time to time he came home looking drawn and depressed, with the news that Captain Evans had been torpedoed, or that Captain Cartwright had been taken prisoner.

Early in 1916 they had news that Victor was wounded, and Mary Ellen knew that her heart lightened. At least he was safely out of those trenches away from that murderous gun-fire, and all the other horrors which seemed part of modern warfare.

Later they heard that he had been brought to England and that he was in a hospital in Park Lane and doing well. They would be allowed to visit him.

Amos whistled. "Park Lane! Must be one of those houses given by the aristocracy for hospitals for officers. Fancy Vic in Park Lane!"

Mary Ellen said. "Fancy me going to London for the first time to see my lad in hospital. That's a nice thing, isn't it? I've heard some tales of the nurses—some of them are artful hussies. I hope they'll not try on any nonsense with our Vic!"

The hospital impressed them, though Amos, being a Councillor, had been to plenty of grand houses, and was able to assume an air which appeared to imply that this was nothing extraordinary in his eyes.

As they entered Victor's room Mary Ellen held her breath, while Amos wore a particularly wooden expression and looked more stolid than ever.

Victor was lying in the rather high, narrow hospital bed, and except for a strapping of plaster down the line of one jaw, he looked very much as he had always done. A little older, perhaps, when you remembered that he was barely twenty, but his eyes were bright and his voice strong as he greeted them.

"This is nice! What an excuse for you both to shake a loose leg in town! Doing all the theatres, eh? Wish that I could come with you. What are you going to see?"

His mother said, "Nay, luv, give us a chance. We only got here at two o'clock and it's only half past three now. We've come straight here, only stopped for a minute to drop our bags and things. Now, tell us, Vic, how are you?"

He smiled. "Grand. Slowly and with the greatest care they are removing all the bits of shrapnel which the Boche gave me as a souvenir, or as a number of souvenirs."

"Where were you wounded, Vic?" Amos asked.

"Come along without Mummy one day," Vic said, "and I'll give you a list in detail. This"—he touched his plastered jaw—"was one of the outstanding bits. However, it's all going on very well, and in a couple of weeks I'm to be moved to Nottingford."

Amos frowned. "What, the Duke of Nottingford's place?"

"Nothing less. The best is good enough for your gallant defenders."

"Then, when you're better, they'll let you out of the Army?" Mary Ellen asked.

"Not on your life, Mummy. I shall be as good as new, ready—if not completely willing—to go back. Oh no, darling, the Army can't do without blokes like your elder son—or the younger one either. He's a sergeant. Did you know? I bet that he makes a rattling good one too."

His mother said, "I call it a shame. You've done your bit, let someone else go now."

He patted her hand. "Darling, the trouble is that there aren't enough *to* go out. They're all wanted, every damned one. This is a big job."

"What's it like, Vic?" his father asked.

Their eyes met, steadily and without wavering. Victor said, "Pretty beastly."

"I thought as much."

They stayed for five days and Mary Ellen felt that he was growing stronger every day. Nightly, on her knees, she thanked God for this respite, and wished that Wilfred might be wounded also. She gave the Almighty explicit instructions as to what kind of wounds would be acceptable and which were to be avoided, and trusted that due attention would be paid to her petition.

A fortnight later Victor Towers was transferred to Nottingford. His first sight of the great grey-stone house, with its majestic towers and vast expanse of shaven lawns, already changing from the grey-green of Winter to the new bright green of early Spring, both delighted and astonished him.

The great trees with splendid wide-spreading branches, with their massive trunks, entranced him. Already their boughs were taking on a hint of "fuzziness"; you could not yet actually see the new buds, but their presence was evident from the change in the outline of the huge branches. As they drove along he saw willows with "catkins" already dangling on them.

His mind went back to Flanders, to the trees which he had seen there, poor, shattered things, broken, destroyed, standing there as mere unsightly stumps. He had always loved trees and the sight had hurt him. He was conscious of a sense of pride and innate satisfaction that these English trees were intact. It seemed a good omen.

He was not a particularly sentimental young man; he had no illusions about the war. It was stupid, illogical, wasteful and generally most unpleasant, but it was something that had to be done, and, like many young men of his age, he believed firmly and honestly that the Allies were fighting "a war to end war".

Meanwhile, he confessed that it was wonderful to sleep in clean sheets, to eat food which was well prepared, and to be away from—the noise. How he loathed and hated the noise, not only of guns, of bursting shells, but the continual confusion of sound which rose when twenty or thirty men gathered together in the Mess. He was not a young man who disliked his fellows; on the contrary, he was popular with his associates. He was interested in their lives. he laughed with genuine appreciation at their stories, and he sympathized with them over the girls who wrote too often or the *one* girl who never wrote often enough.

Now, with the prospect of several weeks' tranquillity and peace before him, he lay back in his ambulance bunk and sighed contentedly.

The whole thing had been a kind of dream; at first he had mentally used the word "nightmare", but now, looking back, he thought that the other word was more fitting.

That awful burst, that noise which he hated, intensified until it became fantastic and unreal. Lying there, conscious with a kind of surprise that he was actually alive. Cold mud silting through his clothes, and hot blood seeping out of his body to mingle with the mud. Being lifted and jolted shockingly over uneven ground. Lying in a tent, C.C. station. More jolting, and finally being in bed. A hard, good hospital bed. People in white overalls jabbing about, making themselves intolerable nuisances, giving grunts of satisfaction when they located a piece of shrapnel. Later, London, and being driven out of Charing Cross Station, hearing people cheering. He had asked a nurse who was with them in the ambulance, "What's the noise—Lord Mayor's Show?"

She smiled at him. "It's a welcome for you all, that's all."

Then Park Lane, and he thought that he had never known what comfort really meant. It was like being home again in his mother's house. People who smiled, who had deft, kind hands, who were only anxious to do everything that lay in their power to help. Wonderful visitors—quite breathtaking. The Queen herself, stopping to say a word to him, and to his room-mate, who was a lord himself. He had listened, of course he had listened, to what she said to "Pudding" Welford.

"I shall tell your mother that I have seen you."

And Pudding's voice, much higher than you'd have expected it to be, for he was a big heavy chap, saying, "Thank you, ma'am, that's very kind."

"I believe that we may expect David home on leave. He will want to come and see you, I'm sure. Good-bye—go on getting better."

When she had gone, Pudding said, "I've known her all my life. She is awfully decent to my mother. Hope David comes. I like David a lot."

"David" had come, and had sat on Pudding's bed and

smoked a great many cigarettes, and had grumbled and used a certain amount of bad language concerning people who couldn't mind their own business and were "everlastingly trailing me". Then he laughed and said that he was going to see *The Bing Boys* and *Chu Chin Chow*, and buying masses of records to take back with him. Then he looked at his watch and said, "I say, that's not the time!" and when assured that it was he jumped up and shook hands with both Pudding and Victor and rushed out as if he had a train to catch.

Pudding said, "Stout fellow that. If only they'd *let—him —alone.*"

The ambulance stopped and the doors swung open, letting in the chilly, damp air of early evening. Victor was tired, some of the wounds ached, he felt "edgy" and suddenly bored. A beautiful woman in uniform greeted them; she had a wide all-embracing smile and really seemed glad to see them. One of the nurses whispered, "That's the Duchess."

A room with two beds, the other occupied by a tall man, who was dressed and lying on the bed reading a book. He scarcely looked up as they entered with Victor, merely glanced at them for a second and returned to his book. He had a long thin face and a narrow head. Victor judged him to be considerably older than himself. What a blessed relief to relax, to wriggle his toes against the smooth, clean sheets, to—just wait for people to do everything for him!

The sister asked if there was anything he'd like. He nearly said that everything was like what he imagined Heaven to be —yes, even after Park Lane—but thought it was possibly early days to begin talking like that.

She leaned a little lower and said in a confidential voice, "I wonder if you'd like a cigarette and"—she paused and her eyes twinkled—"a whisky-and-soda before dinner?"

He grinned and said, "Sister—lead me to it."

"You mean lead it to you, eh? I'll see to it."

The man in the other bed looked up and said, "Can't I be included?"

"You can get up and get one for yourself, can't you?"

Her voice had sharpened a tone and Victor felt that she didn't like him much.

He replied easily, "Lots of things I can do, Sister, only they're so much more pleasant when someone else does them for me."

He smiled as he spoke, and Victor saw that in spite of his long narrow face, there was something particularly attractive about him. His smile changed everything, he looked younger, less certain of himself.

"All right," he said, "I'll come and get it. I'll bring it for"— he jerked his head towards Victor—"for him too."

Victor said, "That's awfully good of you. My name's Towers."

"Mine's Hamish MacPhail."

He followed the sister out of the room and Victor stretched his legs again, revelling in the luxury of the sheets, the good hard bed and the soft pillows. He was still weak, some of his wounds still ached and throbbed; tomorrow, he supposed, the endless probings and dressings would begin again. Meanwhile it was good to know that his journeys were over for a time at least.

MacPhail returned with two whiskies-and-sodas; he set one down on the locker by Victor's bed and stood looking down at him.

"Had a bad time?"

"Not too good, but it's much better now. Shrapnel stuck all over me."

"Damn awful. I just managed a nice tidy straightforward job. I'm going out in three days. Finished with the blasted Army—they've left me with one leg an inch shorter than the other. So back to Scotland and my own business."

"Which is?"

"Oh, estates and that kind of thing. Moors and a nice bit of salmon river. I shall have to marry and settle down. I shouldn't, except that I'm an only son. What do you do?"

Victor sipped his drink and thought that he had never in his life tasted anything which so conformed to his idea of what nectar must be like.

"Well, I hadn't started doing anything. I'd just left school when this show started. When it's over I shall go into my father's business. He's a ship's chandler at Willingbrough."

MacPhail stood talking, and Victor found that he was amusing. He had been in the hospital for three months and was able to give details of the life, impressions of the surgeons and doctors, to criticize the sisters and nurses, even to give an imitation of the Duchess.

His humour was dry, caustic and astringent; Victor felt

that frequently it held a touch of malice or spite. It was evident that he enjoyed talking, and that he expected his listeners to find him amusing. He finished his drink, took his own glass and Victor's, and wandered out again, with a casual "See you later. If you hear me moving about, after the lights are out, don't worry. I get restless."

The doctor saw him when he made his rounds: a young Scotsman with red hair and a freckled nose. The sister stood beside him, stiff and starched. A younger nurse hovered in the background.

The doctor set the palms of his hands in the small of his back and said, "Losh, Sister, this is a back-breaking job, eh? Well, Mr. Towers, they sairtenly did their best tae mak' ye into a colander, eh? You'll get a good night's sleep and we'll hae a proper luke at ye in the morning. Gie him the usual, Sister. Good night, Mr. Towers."

The young nurse stood back to hold open the door for the doctor and her superior to pass out. For the first time Victor saw her face clearly. She was tall and slim, her face was oval and rather pale, but a lack of colour which augured no ill health. Her eyes were very dark, grey, he judged, and wished that he could see them more clearly. As she followed the doctor and sister out, she turned and sent him a smile—of friendliness, encouragement, assurance—he didn't know; all he did know was that it had been a particularly nice smile, and that he wished she would come back and talk to him.

He dozed, was awakened to find his dinner being offered to him. He hoped for a brief second that it might have been brought by the nurse he had seen before, but it was placed on his bed-table by a broad-shouldered orderly in a spotlessly white jacket.

Victor said, "I don't believe that I'm hungry."

"Try and take something, sir. Sister gets worried if you don't eat."

"I'll do my best. Thanks."

He didn't manage to eat very much, he was tired, and a wound in his hip throbbed and stung. Later the door opened and the nurse he had been wishing to see came in.

She walked over to the bed, looked down at his tray and said, "You've not eaten very much, have you?"

"Sorry, Nurse, I didn't feel hungry."

"It's very nice food. The Duchess insists that everything

here is good. Her stock phrase is that nothing is too good for 'the brave boys'. Well, you hear that said so often and it means—just nothing. With the Duchess it really *does* mean exactly what she says. We all have to work pretty hard, but I honestly believe that she works harder than anyone here—yes, harder even than Sister!"

He lay there listening to her voice, wishing that she would sit down and go on talking for a long time. It was a low, rather full voice, beautifully clear, with no slurred vowels, and no high-pitched notes. The kind of voice, Victor thought, that would be pleasant to listen to if you had a raging headache.

She looked down at his tray again. "Now, don't you think that you could manage a little more? That jelly, it's good—made with real fruit juice. Do try."

He felt that he would have done his best to eat anything if it would please her. He picked up his fork and said, "I'll try."

"I'll come back in five minutes. You're to have something to make you sleep."

She came back, and smiled approval when she saw the effort he had made.

"That's better! Now, here's your draught. Take it and get to sleep, and if Major MacPhail is late, he won't disturb you."

"He tells me that he's going in a few days."

She nodded. "Yes, back to his beloved Scotland. He's been here a long time." Victor thought that she spoke the last sentence as if she were talking to herself.

"He's amusing, isn't he?"

"Very, when he wants to be. Like most of these Highlanders he gets moods of black depression. They're a strange race."

She held out the little glass which held the draught. "Take this, and then by the time you're washed and settled down—why, you'll be almost asleep." She watched him drink the draught; it tasted of salt and nothing else, he thought. She picked up the tray and took the empty glass from him and went out.

He lay back, wondering who was going to wash him and "settle him down" for the night. The idea that she might come back and do it filled him with a sense of panic. Of course he'd been washed by other nurses, dozens of times, but somehow—this girl was different. He lay there, apprehensive and disturbed. They ought to have orderlies to do these things, not beautiful girls. No man wanted a woman, however skilful and impersonal she might be, to see him when he was as thin as a rail, covered with scarcely healed scars, bound up in bandages here and there. The thought was revolting.

Then the door opened and she came back with a trolley, and said in a voice which he felt was assumed to give patients confidence, "Now we'll settle you comfortably."

He said, "I believe that I could quite easily wash myself, you know."

"Probably, and possibly after tomorrow I may say, 'Now Mr. Towers, get ready for bed,' but not tonight. Tonight, until they've had a real examination, you're an unknown quantity, and we watch"—she laughed—"unknown quantities very carefully."

He resigned himself, tried to forget his miserably thin body, and the unpleasant scars. Her hands were capable, efficient and very steady. He felt that she knew exactly what to do, and how to do it with the least exertion for herself or her patient. He began to feel faintly drowsy, to realize that his eyelids were heavy, and that his whole body longed for complete rest.

When she held the glass for him as he cleaned his teeth, he said in the slightly peevish voice of a weary child, "I hate this toothpaste, it's beastly."

"Tomorrow you shall tell me what brand you like—we have all kinds in the store here. There, now I'll make this bed comfortable."

"It's all right. I swear that it's all right. Don't bother."

But she made the bed all the same, and he lay back on his pillows completely relaxed and felt the pain in his hip retreat into the hazy distance. From a long way off he heard her voice, that pleasant, low voice, say, "Good night and sleep well."

Once during the night he fancied that he heard MacPhail moving about, but he scarcely emerged from the mists of sleep, and when he woke again it was to find a nurse standing at his bedside with a cup of tea. With a little sense of disappointment—this was not his nurse of the previous night.

She said, "Sleep well? That's good. Take your tea while it's hot, and then go to sleep again. I shan't be in until nearly breakfast time."

"Thank you. You're not the same nurse who was here last night?"

"No, she's off duty. Give us a chance to get *some* rest!

Besides, you can't always have the Beauty Chorus to look after you! You've got to put up with the ordinary kind sometimes." She had a broad, good-natured face, and her smile was infectious. "Monica's one of our highlights."

"Is that her name—Monica?"

She nodded. "Monica Crawshaw. Her father's General Crawshaw, no end of a swell——"

MacPhail's voice from the other bed said, "Oh, for God's sake, Harkess, stop yapping. Come and tell him all about Crawshaw when I'm having my bath."

She took Victor's cup from him, and turned to MacPhail. "From the sound of you this morning, Major MacPhail, I think what you need is a nice glass of liver salts, and not tea. You're looking pretty pasty."

"Oh, mind your own business."

She laughed. "Charming fellow, our MacPhail! I'll bring you your tea *and* the liver salts."

Victor, warmed and soothed by the tea, lay there half asleep. The name Monica Crawshaw came again and again to his mind. Her father was a general. He remembered that he had heard him spoken of as "Cunning" Crawshaw. The "Cunning" was almost a term of endearment, because he had "pulled off" so many things, thanks to his attribute of cunning. He heard Nurse Harkess come back with tea, and in the distance, muffled as if in a mist, heard her speaking to MacPhail. He was grumbling and his voice reached Victor as a kind of growl. He slept and woke again to find her ready to "make you tidy for the day". MacPhail, tall and spare, wearing a magnificent dressing-gown, with a bath towel slung round his neck, nodded, "Good morning."

"Thank heaven," he said, "I am going to escape to the bathroom. This woman will drive you frantic, Towers, I warn you. She never stops talking for a second; her tongue is like the clapper of a mill."

"That last remark," Harkess said, "is one of our fine old Scottish sayings, matured through the ages, along with claymores and haggis."

He had to admit that she did talk, but he was interested. She told him about the hospital, about rules and regulations—which might be broken with impunity, and which must be kept inviolate. He lay there waiting to see if she would speak again of Monica Crawshaw.

She was talking about MacPhail. "Too high and mighty for me. He's never liked me. He tolerates the Duchess, he's reasonably civil to Sister, he likes Monica because she's—well, she belongs to his own class. Swanky, and all County, you know. Not that she ever puts on any side, but—he does. I shall be glad to see the back of him. Let him go back to his grouse and his salmon, his haggis and all the rest of it. There! Now you can face breakfast, and the surgeon and anything else in the day's work. D'you think that you could shave yourself if I get you your things?"

He could and did; he felt better and stronger after his night's rest. He even ate a moderately good breakfast. The examination in the operating theatre was less difficult than he had dared to hope. Apparently the other surgeons who had poked and probed had done their work well, and there was nothing necessary now but for the wounds to heal.

"You're young, and you'll do very well," the surgeon told him. "Rest, eat well, and in about a week we ought to be able to let you get on your feet. Until then, just possess your soul in patience, get the nurses to bring you some thrillers that won't need too much concentration on your part—and go ahead."

Two days later MacPhail left. He shook hands, wished Victor good luck, and that was the end of that.

Harkess said, "There goes old Ship that Passed in the Night! Heaven help the salmon when he gets at them! And oh, the poor grouse! Perhaps he'll send us a brace one day—I don't think."

Victor knew that his strength was returning, knew that his wounds were healing rapidly, and realized with a shock that as soon as they were properly healed he would go before a Medical Board and they would decide his future. He didn't mind what they decided, he didn't mind going back to France, but what shook him was the thought of leaving Monica Crawshaw.

Their conversations never reached the easy-going familiarity which existed between Nurse Harkess and himself. She was always kind, always ready to do anything for his comfort, to change his books, get him whatever he wanted from the store, but he remained "Mr. Towers" and she never joked with him in the slightest degree.

Yet he knew each morning, which meant the beginning of a new day, was filled with the expectation of seeing her.

During his first week in the hospital he waited hopefully for her visit in the evening when she made her rounds of the patients under her charge. She did not come, and in her place a strange nurse came and "settled him" for the night.

He remembered the sense of panic which seized him. Was it possible that she was ill, that she had left the hospital and been transferred elsewhere? In the morning, when he knew that his nerves were on edge, Nurse Harkess said brightly, "Miss our Monica last night? Old Farmley isn't a bad sort, but she's damned starchy and stand-offish."

Victor licked his dry lips. "Where was Nurse Crawshaw?"

"Her day off. She went up to town and saw a show. She had a late pass and got back about two this morning. She'd been to see *The Bing Boys*—of *course*, no prize for the answer to that one!"

His relief was such that he felt he could have burst into tears. He waited eagerly for Monica to come to his room. He was still alone, and found it very pleasant to have the room to himself. When she came he knew that his face flushed, and yet all he could stammer out was that he hoped she'd had a good time in town.

"A lovely time. Doing all the nice things one forgets about down here. Eating particularly good food, talking to lots of people, seeing a show—it's so amusing, I don't wonder that all the men on leave make a bee-line for it. Then dancing, and rushing away at the last possible moment. Oh, it was great fun."

He took his courage in both hands. "When I'm all right again, will you let me take you to town one day? You shall go anywhere you like, see any show that will amuse you. I'd be so delighted."

He wondered if he heard a very slight change in her voice, as she answered, "That is very kind of you, Mr. Towers."

Victor persisted. "But will you?"

She looked at him; her eyes were very steady, good, wide-apart eyes. The silence seemed to last for a long time, then she said, "Yes, thank you. I should like to—very much."

For the rest of that evening Victor felt that his heart was singing. He began to make plans, wonderful plans as to how they would spend the day. He didn't know London very well, but he knew the names of the big hotels, places where he had heard the prices were tremendous. That was the kind of place!

A good band, good food, wine, dancing on a first-rate floor. Riding with her in a taxi, as it were, shut away from the rest of the world. Going to a theatre, walking in conscious that people turned to look at her, that other men envied him. He lay there, dreaming dreams long before he slept. He was very young, he realized, but there was the conviction that unless he could marry Monica Crawshaw he didn't want to marry anyone. True, except in the Army, he had never worked, but there was his father's business, a business which he liked and in which he was determined to carry on the success which his father had made.

He sighed contentedly. Like a small boy, he whispered very softly, "O God, please let her love me," and so slipped into sleep.

CHAPTER SEVEN

VICTOR TOWERS never remembered with any great clarity the names or even the faces of the men who were with him; they came and went, one or two of them died and left a sudden sense of resentment and unbelief with the rest. Death, once you had escaped as far as this peaceful place, seemed so unlikely and even incredible. Another man was put into Victor's room, a pleasant, rather studious fellow, who kept massive-looking books beside his bed, and made copious notes of what he read. He told Victor that "when it was over" he was going to Oxford, and that his ambition was to teach science at one of the public schools.

Slowly everything and everybody were becoming unreal to Victor; the only person who mattered, who stood out with complete clearness, was Monica Crawshaw. Other people he talked with, walked with, laughed with, but they never seemed to have established themselves in his mind as she had done. It was a relief when he was allowed, as he was soon after his arrival, to get up, wash and dress himself without aid from anyone. He felt that with greater independence he ceased to be merely a patient, but that he might justly be regarded as a complete male entity.

She was always friendly, and sometimes when she was off duty they would sit together in one of the garden shelters and talk quietly and almost intimately. The Spring was advancing, the trees were no longer lovely skeletons, but gracious green-clad shapes, ready to give shade, to throw wonderful shadows, and offer rest to your eyes. The primroses bloomed, and when Victor went for long walks into the country, his nostrils were assailed by the scent of violets. He loved to see the brave, bright celandines, looking as if they had been newly enamelled. The birds began to be very industrious, and he would sit quietly and watch them flying backwards and forwards to the nests which they were making.

He was singularly tranquil; he could not but believe that such love as he felt for Monica would be returned, perhaps not in such entirety as he offered his to her, but with a real warmth and sincerity.

He had walked down to the nearest village, and on his way back he overtook her on the field path. He saw her swinging along in front of him; her easy movement, telling of complete health, was a joy to watch. He quickened his steps, and again felt a little thrill of pleasure that he was well again, that his wounds were healed, and that his body was becoming strong, firm and obedient to his wishes. Like many people who have always experienced perfect health, he had felt a kind of shame, a feeling that he ought to apologize for his wounds, his weakness and necessary reliance upon other people to accomplish things which he ought to have been able to do for himself.

He said, "Good morning, Miss Crawshaw."

She turned and smiled. "Hello, Mr. Towers. What a morning! The sun is quite hot, and in this great cloak—I feel suffocated."

"It's grand to know that Spring is really here," he said, "it's such a good time of the year. Makes you believe that the war will soon be over, that life will be as it was before. Gives you—hope about all kinds of things."

He fancied that her face looked suddenly grave, but when she spoke her voice was low and full as always.

"Captain Moscrop brought in a big bunch of violets yesterday. He found them in Templar's Wood."

Victor said, "I found them in Templar's Wood quite a few days ago."

"You didn't bring a bunch back." She laughed. "You were less generous than Captain Moscrop."

"I don't really like picking flowers very much," he

answered slowly. "It's so—final. Once they're picked, well—they're really finished. If you wanted some, I'd get them for you. I know where all the flowers grow, and where all the birds are building nests too! One day if you like I'll show you a wren's nest, and there are plenty of thrushes' and blackbirds'. The wren's is going to be a little beauty."

She said, rather idly he thought, "I should like to."

He felt nervous and strung-up. He wanted to walk quietly beside her, and yet felt impelled to talk. "Summer must be lovely here, but I shall be away long before the Summer. Dr. Robertson says they'll give me a Medical Board any time now. Don't forget," his nervousness was growing and he wished that his voice did not sound so high and rather shrill, "you almost promised to spend a day in town. There won't be much time once I'm posted back to duty."

"I won't forget. I'm going to town this week, on Thursday. I can't ask you to take me then. I've got to meet some people. I shall be busy all the time."

Impulsively he said, "Look, it's really hot. Sit down for five minutes, here in the sunshine. I don't believe you'll be cold."

She sat down on the trunk of a huge elm tree. "This was blown down in one of the Winter gales," she said. "A dreadful night! Now it has to lie here until it is ready to go to the mill."

Seated beside her, Victor pointed to a little shoot, tipped with green, showing bravely. "Look," he said, "it may be dying, but it's dying—game."

Monica nodded and touched the green shoot with the tips of her fingers. "There's a lot to be said for—dying game," she said.

Victor slid his hand along the tree trunk until his fingers touched hers, very gently. He made no attempt to take her hand, just remained very still, watching her.

At last he said, "You do know that I'm terribly in love with you?"

She said very quickly, "Oh, I hope not—not really in love!"

"It's the most real thing that ever happened to me. It's the only absolutely real thing in the world to me. I accept the war, accept the existence of other people, but—except for my mother and father and my brother—none of them are very real. Oh, they're there, they're alive, but to me they're only worth noticing because they happen at the moment to be part of one's environment. You're—the reason for everything. Do you understand?"

"But you don't really know me," she protested. "You just know me as one of the nurses here, and you happen to—well, to like me."

He laughed. "I don't believe that when you are in love—desperately in love as I am—that you *need* to know a great deal. You don't love people because they're religious, or musical, or know how to run their houses efficiently. Maybe you're very glad if they do happen to have those attributes, but that isn't why you love them—nor do you stop loving them because those things hold no interest for them."

"You don't know anything about me!" Her voice was passionate. "For all you know I may be desperately in love with someone now—at this minute."

He shook his head. "I don't believe that you are," he said. "If you had been, you'd have old me—minutes ago."

"Well, if not in love—let'. ay very, very attracted."

"Oh, attraction! That's a different story. I know that I'm young, but after all, that is something which time will put right."

"How old are you?" Monica asked abruptly.

"I shall be what they call 'rising twenty-two' quite soon."

"I'm twenty-four."

"Then with the wisdom of those additional two years, you must realize how completely sincere I am. Listen, Monica dear, wonderful Monica, I'll wait, I'll be patient. I know that I've rather rushed at everything, but I couldn't wait any longer. It's such a big, wonderful thing. I've kept it a secret, and then this morning I felt that I must share the wonder of it—with the person I love best in the world."

For the first time since their conversation began she smiled at him.

"We must go. Look at the time! My dear, there is someone to whom I am terribly attracted—he is attracted to me. Whether it is anything deeper—on his side at least—I don't know. The fact remains that, at the moment, it exists, this attraction, and——"

Victor rose and held out his hands to help her. "And you are going to see him in town next Thursday? Would you like to marry him?"

"I think so—no, I'm certain that I shall."

"I shall wait. If I don't marry you, I don't see myself marrying anyone."

"You're still very young. You may change your mind."

"I doubt that, doubt it very much indeed. There, we must go or be late for luncheon. After all it's Springtime, and hope's everywhere. Young—of course I'm young, and glad of it. I'm fit—or almost fit again—I'm ambitious, I've a good chance to make good, and I can enjoy everything. I've not seen a great deal of the world. We'll see that together. I may not know much about what's called 'life'. We'll make a wonderful life together. I'm not aristocratic, but I come of decent stock, healthy stock, honest stock. I refuse to be depressed! Now, come, we must get back. Thank you, wonderful one, for listening to me."

She shivered suddenly and drew her cloak more closely round her.

"You almost frighten me with your—certainty."

"My dear, not certainty. I'm too humble, too much your very devoted servant to be—certain. Only—hopeful."

They scarcely spoke on their way back to the hospital; Victor left her at the great hall door and walked away to another entrance which led to his own room. His heart was beating heavily, he felt slightly exhausted, tired out. His room-mate was seated by a small table, and glanced up from his notebooks as Victor entered.

"Hello, you look tired, Towers."

"I walked rather far and had to hurry back so as not to be late."

"It's a wonderful morning. I took a turn round the gardens; they keep them well, don't they?"

"I went over the fields. I like watching things, birds, small wild things. If you keep still it's astonishing how many of them come and stare at you. They seem to think that all two-legged things ought to be continually on the move, and when they keep still, they're interested in something strange."

The other man stared at him. "Curious fellow you are!"

Victor laughed. "I'm not scientific, that's why you find me—as the rabbits and field-mice do—curious."

On the Wednesday evening he met Monica Crawshaw in the long corridor. She hesitated, and then said, "Good night, Mr. Towers."

"Good night. You're going to London in the morning, eh?"

She nodded. "I shall be back early on Friday morning. You remember those things you said to me—that morning in the fields? If you really did mean them, I don't want you to *mind* too much, because I'm—I'm going to London."

Victor knew that he did mind, that the thought of her spending hours with—the other fellow, hurt like a dull ache somewhere in his chest. He managed to smile and say, "I only mind because there won't be any chance of seeing you all tomorrow. A day can be a horribly long time, you know."

She nodded. "Yes, I know that too. Good night, Mr. Towers."

"Good night, and have a splendid time."

He thought that Thursday would never end. He tried to imagine what she was doing, lunching in some gay restaurant filled with officers in uniform and pretty women. He wondered if she and this man, who was "the attraction", went to a matinée; if so, what kind of a play—perhaps a musical comedy with nice sentimental tunes. Then she'd go and change. Hadn't she told him that she had an aunt living somewhere in Kensington? He didn't know where Kensington was, but he imagined tall houses with shining front doors and perhaps window boxes. He wondered what she'd wear. He had never seen her in anything except her nurse's uniform. Something soft, long, falling in smooth folds to her feet, or something with a shorter skirt, rather frilly and amusing. Dinner, with shaded lights on the table, and a band playing softly. Dancing, talking, being happy together. Perhaps at that moment this other man was asking her to marry him. He shivered, and moved restlessly in his chair. A man who was writing at one of the small tables looked up, his face sympathetic.

"Got a chill, Towers?"

"No, no, just what they call a goose walking over my grave."

The other laughed. "Grim thought!"

Another man came up. "Come and make a fourth at bridge, Towers?"

Almost eagerly Victor said, "Yes, rather, I'd love to." Anything to get away from his thoughts, to be forced to concentrate on cards, to remember what had been played, and make rapid calculations. Yes, bridge was the thing. He'd play bridge until it was time for "lights out" in the card room, and then go and ask the night sister to give him something to make him sleep. He'd say that he'd been sleeping badly. Then in the morning . . . He said again, "Yes, coming now, Foster."

He played with an intensity that was foreign to him. He played well, but never as he played that evening. His partner grinned at him across the table, congratulating him.

"Grand, Towers, we smote them hip and thigh that time!"

Foster said, "Towers is lucky at cards, I've noticed it."

The third man added, "Lucky in cards, unlucky in love, eh?"

Victor laughed. "Oh, you, you're always handing out those 'wise-saws and modern instances'! Your deal."

Later he went to the night sister and asked for something to make him sleep. The cards had kept his mind occupied, but now he knew that he dreaded the long night.

"Aren't you sleeping well, Mr. Towers?"

"Not awfully well, Sister. Oh, only the last few nights!"

"What did you have before, do you remember? Medenol, was it?"

"I think so, Sister. Whitish stuff."

He took what she gave him, went to bed, and read a thriller with the same fierce concentration he had given to the cards. Finally he felt his eyelids heavy, the words were indistinct, he closed his book and fell asleep.

He woke, stretched his arms above his head, yawning luxuriously. It was morning; she would be back. At this very moment she was probably in her room changing into uniform. He might even see her on his way to breakfast. He would say, "Hello, good morning! Have a lovely gay time?"

He shaved with even more care than usual, and he was very particular about the way he shaved. He eyed his uniform and decided that he must get a new one for that day she had promised him in London before he went back to France. He actually did meet her in the long corridor. His cheerful, carefully rehearsed greeting was forgotten.

He said, "Oh, my beautiful, you're back! What a wonderful start for the day!"

She looked tired and heavy-eyed, not very happy, he thought. Perhaps the man hadn't proved so attractive after all.

Monica said, "Immediately after breakfast you're wanted in the M.O.'s office. I'm tired—danced too long last night, I suppose."

D

"But it was worth it, eh?"

She shrugged her shoulders. "I suppose so."

Victor laughed. "Suppose—suppose—angel, you don't seem very certain of anything this morning!"

"I'm not," she said. "Go on to breakfast, Mr. Towers, you'll be late."

"Can I see you this evening? Do say 'yes'. Yesterday was such a damn awful day."

"If I can, I'll leave a note with the porter."

"Bless you," he said, and went on his way to breakfast.

The Scottish M.O. nodded to him. "Sit doon, I've news for ye. Medical Board i' the mornin'. If they're of the same opinion as myself, they'll pass ye as pairfectly fit. We've cairtainly made a guid job o' ye, ma mannie."

"Will they give me some leave before sending me back, Doc?"

"Och, aye, I'd think sae. That's one o' the advantages o' being in a hospital run bi a duchess! She believes all officers should have a guid leave before going back. Niver doot, you'll get leave. Want it for onything—special? Ah mean any special reason. If so, Ah might pit it to the Duchess. Yon's an awfu' human kind o' body."

Victor hesitated, then smiled. The Scotsman thought what a good-looking lad he was, and reflected for a moment on the uncertainty of life for these youngsters with a certain melancholy.

"I *might* be getting married, Doc. Only *might*, nothing's really settled yet."

The sentimental strain which exists in every good Scot showed itself.

"Have ye told her?"

"That I want to marry her? Rather—what do you think?"

"And does she love ye, Towers?"

"She's a little undecided, but it's going to be all right. I know that it's going to be all right," Victor said.

"That's the speerit! Weel, guid luck tae ye. A' the best. Ten in the morning, aye, here."

That evening when he came down to dinner the porter handed him a note.

I have heard about your Board in the morning. I'll be in the little summer-house by the big beech at nine. M.

Victor put it in his pocket, smiled at the sergeant, saying, "Some of these fellows think that you ought to want to play bridge every night of the year, don't they?"

The sergeant answered, "Not a gime I kere for, sir. Give me a nice gime o' soler, thet's the gime for me, that or nap. Nap's a grand gime."

"I've played nap. It's a gamble, Sergeant, just a gamble."

The sergeant answered heavily, "Come to thet, sir, all life's a gamble, ain't it?"

"Oh, I don't know, some things are—certainties."

"Birth and death, sir. I reckon thet's abart all."

The moment dinner was over he hurried down to the little summer-house. He was terribly afraid that someone might have got there before him. The little place was empty, and he sat down, his heart beating so heavily that he thought anyone passing must hear it. He heard the stable clock strike the hour, and a few moments later Monica was standing in the doorway.

Victor sprang to his feet, and taking her hands in his drew her to the seat. "Bless you for coming. How I've waited for this! I thought that I'd never seen men eat so slowly or so much as the chaps did at dinner tonight. You know that I've got a Board in the morning?"

"Yes, I heard so."

"They're certain—so the M.O. says—to let me have some leave before I'm sent out. Monica, you won't forget that day in town you promised me, will you? May I write to you and tell you when my leave is coming to an end, so that we can—just have our day together? Something for me to take back, to remember. Or," rather wistfully, "perhaps you could manage two days—I don't mean two together, but one day one week and another just before I go off again. Could you?"

She laid her hand on his arm. "Victor, I don't believe that I ought to make promises. I should hate to have to break them—especially to you. You see, I do like you so much, and it would be dreadful to—well, to hurt you. It's all been so strange, and yet I have come to believe that you do mean—all that you've said. You're not only indulging in one of the usual flirtations with one of the nurses, because you're bored in hospital."

"Come, we're getting on!" Victor said. "You must take me

seriously, because it's the most serious thing that has ever happened to me. No, let me write, and just say that you will—well, do your best. I shall know that means exactly what it says, and that your 'best' is something frightfully good. Don't worry about me, I *know* that it's going to come right."

"For you, or for me?"

"For both of us! Once this damned war is over, we're going to have a marvellous time. I swear we shall."

She leaned a little nearer to him, and in the dim evening light he saw that there were tears in her eyes; he pulled her to him very gently, saying softly, "Oh, darling, darling, don't worry. Please don't worry. You're tired, you must get some rest. I expect they'll send me packing very quickly, but perhaps I shall be able to see you for a moment."

Monica raised her head and brushed away the tears which had fallen on her cheeks. Then she put her hands on Victor's shoulders and kissed him, long, very tender, passionless kisses.

"Yes, I must go. Victor, dear Victor, I wish that I loved you as you deserve to be loved."

He smiled at her. "You will, darling, you will—one day."

"Good night, dear Victor. No, don't walk back with me. Remember I'm not supposed to sit in summer-houses with the patients."

"Very well. I'd quote *Romeo and Juliet*, only every man who has been in love has done that; I will say that 'I would kill thee with much cherishing'. There, darling, good night."

The Scottish M.O. was right, he was passed as fit, and granted four weeks' leave before returning to his regiment. They told him that he had made a fine recovery, added a few phrases indicating that it actually paid substantial dividends to lead a clean, healthy life, and never to abuse any of the good things which life provided. He might go on leave at once and he was to report to the Duchess before he left.

She was sitting in her office, her desk covered with forms, letters and various official-looking documents. She nodded to Victor, and told him to sit down.

"As you're a patient no longer, would you like a drink?"

"I should indeed, ma'am."

She indicated a tray on which stood glasses and siphons. "Help yourself, and mix me a whisky-and-soda, Mr. Towers. Where do you live—where is your home, I mean? Willing-brough? I know it. I launched a ship there years ago, before you were thought of. I think the best thing is to catch the London train; it leaves Loughton at three-twelve. We'll send you in one of the cars to the station. Then get the train North, from King's Cross. Remember, no having a good time in town for the night. Miss Mullins is arranging about your warrant now. Ah, thanks, Maude; there you are, Mr. Towers. Was the M.O. right in dropping a very discreet hint that you might be getting married?"

"I hope to, ma'am. It's not settled yet."

"Can't she make up her mind? Tell her from me she's a fool if she lets you go! Well, Mr. Towers, the best of luck! I can't say that we shall always be glad to see you back, can I? But I can say that I hope one day, when this beastly war is over, you'll come and see me. I should be delighted, so would my husband. I mean it. Good luck."

"Thank you, ma'am, thank you for everything. Good-bye. Good-bye, Miss Mullins."

He rushed up to his room and began packing. He was excited at the thought of going home, of seeing his father and mother. What stupendous luck if Wilfred had leave while he was there! He thought of the old stone house which he loved so much, the wide fields which stretched away towards the moors, the trim garden, and the well-kept flagged yard at the back of the house. Yet, the thought of not seeing Monica Crawshaw every day took—he felt—the sharp edge of delight from his happiness. He had grown so accustomed to catching glimpses, however brief, of her every day, those moments had been the white stones on the journey of every day. He would write to her, although he never felt that he was very good at letter-writing. She would understand. The fact that she had kissed him last night, kissed him of her own volition, had left his heart singing. Surely she must feel something for him more than mere friendship. He knew her sufficiently well to realize that she was not the type of woman who offers kisses indiscriminately. He scribbled a note to her, and took it down to the Matron's office. She greeted him with some warmth; everyone liked young Towers; he had never given any trouble, he was handsome, well mannered and never "made fusses".

He put his request very nicely, Matron thought. He was leaving, and from time to time he had lent various books to Nurse Crawshaw, books which he valued. Might he see her for one moment, in order to give her his home address or to take the books himself if she had finished with them? He would not keep her a moment.

"She'll be at luncheon, Mr. Towers. I'll send the note down by my secretary." He watched her broad, kindly face and wondered if he detected the suspicion of a twinkle in her grey eyes. Did she suspect? Was she merely being very kind to a foolish young man who had fallen in love with one of her nurses, and—was leaving that afternoon? She added, "Just wait here, Mr. Towers, I have to go and speak to the Duchess about something. You can speak to Nurse Crawshaw here. If I don't see you again, good-bye and good luck."

"That's very kind of you, Matron. May I smoke here?"

"My dear boy, I rarely stop smoking myself! Of course."

He lit a cigarette and smoked it rapidly and nervously. He tried to think what to say to Monica, and found nothing but a number of clumsy, disjointed sentences came to him. He stubbed out his cigarette irritably. Why didn't words come easily, beautiful words, sentences which would convince Monica that he really loved her, instead of those stumbling, inadequate phrases which sounded in his ears so stilted and artificial?

There was a knock on the door and he rushed to open it. Monica stood there looking uncertain. "Matron's secretary said that I was wanted in Matron's office."

He said, "So you are, wherever I am—you're wanted, badly."

She looked at him; he saw that her eyes were still heavy, she looked—he thought—dispirited. "Oh, Victor!" and a smile touched her lips.

"It's true! I've had my Board. I'm going this afternoon. I go to London, and have strict injunctions from the Duchess to 'go straight home'. Monica, when am I going to see you; when are we going to have that day in town together?"

"It's a long way to come all the way from the North just to spend a day in London, isn't it?"

"That depends on the person with whom you are going to spend it. You know as well as I do that I'd take a much longer journey than from Willingbrough to London to spend an hour with you."

As he spoke he had a feeling that she was only partially listening to what he was saying; her eyes were watching him, but he was certain that she was thinking of something which had nothing to do with his coming to London. He stood silent, their eyes meeting, his anxious, hers puzzled and distressed.

He said, his voice suddenly sharp, "You *will* come, won't you?"

"Yes, yes, I shall come. I'll write to you, and tell you when. I can get your home address from the office. There, I must get back. Good-bye, Victor, I hope you have a good journey."

He took her hands. They were very cold, and lay motionless in his. He leaned forward. "Kiss me before I go." He smiled. "A kiss is such a pleasant thing to—to take on a journey as a memory."

Monica shook her head, an almost imperceptible movement. "All kisses aren't—pleasant things," she said. "One kiss at least has gone through the ages as something—horrible."

He felt that she had laid one of her cold hands on his heart. He was shocked and shaken; he wondered if she were ill, running a temperature in spite of her cold hands. You came to think that quite a number of things might be attributed to a temperature, when you'd been in hospitals for months.

"Monica," he exclaimed, "you're not well, darling."

"Quite well." Then almost wildly, "There, you shall have your kiss, a good-bye one." She kissed his cheeks, gently and softly.

"Not really good-bye," he whispered. "It isn't that, is it?"

"No, my dear. I shall see you again."

She turned and walked out, closing the door softly behind her.

Victor stood frowning, disturbed, distressed. Then, because he was young and hopeful and very much in love, he accepted the solution which gave him the most mental ease. She was beginning to realize his sincerity and the depths of his love for her. The knowledge was bringing problems with it. After all, she was the daughter of General Sir Claude Crawshaw, a baronet, a man of great distinction, and great attainments. He was only a junior officer, the son of a well-to-do ship's chandler. She knew nothing of his family, of his prospects. She was growing to love him, to have dreams of their life together, and she knew that such a marriage might bring considerable opposition from her family. No wonder that the beloved girl was distraught; she had, as they said, "enough on her plate". He'd write from London, he'd send her flowers, and if there was sufficient time he'd go and order books for her. No, he wouldn't though! He'd write, and send the flowers; he'd send the books from Willingbrough, they would be an additional excuse to write to her! He'd send photographs of Mummy and his father, of Wilfred, of his dog, "Haig", of the house, of the garden, of his car, of every blessed thing that he could photograph! He'd begin to build up a picture of his home for her, and then when they met in London—for what he already thought of as that wonderful day—he would ask her to become engaged to him before he went back. They might even go and buy the engagement ring. He had spent little or nothing since he came home wounded; his allowance from Dad was practically intact. He could afford something—well, rather startling. Something that she could show to her family without any fear that they might imagine him either vulgar or parsimonious. Everything was going to be all right.

He went to the desk, tore a sheet of paper from a scribbling-pad and wrote, *Dear Matron, thank you so much. Yours gratefully, V. Towers.*

When the car came for him, the fellows crowded on the steps to wish him a good journey. They were so obviously sorry to see him go, that Victor's heart warmed towards them, and he felt suddenly sad and regretful to be leaving.

"Good-bye, Towers, see you over there!" "Good luck, old man, put one over to the Boche for me!" "See you on Paris leave, eh?" "Not too much of that *vin rouge*, Towers, it's fatal," and so on. Some of their injunctions were not altogether delicate, but as he settled himself in the comfortable car Victor thought that no man ever had such a grand collection of friends. He made up his mind never to lose touch with his particular friends, to write to them regularly, and meet them whenever it was possible. Except for two men, neither of whom he liked very much, one of whom he met in Rheims, and another in Arras, he never saw or heard of any of them again. He never wrote to them, nor they to him. It was like leaving school, swearing eternal friendship, and almost forgetting the other chap's name at the end of a month.

At Paddington he made enquiries; his train left from King's Cross in two hours' time. He got his luggage piled into a taxi, told the driver to take him to a telegraph office and a flower shop, and leaned back to watch "London in war-time".

Last time he had been in London he had travelled in an ambulance, now he was fit and strong again. The taxi stopped, almost shooting him off the seat.

"Telegraph orfice, sir. Over there."

He sent his telegram to Monica, beginning to write the message and then tearing up the form because it was so banal, or far too obviously affectionate. Finally he wrote, *All places that the eye of heaven visits are to a wise man ports and happy havens stop Just the same I wish that I were back. V.*

He read it over—pretentious and pompous, showing off, altogether rather silly. He handed it in, and went back to his taxi feeling disgruntled. The sight of the flower shop restored him a little. He loved flowers, loved colour and beautiful scents. He bought with taste and considerable extravagance. He wrote a card: *London looks very drab, so I am sending these to take them away from the grey skies of London to where—it seemed—there was always sunshine. V.*

In the corner of his railway carriage he lay back and sighed. This was the first time for months that he had been a completely free man, able to direct all his actions, to be without the necessity of conforming to the rules of a timetable. It was strange how the effort had tired him. He felt half exhausted. It was queer to have even a small responsibility given to you, the ordering of a taxi, tipping a porter, sending a telegram, buying flowers, all nothing in themselves, but assuming enormous proportions when you first practised them after months of relying on the efforts of other people.

He leaned back in his corner, dreamed waking dreams of Monica, and slowly fell asleep, and slept for over two hours. He woke, looked at his watch. The time was ten minutes to eight. The train was due in Willingbrough at ten minutes past. He peered out of the window trying to discern familiar landmarks, but everything was hidden by the darkness of the Spring evening. Only when the train rushed through a small station—Flayfield—did he realize that in a few moments he would be home.

He slammed down the window as the train slowed down and shouted for a porter; the old familiar smell of the station reached him. He and Wilfred had always agreed that they would know the smell of Willingbrough station if they were blindfolded.

The porter stared at him, then said, "Nay, it's young Mr.

Victor Towers. 'Ow are yer? Grand ter see you back. Now, what 'ave you got?"

"Only what is in the carriage. That's the lot."

His father pushed through the crowd, shouting, "Hello, Victor! We've got the car here. Look who's with me!" And there was Wilfred, with his broad shoulders and his strong, solid figure, wearing officer's uniform, and grinning his head off.

"Hello, Wilf. What's this? I thought that you were never going to take a commission, that your aim was to be R.S.M."

Wilfred slapped him on the shoulder. "So it was, only Haig said that I should be more help to him if I took a commission. The King said he thought it was a good idea too—so I gave in gracefully."

Pleasant to walk down the dirty steps, to see his father's obvious pride when people stopped him and said, "Got both your boys back, eh? That's nice, Mr. Towers." Or, "Hello, Towers, the family reunited!"

Amos beamed at them all. Victor thought that he would have liked to linger and recount Wilfred's doings and his own.

The car, a larger one than the one which he remembered. Quite a luxury car, shining and gleaming, with a uniformed chauffeur at the wheel.

Amos said, "The other was a bit small. I like your mother to have a bit of comfort when she goes out. I still drive my own old car, but she insisted that Wilf and I brought this one to meet you. She's excited! She was just as bad when Wilf came home, like a hen on a hot grid! Like to just stop for a quick one at the White Hart? It's all right, I told Mother that we might just drop in for one."

Victor caught his brother's wink, and the grin which accompanied it. He knew that their father longed to walk into the rather exclusive saloon bar of the White Hart accompanied by his two sons.

"Until you suggested it, Dad, I didn't realize how badly I wanted a drink! What about Wilfred?"

"I always realize how badly I want one about this time of night."

Amos walked in, trying to look modest and unselfconscious, and failing badly. He ordered their drinks, and Victor watched his eyes roving round the big ornate saloon bar. He saw, too, how his father's face beamed whenever anyone came over and greeted his sons. His evening was made perfect, Victor thought, as they were leaving, and almost collided with a very large, stout man, with a broad, florid face and bright, keen eyes.

"Ah, Mr. Towers, how are you? These your two lads? Ah, glad to meet you, glad to meet you. Just leaving? Well, good night."

As they went back to the car, Amos Towers said in a loud whisper, "That was Sir Walter Merley, the Conservative M.P. Glad you both met him."

CHAPTER EIGHT

VICTOR thought that he had never imagined anything so pleasant as his days at home. He wrote to Monica that, except for the fact that she was not there, he had never been so happy. His mother was overjoyed to have her sons with her again. They all tried to forget that Wilfred's leave was only for a bare ten days, when he had to report to an Officers' Training Camp.

"Never heed," Mary Ellen said to her husband, "he's in England again, away from that nasty fighting and dirt. I only wish Vic was going to some kind of training place. I fair dread his going overseas again. Somehow, Amos, it never seems right to me—they get wounded, they're sent home to get patched up and then pushed off again. Like as not to get wounded again. It's—why, it's inhuman."

Amos nodded. "Aye, love, it's a queer do. Puzzles you to understand it all."

He had taken them both to the store, had them measured for new uniforms, and listened to the little Jewish cutter exclaiming at the width of Wilfred's shoulders, and seen his obvious admiration of Victor's good looks.

"Both of t'em do you credit, Misther Towers. They'll be a grend advertisement for our uniforms! We'll hev half the British Army coming to us for new uniforms ven t'ey see t'ese two young fellers."

One sunny afternoon the two boys drove out into the country, and sitting in the sunshine on a bank where primroses were already showing their sweet, pale flowers, Victor told his brother about Monica Crawshaw. Wilfred listened gravely and with complete attention. It seemed strange to hear Vic talking about becoming engaged, even of being married during his next leave. It seemed only the other day that they had been at school together immersed in the work, the games and the usual domestic politics of school life. A match won or lost, scholarships for the Universities gained, bringing additional credit to the school; the arrival of a new house master, a change of matrons, the tuck-shop under new management: these things had been all-important in their lives. Now that life seemed years ago, miles away, almost as if they had both moved away from it into a different world. They had learned to accept responsibilities, to give orders; Vic had been wounded, and now to make the change from their old life even more marked Victor had fallen in love and was talking about being engaged to this girl whose father was a general and a baronet into the bargain.

He said, "Well, it takes some getting used to, Vic. She hasn't actually promised to marry you yet, has she? You don't think," very anxiously, "that she's leading you up the garden?"

"If you knew her, you'd not think so either, Wilf. It's just —oh, I don't quite know myself, but I'm as certain that it's going to come right as I am that tomorrow's sun will rise."

"Well, good luck. If she's good enough for you, she must be a damned nice girl."

Wilfred was to leave at the end of the week; he would travel to London, and then on to his training camp. The night before he was leaving Victor received a letter from Monica. She thanked him for his flowers, the books which he had sent her, for his letters.

They are very dear letters, I have loved having them. Can you meet me in London on Friday? I still feel very guilty that you should take such a long journey, but you made me promise, and I hate breaking promises. I would meet you in the entrance of the Savoy at half past twelve. If you feel that it is a long way, don't please hesitate to write and say so. I shall understand perfectly.

That evening he said to his mother that he thought he would travel up to London with Wilfred. He added that he hoped she didn't mind; he would be back as early as possible on Saturday.

"Mind, luv?" she said. "Nay, I'd be a funny kind of muther if I minded you having a jaunt to London!" She looked at him, her eyes dancing. "Are you meeting anyone in London, luv?"

He knew that he flushed. Trust Mum to know things, trust her to know without being told. Not that he minded, she always understood things.

"As a matter of fact, I am meeting someone."

"A young lady, I'll be bound!"

Victor nodded. "Right again, Mum. I'm going to ask her to marry me."

"Marry you! My word, this is a surprise. It seems only the other day that I was pushing you and Wilfred in a pram, and now you're talking about getting married. Wonders will never cease."

She settled herself more comfortably in her chair, picked up the khaki sock which she was knitting, and said, "Tell me all about her. Don't miss anything out. How old is she? Two years older than you, twenty-four, a bit over maybe. And what's her name?"

Surprisingly he found himself telling her the whole story, how he had fallen in love with her "almost, you might say, at first sight". He recounted all his hopes and fears, he even told her how she had kissed him the night before he left the hospital.

Mary Ellen listened, her eyes intent on her knitting. She listened not only to her son's words but noted the inflections of his voice as he spoke of this girl he loved. Mary Ellen thought that there was no mistaking his sincerity; it seemed that his voice had taken on deeper notes, new modulations. His words were simple enough, but what coloured them was the manner in which he spoke them. There were no high-flown phrases, no elaborate descriptions; it was the very simplicity of what he said that convinced her how deeply he had fallen in love with Monica Crawshaw.

"Eh, I hope and pray she'll be good to him," she thought. "Our Vic's not like Wilf. Wilf would stand up to unhappiness. It would break Vic. He's always taken things to heart, ever since he was a little lad."

"So, Mum dear," he was saying, leaning forward, his hands clasped, his eyes very bright, the light catching his hair and making it shine, his mother thought, like gold, "you'll wish me luck, won't you? The moment I know that it's all right, I shall send you a telegram."

"It's her that will have the luck, my dear, if she gets you for a husband. Aye, I'll wish you luck. I'll do more. When I say my prayers tonight, I'll ask Him to make you happy. Same as while you and Wilf have been away in France, I've asked Him to luke after you both."

Victor rose and came over to her chair. Her words had moved him deeply; for a moment he wanted to kneel down and ask her to put her arms round him, as she had done when he was a little boy.

He stooped and kissed her smooth, soft cheek. "Darling Mum, what an angel you are."

"Nay, I'm no angel. Just an ordinary muther, who loves her lads. You'll be wearing that luvely new uniform. See as you wear those nice shirts Dad had made for you. Egyptian cotton, it's called. Lukes like silk, it's that fine. Will you be staying with the young lady's family?"

"No, Mummy, she'll stay with her aunt at Kensington. I'll go to a hotel."

"Very well, I'll just slip up and pack a bag for you. No, you will not do it yourself! What a thing! Leave out half of what you want and take the other half of things you don't need."

They were taken to the station the next morning in the big car, Amos and Mary Ellen with them. Victor felt a little sensation of tender amusement. Bless them, they could not resist coming to the station to see their boys off. They were as proud as peacocks, delighted that their uniforms should be faultless, their bags solid leather, heavily polished. At the station, the porter who took their bags was warned in a slightly louder tone than was necessary, by Amos Towers, to "mind, think on, first class for officers". He was an elderly man who had known Amos all his life. He grinned.

"Nay, Amos, Ah've carried bags fer a few officers i' my time. Ah've learned as they 'ave ter travil like wot dukes does. Aye, an' why not? That's what I say—why not?"

As the train moved out of the station, Mary Ellen slipped her hand through her husband's arm. He was growing stout, his hair was not so thick as it had once been, he was short and stocky, but to her he was all that a man ought to be.

"You'd have a job," she said, "to find two lads who luke like ours do!"

"Aye," Amos answered. "Those two could go anywhere, into the highest society, and they'd be all right. Those uniforms we've made, they're proper treats. Like gloves they fit!"

Wilfred was excited at the thought of his coming training. He sat with his long legs outstretched and his eyes half closed, dreaming of the time when he would have pips on his shoulder; one day, if the war lasted long enough, the pips might be exchanged for a crown. There might be bits of coloured ribbon on the breast of his tunic—Major Wilfred Towers, M.C. He was going to be a good officer, just and sane; if he were lucky and got promotion, he'd jolly well see that he earned it. He'd not be just another "gong" hunter, like the general who had come to address them one day when they were going into action, who said that he wished "I could be coming with you, but I must get back immediately to G.H.Q.".

He glanced across the carriage to where his brother sat. Victor, he thought, looked a bit white about the gills, like some chaps looked just before they went into action. Not frightened exactly, but as if their nerves were tightly strung. At Doncaster, Wilfred got out the packet of beautifully cut sandwiches which Mary Ellen had given them, unscrewed the cap of his silver flask, his father's parting present, and when he offered the sandwich packet to Vic, his brother shook his head.

"No thanks, Wilf, couldn't eat a thing. A drink? Ah, that's different. Thanks."

Wilfred refilled the cup of the flask, and raised it in his brother's direction. "All the best luck in the world—down the hatch!"

Again Victor said, "Thanks," and then continued to stare out of the window. Wilfred finished the sandwiches. No use bothering the chap if he didn't feel like it.

They slid into King's Cross station. Victor sighed, a sigh of relief. Had ever a journey seemed so long? His watch showed that the time was five minutes after twelve.

"Wilf, come to the Savoy and have a drink with—with us. I won't ask you to have lunch with us, for obvious reasons. But I'd like her to see you." He laughed. "I'm rather proud of my young brother."

"The Savoy!" Wilfred whistled softly. "I say! I've never

been inside one of those swagger places in my life. I promise that I'll make myself scarce, quickly."

He admired the way Vic said to the taxi driver, "Savoy." Just that, as if he'd been going there all his life. They turned into a kind of courtyard, with what looked like a theatre on one side, and where several porters in smart uniforms stood about, ready to open taxi doors. Through big glass doors, into a great hall, with a flower shop on your right, and long counters where men stood ready to attend to the visitors. Somewhere, a long way off, he could hear music being played. Mentally he registered a vow that, one day, he would come here to meet a beautiful girl. Not as "Cadet" Towers, but as—at the very least—Captain Wilfred Towers.

Victor was raking the hall with his eyes, tapping his leg with the little leather-covered cane he carried. He looked as if he were waiting for zero hour.

"Take it easy," Wilfred said, "it's only twenty past twelve. Women are always late. What about that drink?"

"Yes, yes. Somewhere where I can see the door."

Victor's eyes never ceased watching those swinging doors. Wilfred relapsed into silence, and wondered if being in love made everyone like this. Suddenly Victor sprang to his feet. "There she is!"

He darted away, and Wilfred saw him speaking to a girl in a very well-cut dark blue suit, with a white shirt or blouse or whatever they called such things. She was remarkably pretty, with eyes which, even from where he sat, he could see were very large and set wide apart. They were turning and coming towards him. He sprang to his feet, and Victor introduced him.

Wilfred said, "I'm only a bird of passage, Miss Crawshaw. Victor brought me in for a drink, and now we're going to have another, and then I must be off." He ordered drinks, and when they arrived raised his glass, smiling his pleasant, kindly, engaging smile at them both.

"All we wish ourselves!" he said.

He bade them good-bye, and they watched his tall, muscular figure disappear through the doors.

Victor twisted round so that he could look directly at Monica.

"Well," he said, "darling, have you come to a decision?"

She nodded. "Yes, I've come to a decision."

She heard him draw a deep breath, saw his knuckles show white as he clutched the arm of his chair. "You'll marry me?"

"If you are quite, quite sure that you really wish to, if you have made up your mind that I could make you happy, then—yes, I will."

"Oh, my dear, my wonderful Monica. You really love me?"

She answered gravely, "Yes, I do really love you, Victor."

For the first time he smiled, his lips and his eyes both smiled. He looked very young, very happy and hopeful.

"When did you find out?" he asked. "When did it dawn on you that you wanted to marry me? Oh, there's so much I want to know."

"I think," she said slowly, "that I had begun to know weeks ago. Then so many things about you were so endearing. You were so unfailingly kind, thoughtful, and"—she laughed—" you made it so obvious that you were in love with me. They say that love begets love, don't they?"

"Can we be married when I get my next leave?"

"If you like—if you wish"—she laid her hand for a moment on his—"I'll marry you before you go out again. You will have to get your Colonel's permission, I suppose, but that shouldn't take long."

"You'll marry me before I go out! Monica, how wonderful! It doesn't seem possible. It's the one thing I dreamed of, but dared not even hope for."

His face was alight with happiness, and Monica thought, "I'm right to trust this man, he'll always be kind and good to a woman."

A massive, elderly colonel sitting with his thin, rather desiccated-looking wife, whispered to her behind a freckled hand like a small ham, "See those two, Alice? I'll lay a horse to a hen he's just popped the question, and been accepted. Look at his face!"

She replied in a thin, dry voice, "Well, the girl's getting the best-looking young man I've seen for a long time."

Victor sent off a long and needlessly detailed telegram to his Colonel; together at luncheon they composed another, equally long, to Monica's father. "It's great good luck that Daddy's home on leave just now," Monica said. They telegraphed to Wilfred, to Victor's father and mother. They sat long over luncheon, until it was too late to go to a matinée, and then he persuaded her to come with him to buy an engagement ring.

It all seemed a wonderful dream, driving with her through the streets of London, listening to her voice, holding her hand in his, and from time to time raising it to his lips, entering a jeweller's whose name was almost world-famous. A suave young man attended to them. Victor noticed that he was slightly lame; he thought that was why the poor devil had to stay selling engagement rings to lucky fellows like himself. No, not exactly like he was, for he was the only one who was going to marry Monica.

Monica said, "Not pearls, Victor. They're unlucky."

"And not opals, either," he stipulated.

She said softly, "Don't be too extravagant, will you?"

The young man was the soul of discretion. He brought out rings, called upon them to admire this one or that; money was never mentioned, you might have imagined that the famous firm were going to make them a present of a ring. Sapphires and diamonds—Victor thought it an ideal combination. He followed the immaculate young man into a little office, heard his statement of the price, lugged out a wad of notes from his pocket and paid.

"My hearty congratulations, sir," the assistant offered.

"Thanks awfully. I've been offering myself congratulations for the past two hours. Thanks."

They drove to her aunt's in Kensington, and in the taxi Victor took out the little blue velvet box and, opening it, slipped the ring on her finger.

"It's beautiful, beautiful. Dear Victor."

"We've been engaged for several hours, and all I've been able to do is kiss your hand. Monica, darling, hang the driver, and the people in the street probably can't see us, and if they can—what odds?"

He put his arms round her, holding her close, kissing her cheeks, her eyelids, her mouth. At last she put up her hand and very gently pushed him away. He saw that there were tears in her eyes.

"Darling, what? Tears in your eyes! Monica, why?"

"I don't know. I'm tired, I think, and you're so—so sweet to me."

Her aunt, Mrs. Boyd-Summers, greeted them warmly. She was a handsome, rather stout woman, with considerable dignity. It was evident that she was delighted at their news. She beamed on them both impartially.

"I shall telephone to my brother this evening, Mr. Towers Possibly before you take Monica to dinner, then she can speak to him also. It's all most exciting, and you must see about that special licence immediately. Oh, you brave young things, how I admire you all! Such courage! Are you going to be married from home darling girl, or from here, just a quiet war-time wedding?"

Victor was surprised at the note of decision in Monica's voice.

"The quietest wedding imaginable, Aunt Charlotte. You don't want a big wedding, Victor, do you?"

He hesitated. He had always believed that girls liked big and elaborate weddings, with crowds of guests, and photographers snapping cameras at them from every angle. In his heart he knew that he would have enjoyed it all. Monica in white with a veil and train, bridesmaids and pages, guests in uniform and out of it. Flowers, speeches, driving away for a two or three days' honeymoon amid showers of confetti and cheers.

He looked at her; she was leaning forward, her hands clasped.

"I couldn't bear a crowded wedding—anyhow, there isn't time. Victor only has another three weeks."

He nodded. "I don't think, Mrs. Boyd-Summers, that a big wedding could be arranged in time. And if Monica doesn't want one—that's settled."

"I wouldn't have one!" Her voice was almost passionate.

"Your dear mother will be disappointed, I'm afraid. However, you must be married from here, my dear. A nice, intimate, *cosy* wedding. Just the immediate family. Yes, that's right."

That evening they danced. Monica told Victor that he danced beautifully, and he felt that he had been awarded some coveted decoration. They talked in low voices; he told her of his prospects more fully than he had ever done, he talked of his father and mother with simple, unaffected love and admiration, and of his brother with affection and pride. Listening to him, she thought how his frankness, his simple but evidently genuine praise of his family, touched her. Her own family had never been particularly affectionate. Her father was proud of his wife, his home and his children, but Monica could never remember any great affection existing in the home.

She admired her father for his attainments, she was proud of his success as a soldier, and liked hearing men speak of him with admiration. Her mother was a handsome woman, with rigid ideas, and a narrow outlook.

She had done her duty to her husband and children. The latter she hoped would marry well, and the former on retirement be appointed to some minor colonial governorship. Her elder daughter, Cynthia, had married a clergyman with excellent prospects, the son of a baronet, and the family living, which would be his eventually, was accompanied by a beautiful Georgian house, a garden which was almost famous for its magnificent yew hedges, and a stipend which was eminently satisfactory. Her elder son, Walter, was in the Diplomatic, and doing well; the younger was in France with his regiment.

As Monica listened to Victor talking of his family, she loved the warmth of his words; it seemed that all his life he had lived in an atmosphere so much warmer than she had ever known.

When he drove her home her aunt was in a state of complete satisfaction. She had spoken with Monica's father; it appeared that he was coming to town in the morning, and he would come to the Savoy to meet his prospective son-in-law.

Monica said, "Did he sound pleased, Aunt Charlotte?"

"I have seen your father look as if he were fairly satisfied with everything, but I have never heard him *sound* as if he were pleased in my life. He spoke as he always does, as if each word cost money and he wished to spend as little as possible."

Monica returned to the hospital in the morning. And after Victor had seen her off, he waited, restless and slightly apprehensive, for the arrival of General Crawshaw. He came, a tall man who looked as if he had been poured into his uniform. The rows of ribbons, and the sign of his rank, were impressive. He looked Victor up and down with rather large, very cold grey eyes.

"So you want to marry Monica? Don't see why not, if you can keep her when this show is over. Not a regular, eh? What's your father? Ship's chandler? Never knew one in my life. What's his club?"

Victor laughed. "Except for the local Conservative Club,

sir, he hasn't got one. I doubt if he's been in London half a dozen times in his life. My mother came for the first time when I was sent home wounded and was in the hospital in Park Lane."

"Umph! Got your Colonel's permission? Who is he, by the way?"

"Southern, sir. Ashley Southern."

"I know him. Good fellow."

"I had his reply just before you arrived, sir. He's quite willing, and so, if you are also, I can get cracking getting this special licence. I thought that we might be married, very quietly, next week."

"Don't see why not. Quiet wedding, yes. Don't approve of ostentation in war-time. Bad form—damned bad form."

"Mrs. Boyd-Summers suggested that we might have the wedding at her house. I mean, that Monica would stay there, and we might have a very small reception after the wedding. I should like to get away as soon as possible. My leave is up in just over a fortnight. We might manage a couple of days' honeymoon, loitering about a little on the way to see my people. I hope you approve, sir."

"Oh, I approve. I shan't be here. Back in Flanders. Going in three days' time. Monica's uncle must give her away. I'll write to him. He's older than I am. Got one of these Parliamentary peerages. Lord Crawshaw of Camberford, if you please. Well, I must get along. Well, perhaps we might have another. Drink to your good luck. Sure that you can keep my girl? She's lived—well, pretty soft, until she took up this nursing."

Carefully but briefly Victor explained that his father had promised him a partnership. Eventually the place would be his. It was very successful, well known all over the North of England. He gave the name of his father's solicitors, and asked the General to ask them to give him further particulars.

Crawshaw inspected the card and put it away in his wallet.

"Father's people belong to the North? Grandfather?"

"Founded the business, sir. Ship's chandler."

"Ah! Your mother's people?"

"I couldn't say, sir. Country people. She was an orphan, living with an aunt when my father met her."

"Umph! Shocking the way you young people take no interest in your families. Don't know who your grandfathers were, much less your great-grandfathers. Pity. Well, carry on,

Towers. Good luck, and I hope you and my girl will be happy. She's—well, she's a damn nice girl."

"I discovered that, sir, quite a long time ago. Good luck, sir."

That afternoon he travelled North. He stopped on the way from the station to see his father's solicitors, and begged them to get the licence arranged for as quickly as possible.

The solicitor's sharp eyes twinkled. "Can't give orders, Victor, to the Archbishop of Canterbury. I believe that it goes through him. We'll do our best. I'll telephone you if there is anything to sign."

He drove home, conscious that he felt a little light-headed. It was all so astonishing. Monica had promised to marry him, her aunt had been enthusiastic about it, her father friendly and obviously not displeased. He had put things in train for the licence, and now tonight he would write and tell Monica that the wedding should be fixed for next Thursday, or at the latest Saturday. With luck, in just over a week he would be married. Monica and he would be able to spend the rest of their lives together. No wonder he felt as if he were slightly "alcoholic".

He paid off the taxi and rushed into the house, calling at the top of his voice, "Mummy, Mummy, where are you?"

She came out into the hall to meet him, her eyes dancing, her lips parted in a smile.

"It's gone all right, my luv?"

"Wonderful Mummy, how did you know?"

"Only got to luke at your face, it shines like the sun, like Moses' face must have shone when he came down from that mountain. Come in and tell me all about it."

There was tea, and fat rascals, and Sally Lunns, and the rather gaunt housemaid smiling wisely, so that Victor knew that his mother had not been able to resist "hinting" that he might come back with great news for them all. He grinned back at her and winked.

"Eh, Ah can see as it's alreit, Mister Vic."

"Couldn't be righter if it tried!"

His mother wanted to know everything. She declared that they were right to be married at once, wished to know if Wilf had seen Monica and what his opinion of her had been. Victor talked eagerly, his eyes alight, his face a little flushed with excitement.

Mary Ellen said, "Mind, luv, you'll have it all to tell over again when Dad comes in! Only with me it's the little things that are important; with Dad it will be the big things. Victor, luv, when you have to go overseas again will Monica stay here with us? You know how I'd luv that. I'd feel as if you'd left something with me, for me to guard and treasure until you come back. Ah, I'd take such care of her; so'd Dad, come to that."

"Why, darling, I hope she will. I'd love to think of her here. You see, this house, even apart from you and Dad, means such a lot to me. I've always hoped that if I did get married, there would be room here for my wife and me. I'd like my children to be born here, to love it as I do. I'll write to Monica tonight."

Mary Ellen glanced at him, suddenly selfconscious.

"I suppose that I ought to write to her, your young lady. I'd like to, but my writing isn't what you might call tip-top. I never was much of a scholar, Vic. I'd not like her to be ashamed to show a letter of mine to her family. Dad's different, he writes a beautiful hand, like copperplate, as you know. D'you think we might leave it to him to do, Vic?"

When Amos came home, the story had to be repeated all over again, with promptings from Mary Ellen.

"Nay, Vic, you're going overfast. Tell your father what the young lady's auntie said about the wedding," or, "Vic, you've missed out about the General's ribbons and all that."

She beamed on them both, and Amos listened, nodding pontifically from time to time. A smile hovered at the corners of his mouth, and Victor knew that he was completely satisfied.

"Champagne at dinner tonight, Muther," Amos said. "This is an occasion. I shall be writing—on behalf of your mother and myself—to Miss Crawshaw tonight. I shall also be writing to her father. In case my letter misses him, I shall direct it to General Sir Claude or Lady Crawshaw. You didn't talk any business over with the General, did you?"

"No, only arrangements, Dad. He asked me if I could keep Monica decently—that was about all."

"Ah!" Amos drew a deep breath. "These aristocratic parties are often unbusinesslike. I want him to know, Vic, that his daughter is marrying into a family as well provided for as any in the North Riding." His tone was impressive, his

manner that which he assumed in the Council Chamber. "Time
is short, and we must not beat about the bush. Your wife, or
the lady who has promised to be your wife, is getting a husband
who will not only be a rich man, but"—he paused and stuck
his thumbs into the arm-holes of his beautifully fitting waistcoat—"but," he repeated, "a very rich man—provided that
he has a headpiece on him, and doesn't play ducks and drakes
with what will one day be his.

"Now it is usual for these aristocratic young ladies'
families to talk about—settlements. Seemly, the General
omitted to do this. I shall mention it in my letter this evening.
I don't know if she has money of her own; if so—so much the
better. If she has not, then I shall settle £500 a year on her—
the interest. She can't touch the capital sum, but the interest
will bring her in £500. On your return from France, you'll get
a partnership. That should bring you in anything from
fifteen 'undred to two thousand a year.

"I'm only barely fifty, so I think you'll agree, Vic, I've not
done too badly. Eh?"

Victor rose, and going to where his father stood, held out
his hand. Amos might be slightly pompous, he might even
suffer from a little too much satisfaction, the self-satisfaction
of the self-made man, but he was solid, and with his solidarity
went integrity, ability, industry and complete goodness of
heart.

Victor said, "I'm proud to shake your hand, Dad. Not
because you're being so astonishingly generous to Monica and
me, but because you're the grandest chap I know. Not done
so badly! Show me anyone who has done as well. You're—
well, you're magnificent."

The days seemed to Victor Towers to fly past. He had
never written so many letters, made so many long-distance
telephone calls. Mrs. Boyd-Summers boomed at him over the
telephone wires, but he had to admit that she was wonderfully
helpful. It was she who arranged for the wedding at Saint
Agatha's in Leven Street.

"It's small, Victor dear, but very charming. Quite a
number of war weddings take place there. The vicar is a friend
of mine—the Honourable Reginald Maudesley. Crawshaw is
going to give Monica away. He looks more impressive than he
actually is. Never opens his mouth in the House of Lords.
Oh no, another call, operator—yes. Victor, the Duchess is

coming up from the hospital! Dear Beatrice, I've known her for years. Monica says that your brother will be the best man. She says that he is handsome. It must run in the family."

On and on, but he couldn't grumble, she was really helpful.

They all travelled up to London in the big new car, for Amos was determined to give a dinner at the Savoy the night before the wedding. He was as excited as a schoolboy; only Mary Ellen looked nervous and apprehensive. When Victor told her that the Duchess was coming, she stared at him and said, "Oh, Vic dear, need we have her?"

Amos was astonishing; he organized everything, he interviewed a manager, gave orders as to the table decorations, discussed the menu—his attendances at various municipal banquets had made him very knowledgeable. He was in his element!

Mary Ellen thought that she had never been so frightened in her life. The massive Mrs. Boyd-Summers, and with her a clergyman—he looked delicate, poor fellow, she thought—who in addition to being a clergyman was an "Honourable". The Duchess, laughing a great deal, dressed magnificently, saying, "What a relief to wear real clothes again! I'm growing to hate my uniform." Monica's uncle, a lord, and her mother who was a lady, though Monica's father wasn't a lord. Very confusing. "So sorry, Mrs. Towers, that my husband could not be here. Yes, he went back to Flanders four days ago. Monica looks tired. It's all been such a rush." Mary Ellen noticed that she said "Flarnders", not "Flanders" as they did in Willingbrough, and wondered if she tried to say it that way if she'd feel daft. Wilfred, he was broader than ever; and Victor, her own beloved Victor! When Monica arrived and she saw his face as he went to meet her, Mary Ellen caught her breath. She thought, "I shall remember that luke as long as ever I live. It was as if heaven had opened for him."

CHAPTER NINE

VICTOR's own car had been sent down from Willingbrough, and he and Monica drove to the North slowly, enjoying all the beauties of the English countryside. He told her that he never saw the sign which reads "To the North" without feeling a thrill of pleasure and expectancy. They savoured everything to the full. Monica knew far more of the Home Counties than he did; he was always willing to stop if she told him of an old church, picturesque houses or the like, so that they might explore together. Time, for Victor, had ceased to exist. He had refused to allow his father to make reservations on the route at well-known and expensive hotels. They drove until they came to a place which attracted them, and stayed there.

Monica was a revelation to him. He had never known her so gay, had never heard her laughter come so readily. She was enchanting!

"It doesn't seem possible," he told her. "I think at any moment I may wake up and find it has all been a wonderful dream. Oh, darling, don't get tired of me, will you? I'm such a very ordinary kind of fellow."

In the evenings, sitting in some quaint old country hotel, he would talk of the future. They would travel, go somewhere new each year until they found a place which held everything they wished for. There would be a brief holiday each Winter for Winter sports, when they would rush to Switzerland, and come back bronzed by the sunshine and full of vigour.

Monica agreed that until the war ended, it was wiser for her to divide her time between the Towers' home and her own. Victor was enchanted when she told him.

"I expect," she said, "that what I mean is that most of the time I shall be with your people. It's exciting to be going to stay in a house which I have never seen, and of which I have heard so much."

"I love the place!"

"I think that I shall love it too. Did your mother like me?"

He laughed. "I think she was a little frightened of you, my sweet. She's a very shy person, my beloved mother. The very fact that your uncle is a peer and your father a baronet was sufficient to put her in what she calls 'a flutter'. She said to me, drawing a deep breath, 'Oh, Vic dear, what a luvely young lady she is!' "

Monica sighed. "Yes, but I do so want her to *like* me."

He smiled at her. "My angel, in the North we don't rush into such things as friendship and love——"

She interrupted him. "Victor, how can you of all people say that?"

"Oh, that was different," he said calmly. "I fell in love

with you. That was an exception. We take things slowly; our likes, our loves, are things which grow slowly, and which we guard and prize. I once heard my mother say—she's a great gardener, you know—that her friendships were never annuals. That annuals were easy enough to grow, they only lasted one Summer, anyway. If you wanted to grow perennials, you had to take them seriously, because they'd go on and on. She's the same with her affections, she likes to take them seriously. Once when I was teasing her, I told her that I didn't believe that she loved me or Wilfred until we were four years old, because she'd have to take that amount of time to get to know us."

"What did she say?"

He made a grimace. "I'm afraid that she was rather hurt. She has a sense of humour, but it's not very elastic. She stared at me, and then said in a slightly reproving voice, 'No, you're wrong. Bairns bring their love with them; you love them the minute you set eyes on them. Yes, and before that.' "

Monica nodded. "Yes, I see—and before that. I will do all I can to make her really like me, Victor."

He laughed. "You won't have to try very hard, sweet."

They arrived at Willingbrough; Monica thought that she had never seen such an ugly town, but Victor assured her that the country round about was some of the most beautiful in England.

As he turned the car into the gates of his father's house, Monica said softly, "Victor, it has been wonderful. Every separate minute. Drive slowly, because I do want to say this. At first, I—yes, I wasn't sure that I loved you. There was a kind of doubt. Was it only war-time sentimentalism? Was it something that would wear thin in a short time? Now, dear, dear Victor, I know that it is just something that will last— as long as I do, yes, and longer. There, I've said it! I will make you—as they say—a good wife. I'll be your loving wife always. You do believe that, don't you?"

As he drew up at the front door with its porch supported by two stone pillars, he turned and caught her in his arms. As he spoke she heard his voice shake with emotion.

"My dearest, my wonderful Monica. I don't know, I never shall know, what I've done to—not deserve, because no one could deserve such happiness, but to have such utter content, such wonder, such lovely completeness in my life. There, angel, they're opening the front door, and my mother's servants mustn't find us embracing like this."

Strange to be greeted with, "Glad to welcome you 'ome, Mrs. Victor," and, "Every 'appiness, Mrs. Victor, Ah'm sure"; Mary Ellen bustled out, her eyes shining, her hands held out. Monica thought that their voices alone made you welcome. Broad, open vowels, speech which might be slow but which never degenerated into a drawl, and which carried with it an impression of energy and vitality as well as warmth.

"Come in, come in. Victor, see that Gibbs takes your bags up. Now, I'll lay that you're ready for a cup of tea, my dear."

Monica, her eyes taking in rapidly the charm of the long, low room with its old, beautifully polished Chippendale, its cabinets filled with Spode, Worcester and Derby, sighed with content.

"I'm always ready for a cup of tea, Mrs. Towers."

"Nay, nay," Mary Ellen protested, "I can't have you calling me that. I'd not ask you to call me 'Muther' because you've a muther of your own, and I don't hold with all this 'muthering', any more than I do bairns calling all and sundry 'Auntie'. But oh, no, my dear, not Mrs. Towers!"

Victor was sitting on the arm of his wife's chair, smiling contentedly, and asked, "Make a suggestion, Mother."

Mary Ellen flushed a little, then said, "Why, Victor luv, my real friends call me—Mary Ellen." She added almost defiantly, "It's my name, choose how!"

Impulsively Monica rose and went over to where she sat. Leaning down she pressed her cool young lips against the soft cheek of her mother-in-law, saying, "Thank you, dear, dear Mary Ellen. It's a lovely name and I shall adore using it."

The elder woman nodded, and said half nervously, "Aye, well that's all right then. Now, go back and drink your tea, or you'll have me properly upset. Vic, I don't see that there's anything to grin about. Seemly you've left your manners on the Great North Road."

But she smiled as she said it, and Monica realized the immense bond of affection which existed between her husband and Mary Ellen Towers. It was the kind of warm, beautiful feeling which Monica had never known in her own home. There she had known kindness, she had been given every care, even luxury, but this was quite different. This was something as strong and lasting as the hills which Victor had pointed out to her as they drove along; it was something unshakable, lasting, so deep-rooted that no storm or tempest, no upheaval, could ever shake it.

During the days which followed she told Victor that she had fallen in love with everything and everybody from his mother downwards. She loved the old house, with its shining, spotless cleanliness, the faint smell of lavender and home-made furniture polish. She found the cooking delightful; she had never eaten such perfectly cooked or flavoured food. When she complimented Mary Ellen on it, she assured her that nothing was ever made in her kitchen which she was not capable of making herself.

"That's the secret," she said. "If you keep servants, let them know that there's nothing comes amiss to you. Let them understand that if they can't do this or that—well, you can!"

"Mary Ellen dear, will you teach me how to do all these things? Baking and mending and making floor polish?"

Mary Ellen beamed at her. "Why, my dear, there's nothing I'd like better. With our lads away at that horrible war, it will be something to—well, take our minds off things, won't it?"

The thought of Victor going overseas seemed to come nearer to Monica like a great, menacing cloud, which hung ever lower and lower. A cloud which threatened, which carried with it danger, fear, even death. Her love for him had grown, she thought, with every hour since she had promised to marry him. It obsessed her, she found it difficult to let him out of her sight, even felt a sense of anger when his father carried him off to the store, or took him to visit some of his business acquaintances. To Monica the whole world held only one man —one man who mattered in the least—and that was her husband.

Each day she discovered some new trait which she loved or admired. She did not know if he were particularly intellectual, but as she was not intellectual herself, that did not matter. He was undoubtedly clever. His father had told her that Victor would make a greater success than even he had done.

He added, "And, my lass, I've not done over-badly. But that Vic, once he gets cracking, he's going to show them something, mark my words. It would never surprise me if you found yourself Lady Towers one fine morning."

She loved Victor's good humour, his delicacy, and his innate courtesy. He was all she had dreamed of. It was obvious that he was popular with everyone; when they went into the town together, people of every class greeted him, and showed evident pleasure at seeing him again. Now, each day brought her nearer to the time when he would leave her. She thought of it with a kind of panic in her heart. Things were not going too well in France; even Victor looked grave and disturbed when he read the papers. She knew that Mary Ellen congratulated herself that Wilfred was still at his O.T.C. Six days, five, four, three, two, one, and she woke with the consciousness that today he was going.

Already he was up, dressed, and moving about very quietly, packing the last odds and ends.

"Oh, Victor," she cried, "you ought to have wakened me!"

He came and sat down on the edge of the bed, taking her hands in his.

"Darling, I wanted to let you sleep as long as ever you could. It's not going to be easy for either of us; I wanted you to have every minute's sleep that you could get. I want to thank you, my dear, for everything. You've made life such a wonderful business for me. I can go out now, conscious that I've experienced all that is most beautiful and lovely in life. The past, made beautiful because I found you, the present because you made it beautiful, and the future—because that must be beautiful, most beautiful of all, because we shall spend it together. Take care of my mother; I know that she will take care of you. Be happy, and send waves of happiness over to me in France. Angel, it is nearly eight o'clock. I'll go down and have breakfast with Dad and Mother, then I'll rush up and give you a last kiss. Darling, be brave; otherwise I shall disgrace you. You'd not like a weeping husband to be seen by everyone at the station. There, I shan't be very long."

She lay there wishing that she had insisted on going to London with him, or even to the Willingbrough station, but he had been so insistent, had declared almost passionately that he wished to think of her not among crowds of returning soldiers, not in a grim and grimy railway station, that she had given in, and promised that his last memory of her should be in the old house which he loved so dearly.

She felt that he was away for hours, though the little clock which he had given her showed that she had only been alone for a few moments. He came rushing back to her; she could hear him leaping up the stairs taking several steps at a time, heard his eager feet in the corridor, and then saw him framed for a second in the doorway, before he came and took her in his arms.

She could feel the buttons of his tunic through her thin nightgown; he held her tightly, but even then at that moment of parting Monica realized that he was gentle. His embrace might be strong, fervent, but it never became violent or so intense that it caused real physical discomfort.

He let her go, very gently, and sat watching her as if he wished to photograph her face on his memory.

"Darling, you're very lovely," he said. "Take great care of yourself, don't ever get ill, or be sad. 'Better by far thou should'st forget and smile, than that thou should'st remember and be sad.' Sweetness, I must go. Don't watch me from the window. Just lie here and think how lovely it will be when I come marching home again."

She could scarcely see him for the tears welled up in her eyes, and she clung to his hands, pressing them to her breast.

"Victor, always remember that I love you. Whatever I've said or done in my life, said things that were untrue, done things which were—unworthy, remember that I love you—I think, more than many men have been loved by their wives. I didn't know that such love existed. My darling," she put her hands round his neck and drew him down so that she was able to kiss him. Long, agonized kisses, while her hands stroked his yellow hair.

At last, as if she were exhausted, she whispered, "Go, darling."

Monica lay there, her hands pressed over her eyes, listening, with every nerve quivering to the sounds which reached her. She heard Victor's voice, clear and cheerful, bidding the servants good-bye, heard the car drive up, the noise of baggage being taken out to it, and at last—after what seemed an interminable time—the noise of the car driving away. He had gone. Now even if she flung on her clothes she would not be in time to see him at the station.

Later, for she did not know the time, she kept her eyes averted from the little busily ticking clock, she felt that time was something outside her life, time must always drag slowly and painfully while Victor was away, while their separation lasted. Mary Ellen opened the door, very carefully, and came in. She had obviously been crying, but her smile was cheerful.

"Now, my dear, Alice is just bringing you a nice cup of tea and a bit of toast. I didn't think you'd fancy more than that this morning."

Monica said, "I don't think that I really want anything."

"You will, when you see it. I might stop and have a cup of tea with you, if you'd let me. The house feels—somehow deserted."

The days lengthened into weeks, life in the old house went on in its usual orderly way. Monica lived for Victor's letters, those letters written on odd sheets of paper torn from a notebook, written in places of which she had no knowledge, and often scrawled in some dimly lit dug-out, or through the hideous noise of a bombardment.

They were never very long; they only told her that he was well, that he longed to be with her again, and that she was not to worry about him. As she read them, she realized how very young he was, young and probably lonely, and often frightened. In addition to her love for him, she experienced a great tenderness, a longing to protect and guard him from anything that might dim—even momentarily—the brightness of his youth.

April was over and May had begun when she knew that she must tell Mary Ellen. She had spent long sleepless hours, night after night, trying to argue things out with herself. She loved Victor; the coming of a child would mean everything to him, he would be happy, excited, elated. To confess to him that the child was not his, that she had married him because her former lover had refused to marry her, would most certainly make him doubt the sincerity of the love which she had for him now, a love which had grown to such immense proportions since her marriage to Victor Towers. She remembered his youth, that lovely thing which made him face life like a child who expects nothing but golden days and tranquil nights. To confess to him, particularly at this time, would be to rob his life of the bright charm which made him enjoy everything so passionately. The gold would be tarnished; instead of hope and expectancy, he would know only bitterness and disillusionment.

To tell him now, when he was facing new dangers every day, when he was without the comfort which his mother and father might have given him, seemed terrible. To write one of those letters to which he told her he looked forward to so eagerly, to write the bare facts to him. She could imagine the brightness fading from his face, see his stare of incredulity, which as he read the letter again and again would change to horror, anger and despair. She who loved him more than anything or anyone in the world would have sent his world crashing about his feet, leaving him standing alone in the ruins.

She knew that her courage failed her, that never could she make such an admission to Victor. She had deceived him, and she must go on deceiving him. He should never know, no one should ever know. The whole thing would be a secret locked in her own heart. She would give Victor other children, concerning whom there should be no deception; she would make him the best wife in the world, she would love and cherish him all her life, his wishes should be hers, his happiness her first consideration.

She picked up the photograph which Victor had had taken before he went to France and looked at it intently. His eyes smiled at her, his mouth was kind and friendly. She felt that he was reassuring her, that he understood.

"Darling," she whispered, "I know it's horrible, I know that to deceive you of all people is terrible, but I will make up to you for all my weakness and cowardice. I swear it, dearest. Forgive me, for I shall never forgive myself. I was afraid, afraid of what my family would say and do, what my relations would say—oh, I was afraid of so many things. I never loved him as I love you; when I look back I know that I didn't understand what love meant—until I loved you. My dearest, I may be allowing you to live in a fool's paradise, but it shall be paradise, for I will make it that for you. Perhaps a fool's paradise is better than none at all. There, I am going to tell my last lie, perform my last act of deceit, and tell your mother." She lifted the picture to her lips and kissed it. Then, setting it back on the bedside table, Monica squared her shoulders and went down to find Mary Ellen.

Mary Ellen was in the sitting-room, that pleasant, long, rather low room, where the shining furniture was covered with bright chintz, and she always contrived, even in the depths of Winter, to have flowers. She was sitting at the desk which her sons had given her for Christmas, a little Sheraton affair, elegant and charming.

E

She turned as Monica entered, smiling. "Now that is nice. I've just finished letters to both my lads. It takes me a goodish time, because my pen is not the pen of a ready writer. I always say that the schoolmaster must have been abroad when I went to school! Now, luv, sit down and let's have a nice cosy talk. Monica, what's the matter, my dear, you're white, you're shaking. Do you feel ill, my dear? Here, sit down here. There, I'll get you a little drop of brandy." She bustled away and returned with a tiny glass of brandy. "Just sip it, that's the style. Tut, tut! There, the colour's coming back into your face. Monica, you don't think that—I mean, could it be that—well, that——"

Monica nodded. "I think that is exactly what it is, Mary Ellen. In fact I was coming to tell you, when you found out yourself."

Mary Ellen beamed at her, her comely face shining with delight.

"We'll have the doctor along first thing and he must keep an eye on you," she laughed. "In fact, as Dad would say, he'd better keep both eyes on you."

Monica said, "Would you mind very much if I went home and saw our old doctor there? He's known me all my life, and—well, if you didn't mind, I'd like to see him. Then I'll come back and we'll settle down to wait until Victor comes back and—oh, it will be sheer heaven."

"Mind, indeed!" Mary Ellen was almost indignant. "Mind! My dear, of course go and see your nice old doctor. I think oft-times they're better than these new-fangled doctors—certainly for things like babies they are. No, luv, you shall go just as soon as you like, and then you'll be all the sooner back with Dad and me. Have you told Vic anything about it?"

"I wasn't absolutely certain until—well, until today."

"I must say that you've not wasted any time, my luv. And what for should you? You're both young and that's when folks ought to start a family. Now, here's tea, and a cup of tea will do you all the good in the world. We'll say nothing to Dad until you've seen this nice family doctor of yours." She went over to Monica, and leaning down kissed her with real warmth. "Nay, the very thought of it brings tears to my eyes, bless you both"—she chuckled softly—"bless you, all three of you."

Monica went first to London, where she visited a famous

doctor, who told her that she might expect her baby in November. He was kindly, sympathetic, when he heard that her husband was overseas, and assured her that she was very fit, well built, and that the whole business should cause her very little trouble.

"I'm always glad to find young people starting a family. It's a tremendous link, and binds husbands and wives closely together. That is my opinion after many years' experience, Mrs. Towers. Nothing to worry about, nothing at all. Good luck and some day bring the baby to see me. Yes, yes, I like to have children whose advent I have, as one might say, heralded, brought to visit me. Have you told your husband yet? I should send a telegram, It puts new heart into these gallant chaps—news of that kind."

Her aunt was delighted; she assured Monica that she had "fallen completely in love with your handsome husband and his good-looking brother".

The next day Monica went down to her father's house. She told them that she had seen a specialist while she was in town, and that there was no necessity to call in Dr. Brownleigh.

Her mother was quite willing to accept the specialist's opinion, and said tolerantly that although Brownleigh was a nice old man, she had always thought that as a doctor he was "a dead loss". She was inclined to be slightly patronizing about the Towers, which Monica found very irritating. She had grown to have a real and deep affection for Amos and Mary Ellen. She had found that although they might lapse into dialect and speak with a very decided accent, they had great principles, and there was a certain innate nobility about them which was both simple and splendid. To hear them referred to in a way which was patronizing, and at times almost apologetic, made her furious.

"And do you find that you can really *get on* with Mr. and Mrs. Towers?" her mother asked.

"Get on? Mother dear, I adore them both. They're the most generous and kindly people imaginable."

"I suppose that you'll come here to—er—have this child?"

"No, I shan't. Victor loves the Little Manor, and he'd want his child to be born there. He has a kind of passion for the place."

Her mother smiled. "My dear, really! They've only lived there for a few years. I heard that the father kept a *shop* not very long ago. It's not as if this house were—an ancestral home. Really!"

Stubbornly, Monica said, "Victor loves the house, and so do I."

"Then I suppose there is no more to be said."

There were nights when she lay awake, thinking, thinking. She had come, as she told her mother, to love both Amos and Mary Ellen very dearly, and the very fact that they had given her their kindness and affection so freely and generously made her deception more terrible. They had opened their hearts to her, they had accepted her as they would have accepted a daughter. They had lavished every care and sign of consideration on her—and now she was practising this dreadful deception on them, and on their son.

Then her mind would swing in the opposite direction, and she would reassure herself with the thought that nothing mattered when weighed in the balance against Victor's happiness. Now of all times, when the British were hard pressed, when the Germans appeared to have flung into the struggle every force known to man, when each day brought those casualty lists which always made her heart beat more heavily with fear.

She stayed with her mother for a week, and was conscious that she was longing for the old house, the hills, and moors, for Mary Ellen's kind, warm voice, and Amos's shrewd but kindly comments on everything. She already thought of Willingbrough as "home". She could not bear to stay for one night in London; there were Victor's letters waiting for her, there were letters which he would have written to his mother and father, to Wilfred, who always sent his brother's letters home so that his parents might glean every small particle of news concerning Victor. All these letters, Monica knew, would be given to her to read, and their contents would be discussed and commented upon in detail. The long journey to the North seemed endless; she was full of excitement as the train drew near the big town; she remembered how often Victor had told her that it was a good sign that trade was brisk when a heavy pall of smoke hung over the town.

"The sky is only really clear when the furnaces are shut down through lack of work. They say in the North here—yes, all over the North—that where there is muck, there's money. It's true."

When she got out of the train there was the smell. Victor had told her that he and Wilfred always said they would know they were in Willingbrough by the smell even if they were blindfold. Amos was there to meet her, his face beaming, his hands outstretched to take hers.

"Welcome home, my dear. I was just saying to Muther this morning 'How much longer is that girl of ours going to stay away?' Nay, happen we're selfish, but we've come to set a lot of store by you."

"It's lovely to be back, lovely. You're both well?"

"Champion, my dear. Nice little pile of letters waiting for you."

She laughed; everything seemed smoothed and safe. These people really loved her, missed her when she was away and welcomed her return.

In the car she laid her hand on that of Amos. "I'm coming to like this queer, dirty town of yours," she said.

He nodded. "Aye, it grows on you. No good pretending that it's beautiful as they say London is, or some of these foreign places, but it's a *homely* place. They say that home is the place where your heart is. Well, my heart will always be here because I handed it over to my Mary Ellen over twenty-three years ago."

She thought, "I wonder if Victor will say that after we've been married for twenty-three years?"

Mary Ellen made no attempt to hide her delight at Monica's return; she smiled and chuckled with sheer pleasure. Yes, there were her letters, three of them, and there were others for her to read later on. Victor was well, he said, and Wilf was going overseas quite soon; he had his commission, and how wonderful if he and Vic met!

"Amos, get our Monica a little drink, and then she can slip off to her own room and read her letters in peace. Yes, I had a plate of sandwiches cut for you, luv. Eat one or two; it's not good to drink without eating something, and I know the kind of dinners they give you on trains. Shocking!" She laughed. "Not that I've ever had a meal on a train; I've never taken a long-enough journey. When we went to London to see Vic in hospital we were both that het up, neither of us could have touched a morsel. That's right, Amos. Sit here, Monica luv. How have you been? And you saw your nice doctor?"

"No, Mary Ellen, I stayed the night with my aunt in town,

and went to a very well-known specialist, Sir Marcus Ford. He said that I was as fit as anyone could possibly be. I've promised to take the baby to see him one day."

In her own big, comfortable room, where there was a bright fire burning and vases filled with Spring flowers, she sat down and read Victor's letters. They were very like all the others he had written her, short, and assuring her that he was well. *We've been having rather a hot time, but it might have been worse—though not much! I never really stop thinking of you, loving you.*

Just the letters of a young man lacking any great power of expression, very much in love, and happy in the fact that his love is returned.

Tomorrow she would write and tell him about the coming child. She would tell her last lie to him and then begin to atone for her deception in every way that was humanly possible. It would be a dreadful letter to write, the very writing of it would leave her feeling smirched and disgraced; then— then she would set about making life for Victor Towers as bright and lovely as it was possible.

Mary Ellen came in before dinner; she glanced at the letters which Monica still held.

"Have you written to tell him yet, luv?"

"I'm going to write and tell him tomorrow, or even tonight. I didn't want to say anything until I was quite certain, that was why I went to Sir Marcus Ford. The best man I could find. Then, somehow, while I was staying with my mother, I didn't want to write that *particular* letter. I wanted to write it from his home, the place he loves so much."

"I believe that you're coming to luv it like he does. There, dinner will be ready in just a few minutes."

Monica went downstairs. As she entered the room she saw Amos take an orange envelope from the maid. Mary Ellen exclaimed, "Eh, they give me a turn, those things. I never liked them in peace-time, but now—Amos, what is it? Amos!"

He did not speak immediately, and Monica saw that he swayed a little where he stood. Mary Ellen cried again, "Amos, what is it?"

He raised his eyes and looked at his wife, and then at Monica, as if he were half blind.

"It's Vic," he said.

Monica felt her fingers close on the back of the chair,

she felt that she knew what news of Victor the telegram contained.

Mary Ellen cried, her voice shrill with anxiety, "Wounded?"

Amos shook his head. "No, not wounded, Mother."

Monica held out her hand. "Let me see, please."

She read the bald, conventional words, and thought, "That's the end, the end of everything. This is my punishment. Victor—dead."

CHAPTER TEN

MONICA felt that they lived in a world of unreality, the only things which seemed real were the mechanical ones—the notice in *The Times*, in the local paper, the answering of kind letters, the letters from Victor's Colonel and his brother officers. The rest, the knowledge that they would never see Victor again, that Mary Ellen would never hear him calling, "Mum, where are you?" The realization which must come to Amos that now he would never be there to assume that partnership, and to Monica to know that never again would she smooth that bright head; never now have the opportunity to atone for the sin which she had committed, never be able to make his life the beautiful, happy thing that she had hoped and longed to do.

Wilfred came home on forty-eight hours' leave. A different Wilfred, white and strained, speaking in short, jerky sentences. He asked Monica to come out with him, to walk in the fields which Victor had loved. For a long time he was silent, and then suddenly began to talk.

"Look, Monica, this has hit them both terribly hard. It's hit us all hard. You most of all. They understand that. They may not say much, because they're frozen—yes, that's it, frozen. Oh, they love me, but Vic—he was something special. He had everything, and Dad was counting on his coming into the business."

She said, "Wilfred, I've been thinking, thinking hard. Your ambition is to be an engineer. I know that you'd sacrifice it to go into the business with your father. It would be a wrench, it would mean setting out to do something you never really wanted to do—but you'd do it?"

He nodded. "Yes, I'd do it."

"Need you? Listen, I'm young, I'm reasonably intelligent. Do you think that I could go into the business, and gradually get to understand it all? I would work, and"—for a moment her voice was not quite steady—"it would be—oh, I can't explain, but as if I were doing something to please Victor. Wilfred, do you think that your father would consider—taking me on, to learn?"

He stood still, then swinging round caught her hands in his. In the half light she could see his eyes shining, his mouth curved into a smile.

He said, "Monica! You mean that you want to stay with them? You don't want to go back to live with your own people? My dear, this is wonderful. I know how apprehensive they've both been. Mum said to me only this morning that it was sufficiently terrible to lose Vic, but that they'd have to face losing you. Monica, they think so much of you, and—this baby that's coming. Vic loved this place." He jerked his head towards the grey-stone house. "He told Mum that he always hoped that his children might be born here. Oh, Monica, you'll make Vic's dream come true."

She stared at him, her eyes swimming with tears, then tore her hands from his grasp and said, "Leave me alone, Wilfred. Just leave me alone. It's all too much for me. I shall be all right. I just want to be alone for a few minutes."

He nodded gravely. "I do understand," he said, then walked away in the direction of the house.

Monica stumbled forward; she had been thinking all day of the idea that she should enter Amos Towers' business. It had seemed that the work would be something to fill her life. To return home to her father and mother was to face empty days, filled with trivial matters which would never hold any real interest for her. Possibly a little sick visiting, garden parties, tennis parties, dinners, the various shoots in the district to which women were sometimes invited. Nothing which held any interest for her, all things which removed her farther and farther from the place where she and Victor had been happy, the place which he had loved.

He had wanted his child to be born in that old house. His child! Yet, if she stayed here, and having embarked on this dreadful career of lies and deception, the continuance of those lies and those deceptions meant the happiness—the comparative happiness at least—of three people. Amos would be content in that Victor's widow wished to take an active interest in the firm. Mary Ellen would be happy to have her son's widow, and—as she thought—his child with them, and Wilfred would be able to pursue his chosen profession, and not from a sense of duty be forced to enter a business which actually held no interest for him.

Henry of Navarre, Monica reflected cynically, had said that Paris was worth a Mass, and she—standing there with the wide hills stretching before her—felt that the happiness of three people almost justified the step which she was prepared to take.

The happiness of three people: an elderly man, his wife and their son. The business which Amos had built up, and which, if she remained in Willingbrough, would have a "head" when he grew too old to take an active part in the enterprise; his wife, that dear Mary Ellen, happy because Amos was content, happy in that her beloved Victor's wife would remain with them—and keep her child with them; Wilfred, who longed, once the war was over, to make a start in his chosen profession.

Monica sighed. She felt a sense of satisfaction which pervaded her whole being; she felt that she was doing something which was right, something which bore out her belief of the greatest good of the greatest number. Standing there by the loose-stone wall, where the stone crop pushed its way between the skilfully laid stones, watching the evening light fade, she felt secure and content.

Then, quite suddenly, realization came to her. She raised her hand and brought it down so forcibly on the rough stone that she felt the skin break under the impact. She felt the pain, and that pain helped to bring her to her senses.

With both hands, one of them torn and bleeding, she clutched the wall, whispering softly.

"Sophistry! Even now, can't you be honest? Can't you admit, even to yourself, that you want to stay here, that you'd hate to have to go home and live the life which your family find sufficient? You've known happiness here, and you hate to leave it. The complete happiness may be only a memory, but that memory is more vivid here than it would be in any other place.

"Here, even if you worked and worked hard, you'd be

literally wrapped round with love and warm kindliness. You'd always be—to them—Victor's wife, and your child would be Victor's child. Face it, face it, you want to stay here because you know that your only chance of real happiness is here; but be honest enough to admit that you have no fine aspirations, no real aching desire to make anyone happy except yourself."

She stood there feeling the chill of the evening reach her. She shivered; she wished that she could feel that losing Victor had made her reckless, that losing that bright, beautiful boy had changed her, made her unscrupulous, reckless. She knew herself too well. Knew that under all her foolishness she had in her a very strong strain of hard calculation. She knew what she was doing. She knew that she had not loved, but literally adored Victor Towers. She had longed for a life which would be spent with him, with their children, a life of interest, happiness and colour. Victor had gone and she had reverted to her real type—a woman who planned and calculated. She loved Mary Ellen, she was very fond of Amos, she found Wilfred kind and sympathetic, but in reality what mattered most to her was her own life, and the security of the child which she was carrying.

If—if—if she could have kept Victor, if she had never been so foolishly attracted to the other man, had never been such a fool as to have yielded to him and his importunities, everything might have been so different. Now, driven by circumstances, she felt that she must protect herself, and grasp the opportunity which offered. She was thankful that in carrying out her plans she would inflict no pain on these kindly folk who had been so good to her.

She turned and began to walk back slowly to the house, carefully holding the hand which she had hurt against the stone, for it had begun to throb painfully.

She entered the house, walked down the long corridor hung with old prints of Willingbrough when it was little more than a few farms and a marsh, and entered the sitting-room. Wilfred was standing on the hearth-rug talking eagerly, Amos leaning a little forward in his chair as if he did not wish to miss a word, and Mary Ellen leaning back, busy with her knitting of a khaki sock.

Monica wondered if that sock had been intended for Victor; if so, she'd have to make the foot larger if it were to fit Wilfred.

Wilfred turned to her as she entered, his pleasant face beaming.

"Here she is," he cried. "Monica, I've told them! Told them that you're going to stay with us. That you want to go into the business——" He broke off suddenly. "What have you done to your hand?"

She glanced at her hand, it was covered with blood; she had been so absorbed in her own thoughts and problems that she had not noticed how badly it was bleeding.

"I scraped it on the wall, I think. It's nothing. Nothing at all. I'll tie my handkerchief round it."

Mary Ellen sprang from her chair. "Nay, you'll do nothing of the kind. You, a nurse, and don't know better nor that. Wilf, get me some bandage and some peroxide. Hurry now. Amos, ask them to give you a basin of warm water and a clean towel." She took Monica's hand in her own smooth, firm ones, making little clucking noises. "Tut, tut, tut, whatever have you been doing! That's right, Amos, let's see as there's no grit left. There! Stings a bit, eh? Now, Wilf, there, now that's as right as rain. Sit down and tell us your plans, luv. You think as you'd like to go into the business?"

Monica smiled. "You're making far too much fuss of me. Yes, if Amos will have me. I'm not—I think I can say without being conceited—unintelligent, and I'd work!"

Amos carefully knocked out the dottle of his pipe into the huge ash-tray which stood on the completely hideous "smoker's companion", executed in bright blue iridescent paint, which Mary Ellen had given him for Christmas. He drew a deep breath, and proceeded to refill his pipe, speaking as he did so.

"I'll have you," he said. "I have never been one who talked about 'men's jobs' and 'women's jobs'. You may remember as in the days when women was fighting for the vote, I was allus on their side, eh, Muther? I got a lot of dirty lukes for feeling as I did, but I've allus said as right's right, and wrong's no man's right.

"Well, except when it comes to a matter of sheer physical strength, theer's very few jobs as women can't do as well as men. Naturally, I had my own hopes, same as we all had——"

Mary Ellen said, "Nay, Amos luv, don't dwell on that."

"No, you're right. However, Wilf's set on being an engineer, and—why, if Monica likes to come into my business, to learn the job, right from the bottom—well, we shall be keeping it in the fam'ly. I don't see why she shouldn't make as good a job of it as most men could do. Until—well, until she's got her baby, I suggest that she comes down and—now, what do I mean exactly—I'm getting myself flustered——"

Wilfred laughed. "You mean, learn the ropes, hold a kind of watching brief and find her feet."

His father nodded. "Aye, something like that."

"And you'd really like to have me?" Monica asked a little wistfully.

"If Dad didn't like to have you," Mary Ellen assured her, "you can be very certain that he'd *not* have you, my dear."

"And you really think that, if I try, I can learn the business?"

Amos leaned forward and laid his hand with its broad palm, and short, practical fingers, on her knee. "If you want to learn, my girl, you can and will. It's nobbut sound common sense, and a"—he chuckled—"and a bit o' 'flyness'."

Mary Ellen said, "Nay, Amos, for shame, talking that way! Monica 'ul think that she's going into a thieves' kitchen or summat. Have done. Monica, luv, he's only funning."

That night when Monica lay in bed and sleep refused to come, she went over everything again and again. She tried to justify herself, argued that she would do her best and only her best to make herself useful—more, indispensable—to Amos. She would be a help to Mary Ellen; even the baby would be a comfort to the woman who would regard herself as its grandmother. It all sounded satisfactory and feasible, until Monica flung away her wishful thinking and faced facts squarely. Whatever she did, however she proved her love for, and did her duty towards, these people, she would still be practising a deception, be using a fraudulent means of getting her baby a home and recognition as the child of a man who had died for his country.

In the early hours of the morning, "when the heart beats thin and small", she lay with clenched hands and forced herself to face reality.

"I shall go through with it. I shall be a cheat and a fraud all my life, even towards my child, to whom I shall talk of its 'father', and allow it to believe that the Towers are its grandparents. The fact that I love them both, really and sincerely, only makes my deception more heinous, because it is despicable to cheat the people who have given you their love and trust, and to whom you have given affection. It's no use, I can't turn back now. In addition to all my other sins, I'm a coward. I'm afraid of their awful, terrible disappointment. I'm afraid of my mother's cold eyes, of my father's horror, of the raised eyebrows and frigid voices of my brothers and my sister.

"The Towers may be fond of me, they *are* fond of me, but if I confessed that this child is not Victor's, how could they keep me here; how—even if they were willing—could I stay? My own people would send me away to some place where I wasn't known, and when the baby was born they would have it adopted. I should never see it again. I might be allowed to live at home, but I should live under a perpetual cloud of cold disapproval. I can't face it! It's no use preparing arguments, no good trying to find excuses. There are no arguments which hold water, there are no excuses which are valid. I'm doing an abominable thing, a shameful, wicked thing, and I'm doing it because I'm a coward and can't face life as it would be if I made admissions and confessions."

She began to go down to the store each morning with Amos. At first she was bewildered, there was so much to learn, so much to understand. She studied prices, read letters received from and written to the various firms with which Amos dealt. Slowly things seemed easier; she began to understand something about buying and selling, the way stock should be kept, the prices which were wholesale and others which were retail. She learnt how to check off the items in each order, to satisfy herself that everything was complete. Once or twice Amos drove her down to the docks, and they went aboard some fine ship for which he had provided the provisions.

Amos nodded to the officer who was checking the delivery, nodded too to his own clerk who was counter-checking.

"Everything all right, Johnson?"

"Everything running quite smoothly, sir."

"Good morning, Mr. Mate. It's a long, tedious kind of job, eh?"

"It would be more tedious, Mr. Towers, if we did not have all this stuff on board, yes? I oft-times think, when I'm on this job, where we shall be when these tins of beef or condensed milk are opened, yes? Maybe the other side of the Line, maybe rounding the Cape. Such ideas are provocative, Mr. Towers. Provocative of many imaginings."

"Aye." Amos nodded his head vigorously. "Indeed they are. Now, do you think the Captain is ready for me, Mr. Mate?"

"Indeed, yes. He was here a few minutes ago, saying that he expected you. Please go right for'ard, Mr. Towers."

As they walked towards the Captain's quarters, Amos said, "Yon mate's a Welshman. They're always thinking out fanciful things. They're a strange lot. Now what does he mean by thoughts being—provocative?"

"I think he meant that they awakened more thoughts. Made him imagine or perhaps remember places where he had been, things he had seen," Monica told him.

"Tut, tut, why the devil can't he say so then?"

A tall, heavy man came towards them, his broad, good-looking face smiling and kindly. "Ah, Captain, good morning to you. Johnson tells me that everything's going smoothly."

"That's right. You keep it smooth at your end and we'll keep it smooth at ours. Come in. Not too early for a quick one? I've a box of cigars for you here. You liked the last lot, remember?"

"That's kind of you. Monica, let me introduce you to one of my oldest friends—I think that I may say we're friends, eh, Captain?—Captain Cartwright. This is my daughter, Mrs. Victor Towers."

The wide smile died, the eyes which met Monica's were very gentle and kind, the hand which held hers gave her a sense of the man's sincerity.

"I knew Victor, had known him since he was a small child. A fine chap, they're both fine chaps—it's sad, terribly sad. Come in, Mrs. Towers, come in. There, that chair's comfortable."

He bustled about, ringing for his steward, opening a cupboard and taking out a tin of biscuits. He held them up. "Been all round the world, and I'll bet any money they're as fresh and crisp as ever. They came from Towers', you see, Mrs. Towers!"

Amos watched him, and Monica realized that this man was one of his heroes. He gazed at him as a small boy might gaze at his favourite footballer or cricketer, his expression a mixture of admiration, affection and awe.

He said at last, "He," nodding his head in the Captain's direction, "was caught by the Germans. He was the man who ate his sailing orders! Imagine it. In a prison camp for months, but he got away. Take more than a bunch of Huns to keep him behind barbed wire! One day you must get him to tell you about it. It's grim, but he makes you die with laughing just the same. She's learning the business," he told Cartwright, "yes, her own wish. As soon as she knows the ropes, she's getting a partnership. Aye, we lost poor Vic, but we gained a grand daughter when he married our Monica."

Wherever Amos took her, when he spoke of her to any of his customers it was always the same, he never missed an opportunity of speaking of their affection for her, and her growing knowledge in the business.

Mary Ellen was always solicitous that she did not grow over-tired, always planning new dishes which she felt Monica would enjoy, never failing to do everything possible to make her happy.

Wilfred, too, wrote regularly, saying how content he was to think that his father and mother had Monica with them, what a difference her presence made to their lives, and how full of gratitude they all were to her.

Again and again Monica would go to her room and sit staring into the looking-glass, wondering if she could go through with the deception. It would have been easier, she thought, had they been less loving, less kind, less grateful. Had she felt that she was merely at Willingbrough on sufferance, had they made it quite plain that they only wished to have her there because they felt that they had a duty to her as Victor's widow, and the mother of his child, Monica told herself that it would have been less agonizing. Each time Amos or Mary Ellen spoke to her or of her with obvious affection, it was like the stab of a knife in her heart.

Whitefaced and haggard, she would whisper to her reflection, "I can't tell them now, it's too late. If only I could die when the baby is born, if both of us could die! That would be the only solution."

During the hot days of August, Mary Ellen insisted that Monica should come to her little cottage in the country, where the air came cool and sweet, blowing over the moors from the sea. Together they would sit in the trim little garden, sewing, and Monica came to know the elder woman more intimately than she had ever done. She had known her to be kind and capable, warm-hearted and generous, but now she realized that there were depths in Mary Ellen's nature which she had not guessed. She possessed a shrewdness, a mental keenness of thought, and an ability to sum up individuals briefly and aptly.

"I never had much schooling," she told Monica, "and somehow I've never really taken to reading much. I've never found it all that easy. Something of a task, as you might say. I learnt just enough to get into the Fifth Standard, then my auntie took me away. Then I did begin to learn things! Just hand me those scissors, luv, thank you. Aye, Auntie was a notable housekeeper, and she taught me all she knew. I reckon as my Amos has been happier with a good cook for a wife, with the knowledge that she was able to make every shilling do its duty—aye, and a bit over if it comes to that, with a store cupboard full of jams and pickles and suchlike—than he'd have been if I'd had my head stuffed with a lot of buke-learning. Compound fractions and decimal points don't help you to feed a man or run his home for him."

She asked Monica one day if she wanted to have her baby in "one of these new-fangled nursing-homes. I know as Dr. Heath's very set up with his. They say it's properly up-to-date."

"He asked me," Monica said, "and I told him that I wanted to have it—at home."

"Meaning?"

Monica smiled at her. "Meaning, you silly, *yours* of course."

"Nay," Mary Ellen's bright eyes were brimming over with tears. "Nay, that's our own lass. Dad and me's worried a bit about it. We just felt as we wanted Vic's bairn to be born in the house he was so fond of. Eh, Dad 'ul be right set up when I tell him."

It seemed to Monica that the sun shone a little less brightly, that a very small chill wind blew through the garden. Vic's bairn!

Mary Ellen wiped her eyes and smiled again. "You're a grand lass," she said. "My auntie always said God never closes one door but He opens another. He closed one when He took our Vic, but before that He'd opened another and you'd walked in, walked right into our hearts."

Monica said shakily, "Mary Ellen dear, don't say such lovely things about me. I'm not a *fine* person, not fine as Victor was, as Amos is."

"No? Why, you're fine enough for us. We're quite satisfied, luv."

She began to worry about the date of the baby's birth. True, Mary Ellen said, when Amos suggested that "our bairn might be here to wish us a Happy Christmas, eh?", "Nay, they say the first comes any time—within reason. I mind when our Vic was born, he came ten days before we expected him. Now Wilf was different. He just seemed as if he never would get himself born. Do you remember, Dad, how worried your mother and old Dr. Blackstone got? For ten whole days, there was I not daring to go further than the front door, and nothing happening."

"Then when he did make up his mind to arrive," Amos said, "of all times of the day or night, he chose two in the morning! I mind running to Blackstone and ringing his night bell. Suddenly a voice spoke right in my ear! I nearly jumped out of my skin. He was speaking through a tube contraption in his bedroom! I begged him to come quick, but he was a hardhearted old monkey. 'Nay,' he says, 'she'll be all right while the morning. I want my sleep even if you don't.' "

"And were you all right, Mary Ellen?" Monica asked.

She nodded. "Our Wilf's always been slow but sure. Took his time same as he's always done with everything. Bonnie bairns they were, both of them. Folks used to turn round in the street to look at them when I took them out in the pram. Vic, so fair and pink and white, and Wilf, dark with big dark eyes. Pictures, they were."

It was in October when Monica ceased going to the store. She was walking slowly over the fields, savouring the pleasant keen wind that held nothing unkind in its blowing. The hills were speckled with the bright gold of the gorse, and farther away the moors were already changing to purple. Victor had said that at the turn of the year the moors brought out their royal purple robes. Once a curlew flew over where Monica stood, and a flock of rooks made their way slowly home.

Suddenly a spasm of pain made her cry out. She felt a sudden sense of panic. October the tenth! And Amos had talked about Christmas, and even Mary Ellen had hoped to goodness that the daft lads would keep away and not frighten the poor bairn with their fireworks. Now—it was October the tenth. The sudden pain died away, and she tried to assure herself that it was nothing, but in her heart she knew that she was indulging in wishful thinking.

She walked slowly back to the house and made her way to

where Mary Ellen sat in the sitting-room, by the bright fire. She looked up as Monica entered, smiling.

"Why, you're back. We'll ring for—— Why, my girl, what's the matter? Sit down. What is it?"

"I slipped, and when I got up I had the most awful pain." One lie more or less surely couldn't matter now. "I didn't think I should be able to get home. It's better now, but I felt so shaky."

Her mother-in-law was bustling about, ordering tea to be brought in immediately, a fire to be lit in Mrs. Victor's bedroom, hot-water bottles put in the bed. She set a cup of tea on a table at Monica's side and went into the hall to telephone. Monica could hear her brisk voice speaking.

"Yes. Mrs. Towers. My daughter, yes. Oh, I think so. Out walking and slipped. As soon as you possibly can. I'd feel easier in my mind with a nurse here. Yes, thank you."

She came back. "How are you, luv? Tea's comforting, isn't it? They're sending the nurse round from the nurses' hostel or whatever it's called. Now, a drop more tea. Eh, is it that nasty pain again? Give me the cup. There, there, my luvey, there. Hold my hand tight."

Soon she was in bed, thankful to be there. Amos tiptoed into the room and said, "What's this about falling down? Nay, it's those high-heeled shoes you lassies wear. I'd have the lot prohibited by law. Nasty dangerous things. It's a mercy you didn't break your leg."

The nurse arrived and began moving things, taking this and that out of the room, saying brightly, "We must have plenty of room. I'm a great believer in having lots of space, Mrs. Towers. Space and air, that's what I always say, 'Give me space and air.' Dr. Heath once said to me that 'space and air' might be my family motto. I laughed. 'Well,' I said 'I might have a worse motto.' He agreed. I've done a lot of work for Dr. Heath. Very clever, I think. Go-ahead, if you understand me. Not one of these old stick-in-the-muds. Modern. I wonder that you didn't go into his nursing home. It's very good, up-to-date. I always think that a nursing home gives the patient and the baby a better chance, really."

Monica asked, "A better chance of—what?"

"Well, comfort, everything there to hand, on the spot as it were."

"I wanted to have the baby here."

"Oh, if you fancied it, that's all right. I'm sure it's a very comfortable room, plenty of light, as I say—space and air."

Monica wondered vaguely if patients ever hurled themselves from their beds and murdered their nurses.

Dr. Heath, when he came, was reassuring and efficient. He was a young man, well on the way to making an exceedingly successful career for himself. He had known Victor Towers, and had liked and admired him. He knew that Victor had first met Monica when he was in hospital, and his own belief was that Victor had, as Heath expressed it to himself, "made the most of his opportunities". Admittedly the girl didn't look "that kind", but you never knew. That would account for the hurried wedding, which all Willingbrough knew had been arranged in a few days. Well, it was no business of his, Heath decided. He had a very strong belief that doctors had no right to chatter about their patients' affairs, and despised the doctors who did so. It was evident that the Towers thought the world of Victor's widow. The old man—not that he was so very old after all—was as jumpy as a cat about everything. He had asked dozens of questions, and had grown slightly irritable when Heath protested that he could not possibly answer them.

"But can't you tell if it's all going to be easy and straight-forward?" Amos Towers persisted.

"I can only say that, as far as I can judge, there is no reason why it should not be," Heath replied.

"Would you like a second opinion? Some specialist from Leeds or Newcastle? I don't care what it costs."

"There again, Mr. Towers, I can only say that at this juncture there is not the slightest necessity."

"Ah, but suppose at some—what did you say?—juncture, that there was need, you'd have lost precious time, wouldn't you?"

Heath looked at the irritable, red-faced man before him. He might have grown irritable himself, but Amos was so palpably worried and distressed that he kept control of his nerves.

"If, Mr. Towers, you would like to telephone to Harvey Summers in Newcastle, or to Sir James Bright in Leeds, I am quite willing that you should do so. I only repeat that there is no *necessity* to do so."

"And you don't mind, don't think that we don't trust you?" His tone was almost pathetically earnest and sincere.

"Not in the very least. I understand your anxiety. It's very natural."

"It's that fall that's bothering me. We didn't expect the baby yet, as you know. We thought November at the earliest."

Heath made a mental reservation that he had never felt the same, but he promised to telephone to Newcastle and ask Harvey Summers to come immediately.

The great man was at the hospital performing an emergency operation. His secretary promised that Heath's message should be given to him immediately on his return. The baby was born at half past eleven that night, and emitted its first quavering wail as Harvey Summers came in through the front door.

"Sounds as if I'm a day behind the fair," he said to Amos, who was shaking like a man with palsy.

"Aye, I thought you'd be here sooner. Never heed, just slip up and see that everything is going all right. The bairn's alive, thank God. That's something."

Heath met the specialist, and taking him into another room told him briefly and without unnecessary comment what he believed to be the case.

"Naturally, the Towers are terribly upset over the death of their son, this child's father. I don't wish to add to their unhappiness. They apparently dote on the girl, and after all—that side of the story is no actual business of ours. You agree, I hope?"

"Oh, completely. No necessity to say anything. Now, shall I take a look at your patient and at the infant?"

Later he told Amos Towers that the child, a boy, was perfectly healthy, that for seven months he was a big child. The mother was as well as possible; she was a fine, well-built girl, and had come through it all splendidly.

"Possibly it's as well that your daughter-in-law did slip. If the little fellow had stayed where he was for another couple of months things would not have been so easy. These very big babies often make for difficult confinements."

He was driven down to the station to catch the night express, with Amos Towers' considerable cheque in his pocket. Easy, urbane, assured and rather elegant, he left behind him a sense of reassurance.

Monica slept, still drowsy from the chloroform. When she woke, Mary Ellen was seated by the fire, the child on her knees.

Monica said, "Mary Ellen, may I see my baby?"

Mary Ellen rose, the child in her arms, and walked to the bed.

"It's a bonny boy, luvely straight limbs, and lots of dark hair. He'll lose that, they nearly always do. There!" Very gently she laid the sleeping child down. For an instant their eyes met, and although Mary Ellen smiled, then stooped and kissed Monica tenderly, the girl felt her heart miss a beat.

She thought, "She knows! She kissed me as she did to assure me that she and I will keep the secret. She'll never refer to it, I am certain, but—she knows."

PART TWO

CHAPTER ONE

TEN years, and they had slipped past so quickly and smoothly that it came as a shock to remember that she was thirty-five, that her son was ten years old and chattering excitedly about going to his prep school. She had learned a great deal in those ten years. The vast business no longer held any mystery for her. She had gained her knowledge slowly and surely with Amos Towers as her patient and wise teacher. With each year she had gained confidence and knowledge, until now, when Amos declared that he was going "to take life a bit easy", the thought of being in complete control held no terrors for Monica.

Ten years, during which time Mary Ellen had never shown that she realized that young Wilfred was not Victor's son. That she knew, Monica never doubted, had never doubted since their eyes had met when on the night of his birth Mary Ellen had handed the child to his mother. To the boy she had been unfailingly kind. Monica believed that she loved him dearly, and it would have been difficult not to do so, for he was a splendid boy, straight and clean-limbed, intelligent and eager to learn, while possessing a warm heart and an appreciation of kindnesses which was at once charming and ingenuous.

Only once had Monica felt afraid, and that was when the child's name was under discussion. Amos, who idolized the boy from the first moment he saw him, said that he should be called Victor.

"That's the name for him. A kind of memorial of Vic. Keep his mem'ry green, as you might say."

Mary Ellen, knitting furiously, spoke without raising her eyes.

"Nay, Amos, I don't know that we need anything to keep Vic's mem'ry green. However luvely this bairn grows up to be, there'll never be another like our Vic. I know as Monica feels the same."

That was when, for a split second, the cold hand of fear seemed to clutch Monica's heart.

She managed to reply quite steadily, "No, I don't think that we'll call him Victor, Dad. I'd rather call him Wilfred," she managed to smile, "after our Wilfred, as a compliment to him."

Amos shrugged his shoulders. "Why, if that's how you feel——"

"Aye, and then if our Wilf gets married and has a bairn, he can call him Victor. There, that's settled!" Mary Ellen continued to work at the Dutch heel which she was turning. The dreadful moment was over.

The Peace came, and Wilfred returned home and went off to the Tyne to study engineering, and Monica stayed at Willingbrough.

From time to time she visited her parents and listened to their comments on the boy. Her father said that he was a fine sturdy little chap and must go into the Army. "The only life for a man!"

Her mother said calmly, "Possibly his other grandparents may have plans for him, Claude."

"Plans!" he ejaculated explosively. "What d'ye mean by—plans?"

"I believe that Mr. Towers is exceedingly rich."

"All the better. He'll be able to give the boy a decent allowance to keep him in a first-rate regiment."

It was at that point that Monica spoke. "Papa, unless Wilfred shows some very marked talent or preference for some profession, I hope that he'll go into the business. The business which his grandfather and great-grandfather have built."

Her father stared at her blankly. "Business! A ship's chandler, whatever that is. I remember telling your husband, poor feller, that I'd never known one, never even knew that there were such things. Ships' chandlers! You'll tell me next that you're going into this precious business!"

Mentally she compared this house with her home in the North. Here she was conscious of criticism from her mother and disapproval from her father. They chilled her; there was nothing of the warmhearted affection with which at Willingbrough she was surrounded. Even the baby was treated differently. He was "brought down" by his nurse, exhibited, left for fifteen minutes, then Lady Crawshaw, glancing at the clock, invariably said, "Nurse is a long time coming to take

Wilfred! So bad for a baby to not have its life run with complete punctuality."

At Willingbrough how often had she heard Amos say, since the child was born, "I think I'll just slip off. I might call in and see James Leyton. You come up when you're ready, luv."

How often she had smiled, knowing very well that Amos had not the slightest intention of going to see James Leyton. What Amos wanted to do was to rush back to his own home and make his way to the nursery in the hope that he might find the nurse bathing Wilfred, so that he could stand watching, and, the bath over, possibly be allowed to hold the baby for a few moments.

Now she knew that she longed to be back. True, there were days when what she had done weighed heavily on her, when she worked harder than ever as if to attempt to atone for her deception. She had not been able to nurse the baby, and at the earliest opportunity she had gone back to the business, leaving the child in the care of an admirable nurse. Amos stated that he was "jubious", and gave it as his opinion that she needed at least six months' rest.

Mary Ellen had supported Monica, and Monica wondered if, having reconciled herself to accept the child, she was determined to bind him to herself and Amos as firmly as possible.

Now, in answer to her father, she said, "I am in the business, Papa. I'm the junior partner, and when my father-in-law retires, which won't be for a long time, I shall be in control."

Her father stared at her. "Good God!" he ejaculated piously.

Her mother asked, "Do you intend then to make your life with the Towers, Monica?"

"Yes, Mama. They adore the boy, and they're very fond of me."

"I'm afraid that he'll grow up with a dreadful accent. Such a pity. I remember Mr. Towers had an accent that—well, you could have cut it with a knife. Terrible!"

Flaring suddenly, Monica flashed, "Victor had no accent!"

"I admit, scarcely any, though I—I have a very sensitive ear—should have known that he was a North Countryman."

Her father continued to watch her as if she were something

strange and curious. Her mother continued her embroidery in silence.

Presently Sir Claude said, "Where will he get his education? The local grammar school?"

Very quietly she answered, "Mr. Towers entered him for Harby."

"Great heavens! Does he know what it costs? I wanted to send your brothers there, but—it was beyond me! Harby!"

His wife, speaking in her smooth, even voice said, "My dear Claude, remember that we live in a new world. Not the world we used to know. It is people like—er—Mr. Towers who can send their grandsons to such schools. If it comes to a question of local grammar schools, it is extremely probable that your sons will send their boys to them!"

Her sister had come over to see her, bringing with her two pale children, who Monica thought would be all the better for the air which blew so freshly and so cleanly off the moors. Her sister and she had nothing in common; her sister's interests were entirely bound up in her husband and children, the parish and his chances of advancement. She babbled happily about what the Bishop had said when he came to luncheon, of Hilary's determination—backed by the Bishop—to use vestments, "within reason, of course, Papa".

Monica asked her if she would not like to send the children to Willingbrough for a holiday. Her sister, Cynthia, hesitated, and then said, "But it's a town, Monica darling, isn't it?"

"We live right outside the town. The fields are at our back door. Or I could send them with Nannie to the cottage. That's close to the sea."

"It's very kind of you, darling. I should have to ask Hilary."

Monica knew that they would never come. It was the same when she told her father that Amos had some "rough shooting" and a stretch of river, as when Wilfred came home he liked to get out with a gun or a rod.

"I'm sure that Mr. Towers would be delighted, Papa, if you cared to come up and fish or shoot. I'll get him to write a formal invitation if you wish."

Her father brushed up his short bristling moustache with the tip of a forefinger. Then he said, with what she felt was a valiant effort to be kindly, "You know, Monica, I think you'd better not, m'dear. It's kind of you, kind of Towers, but—

well, I shouldn't know what the deuce to *talk* about. You see what I mean?"

It was a relief to be back in the train speeding North. They meant to be kind, she was certain of that, certain too that her father had gone to the root of the matter when he said that he would not know what "to talk about". Their lives and hers were completely different. Topics which were all-absorbing to them meant nothing to her; things which interested her were completely beyond their ken. She had literally moved into another world, as much so as if she had been translated to another planet.

"Are you glad to be going home, Nannie?" she asked.

The nurse, a pleasant, rosy-faced woman answered, "Well, madam, it's always pleasant to be back in one's own nursery, with all one's own things round one, as you might say. I'm sure that her ladyship did everything to make me and baby quite at home, but—well, there it is, isn't it, madam?"

"He's growing, I think, Nannie."

"Growing! The precious lamb, I should just say that he is. What his grandpa will say when he sees him I do not know. Or his grandma, come to that. They dote on our baby, don't they, my pretty one?"

"Do you think that he is pretty?"

"Well, madam, I should say that you were a very pretty lady, and he's the image of you. His every feature is yours. I can even see little movements of his hands that put me in mind of you, madam. Oh, he's a very bonnie boy is our Wilfred."

It had been good to come home, Monica remembered, and the delight which Amos showed on seeing Wilfred again was almost pathetic. Mary Ellen declared that he had grown, and, as she kissed Monica, said, "It's nice to have you back, luv. We've missed you sadly, have Dad and me."

She felt that, in spite of everything, Mary Ellen had a real and warm affection for her. Perhaps because, whatever her faults had been, she had made Victor happy; perhaps because she was a help to Amos, perhaps even because she was glad that Amos felt that someone bearing his name would carry on the business. Monica never felt, or even dared to hope, that Mary Ellen had forgiven her—how could she? She realized that Mary Ellen was a very wise woman, a woman who while having led a circumscribed and limited life, yet had a broad outlook. It was not, Monica felt, due to great tolerance, but due to the fact that she weighed up advantages and disadvantages and came to a decision regarding them both.

Wilfred at nearly thirty showed no desire to marry. He had done well in his profession, had passed his examinations brilliantly, and went "round the world and back again" enjoying every hour of his life. Had Wilfred married early, had a son, Monica wondered what attitude Mary Ellen might have adopted towards her and her son. As matters stood, Amos Towers was happy, loving his daughter-in-law, lavishing on his grandson something which amounted to adoration. To the world at large Amos might be merely a very successful man of business, energetic, honest and courageous; he was not in the least good looking, he had an open, kindly expression and a ready smile. His speech was, and always would be, heavily tinged with the dialect of the North Country; he read very little, and his knowledge of politics was firm but elementary.

To Mary Ellen he was the finest man in the world, the greatest success in business, possessing all the qualities which she found most admirable in a man. She had loved Victor, she loved Wilfred, but the larger part of her heart was given to Amos Towers. Monica made him happy, Monica was a help to him, and that made Monica in Mary Ellen's eyes a desirable inhabitant of the Little Manor.

When four years ago Amos had been asked to be Mayor, Mary Ellen's pride had outweighed her nervousness of having to assume the position of Mayoress. For several years he had been an Alderman, and whenever he walked with other members of the Town Council to the Parish Church in procession, as was the custom on Hospital Sunday, Mayor's Sunday and other high festivals of the Municipality, Mary Ellen was always there to see the procession pass.

Her remarks at luncheon were invariably the same; the names might alter, but the substance was the same.

"It's about time as William Watson got a new silk hat, Amos. The one he's wearing must know its way to the Parish Church by itself by this time. Poor Harry Jewell begins to luke a bit tottery. I wonder his wife lets him take yon long walk. Seemed a bit out of place, as you might say, for Robert Corner to be laughing and nodding to his friends. After all, it was a serious kind of procession. I must say, Amos, of the lot, you luked the youngest and by far the best dressed of the lot. Your clothes looked—well, they looked just *right*."

He always laughed. "Nay, Muther, not all of them has as good a tailor as what I have."

"Not all of them has kept their figures like what you have!"

Yes, Mary Ellen Towers would accept practically anyone who contributed to the happiness and well-being of her beloved husband.

The boy—Amos loved him passionately. He was delighted when he was old enough to have his first suit made for him, and would spend hours discussing styles and materials which were destined to be clothes for Wilfred. Monica had feared that he might spoil the boy, but Wilfred appeared to possess a disposition which was not easily spoiled. He was a happy child, good-tempered and sunny. He had gone to a small private school in the town which was run for the children of the people who could afford the slightly exaggerated fees. He was obviously both clever and intelligent. He enjoyed learning, and at nine years old was the head of the school. The question of sending him to a preparatory school was discussed.

Mary Ellen said, "Well, I suppose we can find out what's the prep school for Redburgh, eh?"

Amos said, very calmly, "He isn't going to Redburgh. I entered him for Harby when he was two months old. I've made enquiries and there's a very good prep school at Harrogate where they prepare boys for Harby."

"Well, well!" Mary Ellen breathed. "Did you know about this, Monica?"

She nodded. "Yes, Amos wanted to keep it as a surprise for you."

"Aye, well, he's succeeded. It's a surprise all right. Harby. It's one of the best i' the land, isn't it? I've heard as royalty go there!"

"It's *the* best, so I'm told," Amos said. "That's why it 'ul do nicely for our lad. I was talking to Lord Chadfield the other day, well, he's the Earl of Chadfield. He was asking about our Wilfred. It seems that his younger son, the Honourable Marcus, is going to Harby. I told him that was where we were sending our lad. He said, 'You're right to do so, Towers. There's not a finer school in the world. I was there myself, and I tell you it's not only noted for scholarship, and athletics, but they train the character of the lads. The character, and that's what counts in life.' So there you are. He told me a lot too about this Saint Asaph's at Harrogate. Gave me the address. I wrote off. I had a letter from the headmaster this morning. Now imagine it, Chadfield his-self had written, after talking to me, and said that he knew me. That's something, isn't it? The upshot is that Wilf can go at the end of the Summer holidays. Nice healthy spot, not so far off that we can't drive over now and then. So it just remains for you both to get his things together. There's a list as long as your arm."

Mary Ellen turned to Monica. "Proper high-handed, isn't he? I suppose neither you nor me have any say in it, eh? Nay, things have come to something when men make all the arrangements for bairns!"

But she smiled as she said it, and Monica knew that she was both impressed and delighted. She knew too that tomorrow, when Mrs. Towers met some of her friends out shopping, she would explain how busy she was getting things ready for "my grandson to go to Saint Asaph's. Oh, a very good school —Lord Chadfield recommended it to my husband. In fact, he wrote his-self to the headmaster to advise him to take my grandson. Oh, he'll go to Harby later. That's where Lord Chadfield's son is at the moment, the Honourable Marcus."

And tomorrow she would drive Wilfred over to Harrogate, with his new expensive trunks and bags, his bats and rackets, and leave him there. From the moment she left him he would change. He would begin to move in a new world, make new friends, live a different life. His babyhood was past and over, from now he would be—a schoolboy. Then the schoolboy would slip into being a man. She was not unduly depressed; that she would miss him terribly, she knew; he had been so much part of her life. She had worked hard, in order that she might make his position secure. She had made a personal success, and now Amos admitted that she knew as much of the business as he did. Customers liked her; she had a pleasant manner with them all, no matter what their rank or position. She could be businesslike without being brusque, she could discuss prices and terms of payment without becoming too obviously commercial.

It had been hard work and the last ten years had been filled with determination, striving, and finally achievement. Only two things had mattered in those ten years—really mattered—her child and her work. Yet never had she allowed the one to suffer for the other. No matter how tired she had been, and there had been days when she reached home utterly weary, she bathed and changed and spent every moment possible with Wilfred. She never allowed him to see her dusty and untidy after a heavy day possibly spent in the warehouses.

Wilfred and her work had absorbed her, his safety, and her own success, not for her own personal advancement, but ultimately for his.

Amos had once asked her, when they sat in his fine office, having tea, a thing which she had instituted, if she ever thought of marrying again.

She remembered that she was pouring out tea at the time. When she first went to the business, tea was brought in from the general office, in thick cups, very stewed and dark brown. She had altered that, and installed a charming tea service, tray-cloths and the like. The tea was made by her own secretary and she knew that it was something to which he looked forward.

Seated behind his massive desk, stirring his tea, which he liked very sweet, his kind eyes had watched her with concentrated attention.

"Monica luv," he said, "did you ever think as you'd like to get married again?"

She looked up, half startled, and replied, "No, Amos, I don't think so. Why?"

"You're nobbut young, you're very bonnie, and there's plenty who'd be only too glad of the chance to get a wife like you, m'dear."

She shook her head. "I'll use an expression of yours," she said. "I have enough on my plate. I'm learning a business, I've a son and I have a"—she hesitated, then went on firmly—"a family. In addition, no man could find me a house I should love as I do Little Manor."

He smiled at that. "Aye, it's a canny house. But you've met quite a few chaps at the different balls you've been to—the Bachelors, the Yeomanry, the County and the like, and some of them have been mighty taken with you, m'dear."

"The point is, Amos, that I wasn't taken with them." She laughed.

She saw him sigh, as if with relief, but he persisted.

"There's young Dr. Harris——"

"I can't bear him!"

"There's Wilson Blacker, he's young, not bad luking, they say he's clever——"

"And makes it so obvious that he agrees with them!"

"What about Hector Manning? He's rich, he's well educated, been to some public school and a university, writes bukes in his spare time. He made it quite plain at the Mayor's Ball that he was very attracted."

She shrugged her shoulders. "I wasn't. No, don't bother to find me a husband." Her voice softened. "Victor spoilt me for other men."

Amos nodded. "Aye, maybe he would."

Later he returned to the subject.

"I don't want you to sacrifice yourself to two elderly people like Mary Ellen and me. I don't even want you to sacrifice yourself to Wilfred. I want you to have a full life, a happy life, a life of work and achievement."

She went over to him and took his cup. "Listen," she said, with her hand resting on his shoulder. "Remember always that you and Mary Ellen have given me *everything*. Don't ever talk again of—sacrifices, my dear."

Now as she sat in her pleasant bedroom looking at her own reflection in the mirror, she saw a woman who did not look very young, but who on the other hand did not look—old. Her skin was smooth and clear, her hair shone with much brushing, and her wide-set eyes were bright and shining. A woman who looked—content. That, Monica reflected, she was, except for that cloud which always darkened everything for her; that cloud which came from the consciousness of the deception which she had practised.

She was roused from her reverie by a knock at the door, and when she cried "Come in," her son entered. At ten years old he was tall for his age, slim and beautifully built. His dark hair fell over his forehead and he had a trick of pushing it back impatiently. He came over to her and stood by her side, leaning lightly against her shoulder.

She turned and kissed him saying, "Well, my dear, how is everything?"

"Lovely, darling. I believe that I'm going to like this school. I've just been talking to Grannie. I *love* Grannie, don't you? She tells you such nice things. She gave me a purse with money in it, and told me about a book she'd once read. She said that she didn't read many books, but she'd always remembered this one. It was called——" He hesitated. "Called *David—David Copper—Copper* something——"

Monica said, "*David Copperfield.*"

"That's right. Well, this boy was going to school, and his aunt talked to him. He hadn't got a mother. It must have been pretty awful not to have a mother, mustn't it? His aunt was like his mother. Well, when he was going to school she said to him, 'Never be mean, never be false, never be unkind.' I think that I've got it right. She said then she'd be proud of him. Mummy, if I'm never mean or false or unkind, will you all—you, and Grannie and Grandpapa Amos—be proud of me? I'd rather like you to be."

She swung round on the stool on which she was sitting and caught his face between her hands. "Mean and false"; she had been both.

She said, "Darling, of course. I think that it was lovely of Grannie to say that. It's a very wise thing to have said."

He nodded. "I bet that my father was never mean or false or unkind." He turned to look at the photograph of Victor which stood on the table near them. "He wasn't, was he? He's awfully nice looking. I'm not like him, am I?"

"No, you're like me, Wilfred."

He laughed. "Well, you're jolly nice looking. All the boys at school say so. But I'll try to be like him in other ways—and like you too, Mummy."

"Then we shall all be happy, darling. There, let's go down and talk to Grandpapa. He wants to see as much as he can of you as it's your last night."

Amos talked to the boy, and Monica, listening, wondered if he had talked so to Victor and Wilfred. The boy listened gravely, his face serious and intent.

"Mind you, Wilf, don't go throwing your weight about, because there are bound to be lads who've been there longer than what you have. On the other hand, don't let anyone—put on you. Stand up for yourself, and give as good as you take. I mind when your father first went to school, boarding-school that is, one of the other lads laughed at him and called him 'Pretty Vicki'. He was that good looking. Your father soon showed this chap if he was 'Pretty Vicki' or not! I don't want you to be pugnacious, that is, not always on the look-out

F

for trouble, but stand up for yourself. Never tell tales, never sneak on other boys. Speak the truth and shame the devil, as the saying goes. Try to do well at sport, but don't think as it's the be-all and end-all of your life at school. I'd like— why, we'd all like to see you in the football and cricket teams, but if you don't get there—well, we shall love you and admire you for something else.

"Don't listen to mucky talk; it's not clever and it's not funny. Don't do anything you'd not feel as you could tell your muther or your grannie about. There, I've done. That's a grand lad!"

The next morning she drove Wilfred over to Harrogate. Monica was thankful that he was cheerful, and even when she left him he did not cry, as she saw some of the small boys doing. He held his head up, squared his small shoulders, and if his cheerfulness was a little overdone when she was saying "Good-bye", it was a brave attempt to hide whatever emotion he felt at being left in this strange new building, surrounded by strange new boys.

Back in Willingbrough life went on smoothly and uneventfully. She was always busy and their business had never been so flourishing. Amos had opened another branch in Glasgow and talked of expanding still further. He took no steps without discussing them in detail with Monica, and she knew that he valued her advice. For herself, she enjoyed her work; it was so varied, there were so many facets of the business. And it was a source of pride to her that her knowledge of everyone was complete and accurate.

Before Christmas he told her that he wished her to take Wilfred to Switzerland, wished him to take part in Winter sports, to meet more boys and girls of his own age.

"It's all part of his equipment for life," he said gravely. "He'll be a rich man and he'll meet all kinds of 'high-ups'. They'll all know how to do these things, ski-ing and sleighing or whatever it is, and so must our lad. I'll lay as your brothers learnt all these things; as I say, it's part of their equipment."

She took Wilfred down to see her father and mother before they went to St. Moritz. It was obvious that both her father and mother were impressed with the boy. Her mother admitted that his manners were better than those of her other daughter's, Cynthia's, children. His grandfather enjoyed taking him about, showing him off to his friends. "My daughter's boy, at a prep school for Harby." He fired off questions to Wilfred and delighted in his quick straightforward answers.

"How d'you like school, eh?"

"I like it very much. It's a jolly fine school, Grandfather."

"Win any prizes?"

"We only have prizes at the end of the Summer term, Grandfather."

"Top of your form, eh?"

"No, Grandfather, fifth."

"How many boys in the form?" He remembered an ancient joke he used to voice with his own sons. "Five?"

"No, Grandfather, fifteen."

He talked about him to Monica. "Pity you're determined that he shall go into that business. The Army would have been the place for him. Cavalry. He's got good hands, doesn't look like a sack of potatoes like your brother's lads do. They're a miserable pair! Can't think how Wilfred's managed to escape that awful accent, not a trace of it. Nice fellow, I'm proud of him."

He took to Winter sports as a duck takes to water. He was popular with the other children and Monica scarcely saw him all day. She herself found the life of an expensive hotel rather strange. She had lived so long in a slightly restricted society, where people were in the main serious and hard-working, that these light-hearted men and women, anxious to extract every ounce of amusement from their holiday, seemed almost unreal. To dance again every night as a matter of course amused her. To realize that at thirty-five she was still attractive, that her figure was good and that she was actually sought after, pleased her. She was not a vain woman, but she did know that she had consciously limited and restricted her life for the last ten years.

Wilfred sat talking to her one evening as she dressed for dinner.

"Are you having a good time, Mummy? I am! There's a boy here, older than me, who is at Harby. He was awfully interested when I told him that I was going there. That big man who was dancing with you last night is his uncle. He's his guardian. His name's Colonel Lathbury. This boy told me—his name's Gerald Lathbury—that his uncle says you're the prettiest and the smartest woman here. It's true too, isn't it, Mummy?"

Monica blushed, knew that she had done so, and felt furious. How stupid, blushing like some schoolgirl because a good-looking man had praised her looks!

Wilfred laughed delightedly. "Darling, you've gone all pink!"

"What nonsense, Wilfred! What shall I wear tonight! You choose."

That night she danced with Colonel Lathbury, not once but several times. Wrapping herself in a fur coat she strolled out on to the long terrace of the hotel with him. The moon was nearly full, and the sky was very clear and studded with countless stars. The mountains unbelievably white and impressive, with the shadows painted very dark in contrast to the dazzling snow.

"What a night," she said softly.

" 'On such a night, Troilus methinks mounted the Trojan walls, and sighed his soul towards the Grecian tents——.' "

Monica laughed. "Not on such a night as this, because there was a 'sweet wind to kiss the trees and they did make no noise'."

"Ah, but it was a night when 'the moon shines bright'," he insisted.

"Anyway, I agree that the words are so lovely that anything can serve as an excuse for saying them," Monica agreed.

"The whole play is full of the most lovely words. I could get drunk on some of the play, though I have always thought Portia an impudent creature, and I hope that she was as bored with her Antonio to the same extent that he has always bored me."

He talked of books and particularly of poetry, and she decided that he must be the new type of soldier, a type which was much later than her father's time. She felt that her father would instinctively distrust any soldier who declared that he enjoyed reading poetry.

They met very often; she went skating with him, he taught her to ski, and together they sat and talked for hours. He talked well and had travelled extensively. He was interested in hearing about her life and her work.

"I knew that you were unique!" he cried. "You must be the only woman ship's chandler in the world! I must embark on some fantastic attempt to cross the Atlantic in my cockle-shell of a yacht. May I bring her to you to be fitted out?"

"I should give the matter my personal attention," she told him.

She felt gayer than she had done for years, and when she went to her bedroom and looked at her reflection in the mirror, she saw that her eyes were very bright, her lips parted readily in a smile, and her skin had the bloom of perfect health.

"Mountain air, plenty of exercise, change, new interests all doing their work," she told herself, and then laughed aloud because she knew that all those things might have contributed to her well-being, but the chief factor was—without doubt—the companionship and obvious admiration of Colonel George Lathbury.

CHAPTER TWO

THEY had been at St. Moritz for ten days. Wilfred began to regard himself as the oldest inhabitant and to refer in a slightly patronizing manner to new arrivals. Both Monica and Wilfred had acquired a beautiful golden tan, that charming tint which comes only to people with fine, smooth skins. They were both completely happy.

The boy loved the sports and delighted in the fact that he was quick and clever at them. The instructor praised him, told Monica that his poise was astounding, that his movements were clean and exact.

"He's almost the best youngster I've had through my hands. You must bring him next year, Mrs. Towers. He's a champion in the making."

Wilfred told his mother that he had heard from Gerald Lathbury that he and his uncle were staying for a further week.

"They were going tomorrow, Mummy, but Gerald's uncle told him they were staying another week because they were having such a topping time. Are you glad?"

"Yes, darling, I like them both very much."

She was glad, and to herself she scarcely dared admit *how* glad. The big soldier was a wonderful companion, and she felt a new zest for life, a new interest in her surroundings, when she was with him. She met a great many men in business, owners, captains, officers, and liked them tremendously. They were as a rule dignified, kindly and courteous, but they were ships that passed in the night, and she never had the opportunity to get to know them well. The various men her father-in-law had suggested as being suitable aspirants for her hand bored her. There was only young Blacker who seemed to be interested in anything outside his business and the achievements of the local football team. He was so superior, so determinedly an intellectual, that Monica found him insufferable.

George Lathbury was so many things which Victor had been. He was thoughtful and yet capable of being amused by small things. He was enthusiastic and eager, his manners were charming, and he was completely thoughtful for her comfort. He knew the best excursions, knew where at the *rifugo* they would find good coffee or chocolate; he always had a slab of chocolate in his pocket, and having once ascertained her favourite make, never carried any other.

The night after Wilfred had told her that Lathbury was staying for another week, she danced with him, and then walked out on the terrace. This had become a nightly occurrence.

"Have you heard that I'm staying for another week?" he asked.

"Wilfred told me this afternoon."

"Did he tell you why?"

"He told me that you and Gerald were having—his expression—such a topping time. I'm very glad."

"That we're staying or that we're—having a topping time?"

"Well, both, of course."

He laid his hand very gently on hers; it could scarcely have been called a caress, it was as if he wished to establish closer contact with her. She made no movement.

"Monica, I know that it's early days. I've only known you for a week, but hotel friendships, holiday friendships, ripen quickly. Do you like me? Like me sufficiently to let me ask you to marry me—before I leave, when you've come to know me a little better?"

She turned and faced him. "My dear, I'll be quite frank with you. I don't know. I do like you; I believe that I like you more every day, but I never thought of myself as marrying again. It's something I should need to think over, very seriously, very carefully. I'm thirty-five; I know that I shall never experience again the same ecstasy which I felt for Victor. That was something which happens only once in a lifetime. Ask me again, before you leave, and I'll be able to answer you."

"Very well, I'll try to be patient. You see, Monica, I've fallen in love, head over heels in love, with you. I've never cared a great deal for women—oh, there have been a few—incidents—in my life, but they didn't amount to anything much. I never thought that I should want to marry. When my brother and his wife were killed in that motor accident, I took young Gerald, and it seemed to fill my life, until I met you. Then I realized that I longed to marry not *a* wife, but the *only* wife I'm ever likely to want. That's you, my dear."

She kept her promise and thought deeply about marrying George Lathbury. There were so many things to be said in his favour. He was obviously devoted to her, he had shown her photographs of his house in Warwickshire, he had a flat in London. He was rich and could gratify any reasonable wish. He had retired when his brother was killed in order to devote himself to the estate. He had laughed and admitted that he did not allow it to restrict him too much.

"I like travel, like Winter sports, like bathing in blue waters which don't chill you to the bone! With Gerald at Harby, I've plenty of time to take trips here and there and still be back for his holidays."

Monica had always loved travel and had known far too little of it. Her father and mother disliked leaving home; her father distrusted foreigners, her mother disliked foreign cooking. Victor and she had talked of the places they would visit together, but—his life had ended so soon.

Night after night she lay awake trying to come to a decision. To marry George would be the end of her work; she would have to leave the Towers just when they were both growing old and needed her most. Amos was still strong and full of energy, but in the very nature of things a time must come when he would be glad to shift much of the responsibility on to her shoulders. She knew that if she married, Wilfred would lead a divided life. He was literally the light of his grandfather's eyes, and if he was destined to take his place in the business it was obvious that he must spend a great deal of time at Willingbrough.

She thought of Mary Ellen and Amos and her heart filled with love and affection for them both. They had been so good to her, so generous in every possible way; they had received her as a daughter, and Mary Ellen had done this in spite of everything. For ten years she had never shown by word or deed that she knew Monica's secret. Only for a flash on the night Wilfred was born had her eyes betrayed her.

Then lastly came the thought which she had fought against facing—the thought that if she married George Lathbury she would add to her deceptions, her deceits, her lies. She thought of him, big, kindly, intelligent, and so evidently a man of high principles. He might find many things easy to forgive, but she doubted if he would forgive the fact that she had deceived the Towers, palmed off the son of another man as their beloved son's child. She could almost imagine his reaction if she told him the truth. At first incredulity, then amazement, and lastly disgust and disillusionment.

She thought for a moment, "But need I tell him?" and then flung the thought from her. It was impossible to add to the number of people she was preparing to deceive for the rest of her life! The burden was already sufficiently heavy, the weight of her secret too heavy to be borne easily, and to add to it was unthinkable.

She knew that she was not wildly in love with Lathbury, but she also knew that she was lonely, even with her work, the love which was lavished on her at Willingbrough and the high hopes she had for her son. She wanted someone who would be kind, tender, affectionate, who would be a companion to her, and she knew instinctively that George would be all those things. Not the love which she had felt for Victor. Never again would she have that love to offer anyone. But she felt great affection for George, and she admitted to herself that she found him physically attractive.

Lying in bed, watching the twinkling stars which seemed so much brighter than those in England, she clenched her hands and made her decision. She would not, could not, marry George without being honest with him; if she told him he might insist that the Towers be told. That would end Wilfred's hopes and her ambitions for him.

"I've burnt my boats," she whispered. "I can't marry anyone, because I daren't add to my deceptions, and I dare not confess because no one who wished to marry me would give me absolution. I took the risk, I imagined that I was secure, that after ten years I was safe. I shall never be safe. This dreadful thing might be found out—at any time. I should either have to tell more lies, or see my whole world and my son's crash to pieces."

She came down the next morning looking pale and tired under her tan. George was solicitous and, as usual, unfailingly kind. He was leaving the next day and Monica knew that he was longing to ask her if she had come to a decision.

At last, as they sat drinking coffee after luncheon, he said very softly, "Have you thought over—well, about what I asked you?"

She nodded. "Yes, George. It's been very difficult, because I do like you so much."

"But not enough to marry me?"

"It's all too difficult," she said almost wildly. "It would mean giving up my work, and my work means my son's future. I can't leave my husband's people, they've been so good to me. They're devoted to Wilfred. Oh, it all sounds so easy, but it's not! It's insuperably difficult."

"Then your son, your husband's people, and your work mean more to you than I could ever hope to do?" he said gravely, heavily.

"Wilfred must come first. You do see that, surely?"

"I should never stand in his way. It might be good for the boy to have a—well, a father to look after him."

Monica had recovered her composure. She felt cold and chilled. She was hurting this man who had hoped and trusted that she might give him the answer for which he longed.

"It's no use talking about it, George. We shall only succeed in hurting each other. I have thought it all out so carefully, believe me. I've lain awake for hours and—it isn't possible."

He rose and stood looking down at her. "Very well. You're right. There is no more to be said. If you'll excuse me, I have some last-minute packing to do."

She held out her hand. "George—we have been such good friends."

"Unfortunately, friendship isn't what I want, my dear."

She saw him that evening. They danced but he did not ask her to go out on the terrace, and when she went up to bed he held out his hand and thanked her for helping to make his stay so enjoyable.

"On the contrary," she tried to speak lightly, "it is for me to thank you. I hope that you have a good journey."

"Thank you. Good-bye."

"That," she thought, "is the end. Well, it's over and finished. In a few years men won't want to marry me. I shall be growing middle-aged. I must never allow a man to grow fond of me again. I must remember that I have put myself outside the pale for all decent men."

The days dragged. Even Wilfred mourned the departure of his friend.

Several rather callow youths paid Monica slightly feverish attention, begging that she would skate with them, ski with them, go for runs in their bob-sleighs, dance with them in the evenings. They were pleasant enough lads, with tanned faces and rather unruly hair; they paid her youthful compliments and one of them tried to kiss her as they sat drinking coffee out of a thermos flask. She stared at him, almost startled.

"I say, you're not angry, Mrs. Towers?"

"I'm not angry. Only it's rather silly, sitting in the snow trying to kiss a woman old enough to be your mother," she said.

"Oh, my mother! That's a bit much! I'm twenty-one. We all think you've got the girls here beaten to a frazzle. We were all frightfully envious of Colonel Lathbury. Of course, he's such a big-pot that no one stood a chance against him. You know who he is?"

"I know that he's a retired soldier."

The young man whistled. "Whew! He's a good deal more than that! He was captain of the British polo team. He played rugger for the Army too. Oh, he's a first-class person. Still," he grinned his pleasant, impudent, youthful grin, "we're all jolly glad he's gone."

"You talk a great deal of nonsense," she said, but she liked these lads, liked their evident joy of living and their enjoyment of everything. They were unspoilt, eager, and they had their lives before them. They were the age that Victor had been when she married him, the age when he had lost his life and in dying had left such a desperate blankness in her own.

When she left they all came to see her go, standing waving until she was out of sight. Wilfred sighed. "It's been a top-hole holiday."

"You've enjoyed it?"

"Rather, Mummy. Still, it will be nice to be home again just the same."

"I like to hear you say that, Wilfred. Tell Grandpapa and Grannie, it will please them."

Wilfred went back to school and Monica settled down to her work again. She missed the boy, missed his chatter, his endless questions and comments. She felt that Mary Ellen and Amos missed him as much as she did.

Amos grumbled. "It's grand to know that he's at a good school, but by gum, I do miss him. We must think of something to do when it comes to half term, some special treat, eh?"

"Nay, if you had it your way," Mary Ellen told him, "the lad's life 'ud be made up of treats!"

"Why and what for not? He's got all his life i' front of him when there won't be all that many treats coming his way. I'd like to smooth everything for him, bless him, but one can only do so much, try as you like. I'll lay as he was popular in Switzerland, eh, Monica?"

"Why, o' course he'd be popular. Why for wouldn't he be? He's a friendly lad, and he's got a bonnie smile."

Monica assured them that Wilfred had never wanted for friends and repeated what the instructor had said of him. Amos beamed at Mary Ellen. He was, Monica felt, storing it all away to repeat to his friends at the Club.

"He must go next year," Amos declared. "It's all part of his education, part—as I have said before—of his equipment for life. Now I've a surprise for you both. Mother and me's taking one of these cruises. Aye, you needn't stare, Mary Ellen luv. I've gotten it all settled. It's called a luxury cruise. We'll be away for three weeks. It says 'Follow the sun', and that's what we're going to do. Madeira and the French Riviera, and Capri, Naples, and one or two other places I've forgot for the moment. Now, will you be able to manage, Monica, my dear?"

Mary Ellen said, "Why, Amos, you beat everything. Going off and doing things all secret like, not saying a word to nobody. Will it be dressing for dinner every night? My word, you must give me time. I'll have to get some new clothes. I'm not having anyone luking down their noses at me! It's going to cost you summat, my lad, before you've done."

He nodded, rubbing his hands and smiling contentedly. "That's all right, Muther. I'm not one to spoil the ship for a happorth of tar. Order what you like and I'll give our Monica time off to go with you to Hallam and Rose's. That's right, and I'll not dock the time off of her wages neither."

Monica laughed. "I should like to see you try, Amos. If you did, while you were on this cruise I should rob the till!"

"And you'd be right to," Mary Ellen agreed. "Old skin-flint!"

The evening before they left Monica was standing in Mary Ellen's bedroom, helping her to put the final touches to her packing.

"I hope you have a lovely cabin, Mary Ellen."

Mary Ellen looked at her, pursing her lips as if she were almost shocked. "Nay, it beats me where our Amos gets his ideas from. It seems that we're not having a cabin, not having those bunk things. We're having a state-room, it's called, with our own private bathroom. He's getting some grand ideas in his head, is Amos. Mind you, proper *beds*!"

Monica laughed. "He says that only the best is good enough for you."

"Aye, but think on, Monica luv, it's all wunderful, come to think of it. Me dressing for dinner, changing my dress a couple o' times a day, and—when we started, when I met Amos, I was a general servant. Not a cook, nor yet a parlourmaid, just a general servant. Makes you think, doesn't it?"

They departed, like children going on holiday, with much brand-new luggage and expensive travelling-rugs, which Amos told Monica was a sure sign that you were "somebody", as all the "high-ups" carried travelling-rugs. The house seemed very silent without them, and the evenings very long. She found it sufficiently easy to run the business; the staff were all well trained and highly efficient, everything was done with method and system, the place ran like clockwork.

In the evenings, when the house was so quiet, Monica found herself forgetting to read and sitting staring into the bright fire, thinking of days which were past. She remembered the garden of her old home, the rare visits of her father on leave, bringing Indian shawls, terrible brass trays, numbers of ebony elephants and carved boxes. She did not remember that she had enjoyed her childhood particularly. Her brothers had been overbearing; they had regarded their sisters as things provided by Providence to attend to them and to fulfil their wishes.

She had been a reserved, shy child, and had loved to take herself either to the attics or to the fork of the gnarled apple tree at the end of the orchard, where she could read quietly and undisturbed.

Those books she had read—or wasn't "devoured" a better word?—*Little Women* and *Good Wives*, *Midshipman Easy*, *The Dog Crusoe and his Master*, *The Young Fur Traders*, *Coral Island* and *Treasure Island*—which had always frightened her a little; the two *Alices*, and even *The Swiss Family Robinson*, which had resulted in her disliking all Swiss people because of the incident of the monkeys! Then had come Jane Austen, the Brontës, Mrs. Gaskell and Charlotte M. Yonge.

Wonderful days, hot Summer days when she sat in the apple tree and read with the scent of honeysuckle coming to her, and all sounds emanating from the house reaching her dimmed, softened and beautified. Winter days when, wrapped in a huge old fur rug, lying on an old moth-eaten sofa in the attic, she had lain sucking toffee and reading—transported to another world. Even now, she remembered a book which she had never heard of again—*The Cruise of the Crystal Boat*. One of the early visions of aeroplanes. It had held romance, fear, suspense—everything. She had never heard of it again, and when she searched among the shelves in the nursery she had not found it.

There had been days when her mother said, "I have to pay some calls this afternoon, I shall take one of you with me. Now—which?"

Monica had hated "paying calls", but her sister Cynthia had looked forward to it as a treat. From her early childhood Cynthia had been socially minded! So Cynthia invariably went with Lady Crawshaw and Monica was left to read and allow herself to be transported to the farthest parts of the earth.

Then they had been sent to boarding-school and the remembrance released another series of pictures in her mind. She remembered the clean, cold smell of the school, the rather handsome, severe face of the headmistress. The other mistresses —Miss Dawson, short, fat and kindly, who taught history and literature; Miss Walsington, who was considered by the girls to be "too divine", and who in retrospect had been a tall, rather ungainly woman of thirty, with a Greek profile slightly marred by the fact that it always appeared rather larger than life. Miss Regan, an Irishwoman with a

temper that flared like tinder, and a beautiful smile; Miss——
Oh, she could remember what they all looked like, but their
names had been forgotten long ago.

Cynthia had been a success at boarding-school, not because
she was clever, but because she was both pretty and obedient.
She always looked charming; her exercises might be badly
done but they were always neat and clean. Monica's exercises
were correct but untidy. When she realized that she knew the
answers to questions, when she was told to write an essay
which interested her, then her pen rushed forward, unable to
keep pace with her thoughts. The results might be excellent,
but they were smudged and blotted, badly spelt and untidily
written.

The girls had talked a great deal about love; they had
whispered about sex, and had fallen in love with every male
in the vicinity, from the music master, who was tall, thin and
rather elegant, to the boy who cleaned the boots and who was
cherubic, with red cheeks and fiercely curling hair. There was
a young man whom they often passed when they were walking
in the town, where they were allowed to go twice a week, "two
girls together". He was tall and rather smart, and somehow—
Monica could never remember how—they discovered that his
name was Harold Pensover. None of them ever spoke to him,
but they all loved him.

One morning, Bessie, the maid, told Winifred Balstone
that she wanted to "finish early".

"I want to get off to 'ave a luke at Mr. Pensover's wedding.
Yes, he's getting married this morning at twelve. Yes, to Miss
Lydia Summers."

Winifred managed to breathe, "Where—is—the wedding?"

"At Holy Trinity, miss. She's such a lovely young lady.
Her father's vicar there. It's to be fully choral!"

Winifred told Cynthia, and Daphne, Maud and Clarice,
that she felt that the end of everything had come so far as
she was concerned.

They all agreed that the best thing for them all was to
enter a convent as quickly as possible. They were none of
them Catholics, and no one seemed able to advise them how
to enter a convent, or tell them what happened exactly when
you had entered.

A year later, Bessie said to Daphne, "Last night Mrs.
Pensover had the loveliest little baby girl, I'm told."

Daphne replied, "Who on earth is Mrs. Pens—whatever you said?"

Then they had left St. Marcia's, and were sent to Paris to be "finished". Monica loved Paris and hated the school. It wasn't really a school; it was like a private hotel. Each girl had her own bedroom, there were no "set lessons", no actual time-tables. The girls attended "lectures" and were taken to visit galleries, to the Opera and to—carefully selected—theatres. Here again Cynthia was a success. She loved wearing nice clothes, she hated the galleries, she was not interested in either music or the drama, and her French remained shocking to the day she left Paris. She was pretty, she had charm, and she could make herself appear absorbed in the subject on hand. Monica, who loved Paris, who was hungry to understand pictures and painting—though she had not the slightest aspiration to be an artist—who listened to music in a manner which was almost avid, made far less impression on her teachers.

Cynthia standing before Murillo's "Immaculate Conception", her hands clasped and breathing "O-o-oh" softly, almost passionately. The governess smiled approval and registered that Cynthia "had a heart".

Monica stared at it, absorbed and entranced, but stated that she preferred his "Le Jeune Mendiant". The governess confided later to Madame Grossmont that she felt that Monica "tried to be different" from the others; that Cynthia had a "natural appreciation" but that Monica tried to draw attention to herself by admiring pictures which were, obviously, not the best, although no doubt—good.

Their time in Paris came to an end. Everyone promised to write to everyone else; Cynthia exchanged "keepsakes" with other girls, as she had exchanged confidences. Only one girl seemed to wish to hear from Monica, a tall, plain girl with a clever, ugly face who was always scribbling, scribbling, scribbling. Her name was Nora Howes, and they wrote to each other for several months. Then the correspondence dwindled to cards at Christmas, and finally ceased. Only a few years ago Monica had seen her name again—Nora Howes, whose novel, *Dandelionclocks*, had made a stir in literary circles on both sides of the Atlantic.

They returned home and Cynthia adjusted herself to the life there as easily as she had attuned herself to the life in the

Paris finishing school. She enjoyed paying calls with her mother, going to tennis parties; although she never played well, she was quite satisfied to know that she looked charming. Then she met her aristocratic young clergyman, and fell in love with him. Her whole life, to Monica, seemed to be bounded by his activities, his prospects, and his relations. The wedding took place when Monica was twenty-one and Cynthia a year younger. For two years Monica "mooned" about. Looking back now on the full and absorbing life which she led, she wondered how she had borne it. Life had never been full, it had only been consciously, almost forcibly, filled with trivialities. She enjoyed dancing—but there were so few dances; she enjoyed playing games, but became bored when they were merely an excuse for a "social function". Various young men flirted with her, two asked her to marry them; she refused them both. Her mother looked anxious; to have a daughter of twenty-three, unmarried and with no prospect of marriage, seemed to her a definite stain on the family.

The war began and Monica decided that she would take up nursing. She went to the local hospital and went through the laborious training, taking everything in her stride, and winning restrained praise from her superiors.

"Crawshaw is always willing to lend a hand," "Crawshaw never minds putting in an extra hour or two," "You can depend on Crawshaw," and so on. At first she hated it all, the sights, sounds, smells were all repulsive. Slowly she came to accept them all; they were part of the job. She emerged a fine and capable nurse; she could exercise discipline without losing the goodwill of the patients; she could do her work efficiently and without apparent hurry. The men liked her, she was pleasant to look at, her hands were firm and steady, she never fumbled. The Matron sighed, "I wish I had a dozen like Crawshaw!"

Then the Duchess "dropped in" one day to see Lady Crawshaw. She was energetic, handsome, patriotic. She had turned her splendid home into a hospital for officers.

"I'm determined that they shall have the best and only the best. I've told Nottingford and he agrees. After this war we may all of us be poor as church mice, but while we've got it—and both he and I have 'got it'—let's make some decent use of it! I don't want a staff of nurses who are just a transported beauty chorus. Naturally I'd like decent-looking girls, but they've got to be efficient. What about your girls, Millicent?"

"My dear, Cynthia's married—why, you were at the wedding! Monica's nursing at our local hospital, I believe," with a slight stress on the last word, because it was such bad form to scatter praise about your own children, "that the Matron thinks quite well of her."

"Would she come to me? I see to it that my nurses are comfortable, treated decently. The Matron is a fine woman, and the place is beautiful. I'll write to your girl and suggest it. If she turns it down, she's a fool! I'd like to have her. I remember her, attractive creature, nice eyes and a good skin. You'd like her to come?"

"My dear Beatrice, I should be delighted."

In due course Monica went to the hospital run by the Duchess. It was a beautiful place; even with the exigencies of war there were sufficient gardners to see that the grounds were immaculately kept. The food was excellent, and the rooms exceedingly comfortable. The hospital had been designed to accommodate wounded officers who were well on the way to making a recovery, but again and again when things went badly in France or Flanders, men were rushed to the hospital who were still dangerously ill.

The Duchess almost gloated. "They may well send them here! Our theatres are as good, as modern, as anything they have in England. I've got surgeons who are wizards, nurses who know everything there is to be known in their particular job. There's not a hospital in England where they get better or more skilful treatment."

Looking back, Monica remembered what nice fellows they had been, taking them by and large. True, there had been men who were surly, who were difficult, consistent grumblers for whom nothing was ever right, but the majority of them were plucky souls, grateful for what was done for them, and ready on the slightest provocation to fall in love with their nurses.

She had laughed at them, made gentle fun of them and their sentimentalizing, mocked their sighs and smiled at their protestations. They were so extravagant in their avowals that they loved her; there was no limit to their declarations of eternal devotion.

"And you said all this to the nurse at Westthorpe, didn't you?"

"Oh, Nurse, what a beastly thing to say!"

"It's true though, isn't it?"

"Not a bit like it! This is completely different."

They all said the same, all stared at her with wide eyes, all gave vent to gusty sighs, and all tried to look unutterable things.

"Nurse," trying to catch her hand, some lad would ask, "could you ever love me? Honestly?"

"I love you all," she told him. "I think you're all the nicest boys in the world."

One evening Nurse Harkess told her that "they caught a tartar this time. He's in that room with two beds, you know, number eight. We've had a few of the grumbling, grizzling type, but this one—he beats the lot. Sister told me that he's some tremendous swell—no, he's only a major. I mean in civvy street. Has estates or something. Let's see what the Crawshaw charm can do with him, my girl, eh?"

When she saw the patient the next morning, he was lying perfectly still, his eyes were closed, and the lids looked heavy and dark; there were shadows beneath his eyes too. His dark hair looked damp, as if he had sweated during the night. His nose was high-bridged, it jutted out from his face, and his mouth was shut firmly, the lips rather tight and narrow. Not handsome and yet, as she watched him, Monica had to admit that there was something very striking about his face, some dignity, the face of a man accustomed not only to giving orders but to having those orders obeyed.

The heavy lids were raised. The man said, "Oh, not the same bouncing creature who was here last night. For God's sake, keep her away; it's like having an overgrown cart-horse in the room."

Monica replied, a little primly, "If you mean Nurse Harkess, she is one of the best nurses here. *Everyone* likes and admires her——" She paused and added, "Everyone."

"Possibly—until I arrived. I'm the exception."

"I'm afraid that you'll have to be reconciled to the fact that Nurse Harkess and I will be looking after you most of the time you are here."

He muttered, "I shall make a very speedy recovery, be sure of that."

"I hope so, I'm sure," Monica said crisply, and began her work.

He grumbled consistently; nothing was right; how could he possibly clean his teeth—very excellent teeth they were too, she noticed—if she didn't prop him up better, didn't put the basin where he could reach it, and why did she smother the toothbrush with paste? Who, he asked, was the under-bred little Lowland Scot who had examined him yesterday?

"I think you will find that Dr. McBain is one of the cleverest surgeons possible."

"Huh! He talks like a Glasgow shop-keeper! And the Matron, is she another paragon?"

"Matron is—exceptional."

"And all the nurses and sisters—angels, no doubt?"

"I'd not say that, but I would say that they are all efficient."

"The Ministry of all the Talents, eh?"

"Indeed, you might say so, and not be very wrong. There, your breakfast will be along very soon."

She went out closing the door quietly, though she longed to bang it defiantly. What a detestable man! She didn't doubt that serious wounds were unpleasant, but she had nursed other men, far more badly wounded than this Major Hamish Mac-Phail, who had grinned cheerfully through everything, who had faced the most excruciating pain with a stoicism which was magnificent.

She met Nurse Harkess in the corridor as she was going to breakfast. "Well, have you met the grizzly bear, Crawshaw?"

Monica wrinkled her neat nose in disgust. "We're not going to find life a bed of roses while that little ray of sunshine is with us!"

Harkess laughed. "We'll learn him to be a toad!" she announced.

"He *is* a toad," Monica agreed. "We've got to make him conscious of the fact."

"Get along to breakfast, Crawshaw. The eggs are lovely." She yawned a trifle noisily. "Gosh, I'm all in. That nice lad, Calmenny, went in the night. Pity those good types have to go, and things like this—animal are left. I liked Calmenny."

Monica started and shivered. The fire had burnt very low, the room felt chilly. She had been so absorbed in her thoughts that she had not noticed it. She stared at the clock; the time was half past eleven. Tomorrow was a hard day; she must go to bed; she had allowed her thoughts to take complete possession; indeed it had seemed that she had actually listened to Harkess, had felt a sense of grief that poor young Calmenny had gone. She remembered him so clearly; he had been so anxious to live. Pernicious anaemia. He'd been engaged to a girl with fair, fluffy hair, she remembered.

"Nurse, when I'm better, if anyone ever offers me *liver* in any form whatsoever, they'll do so at their own risk! Liver, how I loathe it and all its component parts, and extracts and juices!"

Poor Calmenny.

She rose, gathered up her bag, her book, turned out the light, and walked slowly upstairs.

CHAPTER THREE

DURING the day Monica's work absorbed her. She never ceased working at top speed. The place had grown so large, with the various additions which Amos Towers had made, that her morning round of inspection was in itself a long business. A word with each head of the various departments, giving advice on this point or that, asking questions, listening to proposals; the great stock-rooms, which seemed to contain everything in the world which was connected with either food, or the working of a ship, the clothes of its officers and crew, the medicines to keep them in health, the material with which to bind their wounds should they be physically hurt. The smell of new ropes, of canvas, the faint scent of tar and paint, solignum and turpentine. Casks of strongly smelling pickles, great tubs of grease and oil, tins which held fruit, jam, meat and fish, tins with bright labels, and words calculated to sell the goods which they contained. Soap in tubs, in bars, in cakes— these, the superior kinds which were scented and chosen according to the taste of the individual. Everything kept with meticulous care, everything shining, clean and spotless; lists which were carefully altered with each sale, and then sent to the typing office so that a new and immaculate list might be ready for the following day.

Amos said, "We sell stuff for the ships. I want no captain or officer—no owner, come to that—visiting here and saying that my warehouse and offices aren't as clean and shining as his own deck. Let's have it all shipshape and Bristol fashion."

Back in her own office, which Amos had furnished with dignity, and even luxury, she sent for her secretary. Letters were read, replies dictated. The list of appointments for the day were submitted to Monica.

"Captain Carter at eleven, Dr. Murray Brown at eleven-thirty. Sir Reginald Harvey at twelve. I wish that I could tell him to take his orders somewhere else! How those tramps of his get past Lloyd's beats me! Old skinflint, he's worth three-quarters of a million and he grudges every penny he has to lay out for the ship and the crew. Then luncheon—oh, on S.S. *Mersey Lily*. I suppose I must go. It's their latest ship. Never mind, I always enjoy talking to Captain Reid, he's shrewd and amusing. Very well, Miss Meadows, I'll get back as soon as I can, but Captain Reid is certain to want to show me the wonders of the *Mersey Lily*. If Captain Carter is there, I'll see him at once."

So it went on all day, and she managed to get back from her luncheon only to find a further list of appointments, interviews and obligations which must be met. At six o'clock she signed the last of her letters, ordered her car and drove back to Little Manor; tired to death, feeling dirty and dusty, but with the realization that she had done a good day's work, and done it to the very best of her ability. Even then, there was a letter to write to Wilfred, in answer to his last one to her. Even his writing gave her a small sense of shock, it was growing so formed, developing character, it was not the writing of a small boy any longer.

Orders to give for the following day, listening to cook's complaints about the quality of the meat from Allwyns, the wickedness of hens who laid irregularly, and the difficulty of obtaining a proper and regular delivery of ice.

"Mr. Towers did say, m'um, as he thought of puttin' in one o' them new-fangled machines wot make ice and keep food fresh for days. It 'ud be a little godsend, I'm sure."

"We'll talk to him about it as soon as he gets back, Cook. In the meantime, point out to Baines that we're good customers and he must treat us properly—or"—she laughed—"we shall know what to do."

Then upstairs for her bath. Whenever she was growing tired the thought of that bath sustained her. Hot scented water, well-warmed towels, scented soap which came from Paris, clean, smooth clothes, and a general sense of being able to relax and forget the affairs of Amos Towers Limited for at least twelve blessed hours.

Downstairs again after a leisurely toilet, to find the tray and cocktail shaker waiting for her, to sip the ice-cold drink slowly, savouring it, luxuriating in its freshness and coolness.

Dinner eaten alone, with well-shaded lights on the table, shining silver and twinkling glass. Dishes which were prepared exactly as Monica liked them—simple things, perfectly cooked, and beautifully served.

Cook said in the kitchen, "Nay, it's not as she eats a lot, for no one could say as she does, but whatever she does have must be the best. T'soup, why she only takes a spoonful as you might say, but it's got to be strong, wi' the right flavour. She likes a couple of cutlets, but they must be proper small, and tender. She'll never luke at greens as is a bit on t'watery side—which mine never is, I'll say that. If it's creamed per-tatoes, eh, there mustn't be such a thing as a lump, no matter if it was no bigger nor a Carter's Little Liver Pill! Savoury must be just so! She likes a change, allus notices them. 'Savoury very nice ter-night, Cook,' or 'Just a hint too much tarragon, didn't you think?' Nay, she's a 'noticer' is Mrs. Victor."

Dinner over, she returned to the drawing-room, there to sit with the coffee-tray at her elbow, the cigarettes to her hand, and a bright fire dancing and leaping in the shining grate.

"Please tell Cook that dinner was excellent tonight, Lizzie."

"She'll be pleased, m'um. She was a bit worrited over that cheese and sparrer-grass flan. I'm glad as it turned out all right."

"Delicious. We must have it again when the master and mistress get home. They'll enjoy it as much as I did."

Lizzle reflected, "She allus says 'the master' and 'the mistress', never tries to set herself up as mistress here. Knows her place, and egspects you to know yours. I like it!"

Then, slowly, with only the reading-lamp to throw a soft ring of light, Monica would put down her book and stare into the bright, crackling fire; slowly her thoughts, her memories, took possession of her.

When had she first been conscious of the attraction which MacPhail had for her? Was it as he grew stronger, and he seemed to grow—with her at least—less difficult, less captious and overbearing? Harkess declared that he was worse, that his temper was less tolerable every day, but Monica had seen his mouth soften, his eyes grow brighter, and had heard a new note in his somewhat harsh voice. Once when he had laughed openly at something she told him, she felt that it was astonishing how much younger he looked.

"You ought to laugh more often," she said.

His expression hardened immediately. "Why—I've nothing much to laugh at."

"Nonsense, there are always plenty of things to laugh at. As a last resource, you can always laugh at yourself."

"I don't find myself amusing," he snapped.

"You certainly don't try to make other people find you so," she retorted. "It's such a pity."

He stared at her, his eyes very keen and searching, then said, "I might try, if I thought that it would please you, my dear." Then stretching out a hand, he took hers and drew her nearer to the chair where he sat. "I should like to—please you. If," he smiled, "it wasn't too much trouble. I hate—taking trouble, except to ensure my own comfort. Do you like me, Monica?"

She started, felt her cheeks crimson, and drew her hand away.

"Do you?" he persisted.

"Sometimes; sometimes I detest you. I'm sorry for you."

He laughed. "Sorry for me! In heaven's name—why?"

"You miss so much," she told him gravely. "You're better, this is a beautiful place, you're looked after marvellously, and there are plenty of nice men here, ready to be friends."

"Pah! I loathe these healthy, hearty, Army types. Shouting their heads off over the latest dirty story, longing to tell you about the women they've slept with—in detail—and incapable of a single original thought. What on earth have I in common with them?"

Monica looked at him critically. "What an utterly self-sufficient prig you are," she said slowly, and had the satisfaction of seeing a touch of colour show on his rather high cheek-bones.

He turned back to his book; she did not speak again, but finished what she had to do and walked out.

Yet she knew that she felt his attraction, knew that if he tried to exercise it she would find it difficult to resist. There were times when he talked pleasantly and easily about his home. If he loved anything, she thought, it was his home. He seemed deeply imbued with a passion for it—the salmon river, the hills, the deer, the wide views of the sea in the distance, the changing colours of the heather in the different seasons. His home, the old house where he and his forebears had lived for centuries, was all tinged with romance for Hamish Mac-Phail. His voice changed when he spoke of these things, it grew softer, he used expressions which were charged with colour and imagination.

He told her stories of the gillies, the crofters, the shepherds and their families; spoke of their devotion to duty, their complete loyalty, and their innate love of learning. He recounted the sacrifices they made in order to send their sons to some seat of learning, of their pride when they were able to refer to "Our Jamie, the minister", or "Jock, him that's a doctor i' Edinburgh".

"Heaven knows how they manage to do it. Simply by self-denial, will-power and—pride. To them it's their great achievement to see their sons start off in one of the—learned professions. Jamie with his manse and his—usually—miserable stipend, Jock with his brass plate in Edinburgh—these are things worth striving for. They don't mind living on oat-cake and porridge if they can talk of 'my son, the minister' or 'my younger son, the physician'. Ah, a great, courageous people, the salt of the earth."

Monica liked him best when he spoke of such things and such people. It seemed that he stripped off his irritability, his cynicism and his intolerance when his mind went back to his homeland. He told her that there was very little money, certainly nothing to spare to keep the great old house as it should be kept.

"Threadbare carpets, worn-out curtains, old-fashioned baths, with huge brass taps which always need polishing. To keep the place properly would need an army of servants, and I've not got the money to feed them, let alone pay them wages. But I'm hanging on, and one day—who knows?—my luck may turn." He laughed. "I ought to marry money, I suppose; that's the solution."

She knew that she was coming to think about him more and more, knew that even when his temper was ugly and his nerves on edge she welcomed an opportunity of talking to him. Sometimes she would find him watching her as she moved about the room putting everything in order, and once, catching sight of his face in the looking-glass, she started. There was an expression on it which she had never seen before. An expression which held the quality of hunger; his eyes were very bright, his lips a little apart, he seemed to breathe more rapidly than usual. Resolutely she turned her eyes away from the reflection. She felt that she had been spying upon him, felt the same sensation of guilt that she might have felt had he discovered her reading his personal letters. She tried to forget what she had seen, but the memory of MacPhail's expression refused to be banished and remained with her all through the day.

Two days later—she remembered that it had been Nurse Harkess's day off duty—she entered his room with some fresh flowers. The Duchess liked to know that there were flowers in every room; she believed that it was good for the morale of the patients. They were "issued" three times a week, and "doing the vases" was a special duty allocated in strict rotation to the nurses.

MacPhail was standing at the window. He turned as she entered, and smiled.

"Ah, it's the bouncing Harkess's day off duty! God be thanked for small mercies."

Monica laughed. "Do you mean that I'm a—small mercy?" she asked.

He watched her gravely as she set down the vase and rearranged one or two of the flowers to her own satisfaction; she stepped back to view the effect. MacPhail caught her arms and held her close to him.

"Monica, what are we waiting for?" he said hoarsely.

She repeated, "Waiting for . . .?"

"We're in love," he said, speaking very rapidly. "You know that's true. We've been falling more and more deeply in love for the last three weeks. Monica, come out tonight after dinner. Oh," in a tone of sudden exasperation as she made a sound of protest, "they all do it. Even your Harkess goes walking away towards the pine wood with that red-headed nitwit Barrass. I've watched them all from this window— Willis, Preston, that fair girl—Manners. I tell you they all do it. Monica, come out tonight, just for half an hour.

"How can I ever talk to you here? Invariably someone

comes blundering in and we have to pretend that we've been discussing a film or some damned silly book. I want to talk to you—really talk." His voice had lost its tone of irritation, it was gentle, and persuasive. "I want to tell you how lovely you are, how smooth your skin is, how soft your hair. My dear, I'm in love, terribly, hopelessly in love, and I want to talk to you"—he smiled—"without the shadow of a thermometer or a dose of linctus between us. Monica, you'll come?"

She nodded. "I'll come."

"Nine o'clock, at that little iron gate that leads to the small wood."

"Very well."

She left him, her heart thudding against her ribs. She knew that she was being foolish, knew that no matter what other nurses did, the whole thing was wrong for Monica Crawshaw. At that moment she almost hated MacPhail, and yet when he had held her to him she had known that he had a fascination for her which she could not resist.

It was inexplicable, a mystery, and yet it existed as a fact, as something which was too strong for her. For days she had known that the moment through which they had just passed was drawing nearer and nearer. It was as if she had felt it coming closer.

She went about her work feeling that nine o'clock would never come. She argued with herself that she would tell him frankly that she would not come out again, and as she tried to imagine the words and phrases which she would use she knew with perfect clarity that they would never be spoken. She might know that in meeting him she was doing something foolish, something which was definitely wrong—for her, and yet she realized that she was incapable of refusing when he asked her to meet him.

She ate very little. Morrison asked her, "Crawshaw, got a headache? You look pasty; not like you."

"I'm all right. Not very hungry tonight."

"I don't believe that you go out enough," Willis declared. "Matron's always preaching about the benefits of fresh air."

Someone asked, "Is that why you go out every evening, Willis?"

Willis winked broadly. "That—and other reasons, my dear."

"I'll admit that—the other reason—or one of them—is a good-looking bloke."

"Oh, my taste in 'blokes' is excellent, believe me."

Monica watched the hands of the big clock nearing nine. She was nervous, filled with apprehension. The nurses were rising, leaving the dining-room. She got up and caught her big cloak from a peg where it hung in the long corridor.

Willis passed. "Going out, Crawshaw? It will do you good."

The night was crisp and sweet, there was a hint of frost in the air, and she walked briskly. MacPhail was waiting on the other side of the small iron gate. She joined him, and he slipped his arm round her and together they walked slowly into the wood. Neither of them spoke. Suddenly he turned and caught her in his arms. He kissed her passionately, repeatedly, whispering that he loved her, that she was the loveliest thing he'd ever seen, praising her hair, her eyes, her soft mouth. When he released her, she put out her hand and laid it on his shoulder; she needed support, her knees were shaking. For the first time in her life passion had touched her.

He said, "There's a felled tree here. Let's sit down. Pull your cloak round her; you'll not be cold."

"No, I shan't be cold."

He slipped his arms round her, and pulled her head down on his shoulder. He talked quickly, softly, and the sound of his voice seemed to dull her senses like an insidious drug. She heard his voice as something piercing the mists of languor, of mental drowsiness. It was a soporific, overcoming her power to think and reason.

She felt that she had been sitting there for hours, for weeks, for ever. Making a violent effort, she moved from the circle of his arm.

"I must go. Yes, I must go now—at once."

"Monica, not yet. You can't go yet."

"I can. I must. Good night."

"You'll come tomorrow?"

"Yes—I don't know. Perhaps. I'm not sure."

She turned and walked back to the hospital. He did not attempt to follow her, but stood watching her figure disappear in the darkness; then, after lighting a cigarette, he walked back slowly to the door which led to the sleeping quarters.

The next day at tea-time Harkess announced that for two pins she'd tell Matron that she refused to do anything for MacPhail.

"The man's a swine. He's like a bear with a sore head. I wonder if he's been losing too much at poker. Oh, they play pretty high, some of them. If it's not that, he must have had a row with his girl, whoever the poor damned fool is. I pity the woman who has much to do with that devil."

Monica did not raise her eyes; she tried to keep her hands from shaking when she lifted her tea-cup. She had promised to meet him again, and again she was going through all the agonies of indecision, of doubt and uncertainty. At one moment her mind was firm, determined. Last night should be the first and last time, the whole thing must end. She didn't love him, of course she didn't love him. The idea was ridiculous, fantastic. A few seconds later she knew that she longed to feel his arms round her, to experience again that strange, half-hypnotic effect which his voice had upon her; a sense of sinking into a deep, untroubled pool, where the water was soft, where there was complete forgetfulness.

She met him as before. He smiled, and kissed her.

"I nearly didn't come," she whispered.

"I think if you hadn't I should have come back to the hospital and dragged you here."

Again they sat together on the tree-trunk, again she listened to his soft, muted voice. Again she felt as if some drug were overcoming her; felt her strength growing less, was conscious that her resistance was becoming non-existent.

She felt his fingers—those long, slim fingers—unbutton the front of her uniform, felt his hand slip inside, stroking her smooth soft flesh. She twisted from him, saying, "No, no! Don't do that!"

She heard him draw his breath sharply, then he whispered almost savagely, "Be quiet, you little fool! Keep still! I shan't hurt you."

Then his voice changed. Once again it was soft, caressing, very low and tender. He was asking her to make promises, and she knew that she was incapable of refusing.

"You'll come tomorrow?" he whispered.

As if she were still half asleep, she answered, "Yes, I'll come."

For a fortnight she met him every evening; there were

times when she hated him, hated herself; other times when she experienced a sense of sickening panic, desperate fear.

Once she told him, and he laughed softly and kissed her.

"Do you think that I can't take care of you, silly one?"

"I don't know——"

"Then you ought to know! No, you can trust me."

She wasn't happy; she doubted if she loved him at all. There were tones in his voice sometimes which were so cold, so cruel, so devoid of any humanity that she shivered.

Once she told him that she was afraid of him sometimes. She fancied that she detected a tone of self-complacency in his voice, when he answered.

"Afraid of me, eh? I wonder why? Can you tell me—why?"

"I don't know——"

"You never do know the answers to questions, my sweet," he teased. "You're vague about everything except your work. Never mind, I'm in love with you; that's all that matters."

One evening he said quite casually, "I shan't be coming out tonight. I've promised to play bridge."

She stared at him, surprised, dismayed by the baldness of his statement.

"You're going to play bridge?" she said.

He nodded. "Yes. Nothing against my playing bridge, is there?"

"Nothing."

He laughed. "Good God, you're offended because I want —a night off! You're like all the rest of the women. You think a man should want to spend his life making love. Be reasonable."

That night Matron announced that tomorrow would bring a new intake. "We shall be packed," she said. "No more single rooms. I'm afraid some of them won't be particularly pleased. That can't be helped; they must make the best of it. The ambulances should be here in the early evening. Yes, from London."

Harkess said to Monica later, "Now the fur will fly with old man MacPhail. He won't care for sharing a room. However, he won't be here much longer. I think he's going in about a week. So McBain told me."

He was going, and he had never mentioned the fact to her.

McBain knew, Harkess knew, only she was ignorant, and surely of all people she had a right to have been told.

Trying to speak evenly, she said, "Who is coming into MacPhail's room?"

"A 'loot', called Victor Towers. I wish it had been a general. He'd have made MacPhail toe the line; he'd have stood no old buck!"

The next day, when she had entered the room with clean linen, and had begun to make up the bed, MacPhail glanced up, scowling.

"What's that for?"

"A new patient. Intake this afternoon."

He shut his book with a slam. "Blast it! It's damnable, crowding us like this. I've a good mind to speak to the Duchess."

As she smoothed the counterpane Monica said very calmly, "Why don't you?"

He stared at her, his expression hostile. "Still sulking about last night?"

"No."

He smiled. "That's a lie. Well, come out tonight, won't you?"

"I shall be busy. We don't know what time—exactly—the ambulances will get here."

His smile died. He rose and came over to her, taking her hands in his. She met his eyes squarely, steadily. She realized that she felt nothing. He had become a habit, a drug to which she had grown accustomed.

"I shan't be here much longer," MacPhail said softly. "I may go in about a week——"

"Yes, I heard so."

"Monica, don't spoil it all. It's been so wonderful, so very wonderful. Let's get as much happiness as we can, my dear. I'm sorry, dreadfully sorry, if I hurt you; I was thoughtless. I'm a stupid fellow, clumsy. Forgive me, Monica, say that it's all right again."

"Yes, it's—all right. There, I must get on. I have a lot to do."

She would have drawn her hands from his but he held them firmly.

"You will come tonight. Say at least that you'll try."

She jerked up her head as if she were in need of air, as if

she wanted to fill her lungs; she felt her strength ebbing, knew that unless she struggled she would promise to meet him.

"I'll—I'll try. I can't promise."

He leaned forward and kissed her, softly, almost tenderly. "Darling, I am sorry. Say you forgive me."

"I forgive you," she said, and drawing her hands from his she went out.

She remembered so well the sudden stir when the ambulances arrived, the bustle, the clear but very warm and kindly voice of the Duchess, the hurried footsteps of Matron and the little group of fluttering nurses waiting to accompany their patients. The sister, behaving like the staff of some general before an engagement, calm, efficient, ready to take orders and to deal with them swiftly and accurately. Stretchers, glimpses of tired men, men with white faces and half-closed eyes.

"Not too bad a journey?"—encouragement in the voice of the Duchess.

"No, thank you, not too bad. Glad to get here all the same."

"Beautifully sprung, these ambulances"—a laugh. "They should be, they're Rollses, y'know."

Sister disappearing upwards in the huge lift, Harkess saying that she had gone up with "our patient". Asking excitedly if Monica had seen him. "A heart-throb if you like," Harkess assured her. "I've never in my life seen such a lovely young man. He's like those Greek gods you hear about."

Monica remembered how she had first seen him when the doctor was on his rounds. MacPhail was not there. The new man lay with his eyes closed, and she stood and stared at him. Harkess was right, he was—beautiful. Terribly thin, and with violet shadows below his eyes; the lids, too, were faintly tinged with the same shade. His hair looked startlingly golden against the white pillow. As she stood watching him his eyes opened slowly, as if to lift the lids was an effort. They were dark blue, and they met hers. She wondered how any man came to be so beautiful, and yet there was not the slightest trace of effeminacy in his features. They were strong and well cut.

Later Monica met MacPhail in the corridor. He was scowling, and stopped her. "Are you coming out?"

"I can't possibly. I've this man, and the Major in the next room, and two more people in number seven. I haven't a minute."

"I suppose that you're all fluttering round the pansy boy with the golden hair! I hope that you were impressed by his silk pyjamas. Magnificent! I believe that his father's a grocer or something of the kind. Good lord!"

"I can't stop," she said.

"I see. Good night."

Towers hadn't managed to eat very much of his food.

"Try, just try. It's very nice. The food here is all beautiful."

"I'll try. Thank you, I'm sure it's first-rate."

When she came back he had finished his supper. She praised him, and he flushed a little and smiled. She gave him a sleeping draught and returned quite soon to wash and settle him for the night. He flushed again, and seemed visibly distressed.

"Honestly, I could quite well get up and wash. I'm really quite able to do that. I mean—oh, I hate to give you all this trouble."

"My dear boy," she said, "you certainly cannot get up and wash. This is my job, remember. I shall put a screen round you in case Major MacPhail comes back."

"He commented on my pyjamas. They're not too—well, too much of a good thing, are they? My mother bought them for me when I was in the place in Park Lane. They went shopping in a very big way for me, bless them."

"They're exceedingly splendid and gorgeous pyjamas."

MacPhail made it obvious that he resented Tower's presence. He occasionally made some attempt to be pleasant to the newcomer, but usually his remarks were edged, and Monica knew that her anger flamed when she heard the elder man talking to this "Golden Boy". That was what Harkess called him. Either the "Golden Boy" or the "Golden Lad".

MacPhail heard her one day and cut in with, "You know what happens to golden lads, don't you?"

"They get well," she retorted, "get well and finally come back covered with glory."

"They don't," he assured her. "They don't indeed."

Towers spoke. "It's all right, Nurse, he means that they come to dust. Well, come to that, so does everyone. 'Golden

lads and girls all must, like chimney sweepers, come to dust.'
That's right, isn't it?''

Ungraciously MacPhail said, "That's right. I don't know
how you knew."

Monica was kept busy; the place was full and the nurses
were run off their feet. She found it difficult to get out to meet
MacPhail, and he made no attempt to hide the fact that her
inability to do so angered him. One evening he told her that
he was leaving the next day. She had expected it, and yet the
news came as something of a shock. That evening he was as
she had known him first: kind, tender and exercising the same
tremendous fascination for her.

"How I hate leaving you," he said. "Monica, my sweet, I
shall be in London for nearly a month. I have to see to some
business, and see some people. I'd rather be here with you,
snatching these few minutes. Finding you, each time, more
adorable. Listen, you get week-end leave sometimes. Darling,
come to Town and spend a week-end with me. Think of it, no
disturbance because Towers has to be washed or fed or have
his damned golden hair brushed! Just you and me. Darling,
say that you will. When is your next leave? The week-end
after next. Sweetheart, say that you'll come. I know that I've
been difficult—very often—it's because I never seem to get
you all to myself. It's all been—just snatches. You'll find me
so different. The very fact that we could look forward to two
whole days together would—make me different."

His arms were round her, his voice was very low, immeasurably tender and pleading. She turned to look into his
eyes. Yes, even they were different. The hardness had
vanished; he looked years younger. His lips had lost their
compression, his mouth smiled. Again that dreadful sense of
being drugged, of knowing that her strength was deserting her.

"Monica, Monica darling, answer me."

"Yes, I'll come. Leave me your address and I'll write and
tell you the train."

The next morning MacPhail left early. She only saw him
for a moment when he pressed a leaf torn from his notebook
into her hand, and whispered, "You won't forget. You will
come? Promise!"

"I promise," she said.

G

CHAPTER FOUR

His going left less sense of deprivation than she had expected.
A new patient was occupying the other bed, MacPhail's bed;
a quietly spoken fellow, who was always reading dull-looking
books, and making copious notes in black-backed notebooks;
a neat fellow, who always went to the window and stood on
the balcony to sharpen his lead pencils.

"I don't want to make a mess, Nurse," he assured her.

Towers was better, the colour was returning to his cheeks,
the gold of his hair seemed to have grown even brighter. He
was allowed to get up, to take baths, and to shave himself.
He still had to rest for the latter part of each day, but he was
—as Matron said—"well on the mend".

After her weekly day off duty, Towers said to her in the
morning, "It was an awfully long day yesterday."

Monica laughed. "I'm sure that Nurse Harkess was terribly
good to you—you're one of her pet patients."

"She was—oh, she was," he assented eagerly. "But—well,
she isn't you."

When she told him that she was going to London for the
week-end, she fancied that he looked disappointed. He asked
if she was going to have a gay time. She nodded, at the same
time wondering if the time spent with MacPhail would be
gay. Certainly not if he were in of one his black moods.

Towers said, "Dancing, and theatres, and meals in hotels
with lots of lights and a good band playing. . . ."

She nodded. "Probably."

He hesitated, then the words came very quickly. "When
I'm discharged I'm certain to get some leave. Would you come
to Town and meet me? I don't know London awfully well,
but I'd do whatever you wished—dance, theatre, anything. I
don't dance badly. Oh, do say that you will. I should look
forward to it so much. Will you?"

She looked at his shining eyes, heard the urgency in his
pleasant voice, and thought as she had thought so often, "How
nice he is!"

She smiled. "I think that it would be great fun. I can stay
with my aunt who lives in Kensington. Yes, we'll do that—
when you're really better."

Towers sighed; she could actually see him relax, and knew what an effort he had made to put his request to her.

"That will be something to look forward to. I shall think that my time is coming, while you're away."

Was it when she returned from the visit to London or just before she left that he told her that he loved her? She could never remember clearly. He told her very quietly; he made no attempt to grow sentimental, just stated the fact, and later said very softly, but with a kind of confidence, that one day she would marry him.

"I shan't be good enough for you, because no one could be that, but I can love you and take care of you always—and that's what I shall spend my life doing."

She had been startled but in some strange way not surprised. He told her that he was twenty-three, adding, "Very nearly, that is."

She was twenty-four, and tried to tease him that he was far too young to think of marrying anyone.

He said, "If you are only two years older than I am, you should be two years wiser. You ought to know that I'm serious. I've never been so serious about anything in my life."

She supposed that her week-end with MacPhail was a success. He was in high spirits, he had arranged everything; they stayed in a hotel which offered every possible comfort. Her room was filled with flowers; he had bought sweets and scent for her. They danced, and he said that she danced divinely. They ate exquisite meals, making them last for a long time, so that they could talk quietly and intimately. She lay in his arms; he talked in that strange low voice which was so disturbing and, Monica felt, dangerous.

"Whatever happens," he said, "you must always belong to me."

She answered, feeling as if she were drifting into a great sea of sleep, and deep unconsciousness, "What—could—happen?"

"I don't know. Life's strange, darling. Strange and difficult."

"Not now." Her voice sounded muffled in her own ears. "Not when we're together—like this."

"No, not when we're together."

The next day he talked to her of his own affairs, told her how difficult everything was. His father was growing old, he had lost the ability to hold the reins and to give directions. He disliked the idea of letting the fishing or the shooting.

"I dislike it," MacPhail said, "but when needs must . . ."

He never asked her about her own life. He had alluded once or twice to her father, praised him for being such a fine soldier, but he seemed completely incurious as to her life or the environment in which she had lived before she came to the hospital.

He went with her to the station; he bought her papers and was kind, attentive and charming. He said that she must come to Town again, adding that everything had been wonderful. She leaned from the carriage as the train drew out of the station. He had turned and was walking away towards the barrier. Monica sank back in her corner, feeling inexplicably chilled and disappointed.

Even now she could remember the sensation. It was as if the curtain had been rung down on a wonderful play, as if the lights in the theatre had been extinguished, and she was walking out into the cold darkness. She felt confused and disturbed, and yet could give herself no valid reason for being either.

"I'm being stupid. I'm probably tired. I've lost the knack of dancing until the small hours, of tearing about in taxis, of never relaxing for a moment. My work at the hospital is hard, but it's like a machine which runs smoothly and easily."

As the train carried her back to her work, her depression grew. Doubts, fears, which she tried to fight down, beset her. Did Hamish really love her? She remembered that he had told her so hundreds of times, but he had never mentioned marriage. Never spoke of a possible life—together. He had told her that he was poor. Once he had said that his only solution was to marry money! She recalled how his whole voice, his manner of speech, his expressions had changed when he spoke of his home in Scotland. Did that mean more to him than love, happiness? More than spending the remainder of his life with the woman he loved and who loved him in return? She shivered.

The chauffeur who met her at the little station took her bag, and hoped that she had spent a pleasant week-end. He thought, "Bin burning the candle at both ends, same as most of them do when they get week-end leaf. She looks tired out."

Monica assured him that she had had a wonderful time.

He grinned and said, "Thet's right, Nurse, you're ondly young once, eh?"

She was glad to be back at work, glad to see young Towers again, and to see his whole face light up when she walked into the room. Even the quiet fellow—what was his name? Grimshaw, Gridley, Gorley—she couldn't remember—looked up and smiled, saying, "Why, this is nice, Nurse Crawshaw. We've missed you, haven't we, Towers?"

Towers, his blue eyes shining, said, "Quite a good deal," and laughed as if he and she shared a secret.

Monica Towers shivered suddenly. She rose and added some of the small logs which lay in the box by the fire, watched them thoughtfully as the flames began to lick round them. Then she walked over to the table where the siphons and spirits had been placed, as they were every evening, and poured herself out a moderately strong whisky-and-soda. She carried it back to her chair, set it down on the little table, took out a cigarette from the big silver box, lit it, and, leaning back, smoked slowly and quietly.

How well she remembered the days that followed, the days which slipped into weeks, and which brought no letter from MacPhail. He had sent her flowers from London, magnificent flowers, enclosing a note scrawled on the back of his visiting-card. Victor Towers, never attempting to persuade her to go out with him, always ready to talk, to lend her books to read, and to be quietly charming. He told her about his father and mother—it was evident that he adored them both—about his brother Wilfred, who, he stated, was the finest fellow he had ever known. He told her of his prospects, not boastfully, but without either exaggeration or underestimation. Always, too, he insisted, quite calmly and with complete certainty, that one day Monica would consent to marry him.

She reflected that she ought to have resented it, ought to have told him quite firmly and definitely that she had no wish to marry him, and that she could never even consider doing so. She didn't, because never from the first had she felt resentful of his assumption. He was so gentle, he made no demands, asked for no particular favours. Then, too, at the back of her mind, fear was growing. A dreadful, unsleeping fear, which seemed to lie in wait for her. She might be immersed in her work when suddenly fear would push itself forward into her consciousness, as if it were a living thing, mocking her, saying, "You can't get rid of me. You may pretend to have forgotten, but you know that you can't. What are you going to do?"

She slept badly, and when she slept, woke feeling exhausted. The other nurses told her that she wanted a holiday, and she only shook her head and protested that she was all right, not tired; she would ask for a holiday when she really needed one. She wrote to MacPhail, never putting her fears into words, only referring to her visit to London, asking how long he was remaining there, and saying that she would be coming up on her free day to see her aunt.

He replied—after a long silence—evasively. He would love to see her; he was tremendously occupied; there was so much business to be seen to. He had been discharged from the Army, and was now able to examine the mess and muddle which his father had achieved during the time MacPhail had been overseas. She folded his letter and pushed it back into its envelope, feeling chilled and dispirited.

At last the vague fear took shape and became a certainty. She remembered how she had lain in bed, her face pressed into the pillow, afraid that she might cry out in despair. She went to Matron and asked for special week-end leave. The Scotswoman listened to the reasons which Monica gave her. The story was completely credible: a brother on leave, going back overseas, a small family reunion to "wish him luck". Her father, too, was on leave, and she had not seen him for a long time.

"But, Nurse, ye should have asked for leave to go home for a wee while. Worrk is all right, but after all you're not machines, and family ties are strong. I'm not all that haird on my nurses, surely. And ye've worked verra weel. Aye, ye can have the week-end."

She walked over the fields to the village and sent a telegram to MacPhail. He was living in some chambers in Jermyn Street.

Coming tomorrow. Meet me at the Savoy one o'clock. Monica.

Slowly she walked back towards the hospital, and tried to prevent herself speculating what would happen when she told

MacPhail of her fears, those fears which had proved to be certainties.

She saw Towers coming over the fields; he caught up with her, and she found herself sitting beside him on a fallen tree-trunk. She remembered that other fallen tree, where she had sat with MacPhail. She told Victor that she was going to London, and saw some of the brightness fade from his face. He had asked her if she was going to see anyone in particular. Even now, she never knew why she had told him that she was going to meet someone who "attracted" her; gravely he had asked if the attraction was mutual. She said that she thought it was.

Again he told her that he loved her, that unless he married her he never wished to marry anyone. She listened, and suddenly realized that this handsome, essentially kindly, pleasant young man might mean—safety. The realization that she could harbour a thought so base, so unworthy, shocked and shook her profoundly. This was another fear; this was something else which would continue to force itself into her brain, the words—safety, escape, protection, ran through her mind. She scarcely heard what Towers said; his words reached her blurred and indistinct.

They walked back together. Monica felt light-headed, uncertain of herself. The dread of meeting Hamish was growing; she fought against the certainty of what he would say. There would be no more tenderness, no more whispered phrases; he would no longer speak in that tone which had acted on her like a drug. Instinctively she knew that.

Again Victor reminded her that she had—almost— promised that one day she would meet him in London when he left the hospital.

"Whenever you wish, wherever I am—I shall be there," he said.

She left the next morning for London. She felt cold—she shivered again now, though the logs had caught and were burning bravely, when she remembered that journey. No train had ever been so slow, no train had ever tarried so long at insignificant country stations, no book had ever been so utterly incapable of holding her attention as the one which she tried —vainly—to read.

She drove to a hairdresser's, one of the best in the West End. She tried to talk brightly and with reasonable intelligence to the delightful young man who set her hair so swiftly and surely. She dreaded the moment when he would stand back and say, "There, Miss Crawshaw, and very nice it looks. It's beautiful hair!"

At the Savoy she washed and made up her face with discretion and care, then walked out into the big entrance hall to wait. The clock showed that the time was ten minutes to one. She ordered a cocktail and tried to sip it very slowly. Her hands were very cold, her eyes felt that they were burning in their sockets.

MacPhail entered, and for a brief second she felt the old attraction for him. He was so tall, so slim; he held his head at an angle which might be autocratic and arrogant, but he looked distinguished. He stared round, saw her, and came over to where she sat.

She said, "Were you surprised when you got my telegram?"

"I was. I've only managed to get here with the greatest difficulty. I told you how damnably busy I am. I have an appointment at three."

She smiled; her face felt stiff. "That still gives us time for luncheon together."

"Are you staying the night? I've got to go into the country."

"Yes, with my aunt in Kensington."

She suggested a cocktail; he shook his head. Rising she said, "Then let's lunch, shall we?"

She forced herself to eat. Even now she remembered the food they ate; to her it tasted of nothing, she might have been eating dry bread. MacPhail appeared to enjoy his luncheon; he became a little more talkative, told her that she looked charming, that he had never seen her hair look so nice. He asked after various people at the hospital.

"How's my *bête noire*, the bouncing Harkess? Still bouncing, eh? And the Golden Grocer or whatever he is? Still luxuriating in gorgeous pyjamas?"

"Those pyjamas seem to have made a lasting impression."

"They have, believe me. Imagine people of that kind indulging in such things as silk pyjamas! The world's turned upside down."

"As a matter of fact, Towers is an exceedingly nice fellow."

He stared at her insolently. "Good lord! I gave you credit for better taste."

She drank her coffee, slowly, trying to brace herself for the moment when she must tell him that she wished to talk to him in private.

Monica said, "You're living in Jermyn Street? Nice rooms?"

"Tolerably. The man used to be a butler of ours, years ago, when we could afford such things as well-trained servants."

"I'd like to see where you live," she said.

MacPhail hesitated. "I don't know that I ought to take you there—I mean, after all, it's not quite the thing for girls" —he paused and smiled—"attractive girls to visit men in their rooms, is it?"

She contrived to laugh. "My dear, don't be old-fashioned and stuffy."

"I have an appointment at three——"

"It's five minutes past two," she glanced at her watch. "Plenty of time."

"Oh, very well." But he was ruffled and showed it. He called for the bill, but Monica took it from him.

"I asked you to have luncheon with me," she said. "Oh yes, for once."

He scarcely spoke as they drove to Jermyn Street. He opened the door of a tall, narrow house, and went before her up the stairs. The house was sufficiently well furnished, but after the meticulous cleanliness of the hospital, after the well-aired rooms there, this place smelt dusty and stuffy. MacPhail opened a door on the first floor, held it open for her. The first thing she saw was a large and very beautiful photograph, a woman of about thirty, she judged, handsome and well groomed.

She walked forward to examine the photograph more closely.

"Nice-looking woman," she said.

"That's the woman I'm going to marry," he said, his voice harsh and determined. "We became engaged a week ago."

Curiously enough, she felt no surprise, felt nothing, not even a sense of dismay. She had never felt in her heart of hearts that Hamish would marry her. He had never spoken of marriage, only of being "in love".

She said, "Is this the rich woman you told me you would be forced to marry?"

"She is rich. She is also very charming." His tone was cold.

Monica swung round and faced him. "You know why I wanted to see you today, why it was important that I should see you?"

"I didn't attempt to find reasons——"

"But there is a reason," she said. "I'm going to have a child, and it is yours. What are you going to do? Break off your engagement and marry me?"

His usually pale face flushed; he stared at her, his lips set into a thin line, his jaw working as it did when he was angry.

"You fool!" he said. "Good God! Surely you know sufficient to take care of yourself. Break off my engagement! Most certainly not. How am I to know that this child is mine? I know you nurses. Haven't I watched them, trailing out night after night with some fool to make love in secluded corners?"

Speaking very calmly she said, "That's not true. There may be some idiots who—play that game. The majority don't, and you know it. Tell me what I am going to do!"

"Do? What are you going to do? Do the same as other women do when they get into a jam of this kind. You're not a fool. Surely you know enough—to know what to do. Do you mean to tell me that Harkess or Manners or Willis couldn't tell you—what to do? If it's a question of money, I'll pay; that is, I'll give you the necessary money provided my name is kept out of it."

She stared at him, then picked up her handbag and her gloves very calmly, and with her open hand struck him across the face.

"Damn you! How dare you do that!" The impact of her hand on his cheek smarted; instinctively he put up his hand and felt the skin burning. "How much good d'you imagine that kind of thing is going to do you?"

"So much good," she told him, "that I feel better already. I've been a complete fool, and worse. Never mind, Hamish, don't be afraid. I shan't bring your sacred name into this, I can manage alone—and I will." She laughed. "To think that I thought you attractive, to think that I listened to your sentimentalizing about your home, your gillies, shepherds and the like! You care nothing for any of them. All you care for is—yourself, your wishes, your desires, and your gratification. You rate yourself as something better than other people, you sneer at Harkess, you sneer at Towers—either of them is better, more honest, more sincere than you could ever be. You won't worry about me; you'll never worry about anyone except Hamish MacPhail—and there never was anyone less worth worrying over! When I came up to town this morning I still had some faint hope that you might—behave decently." She laughed. "Thank God, you've cured me of the slightest feeling of affection or respect which I ever had for you. I was *infected* by you, your voice—oh, you use it so well—was like a drug. I became a drug addict. A stupid, weak, senseless thing that craved—imagine it!—*craved* for proofs of what I was fool enough to believe was your affection. I listened to you, and I almost believed you. Never quite completely, because the things you said never quite squared with the thing you did. You were given every care, every attention, and did these things light the faintest spark of gratitude in you? Never. I wanted to love you; it seems ridiculous now, but I did. How you must have laughed!

"I don't know how things will work out for me, but I shall be relatively happy if I never see you again. It isn't going to be easy, it isn't going to be smooth sailing, but I shall come through. It's late in the day for me to talk about my honour—but such shreds as are left I shall keep. But," she threw her arms wide, "I'm cured! How dreadful if you had—what's the expression?—done the right thing, and—another phrase—made an honest woman of me! I should have been tied to you—for life. I'm free. If today you had been even moderately kind, solicitous, that would have been terrible, for I might have taken away regrets, might still have remembered you as someone who, in spite of everything, had redeeming characteristics. Now, I can just try to wipe my memory clear—and clean—of you. Good-bye, Hamish—the MacPhail of Philochery. The laird. I remember you once told me that you felt you were the 'spiritual father' of your people. *Your* people!

"Don't write to me. Don't send me offers of help. I shall only send back your letters—unread. I may have made a general mess of my life, but at least I'm seeing clearly at last. Don't come down with me."

He stood, his brows drawn close together, his face white except where the imprint of Monica's hand still showed scarlet. His mouth worked. He spoke with difficulty.

"Listen to me. What are you going to do?" he asked.

"I have told you that I shall—manage. Good-bye."

She walked out, and ran down the thickly carpeted stairs.

She drove to her aunt's well-ordered, comfortable house in Kensington.

"Monica dearest, I'm delighted to see you! How well you're looking! Hard work agrees with you! Is some charming young man coming to take you out dancing? No! You surprise me. We'll just have a cosy evening. Go to a show and sup afterwards eh? Delightful. How is the Duchess—charming creature? I'm so fond of her, and I believe old Nottingford is devoted to her. Now let's have some tea. It's early, but as I say, it's never too early for tea."

"Lovely. Let me just go and tidy up. I feel filthy. London is wonderful, but after the country—it is dirty, isn't it?"

She felt astonishingly happy; she felt that she had thrown off a great weight which had been unbearably heavy. She would not think, would not attempt to make plans; she only knew that she had ended everything with MacPhail and that she was thankful.

As they sat drinking the exquisite China tea which her aunt always used, the telephone rang. Monica experienced a sudden sense of panic. Weeks ago she had told MacPhail her aunt's name, in case she was ever in town and staying with her. The immaculate parlourmaid entered.

"Excuse me, Miss Monica, a gentleman to speak to you."

"Did he give his name, Burton?"

"No, miss. I'll ask."

She turned to her aunt. "I've no idea who it can be. Possibly some patient who left weeks ago. I don't want to see anyone. It's so restful here."

The maid re-entered. "The name is MacFrail, miss."

Monica frowned. "MacFrail? I don't know the name at all. Burton, just say that I'm sorry. Ask him to write. I'm afraid that I don't remember him. Thank you. Yes, Auntie, and you said that . . ."

She could hear Burton's well-trained, house-parlourmaid voice. "No, sir. I'm afraid not, sir. Miss Crawshaw is engaged at the moment, sir. Thank you."

He had telephoned. How angry he would be, and how little it mattered to her! She went on calmly drinking tea and talking to her aunt. Later she rested and slept for an hour. Then bathed and dressed, and came down to eat perfect sandwiches and to drink a whisky-and-soda before they left for the theatre. The play was amusing; Monica laughed immoderately. Her aunt glanced at her from time to time, thinking how attractive she was, and how she had retained all her capacity for enjoyment through all the hard work she had done since the war began. By far the nicest of the family— Cynthia was a fool, and the boys both self-satisfied and self-centred. Monica was different. She wished the girl would marry, and marry well. She'd make a splendid mistress for any place; look well at her husband's table, never bore him; have attractive children and bring 'em up properly.

The curtain fell. "I've a table at the Berkeley."

"Lovely, Auntie."

The head waiter hovered round Mrs. Boyd-Summers. Waiters liked her; she knew what she wanted and she knew how to be pleasant and yet retain her dignity. She appeared to know everyone. Young men on leave came to her table, and she greeted them all warmly, kindly, and without a trace of the regrettably flirtatious manner which so many women of just over middle age employed when talking to young men.

They were eating their excellent whitebait when Monica, looking up, saw MacPhail entering the dining-room with a woman; the woman whose photograph she had seen that afternoon in Jermyn Street. Their eyes met; hers never wavered. She fancied that his narrowed, as if he were not quite certain what course to adopt, but she turned again to her whitebait.

Mrs. Boyd-Summers said, "That's Mrs. van der Plast. With that tall, thin man."

Monica said, "And who is Mrs. van der Plast?"

"American. Fabulously rich. Railways, oil—I forget. Husband died two years ago. I believe that she says she wants to marry an Englishman. I've met her once playing bridge. She plays like a cut-throat! Good-looking woman, eh?"

"Most attractive."

"I wonder who the man is."

Monica said, "No one I know."

"Face like a good-looking shark."

Her niece giggled—it was surprising how easy it was to giggle.

"I've never been at close quarters with a—good-looking shark."

Sunday was relatively peaceful. There were amusing people to luncheon, and later she drove to Hampton Court with her aunt to visit some elderly lady who lived in the Palace. Monica enjoyed herself, with a strange determination to live every minute as it came. Only when she was in the train, a train which felt deplorably cold, did she lean back and allow herself to think.

She was going back, and she must make plans. She scarcely knew what she had hoped MacPhail might do when she told him of her condition. In her heart she felt that she had known that he would refuse to marry her. He had said that he must "marry money", and he had lost no time in becoming engaged to the American millionairess. The incident was closed for good and all. She, Monica Crawshaw, must face the music. Again and again she thought of Victor Towers, and each time beat back the thought with an intensity which left her feeling weak and exhausted. She knew that he was in love with her; more, she felt that he loved her deeply and sincerely. It might be a love heavily tinged with romance, but she knew sufficient of the "Golden Lad" to understand that he was not solely motivated by romance. There was something much deeper, more profound and, above all, completely honest.

She clenched her hands. "I mustn't do it; I mustn't even think of it. It's vile, base, unthinkable. I've got into this mess and I mustn't attempt to save myself by dragging someone else down into it all. I shall find a way out, and if I can't find one, then I must face the music."

Her "other self" argued gently. Why should she be dragging anyone down? Couldn't she be prepared to make someone —not of necessity this "Golden Lad"—a good, loving and completely faithful wife? She was young, she could have other children. How many men went to their wives in a state of virginity? Surely what could be forgiven one might well be condoned in the other?

Again with her hands clenched she murmured, "I won't. I won't. It's unthinkable. Deceit, fraud, lies! There must be, there shall be, some other way. I will find it! I shouldn't only feel that I had ruined his—the man's life, whoever he was, but that I had ruined my own."

Nottingford, and the car which was always sent to meet nurses returning to duty. The smiling Matson. "Hope you've had a nice time, Nurse."

"Lovely! I stayed with my aunt. She's great fun. Never like an aunt, she's so young."

Matson nodded. "I've an auntie like that myself. Proper
caution."

"Are we waiting for someone?" Monica asked.

He nodded towards the platform. "Nurse Vincent—been
to Portsmouth to see her brother, I b'lieve. Train's due now,
Nurse. Here she comes. I'll just go and help with her bag.
These porters is old and they're not exactly breaking their
hearts for jobs."

Monica got into the big, comfortable car and settled herself
in the corner. She was back, and now things had to be faced.
There was no waiting for this or that; she must make decisions. Vincent got in and settled in the other corner.

"Hello, Crawshaw, have a good time?"

"Wonderful. And you?"

"Oh, the Navy always gives one a good time. What a
relief after that eternal hospital! Though after all, the Duchess
is pretty decent. Cars always laid on."

"It's not such a bad life," Monica agreed.

At the hospital she ran into Harkess, who greeted her with
warm affection.

"Listen, Crawshaw. Wait a minute, I want to tell you
something. Let's make a cup of tea, shall we?"

"I'd love one."

Harkess made the tea with her usual rather boisterous
efficiency.

"Crawshaw, has it struck you that our Golden Lad is in
love with you? No, don't interrupt. He is. Last night he
played bridge for a little, then went to Night Sister and said
that he wanted a sleeping draught. Said that he'd been having
rotten nights. That's news to me, isn't it to you? I should have
said that he slept like a baby. This morning he told me that
he'd slept well, and when I asked what he wanted to take
draughts for, he said, 'I was worried, Nurse, and I was afraid
I should lie awake—thinking.' Now I'll tell you. He thought
you'd gone to meet some bloke in town, and he was jealous.
Hence the draught. You haven't got a boy, have you?"

Monica answered very steadily, "I haven't, my dear."

"No one you're fond of at all—in that way?"

"No one at all! I swear."

"Then why not marry the Golden Lad? He's far and away
the nicest patient you and I have had through our hands. My
hat, how different to some of the brutes—that MacPhail, for

example! He thought that he was lord of the earth, despised the Golden Lad because his father's a wholesale grocer or something——"

"His father's the biggest ship's chandler in the North," Monica told her.

"I'd not care if his father was a chimney sweep! That boy's all right. He's a gentleman. You can't miss it. There's some school—Winchester, I believe—where the school motto is, 'Manners maketh the man'. Well, that's like Towers. Monica, you might do a lot worse."

"My dear, he hasn't asked me yet——" She stopped short, for virtually Victor had asked her. "At least, not absolutely definitely."

"Oh, then you do *know* that he's in love with you?"

Monica nodded. "I suppose I do, Harkess."

Harkess rose, picked up the empty cups and set them carefully on a side-table. She came back to where Monica sat and laid her hand with its broad, capable palm on Monica's shoulder.

"Don't be a fool, my dear," she said. "Lads like this one don't grow on every tree. He's not only 'golden' to look at, he's gold all through. There, get to bed, you're looking tired."

CHAPTER FIVE

THAT night Monica sat very late watching the fire and allowing her mind to go back on the events of so many years ago. She saw it all so plainly—her room at the hospital with a little pile of clean laundry lying on the bed, the feel of the beautifully starched aprons and caps, the stiff cuffs and collars. She remembered the view from the window, the wide gardens, and the tree-covered slopes in the distance. The sound of the gong announcing the nurses' breakfast, the chatter of voices above the rattle of cups. Her morning duties—lighter now, for many of the patients had gone, and they were expecting an intake at any moment. The sharp, antiseptic smell, the shining corridor, the patients' rooms—neat, tidy and impersonal.

Victor and the quiet fellow returning from breakfast—

they were up and about now; Victor expected to go before a Medical Board very soon. He looked well, his eyes were bright and clear, and even in his shabby uniform he contrived to appear smart and well groomed.

"It's an awfully old uniform," he said to her, and laughed. "I shall have a new one for the day I come to meet you in town."

Slowly, almost painfully, Monica knew that she was growing to be very fond of him. She liked to listen to him talking; not that he ever plunged into any particularly intellectual subjects, but he spoke pleasantly, and even with a certain amount of colour, of flowers, birds—he apparently studied them considerably—the books he had read, and most of all he talked of his home. A long, two-storeyed grey-stone house, looking out over the fields and away to the moors. "It's not a grand place," he assured her. "My father bought it when my brother and I were youngsters. It's an old house, and it feels old and kind and friendly. The windows have small, old-fashioned panes, except in my father's study, and he insisted on putting in a modern window. However, it's at the back of the house, and doesn't show much. In France, I used to think a great deal about that house, used to feel nostalgic, and rather home-sick for it. I used to think that it would be pleasant to grow old there, to watch your own children growing up to love the old house as you'd done. I like poetry, you know. I've learnt a lot of it by heart, and I used to say it over to myself, in the trenches, when things were quiet." He gave his soft laugh. "You can't remember much poetry when things are *not* quiet. I used to say, 'My wages taken, and the long day done, and in my heart some late lark singing.' I don't know why, but that always brought such a clear picture of Little Manor. A feeling that some day, when the long day was done, and I took my wages—whatever I'd managed to earn in life, oh, I don't mean material things, I mean patience, decency, a little philosophy, things of that kind—the late lark would sing in my heart at the thought of going to the grey house that was waiting for me. To hand over to my sons, and sit back and watch the changing seasons, see the moors put on their different robes, look for the splashes of gorse shining like burnished gold.

"That's what you must want when 'you are old and grey and full of sleep, and nodding by the fire'. A house that's a home, a place where some—the only person who matters—no, not the only person who matters, but the person who matters most, is waiting for you."

He stopped and looked at her intently. "Do you think I'm very silly, Monica? Ought I to be telling you about my new car I'm going to have, and what the Major said to me, and what my batman said about the Major? Instead of talking about my home and poetry?"

"I like to hear you," she said, and wondered exactly when he had begun to call her "Monica". When they were alone? She couldn't remember and yet she never resented it.

She began to learn little things about him, and they seemed to grow in importance. He loved dogs; no, he didn't mind what breed, so long as they were "kind dogs". It appeared that he held the belief that very few dogs were not kind. He liked music, in rather a "limited, incurious kind of way". He couldn't read thrillers, because, he said, "the first reference to a murder makes me shiver". He loved colours, bright colours such as "the yellow of celandines, the kingcups, the heavenly blue of harebells and bluebells, and the golden red of chrysanthemums—not the opulent, curled kind, but the small ones that grow in gardens.

"The scent of roses, the old-fashioned kind that grow in cottage gardens. One day when we 'are old and grey and full of sleep', shall we make a rose garden? Not filled with the new kinds, not the one that wins at the Chelsea Flower Show, but the old white ones, the cabbage roses, the generous kinds. Rose trees and fruit trees, espaliered against an old red-brick wall. Fruit trees with apricots, and garden peaches. A hot-house peach is a poor thing compared with those that grow against a warm old wall."

She laughed. When he talked to her that terrible fear and the dreadful uncertainty were driven into the background.

"They take a long time to grow, don't they, those trees? And to make a rose garden takes a long time too. My mother has one, and she says that it takes a lifetime. Nearly as long as to make a good lawn."

"Pooh! We're young, darling. We may both live to be ninety. That will give us quite a long time to work on the garden."

Then one day he told her that he was to have a Medical Board in the morning, and that if he were passed as fit he would leave practically immediately. He begged her to come out with him that evening. Monica's mind rushed back to the first time she had met Hamish MacPhail, and for a moment her impulse was to refuse. Then, meeting his clear, honest eyes, she knew that this man was different from MacPhail. She could trust him; there would be no pleading for anything more than he could ask for frankly and openly. He was going away; he wanted to sit and talk with her quietly and undisturbed because it might possibly be the last opportunity he would have.

"Yes," she said, "I'll come. The path that leads to the pine wood. I'll be there at nine, Victor."

He said, "Thank you," gravely and quietly, but she had seen how his eyes lit up, and knew that he was happy.

Monica was terribly disturbed, knew that a change had taken place in her sentiments towards Towers. She had always liked him, always found him courteous and considerate. When he first came to the hospital, and his various wounds needed daily dressings, dressing which caused him considerable pain, he had shown great fortitude. Since her meeting with MacPhail in London, it had been impossible not to contrast his brutality, his cynical attitude, with what she believed might have been Towers' under similar circumstances. Her whole relationship with MacPhail had been a series of small scenes, evidences of selfishness and intolerance, and great storms of physical passion which he seemed to regard as the solution of all quarrels and differences.

The satisfying of his physical desires, the achieving of that sense of domination which he enjoyed, his demonstration of power and mastery, these were the things which had appealed to Hamish.

She looked back on her association with him with a kind of horrified unbelief. Had it all really happened? It seemed like some dreadful dream in which she had become someone other than herself, and yet had lost the power to assert her own individuality.

That night she met Victor; he was waiting as MacPhail had waited. He came forward eagerly holding out his hands. The gesture might have seemed stilted and overdone, but it was evidently so unselfconscious that instead it became an unspoken declaration of the value this meeting had for him. They walked on to the little summer-house, and he was solicitous that she should not feel cold. He didn't fuss, he didn't attempt clumsily to wrap her cloak more closely round her, his movements were swift and exact.

"There," as he laid one fold over the other, "there, now you won't be cold, will you?"

Very carefully he slipped his hand under her heavy cloak, and held hers. She remembered how cold it had been and how comforting it was to feel the warmth of his.

He said, speaking very softly, "If I go tomorrow, because I've heard that the new intake may arrive then and they'll be glad of my bed, I shall go to London and then home. They're bound to give me some leave before they send me out again. Bound to. Probably about three weeks. If—if during that time you can get to London and will let me come and see you, will you write and tell me?"

"But, your home—it's such a long way from London."

"A long way, my dearest; nothing could be a 'long way' if it meant I should see you at the end of the journey. I don't want to get sentimental about going overseas again, but it may be ages before I get leave again, and—well, it is rather important to me to see you again."

She answered, "Yes, I will. You shall see me again. I promise that."

"I wish," he said just a little wistfully, "that I could hope you'll be a thousandth part as glad to see me as I shall be to see you."

They talked in low voices, not of love, but of ordinary things: of what he planned to do at home, of how magnificent it would be if his brother Wilfred were home on leave at the same time. He asked her if she would write to him, and rather regretfully admitted that he had never been able to write what he called "good letters".

"I shall copy a poem from some book of poetry and send it to you as something I've written," he said, and laughed.

The stable clock struck the half-hour. Monica said, "I must go."

"Such a short time," he sighed, then added quickly, "but it is something to look back on. Tomorrow we shall both be caught up in this gigantic machine. You'll be hurrying about, and I shall have to go and face the Board. We're really saying 'Good-bye' now."

She turned and on a sudden impulse leaned forward and kissed him.

She heard him draw his breath sharply, then she rose and walked back rapidly towards the hospital. She entered by one door, Victor by another.

In her room she sat on the bed thinking, thinking, thinking. Why had she given way to that impulse to kiss him? Why did she wish so passionately that she might see him before he left—if the Board passed him, which she was confident they would do—tomorrow? Her head ached, and she undressed quickly and lay on her bed, pressing her cold fingers to her temples.

"Why? You know why! Because you love him, as you have never loved anyone in your whole life. He's broken down all your defences, he's shown you what kind of man he is—gentle, chivalrous, tender. All the things you've imagined a man might be. He'd go on being those things all his life. He'd marry you and wrap you round with love and thoughtfulness. You want to marry him, you want to spend your life with him, and you can't, daren't, must not, because it's impossible to be honest with him. To tell him that you are carrying another man's child! You could never face the disillusionment in his eyes. You'd be robbing him of something that is precious to him. He would never be angry, he'd not say a word in reproach, but you would know that you had killed something that was precious to him, something which he believed to be beautiful."

She answered herself. "I know, I know, and yet I do love him. I never knew what real love meant until now. That other —that time when I thought so much about Hamish, that wasn't love. That was attraction, a physical attraction. Victor is immeasurably handsomer, but he hasn't got that animal magnetism. Victor is all the things at which Hamish would sneer—he isn't and never could be overbearing, or arrogant, he doesn't want to exercise mastery over people, he wants to treat them decently, fairly.

"I'd make him happy, I'd devote my whole life to him. I'd give him children—beautiful children. I'd love his old house as he does. I'd teach them to love it too. He's rich. I don't care if he lost every penny, I should still love him the same. I'd be ready to work for him—I'd glory in working for him. Oh, God, isn't there any way? Any way . . ."

She lay awake until the sky began to turn grey on the

horizon, heralding a new day, and then from sheer exhaustion she fell asleep.

The rest of the day was confused. She thought that she saw him for a moment in the corridor on the way to his Medical Board. He spoke, and she answered mechanically. Later she wasn't quite certain whether she had seen him, spoken to him or only imagined it. Then at luncheon a message was brought that Matron wanted her to go to her office at once. Vaguely Monica wondered if she had committed some fault. Had she been seen sitting in the old summer-house with Victor? What did it matter?

She had seen Victor in the office and promised to see him again. He had left her, and she went back to her work with her mind racing. Nothing mattered, nothing was important, but that she should marry Victor Towers, share his life, make him happy. She could do it, she knew that she could.

Flowers came from London, splendid, bringing fragrance and colour. He sent a telegram, he wrote, he sent her books, and with each letter of his she read she knew that her love for him was growing stronger and stronger. Days passed. She knew that before long he must be going overseas. Everything, except the fact that she could not lose him, was blotted out.

The old fear of the possibility—the probability—that she was going to have a child receded. Her longing to see Victor, her inability to face life without him, was growing. It was with difficulty that she did her work, smiled, and behaved in an ordinary way.

Harkess said, "It's my opinion that you're missing the Golden Lad. Why don't you see him on your free day? You know as well as I do that Matron's never hard on—love affairs. Go on, Crawshaw, wire to him to meet you in town. The poor devil's going back to France, and from what you hear it's not exactly a picnic."

Her smile a little twisted, Monica said, "You don't have to tell me that." She paused, then said, "I will wire to him."

Her own desire for him, her love, her determination to spend the rest of her life with him, had conquered. Honour, decency, truth, integrity—they had gone by the board. Only Victor mattered.

She met him at the Savoy; with him was his brother for whom he had such an admiration. Good looking, broad shouldered, with a voice which was kind and friendly. Monica was not a conceited woman, but she saw admiration in his eyes. Wilfred approved of her!

He left them and she was able to turn to Victor, and see again that "golden" quality which, since he left the hospital, had haunted her. He looked better; she fancied that he had put on a little weight. His hair might have been burnished; his eyes were like summer skies. He leaned forward, asked her if she loved him. She answered, thinking what a poor pale word "love" was to express what she felt for him. He asked if they could be married during his next leave. Monica drew a deep breath.

"If you like, I'll marry you before you go back to France," she said.

The colour ebbed from his cheeks, then came rushing back; he was almost inarticulate, then he began to talk very rapidly. If he liked? It was what he had longed for and dared not hope for. He would arrange everything. He sent a telegram to his Colonel, he sent telegrams to his parents, to Wilfred, to Monica's parents, and as he wrote them out he kept stopping and turning to smile at her, as if to assure himself that it was all true.

They lunched. He was gay, ready to laugh easily, and yet lapsing into sudden silences, and assuring her that they meant nothing except that he was "a little bowled over at the thought of all my dreams coming true".

He insisted that they should go and buy an engagement ring. She felt it strange and yet wonderful to be sitting beside him in a taxi, shut away from the world, with his hand clasping hers. For the first time for weeks her fears had receded. She had one fixed determination, and that was to make Victor happy; if she spent all the years of her life making life a joyous, happy thing for him, surely her sins might be forgiven? She was young; they would have other children, beautiful, healthy, laughing children. She would forget the past, forget MacPhail and his brutality, his sneers; forget, too, the thing she had done, the wickedness and the stupidity. Only Victor mattered, Victor and the life which lay before them.

As she remembered it all, she twisted her engagement ring on her finger. How carefully he had told her to have exactly what she wanted. They had agreed—"not pearls, for pearls mean tears". As they drove away, he slipped the ring on to her finger, and took her in his arms.

"We've been engaged for hours and hours. I don't care if the whole world sees us. Let them!"

Her aunt, an incurable romantic, had been delighted at Monica's news. It was obvious that she approved whole-heartedly of Towers. Monica watched her eyes appraising him, approving of him, admiring him. She would attend to every-thing. She poured out a stream of instructions. Victor must do this and that, Monica must do that and this. Victor, eager and yet methodical, made notes in his little book with the gold corners, saying, "Ah yes, yes, indeed. I see." When he took his leave, promising to come back for Monica later, her aunt turned to her.

"My dear child, what a delightful young man! Your sister's pale priest fades into nothingness compared with that charm-ing young man. Sit down and tell me all about him. What Towers are they? There are some in Worcestershire, I seem to remember. Oh, not those! Then—tell me, I must know—everything."

That night they danced, and the next morning he went with her to the station. They would meet again the evening before their wedding. In ten days everything should be ready.

He laughed softly. "It's like the most stupendous miracle."

Back in the hospital she told Harkess, who beamed at her and grew faintly sentimental. She had an interview with Matron, who, being a true Scotswoman, also grew sentimental. "Aye, it can a' be arranged. I'm losing a grand nurse, and Towers is gaining a grand wife. Gawd bless you baith."

The Duchess, an ex-musical comedy star, frankly wiped her fine eyes, and said that nothing could have pleased her more.

"A nice boy, Monica, and as for you—why, I've known your family for years. You're all straight as a die, and you'll do your duty to this boy. I shall write to your aunt tonight, and announce that I've got to be asked to the wedding. Never mind how quiet it is, I intend to be there." She laughed her pleasant, rich chuckle. "I'm not going to lose the chance of seeing that beautiful young man again, even if it's only to see him marrying another woman. My dear, I am so glad for you both."

Victor's father wrote. His letter looked as if it had been

engraved from a copperplate. It might be trite—*"we shall not be losing a son, but gaining a daughter"*—parts of it were stiff and formal, but Monica remembered that it had pleased her.

The next time she saw Victor was at the dinner-party which Amos Towers gave the night before the wedding. The man was a dynamo. He organized everything; it was obvious that he was, Lady Crawshaw said, "a self-made man". Monica answered coldly that he appeared to have made something very good and eminently successful.

Her mother replied, "I sincerely hope so. Your young man is charming, but I have to admit that the father and mother are something of a shock."

Stoutly Monica said, "I think they are both charming. So does the Duchess, Mama."

"She has a perfect passion for what she calls—democracy."

They had all been adorable to her; she felt warmed and stabilized. Fear was retreating, she was blotting it out, determined to think of nothing but the fact that she was marrying the man she loved. She watched him, tried to hear what he was saying to the Duchess at dinner, felt a thrill of happiness when their eyes met and he smiled at her; his very smile was a caress.

Monica felt a sense of personal pride because it was evident that everyone either loved him or liked him exceedingly. His brother, who appeared to be a matter-of-fact young man, spoke of Victor using phrases which were almost lyrical.

The little woman with the bright friendly eyes—Victor's mother—made no attempt to hide the fact that to her Victor and Wilfred were the finest young men in the world.

"There they are," she said to Monica, in her quiet voice which was rendered so attractive by its North Country accent, "the three finest men I've ever known, or ever will know if it comes to that. I never thought to find the equal of my Amos, but—thanks be for it—his two lads are fair models of him—in character. I don't say i' lukes, for they're handsome, and Amos never was that, though he's always looked what he is—right wholesome."

Only when she stood beside him at the altar did her conscience stab her. She felt a pain which was almost physical. She was standing there with him, making promises—before God—and at the same time she was practising a deception so base, so despicable, as to put her outside the pale of decent men and women.

Then she heard his voice, "I, Victor Harold, take thee ..." and realized that it was so full of happiness, that when he spoke the fine old words which followed, he uttered them with such sincerity and proud determination that her mind steadied again. It was done! It was impossible to draw back; all that was left was to repeat her own vows and determine to keep them inviolate for the rest of her life.

Their honeymoon, so brief, was a continual happiness. Victor was so eager about everything. She was surprised at the extent of his knowledge. He would stop at some old church and tell her things concerning it which betrayed a real depth of thought, and a vital interest. He was thoughtful, tender, considerate, and never ceased from impressing upon Monica what a fortunate fellow he was, how he was going to make a success of his life, "because I must stand well in your estimation".

"You don't think that I shall stop loving you unless you make a tremendous success, do you?" she asked.

"No-o-o, not quite, but if you love anyone, and you've told me that you do love me, you want them to make a success for your own satisfaction and—well, justification. You chose me! You might have married anyone. Oh, you know that I'm right. You're lovely, young, well bred. You could have had opportunities, but you chose me!" He laughed. "Thank heaven you did, darling. It's only natural that you want to be able to say, 'My husband's done very well.'"

She smiled at him fondly. "You're very young, darling."

"And that's a nice thought," he answered. "Isn't it a nice thought? Think of the time we shall have to spend together! How dreadful if you and I were sixty! We shan't mind when we *are* sixty, because we shall have nearly forty years to look back on."

She remembered the first sight of his home and how delighted Victor had been when she said that it "has a welcoming look".

Later he repeated the phrase to his father and mother, and they had smiled and nodded. Amos said, "Aye, I like that—a welcoming luke. That's what we always wanted it to have."

Those days before Victor left for France, how wonderful they had been. Filled to the brim with warm, joyous happiness. He and she were like children, forgetting everything in the excitement and ecstasy of being together. The world was wonderful, they were living in the Springtime of life; the sun shone everywhere—they lived for each other, rejoicing in the fact that they were together, refusing to think of the parting which drew nearer every hour.

Then he went, and so soon after—everything ended. Even now, when Monica thought of it, she closed her eyes as if to shut out the agony of the days which followed.

A week before she had congratulated herself that she was young, that she had years before her in which to atone for everything, in which to give Victor such happiness as rarely came to men. Now, after a brief time of complete content, it was all over, and she had to face life alone.

Her misery had been complete; now—after many years—it still caused her deep unhappiness to think of Victor, to imagine what their life might have been together. His father and mother—as she thought of that dreadful time, her face lost some of its wretchedness, her lips softened, she almost smiled—how good they had been to her. She had understood then that she could not bear to leave them, that to return to her father's house was unthinkable. When she had told Wilfred that she wished to remain in Willingbrough, he had shown his delight openly. Later Amos and his wife had both given her their assurance that her decision had given them great comfort.

She had been treated like a much-loved daughter. They had been incredibly kind and tender before her child was born. Nothing was too good for her, nothing should be too good for the child.

Then—when the child was born, and Mary Ellen put him into her arms, she understood that Mary Ellen *knew*. How she came to know Monica had never attempted to discover. Her manner had never changed; she had continued to be as kind, as considerate, as affectionate as ever. Only when it came to choosing the child's name, and Amos had wished to call him "Victor", had she elected, rather, that he should be called "Wilfred".

The years had slipped past, busy, crowded years, years in which Monica had worked to carve out a position for herself. She knew that Amos could not do without her, she knew that he trusted her and her judgment. He relied upon her absolutely. Mary Ellen never ceased to show her affection; whatever she might know, whatever she might have felt by instinct, she never let the slightest hint of her knowledge become evident. Both Amos and Mary Ellen loved Wilfred; that fact could not be questioned; he was their hope for the future.

Amos said, "Nay, I doubt if our Wilfred 'ul ever marry now. He's a rover is Wilf, a bit of a rolling stone, though," he chuckled, "I'll admit as he contrived to gather quite a nice bit o' moss on his travels. One thing's certain, he'll never settle down in the business. So, Monica, one day you'll have to tak' over, and hold the fort for young Wilfred. And," he leaned forward and patted her hand, "grandly you'll hold it an' all."

Monica wondered what she would have done if Wilfred had married and had a son. As things stood she was not robbing Wilfred of a penny; rather she was prepared to give the rest of her life to safeguarding his patrimony. If he had had a son she would have been forced to make admissions. . . .

She shuddered. Would she have been forced? Would she not have clung to her deception and allowed her son to profit, to inherit a great business to which he had no claim whatever? She didn't know, she dared not speculate.

Monica rose. She felt chilled, her thoughts had completely possessed her, she had forgotten how late it was, and—a hard day lay before her. She emptied the ash-tray, set her empty glass back on the tray, and halted for a moment before the large photograph of Wilfred which his grandfather had gone all the way to Newcastle to have taken, because he "didn't fancy the chap i' Willingbrough".

The handsome, boyish face looked out at her; she smiled back at it. She felt a thrill of pride in his good eyes, set so well under their level brows. His forehead was wide and his nose so well shaped, the mouth was generous and finely formed. His whole expression was frank, open and intelligent.

She spoke softly to the pictured face, whispering the words, "Oh, my darling, how much I love you! I've tried so hard to make you grow up like Victor, tried to teach you not to do anything he would not have liked, of which he would not have approved. I believe that I've succeeded. So often I find myself thinking of you as—his son. I've done so much that was wrong, wicked, despicable, but you're blameless, and—I might even find some comfort in the fact that you make Amos Towers very happy, and I think one day you'll make him very proud.

I know that—whatever Mary Ellen knows—she loves you, loves you dearly, and to me—God only knows what you mean to me. There, good night, my darling."

CHAPTER SIX

AMOS TOWERS told himself that he was growing old. Not feeble, but the machinery was slowing down. He moved less quickly, he found it difficult and a little disturbing to be forced to make very rapid decisions. He knew that his brain was as clear as the brains of other men who had reached his age, but faintly he resented the fact that it was not noticeably clearer.

He went to his business every day, but lately he had taken to coming down about the middle of the morning, and allowing Monica to get there first, to deal with the post—unless anything very important presented itself, in which case she brought the momentous letters to him when he arrived. He found that he looked forward with something approaching eagerness to the moment when the mid-morning tea was brought. If he went back to Little Manor for luncheon, he allowed Mary Ellen to persuade him to "drop off" for what Amos referred to as "a few minutes while I lose myself", and which was, in point of fact, never less than half an hour. If he had to lunch in Willingbrough with business associates, he liked to "drop off" in the big leather arm-chair in his own office. Monica had a card printed, "Do not disturb", and he hung it on the door to ensure quiet. Monica thought of everything.

On a fine hot afternoon in early September he had finished his doze and was back at his desk. He still felt tired, and decided that it would be very pleasant to have a comfortable sofa installed in the office. You got cramped "dropping off" in an arm-chair, however large it might be.

"Dash it!" he thought. "I *will* have a sofa, a nice one; I'll have a thickish rug for Winter and a light one for Summer, kind of dust rug like you have in cars. I'll speak to Monica about it."

That sent his mind off thinking of Monica. They'd been

lucky, Mary Ellen and he, to have such a daughter-in-law. She might have turned out flighty, not caring for anything but rushing about and spending money. Instead, there wasn't a finer business woman in England, or one with the same grasp of affairs.

He chuckled, thinking, "No man ever had such luck as what I've had. Barring us losing poor Vic, everything's gone smooth for me. Mary Ellen—an' I got to know her bi chance as you might say, because she was wearing over-tight shoes— what a grand woman she is, what a companion, what a prop and stay! Nay, everything's been champion, always barring about poor Vic, and thanks be, he left us a lad you couldn't find the equal of, choose how."

The door opened and Monica came in. She held a sheaf of letters in her hand. Amos pulled down the corners of his mouth, and said, "Slave-driving as per usual, eh? Now what's to do?"

She sat down opposite to him, smiling. "I shan't keep you long. Farnham's will have to have a pretty stiff warning. Their last delivery of oilskins and sou'westers are very poor. Shall I write?"

"Aye. Mak' it stiff and all."

"Richardson's want discount, and they have kept us waiting nearly seven months. What about it?"

He scratched his chin. "Nay, don't be overhard, luv. Money's tight, and I don't fancy as Richardson's do t'business they used. Write an' point out that it's *us* doing them a favour as they're old customers of ours."

"Very well. Captain Fergusson's complaining that we sent him short measure in the delivery of wines and spirits." She laughed. "I've never known the time when he didn't grumble. I fancy he could account for the shortage if he ever remembered how much he drank, eh?"

"Aye, he's a lad is yon. Just jolly him along a bit, and he'll settle down. Or send him down a quarter of a dozen bottles with my compliments. Make it clear as it's a *present*, not an acknowledgment as we've been wrong."

"We haven't been wrong!" Monica assured him. "There, that's all. You look tired, Amos." Her tone was warm and sympathetic, for she was devoted to this keen little Yorkshire-man, who could strike hard bargains and whose heart had remained very tender.

"Nay, I don't know." He told her about his idea of install-
ing a sofa, and she made a gesture of impatience.

"Amos, I'm a fool! I ought to have thought of it months
ago. It will be here tomorrow—I'll see to that. Not one of
those cold leather things, either. Hello! Tea-time—how nice!
You enjoy your afternoon tea, don't you?"

He watched her with loving eyes. "Why, I like most things
as you and me share, Monica luv. Aye, thank you. I was just
thinking this afternoon as I doubt the machinery's slowing
down a bit. And why not? I'm nearer seventy nor sixty. I've
worked hard all my life; can't expect the engine to run for
ever, can you? I mind once reading a bit of poetry somewhere;
it went like this:

> I warmed my hands at the fire of life,
> It sinks and I am ready to depart.

That's as near as I remember it."

She laid her hand on his shoulder. "Listen, this particular
fire of life isn't going to be allowed to sink for many, many
years. We shall all be ready to throw on those extra lumps of
coal, and this idea of a sofa—well, that's just another nice
shiny big lump of coal. I had a letter from Wilfred this morning. He'll be here at the end of the week. Think of it; this will
be his last year at school."

Amos shook his head. "Wunderful! Seems only the other
day we were sending him off to his prep school, and now
Captain of the School at Harby. A chap was saying to me only
the other day as it was the finest school i' England. I said,
'Tell me something I don't know. That's why we sent my
grandson there. I'll lay he's the finest lad in the finest school
an' all.' Nay, he did laugh. Mind you, it's true."

Monica sat down. She sipped her tea slowly, then set down
the cup.

"He is a fine boy," she said. "In some ways he is remark-
able. Well, he's got you and our dear Mary Ellen to thank
for what he is today. If you and she had not given me a home,
I should have been forced to go to my own family. They're
upright people, good people, but they haven't got the warmth
and the kindliness that you have. He would have been turned
out to—the regulation pattern. He would have learnt to say
that this 'was done' and that 'wasn't done'. My mother always

longed to live abroad, which is strange, when the whole time she compares even the clean, thrifty Swiss unfavourably with the British, and still clings tenaciously to English cooking and dishes of the most completely unimaginative kind. If I had been with them, Wilfred would have spent long and rather boring holidays at Montreux. Instead, he goes once a year when he goes for Winter sports and hasn't time to get bored. What I should have done I don't know—played eternal bridge for small stakes every day of my life. No, both Wilfred and I have everything—yes, everything—to thank you and Mary Ellen for."

The intensity in her voice made him turn and look into her face; she was still a good-looking woman and she was over forty. Her eyes were very bright and her cheeks had flushed a little through the earnestness of her words.

Amos raised his hand and patted hers. "Nay, luv, you've had mor'n a hand in making the lad what he is. As for Mary Ellen and me, I was just thinking today that no two folks ever had a dearer and sweeter daughter. Our Wilfred's a fine son, and you—well, you're my ideal of what a daughter ought to be."

The moment of intensity had passed. Monica smiled back at him.

"Much as I love these mutual admiration society meetings," she said, "I have work to do. I adore being praised, I revel in hearing my son being praised, but—you remember the old saying that time and tide wait for no man. As we're ship's chandlers, that saying applies particularly to us. The last lot of stores for *Helena* must go at once. She sails at high tide tonight."

Amos was failing, Monica knew. There was nothing fundamentally wrong with him; it was just as he said, "the machinery was slowing down". She knew that while he was still the ostensible head of the huge business, more and more responsibility devolved upon her. It was inevitable that such a business entailed tremendous strain; there was a continual necessity to keep abreast with the times. Goods which had been popular ten years ago were now outdated; the very foods which people ate had changed. Little Peters, the master tailor, told her, "Changes all the time, Mrs. Towers. Leetle t'ings, maybe, details, but the changes are there chust the same. Materials—they've changed, styles, oh, one must be alvays on one's toes. Alvays."

Peters had his one department, she had literally dozens· And she had determined from the very beginning to have complete mastery of the details of each one. She must know just a little more than the head of the department; her knowledge must be more comprehensive, absolutely complete.

For eighteen years she had worked in this huge building, larger than ever because they had expanded so much in the past few years. She had seen employees come and go, she had seen the installation of this time-saving device, the centralization of despatch and delivery. Working slowly and carefully, she had offered suggestions, tentatively, and she had never allowed Amos to feel that she was attempting to usurp his authority or his power. The casting vote, the first definite suggestions, had always come from him. She had been merely the prompter, the spirit of modern ideas and improvements.

She had contrived to keep alive her sense of romance and adventure which she felt permeated the whole business. She had talked to her son, when he was very young, making the whole thing seem colourful. She had talked of the places where the goods which they supplied would go, the hazards through which every ship must pass before it reached a safe harbour. She had fired his imagination; he had been alert, interested, and he had noticed every change or improvement.

"I say, Mummy, that house telephone system's jolly good," or, "Those new adding machines! They're marvellous! It's like magic."

She had gone from the romantic side to tell him of the great Merchant Navy of Britain. She had told him stories of heroism, of determination, of tremendous battles fought against the elements, of courage shown in the face of terrible odds—sickness, danger, even deprivation. She had read to him, her voice thrilling a little with pride, Kipling's poems about the sea: "Where are you going to, all you big steamers . . .", "The wreck of the *Mary Gloucester*", and many others.

She had insisted that the men who brought so much of Britain's food and wealth had a great duty owing to them from the people—ship's chandlers—who sold the food, the clothes, the medicines and small luxuries for the men who manned those ships.

Her ideas had taken root; more, they had grown and developed until now Wilfred looked forward keenly to the

H

time when he might begin to follow the same profession as his grandfather and his mother.

He came home after his holiday looking handsome, tanned and full of vitality. It was pathetic to watch Amos Towers with him. The old man's eyes followed him everywhere; his smile, when Wilfred talked to him of his plans, ideas, hopes and the like, was positively beatific. Mary Ellen loved him, there was not the slightest doubt about that, but with Amos his love had become something "only this side idolatry".

Wilfred told Monica that he had been discussing with his grandfather what were the first steps he should take to learn something about the business when he left school.

"I shall be nineteen, Mummy, and I've told Grandfather that I want to see where the ships go, where so much of the stuff which they bring back is grown or produced, and he thinks it's a fine idea. He's going to make that possible; in fact, he's given a trip to me as a birthday present."

Monica laughed. "If a birthday hadn't been convenient, Wilfred, that precious old man would have found some other excuse, bless him. Yes, go on, my dear."

"I'm to have a trip round the world, not just to dash round as fast as I can, not to do a 'Round the World in Eighty Days', but if I find some place which seems interesting—I can spend a week, two weeks, there. He's going to discuss it with you, together. He says that you will work out all the details. I think it's grand!"

"Don't make it too long, darling. I want you to go, I always want you to see as much of the world as possible, but" —wistfully—"I shall miss you, and don't forget that Grandfather isn't young any more."

"I promise that I won't, because I do want to get to work, and more still I want to work with you, Mummy."

They were very close, Monica and her son. They spent holidays together in the Winter when they went to Switzerland or North Italy. They had toured most of England in Monica's car, and Wilfred had always been her ideal travelling companion. She had never tried to hold him too tightly, remembering a saying of her father's, "The tightest rope snaps first."

The old fears, she felt, had grown dulled with the passing of the years. Sometimes she wondered what she would have done if Wilfred—Victor's brother—had married and had children, sons. Well, Wilfred had not married and at thirty-nine showed no disposition to do so. He had risen in his profession, and was holding a fine position as consultant and adviser in engineering to one of the world's greatest lines.

Amos always asked him, when he came home, if he had no intention of settling down.

"I have settled down, Dad. I'm a very respectable citizen."

"Nay, you ought to have a home of your own."

"I have, and both you and Mum approved of it, approved of the way it's run."

"You know very well what I'm driving at, Wilf. You ought to have a nice wife and some bonnie bairns."

Wilfred always shook his head. "I don't think so. I'm very well as I am. I've two damned good servants, neither of them young enough to welcome a mistress over them. I can go off for the firm where I like, when I like. I'm away for more than half of each year. A wife would find it a lonely kind of life, Dad."

Monica refused to wonder what might happen if Wilfred changed his mind. She had become accustomed to believe that he was confirmed in his bachelorhood.

The Summer came round again. Wilfred left school and the plans were ready for his world tour. He was excited and full of plans, and Amos was almost as elated as he was. He fussed about the boy's clothes, the various suits he would need to meet the requirements of the changes of temperature, until Mary Ellen expostulated mildly.

"Eh, Amos, you might be fitting out a whole crew—captain, officers and men—the road you're going on! I'll lay as he never has half the things you've got for him on his back!"

"I'm not skimping the lad for anyone, Muther."

"Nay, no one said anything about—skimping, luv. Well, have it your own way. Same as you've always had all your life."

"Now listen to her, Monica. Me as never raised my voice i' my life. I've been a hen-pecked husband for years, and well she knows it. I oft-times think as it's seeing me, and what a miserable crushed kind o' worm I've always been, as has kept our Wilfred from getting wed."

Mary Ellen would chuckle. "Hark at him! Nay, lad, save your breath, for Monica knows better nor to believe a word of what you say."

Wilfred was away for nearly a year, and his letters never failed to be full of interest and enthusiasm. They were read and re-read, quoted by Amos to everyone with whom he came in contact, and treasured by his mother. The excitement when the date of his return was fixed became intense. Amos could talk of nothing else.

"I'll lay as we'll see a change in him. He's not a boy any longer. Nearly twenty! Tut, tut, scarcely seems possible."

Mary Ellen insisted that his bedroom must be repapered and painted; he must have new curtains, a new carpet. When Amos said that she was pampering the boy, she replied, her eyes twinkling, that she left all the pampering for him to do, "and mightily successfully you'd do it. Only Wilf's muther and me have too much sense to let you get away wi' it."

He returned broader, Monica thought, taller, looking bronzed and handsome. His manner was assured without being aggressive. He talked intelligently of what he had seen, and gave them all the presents which he had brought for them with an unaffected pleasure and affection which Monica found both charming and touching. Amos said, "Why, we sent you away a well-grown lad. Dash it, you've come back a well-grown man!"

"Nearly twenty, Grandfather. Five foot eleven and a half."

"Aye. You're taller nor what your poor father was, isn't he, Monica?"

"I believe that he is—why, yes, of course he is. Victor was five ten."

They were sitting in the pleasant drawing-room; the windows were open and the soft air brought with it the scent of old-fashioned flowers—stocks, pinks and honeysuckle. Monica let her eyes wander round the little group, watching the three people she had come to love best in the world.

Amos, smoking contentedly, his white hair shining in the light of the lamp which stood near his chair, his fresh, pleasant face alight with happiness. Mary Ellen, her fingers holding her rapidly moving needles, knitting something for one of her men as usual. Monica wondered how many socks Mary Ellen had knitted in her life—the number must be tremendous. Her hair was very grey, but her eyes were as bright as ever, and still capable of twinkling when she quietly enjoyed something which amused her. And, lastly, Monica's eyes rested on her son. She had almost come to think of him as her son—and

Victor's. She had wronged him by bringing him into the world, she had sinned, lied, deceived; she had tried to atone, to bring him up with high ideals, with the same gay and kindly attitude towards life which Victor had held. She had been faithful to Victor's father and mother; she had worked very hard, and would in all probability work hard all her life. In this quiet room, with the sound of her son's voice in her ears as he told his grandparents about the beauties of some country which he had visited, she sighed with content.

"I think," she thought, "that it is possible that God has forgiven me. That out of what was bad, evil and horrible, good has emerged. I thought that I had lost all my happiness when Victor was killed. I shall never know that complete, satisfying happiness again. It doesn't come, I suppose, twice in a lifetime. This is happiness of another kind—we're growing older, watching Wilfred grow up, assume responsibilities, take his place in the world. It's very, very good."

Mary Ellen was saying, "Did you meet a lot of nice people? When Grandpa and I take those cruises there always seems to be so many nice *young* folk on the ships. It's a treat to watch them playing games on deck, swimming in the pool, and dancing at night."

"I met some topping people, Grannie. Plenty of dancing, and all the rest of it."

His grandfather said slyly, "I'm wondering if you found anyone *'specially* nice, Wilf."

Monica saw Wilfred flush under his tan. It mounted slowly until his whole animated face was suffused. He laughed softly.

"Grandfather, you're a wizard! I was waiting for one of you to give me a lead, and you've done it! I did meet—someone."

"You fell in love with her?" Monica asked softly.

"Hook, line and sinker, Mummy. She's adorable, a year younger than I am. She was travelling with her mother. Her mother's American. They're both mad about travelling. I caught the boat on the homeward trip at Cape Town, and that's where we met. I'm certain that you'll like her—well, more—certain that you'll love her. Her mother knows all about it, and she approves. She wants me to go to stay with them. They've got a place in Scotland."

"And what's the name of your young lady, Wilf?" Mary Ellen asked.

"Phillida. It's nice, isn't it? It is nice, Mummy, don't you think?" His tone was almost anxious.

"Charming, darling."

"And you reckon as you're engaged to this young lady?" Amos asked.

"I haven't given her a ring yet, of course. You see, they went straight off to Scotland, and I came back here. But when I go to stay with them I shall take one."

"Aye, we must see that you get something really smart."

Monica laughed. "Amos is content now that he finds he'll be able to lavish money on you, Wilfred!"

"Nothing of the sort, Monica. I won't have the lad cut a poor figure before a lot of swells. I s'ppose they are swells, Wilf?"

"Oh, rather. Phillida told me this place in Scotland has been in the family for years. Her father's a baronet, but I promise you that she's as simple and unaffected as anyone you can imagine. I can't wait for you to see her. She can come and stay here, can't she, Grannie?"

"What's her name, luv, besides Phillida?" Mary Ellen asked.

"I'm so excited that I'm missing out all sorts of things," he admitted, laughing. "Her name is Phillida Margaret MacPhail. Her father's Sir Hamish MacPhail and their place is—— Mummy, what's the matter? Are you feeling ill? Let me get you a drink, darling."

Monica nodded. She could not speak. This was the end of her treasured happiness, this was where she was called upon to pay for everything. Fate had chosen this way, to make her pay and hurt her son at the same time.

He stood beside her, holding a glass, and saying, "Darling, drink that up. What was it?"

"I think I'm overtired," she whispered, "and this room feels suddenly awfully hot. I'm all right now, yes, really. Don't look so worried, Amos dear. I'm better now."

"I doubt you want a tonic, my dear. It's this warm weather, and you work overhard. I wish you'd spare yourself a bit."

Mary Ellen said smartly, "Why, Amos, you ought to see as she doesn't work overhard. You should be more considerate with the poor lass. Monica luv, slip away to bed, and I'll bring you some camomile tea to make you sleep."

"Sleep!" Monica felt a sudden spasm of ghastly mirth. "Sleep!" she thought. "I feel that I shall never sleep again. I must think, plan, decide what I can do. I shall have to tell lies, practise deceits again. Horrible! I imagined that I had reached safe harbour. Of all the girls in the world—millions of them—why *this* girl? It's hideous, horrible!"

She said, "I believe that I will go to bed, Mary Ellen dear. I shall be as right as rain in the morning. Good night, Amos. Good night, Wilfred darling. It's so lovely to have you home again."

As she kissed him she felt that no one could endure the agony which she felt, that no one could bear such suffering—and live.

She undressed and, standing in her nightgown at the open window, looked out over the fields away to the moors and hills which Victor had loved. The cool night air soothed her; she felt a little soft breeze caress her feverish forehead like the touch of a gentle hand.

Mary Ellen came in with the camomile, and clicked her tongue in reproof to find Monica not in bed.

"Tut, tut, standing there in that thin gown with all the winds of heaven blowing round you. You'll catch your death. There, come your ways into bed, do! That's better. You weren't upset about Wilf and this young lady, were you?"

Mechanically Monica answered, "No, of course not. She sounds very sweet. Such a pretty name, isn't it?"

"Aye. I wish she wasn't such a swell." She laughed softly. "Lukes as if this family is set on marrying these swell young women. First Victor marries you, now Wilfred's going to marry a girl who's father's a titled gentleman. Well, if Wilf's as happy as you and poor Vic were—though it didn't last long, more's the pity—he'll be all right. There now, lie down and try to sleep, my dear. Why not have a long lie-in in the morning?"

"I can't, it's impossible. Too much to be done, dear." A sudden thought came to her. It was horrifying how quickly lies came once you began lying. "I meant to tell Amos tonight; I think that I must go up to Liverpool and see how the new manager is doing. It's a young branch and wants nursing. While I'm there I might run up to Glasgow. McFee's a good man, but he likes to have personal visits from," she laughed, "the heads of the concern. It gives him confidence, and like all Scotsmen he loves a little praise. No, I must be up bright and early. Good night, and thank you for the tea. It's made me quite drowsy."

Mary Ellen Towers lay awake that night long after her husband slept soundly and, it must be confessed, a little noisily.

Her thoughts were disturbed. "It's come at last," she mused. "Exactly what I don't reitly know. It's as if something was coming closer and closer. Monica taking that queer turn when Wilf told us about this young lady. What can Monica know about her? Then this rushing off to Liverpool and Glasgow all on a sudden. Well, I've stood by her and stood by the boy—and a good boy he's turned out, that I will say. I shall go on standing by 'em.

"I mind the night the lad was born, and there was my Amos in a right taking, longing for this grandchild. Sending off for a specialist in Newcastle, when it was as straightforward a confinement as ever I saw. I held the bairn, sitting by the fire, while his muther slept, and the whiffs of chloroform they'd given her wore off. I watched him, trying to see if there was any likeness to my poor Vic, then it came to me—a seven-months baby, never! Never i' this world or any other. His little nails, eyelashes, eyebrows were perfect. I didn't understand it then, I don't understand it now, but—I've grown to love both Monica and the boy. I've kept a still tongue. They say that a still tongue makes a glad heart. Let's hope it's true."

She gave her husband a gentle push, and said as she might have spoken to a child, "Amos luv, turn off your back; you're making enough noise to wake the Seven Sleepers. There, that's better!"

In the morning Monica drove down to the office very early. She had been at her desk for an hour when her secretary arrived.

The girl said, "Oh, Mrs. Towers, I'm not late, am I?"

"No, my dear, prompt—as always. I had a great deal to do, and I must be off to Liverpool this morning. Find out the best train for Liverpool, send down for my ticket, and then get through to the Adelphi Hotel and book a room for me. I shall spend the next day there—tomorrow that is. Then I go on to Glasgow. Book a room with a private sitting-room for me at the Central, for the following day. I can travel on the night train."

"A sleeper will you want, Mrs. Towers?"

"If it fits in, yes. I'll make my appointments when I get there."

"Very good, Mrs. Towers."

"I shall only be away three or four days. See that Mr. Towers doesn't try to do too much. I don't want to come back and find that he's had plans got out for a new warehouse and that the building is already started!"

She heard Amos enter his office and went out to tell him of her plans. He nodded; he never questioned her decisions, and he himself hated visiting either Glasgow or Liverpool. If Monica thought they needed a visit, he was content, and believed wholeheartedly that she was right.

She returned to her own office to find a sheet of paper on her desk. To it was fastened a railway ticket, and on it was written:

Car will be here at 10.20. *Train for Liverpool* 10.32. *Room No.* 268 *booked at the Adelphi, Liverpool.*

Despite her misery and anxiety, Monica nodded approval. That girl was good; she must be encouraged, given a chance to make headway.

During the journey she lay back, closed her eyes and reviewed her plans. They had taken shape during the long hours when she had lain awake. Her face was very pale, her eyes were heavy and shadowed. She knew that before her lay an interview with MacPhail, the result of which—if it were satisfactory—must be that pain and disappointment would be inflicted on Wilfred, that she would have to watch him suffer, possibly see him disillusioned and wretched.

Looking at the position, she blamed no one except herself. She did not blame MacPhail except for his brutal refusal to shoulder his responsibility. The initial wrongdoing was hers, and hers only. She had allowed herself to be swept off her feet by a physical attraction; she had indulged an appetite, and she had never—she had known it when she fell in love with Victor Towers—loved the man who was the father of Wilfred and of the girl with whom Wilfred had fallen in love. She shuddered.

To confess now to Amos, to Mary Ellen, to Wilfred, was impossible. Her courage failed her even at the thought of

confessing. Too many people, too many issues, were involved
to make such a thing possible: Amos growing old, being told
that the boy he literally adored, on whom all his hopes were
centred, was not his grandson, not the son of that "Golden
Lad" who had "come to dust" twenty years ago. Such a knowledge would ruin irretrievably the remaining years of his life.

Mary Ellen would take any hurt or disappointment inflicted on her husband very hardly. Monica believed that she
would far rather that he remained in ignorance. She wondered how much Mary Ellen did *know*. After twenty years she
remembered that sudden expression in her eyes when she
first laid Wilfred in his mother's arms. She recalled exactly
her sensation of shock as she realized, "Mary Ellen knows."

And Wilfred, her so dearly loved son, his future—now so
bright, so assured, so hopeful—would lie in ruins. Better far
that he lose the girl with whom he was in love, than that he
lose what he regarded as his family, the prospects which were
his, and—again she shivered—possibly experienced a revulsion
against his mother.

He was young; even if he lost this, his first love, there
were years lying before him which might hold other loves,
greater affections than could be experienced completely by an
inexperienced boy of barely twenty.

That night she took a drug to make her sleep, and in the
morning went to the warehouse and inspected everything. The
manager was a hard-headed Yorkshireman who had been employed by Towers for a number of years at Willingbrough. He
had been a sailor, and as the result of an accident had lost a
leg. His nautical determination to keep everything "shipshape
and Bristol fashion" had delighted Amos, and when they
opened the Liverpool branch he had placed George Mason in
charge.

"I shall tell Mr. Towers that I am delighted with everything," Monica told the broad-shouldered, stocky manager.
"This is how a place ought to be kept—from the warehouse
floor to the ledgers."

He fingered the little clipped torpedo beard which he wore.

"Why, if you're glad, Mrs. Towers, you can bet your life
as I'm glad an' all. Mind, at first it was only smallish stuff we
handled, but—onless I'm very mooch mistaken—before very
long I'm going to give you and Mr. Towers a surprise. Aye,
an' it 'ul be a good 'un, a big 'un."

She laughed. "I believe that you have something up your sleeve, Mr. Mason!"

He grinned. "Aye, that's why I have my tailor mak' the sleeves a bit on the wide side. I'll be at the train tonight to see as everything's all reit for you."

Later, when Monica lay in her sleeper, she wondered how anyone's brain could shut out certain things and concentrate—lucidly, clearly and exactly—on others. Mason had said, "D'you think, Mrs. Towers, as the Boss 'ul consider starting a rope walk? Place wheer we could make our own ropes? Specialize a bit in ropemaking?"

Her worries had slid automatically into the background and she had flung herself into the proposed project; she had asked for figures, the amount of labour required, the ease or difficulty with which materials might be bought.

He had said, "I don't like the luke of things—international things."

Immediately she had experienced a sense of panic. What did he mean, what did he know, on what did he base his statement?

"Germany, same as always," he said. "I see and hear a lot, and—I don't like it, that's flat."

Her panic grew, he meant—a war. Her present problems were forgotten; the fact that Wilfred might be forced to give up the girl he said he loved sank into insignificance. Her one thought was, "He might have to fight. I might lose him as I lost Victor!"

Now, with the sound of the wheels in her ears, she sank into sleep, trying to reassure herself that international politics would be managed by men with wiser heads than hers, and that Mason was an alarmist who knew no more, in actual fact, than the average man in the street.

CHAPTER SEVEN

GLASGOW looked very gloomy, Monica thought. She admitted that it held some of the kindest, most open-handed people imaginable—what rubbish people talked about the meanness of the Scots!—that it had encouraged learning and art, and that many of its sons were men possessing great energy, ability and rectitude. Nevertheless, Glasgow remained a gloomy town.

She went to her room and telephoned to the warehouse, asking McFee if he could possibly send her a shorthand-typist.

"I have so much to get through, and I must have someone to take down letters and answer the telephone. I should be so grateful."

His voice came back to her, precise and rather clipped. "Why, Mistress Towers! A grreat surprise, and if Ah may say so a pleasure. Ah hope you'll be paying us a veesit, Mistress Towers. Ah can assure you we're ready. Everything in orrder onny hour o' the day or night. The shorrthand-typist—aha, the very gairl; Ah'll send her doon immediately. The name? Kirsteen Fish. Aye, a strange name, but a grrand gairl."

Monica washed, changed and waited for the excellent Miss Fish. She arrived, a tall girl, with reddish hair and a fine skin, her small well-shaped nose covered with freckles. She carried a portable typewriter and a portfolio.

"How do you do, Miss Fish? This is very kind of you."

The girl smiled, a pleasant; wide smile, showing beautiful teeth.

"Not at all, Mrs. Towers. It's an honour, I'm sure. Noo, shall we stairt right away, or are there instructions you wish to give me?"

Monica said, "I want you to do some telephoning for me. I hate the telephone. Yes, indeed I do, business woman though I am. I want you to get Joseph Cameron, a jute merchant in Renfrew Street."

Before leaving Liverpool she had ascertained that Cameron was away on holiday in Spain. "Then I want to speak to Mr. McNeil. His office is—now, where is it?—he's a solicitor. After that—and this is more difficult, for I'm afraid that I don't know his address. It may be a long-distance call—Sir Hamish MacPhail."

Miss Fish answered, "No deeficulty at all, Mrs. Towers. His home is at Philochery, and that's only about thirty miles away. Most days he's here in Glasgow, except when he's fishing or shooting. A grreat sportsman is Sir Hamish. I might be able to find him at the Scottish National Club. D'you mind if I try there, Mrs. Towers?"

"Try where you like, my dear. Only it's important that I speak to him. I'll be frank with you, and tell you—in confidence—that it's a matter of business, big business. I don't want it chattered about, you understand? Otherwise—well, until things are signed, sealed and delivered, it's better to keep a still tongue, and the less people know about your business— the better."

The girl nodded. "Ah understand pairfectly, Mrs. Towers. You can rely on me—eemplicitly."

Monica moved restlessly about the stiff, impersonal sitting-room. How strange that she was to speak with MacPhail after all these years. Twenty years. . . . She wondered if he had changed, if he would find her changed, and all the time her plans regarding what she would say were jostling each other in her head.

Twenty years ago—more than twenty years ago—she had waited for him with a sense of excitement, she had listened to his voice, trying to detect from its inflexions whether his mood was good or bad. Now she knew that she could speak to him calmly, and with decision. She would dictate, she would make demands. Twenty years had taught her a great deal.

She turned back to Miss Fish. "Do you know Sir Hamish?" she asked abruptly.

"I'd not say that I *knew* him, Mrs. Towers. I've haird him speak many times, seen him many times, o' course. He's a very well-known gentleman about these pairts."

"I see. Well, get those numbers for me, and then while I'm on the telephone go down to the station and buy some flowers. These rooms are only bearable when they have plenty of flowers." She laid down a pound note, and smiled. "Get something nice, never mind what they cost."

Five minutes later Miss Fish returned and referred to her notebook. "Mrs. Towers, Mr. Cameron is away in Spain, Mr. McNeil will be in his office in about an hour from now. He'll call you. Sir Hamish is at his club—the one I told you about —the number is here."

Monica felt a sudden chill; she fancied that her heart missed a beat, but her voice was steady when she spoke.

"Get him, please. I'll speak to him."

Kirsteen Fish thought that this was indeed the romance of commerce. Here was this lady, still young, and still very attractive, wearing most beautiful clothes—she knew enough about clothes to recognize expensive simplicity when she saw it. There she was, this Mrs. Towers, sending for—aye, sending for—these important men, bidding them to come and speak to her. It was astonishing!

Monica listened, her heart hammering suddenly.

"Ah, good morning, Sir Hamish. A lady wishes to speak to you. Mrs. Towers. A business matter. Yes, she'll speak to you herself. Mrs. Towers, please."

She handed the telephone to Monica, who nodded towards the door and whispered the word "Flowers", then as the door closed she spoke.

"Sir Hamish MacPhail? This is Monica Crawshaw. Ah, yes, we met when you were in hospital——" She heard a slight exclamation. "I thought that you might remember. I must see you, and immediately."

His voice was harsher than she remembered it. "I don't quite see any point in seeing you. What do you want?" There was a slight pause. "Money?"

She laughed. How she contrived to laugh she did not know; it was certainly from no sense of amusement, for her anger flamed in her heart. He hadn't changed; he might be laird of this and that, he might be a notable person here, but he was the same insensitive, self-centred man he had been over twenty years ago.

"Money!" Again that laugh. "I most certainly don't want money. I imagine that I could buy and sell you and scarcely miss it. I want to see you," her voice deepened, "on a matter which is so desperately important that I can say I *demand* to see you. A matter which affects us both, which affects our families—it is urgent."

"Can't you be more explicit?" the harsh voice demanded.

"Impossible. Please tell me when to expect you."

"In half an hour—the Central, eh? I'm leaving Glasgow at midday."

"In half an hour. Very well."

Monica felt that the first round was over, that the bell had gone and she could lean back in her chair and relax, allow her strength to come trickling back. Half an hour.

Miss Fish returned, her arms filled with flowers; their entrance into the room seemed to bring light and sweetness. She showed them to Monica, hoping that they were what she liked.

"Now, can you find a chambermaid to give you vases, and can you arrange them? Then telephone to Mr. McNeil and say that I can see him about a quarter past twelve. Thank you, my dear, that's splendid."

During the half-hour which followed Monica was busy in her bedroom. She did her hair, used a little impossibly expensive scent with care, polished her nails, and tried desperately —all the time that her hands were busy—to dispel the fear which gripped her.

"If I win this battle," she thought, "this is the last—the final. If I win now I can go on, living my life, working hard, conscious that Wilfred is safe. If I lose . . ." She shuddered, then mastered herself. "I can't lose! It's impossible! I must win—I shall win!"

The telephone shrilled. "Sir Hamish MacPhail, madam."

"Please send him up. My secretary will meet him."

She called, "Miss Fish, will you go and bring Sir Hamish to this apartment? Thank you."

Monica sat down, rather heavily, for she felt that her strength had ebbed away. She clenched her hands, took long deep breaths to attempt to steady her heart, then rose, re-powdered her face, gave a touch to her hair and—waited. A knock at the door.

"Yes, come in."

"Sir Hamish is here, Mrs. Towers."

"Very well, Miss Fish. Will you come back after luncheon?"

"Sairtenly, Mrs. Towers."

Even then, when she knew that he was waiting, impatient and resentful, she delayed. She chose a clean handkerchief with extreme care; she picked up her handbag and examined its contents, then walked very slowly to the door and entered the sitting-room.

He was standing staring out of the window. As she entered he spun round. He saw a woman of middle age, beautifully groomed, exquisitely dressed; her light brown hair was touched at the temples with silver threads. She held herself erect, her eyes met his calmly, she was obviously complete mistress of herself.

Monica saw a tall man, rather gaunt, with a long, narrow face, and hatchet jaws. His eyes were heavily lidded, his mouth turned down at the corners. A hard face, a face which, she thought, held disappointment and disillusionment, and a fierce resentment that he should have experienced either.

He barked, "Well, what is it?"

She thought, "The first point is to me. He's rattled, I'm quite calm." She said, "Won't you sit down? Can I offer you something to drink? Ring the bell, will you?"

He said, half sulkily, "You can telephone, you know."

"Of course. Please telephone for the floor waiter. Thank you."

They sat in silence, but Monica felt that while the silence disturbed MacPhail she drew added strength from it. The waiter came, she gave her order, and then turned to him.

"You were surprised to hear from me, of course, but the matter is urgent." She repeated, "Urgent. You know nothing about it?"

"I have no idea what you're talking about."

"Ah, let me explain. Your wife and daughter have lately returned from a long sea voyage. On the voyage they met a young man with whom your daughter fell in love, and he fell violently in love with her. I gather that your wife approved of the attachment. She invited him to stay with you in Scotland, when he was going to ask for your permission to marry your daughter. The young man is—my son."

"What if he is? What has it to do with me?"

"He happens to be your son also," Monica said.

MacPhail sat, his hands hanging between his knees, staring at her, his mouth sagging a little. Monica did not move. Surely this was the end of the second round. They were waiting to enter the ring again.

MacPhail said hoarsely, "I don't believe it. You can't prove it."

"I can prove it. You see, I took the precaution of seeing a specialist, of confiding in my own doctor and a second specialist." How easy lies were when you got into the habit of telling them! "They are all still alive. They all believe that my husband and I had—intimate relations at least two months before we were married. It was war-time, they were tolerant, and the man was going to marry me! My son"—she paused—"*our* son was born seven months after my marriage."

He rose and took several turns up and down the room, then stopped at the table and poured out a stiff whisky-and-soda; he drank it thirstily and set down the glass with a clatter on the metal tray.

"I don't admit that he is my son. Damn it, I wasn't the only man!"

"That," Monica said slowly, "is abominable. You know very well that you were—the only man; more, you know that you were the first man who had ever made love to me. I came to London to meet you, I told you—my condition, and your only suggestion was to offer to pay for an operation—provided that your name was kept out of it! It's not a pretty story."

He licked his lips and his eyes shifted uneasily as they met hers.

"Then I suppose that you tricked some damn fool into marrying you, eh? Is that what happened? I don't think that your part of the business is any more meritorious than mine, after all."

She spoke quietly, slowly, her control was returning, she felt capable of fighting this thing out. She would make everything safe for Wilfred, even if the process was painful to her.

"What I did or did not do does not affect the present issue. I tell you that your son wants to marry his half-sister. That is the whole point. I am going to suggest—no!"—her voice sharpened—"I am going to *instruct* you how to make this impossible."

She saw him stiffen at that; he was not accustomed to being spoken to in that way—it was for him to give orders, for him to make demands, for him to dictate.

"And how, if you please?" The question came sharply like the crack of a whip. He repeated, "And how?"

"I shall tell you. Please give me a drink—very small. That's right. Thank you. Your wife is an American. She was married before she met you, therefore one may deduce that she has a number of relations and connections in the States. The political situation in Europe is not particularly—secure; it will, I am assured, grow more and more disturbed. I don't think that anyone who is not blind does not see the ultimate end! I suggest that it might be wise to send your daughter to America —there is no need to alarm her, poor child, but on the other hand she is—I think—your only child—and the mental distress and apprehension for you in case of, well, a flare-up would be terrible. I advise you to book passages for your wife and her daughter quite soon. If you wait it might look as if they were—running away. Now, anyone will accept that they wish to visit relatives."

MacPhail stared at her, his face furious, his head lowered a little like a bull about to charge. She saw the veins stand

I

out on his neck and his temples. When he spoke his voice was more harsh than she had heard it before.

"And why can't your precious son——"

She held up her hand. "Our son, remember."

He shook his head as if tormented. "Why can't he go abroad? Why can't he go abroad and stay abroad? Plenty of places where a young man can go—rubber, coffee, tea-planting! Send him. Leave my daughter here."

Monica answered very calmly, in a voice which was studiously "reasonable". "Because his career is waiting for him. His grandfather is very rich, very successful. My son is his heir. Why should he throw away everything—when I can prevent it?"

"Career! What is this career?" he demanded.

"Probably the most successful ship's chandler in the country."

He stared at her, even started back a little before he spoke. "Good God! You didn't marry the—the Golden Grocer, did you?"

She rose, dusted her finger-tips together as if she wished to rid them of something which had defiled them. She spoke very coldly.

"There is nothing more to be said, I think. I did not wish to go to Lady MacPhail, but you have forced me to do so. I am sorry that we have both wasted our time. Good-bye."

That roused him; he started forward, crying, "You're not going to tell my wife! You mustn't do that. She's a New Englander, rigid—she'd never forgive me. It would be terrible. But how do you know that she'd see you?" The last question came with a hint of defiance.

"I have a lawyer here in Glasgow, McNeil. He's very good, very trustworthy. I have all the necessary papers with me. I shan't deal with Lady MacPhail. He will."

"What about your—your husband's family?"

"That is my affair. Good-bye."

He hesitated; she watched him closely. She had him "on the ropes".

She said, "I am sticking at nothing to prevent my son doing something which would ruin him in every way. Your daughter is half American; she's young, she'll probably marry an American, anyway—she won't be here where she can meet my son. That is all I have to say."

Slowly MacPhail returned to the table where Monica sat. He hesitated and then dropped into a chair. He leaned forward, his hands clasped.

"Listen, Monica," he said, "why should I be deprived of my daughter, of whom I am very fond? Why can't you send your son abroad? Let him marry some other girl. Why must I be penalized?"

She smiled, a smile without any hint of amusement. "Because this time I make the decisions," she said.

"It's completely unfair. I didn't ask your precious son to fall in love with Phillida!"

Impatiently Monica said, "Oh, don't talk so stupidly! Is your daughter going to America—or anywhere else which will take her out of my son's reach—or not? I'm tired of this interview. I have work to do. I want an answer—yes or no."

He stared at her, his eyelids dropped so that his eyes were almost hidden, his voice grated on her ears.

"You've turned yourself into a damned hard woman, haven't you?"

"Yes, thank God," she rapped out.

"Suppose that I grow vindictive and let your son come to visit us. Suppose *I* tell him who he is—what then?"

This time she laughed. "But you couldn't prove it, could you? I have the proofs; you can't ferret out all the obstetric specialists in London; you can scarcely visit my own doctor, or discover the name of the specialist who came from Newcastle! Very well, leave it, and I will get in touch with Lady MacPhail. There is no more to be said."

He stood up; his face was white, his eyes looked venomous, his mouth a trap.

"I will speak to my wife tonight."

Monica nodded. "I have been told that the international situation is rapidly becoming worse. Britain has given too many promises, pledges and the rest of it. This German madman will make England a very dangerous and uncomfortable place, I imagine. Your wife, as an American, can safeguard herself and her daughter. I suggest that as the line for you to take. I can *rely* on your keeping your promise?"

He snarled suddenly, "Oh, damn you, yes! My wife isn't particularly fond of me. She wanted to be Lady MacPhail— but I am devoted to my daughter. It's a big price to have to pay—I run the risk of losing her altogether."

Monica said lightly, "Oh, the distance between America and England grows less and less every year. Then—remember that the wages of sin are never very pleasant."

"A sin," his lips curved into a sneer, "which was not only committed by me, remember."

Her voice was sombre when she answered, "I have been taking those wages for more than twenty years. Please go. Please have a notice in *The Times* to say that Lady MacPhail and her daughter have sailed for America and that no letters will be forwarded. I shall expect to see it as soon as possible. That is all."

Their eyes met. Neither spoke and MacPhail turned and walked out.

She sat there, very still, feeling drained and exhausted. Was this the end of the necessity for lies, subterfuges and deceptions? Had she at last written "finis" to this story which had run, it seemed, through all her life? Had she at last made everything safe for Wilfred? Poor Wilfred, to have his first love affair shattered to pieces, to have come home so filled with hope and happiness and now to have to face losing it all.

Ah, well, he was young, and youth, she reflected, renews itself. There would be Springtime again for her son; he should have everything possible to make him happy, to make him forget Phillida MacPhail. She would plan his holidays, discover what he wished most to do—and he *would*, he *must* forget.

She roused herself, and began to work. Long training had taught her how to put her own affairs into the background, and to fling herself wholeheartedly into whatever work presented itself. She saw the firm's solicitor; she visited the offices and the warehouse; she made suggestions, praised whenever possible, and tempered her criticisms as extensively as she could. The manager was delighted and reassured; his anxiety had been almost pathetic, his eagerness to gain her approbation rather wistful.

"You're doing very well," Monica told him. "Remember that Mr. Towers and I are always ready to help in any way we can."

"That's a great help, Mrs. Towers, that assurance. Not that Ah think for one moment that—given health and strength —Ah'll not be able to satisfy you baith, and to live up to the high standard which you and Mr. Towers have inaugurated. When Ah say that Ah shall do my best—well, Ah mean it."

He said to his wife that evening, "Ah think that Ah may say Ah acqeeted myself weel, Alice. Yon Mrs. Towers is a clever woman; more, she's a nice-like woman, and forby, a bonnie woman."

Monica travelled back on the early train. As she was leaving the hotel a letter was handed to her. It was heavily sealed and marked "Private and Confidential". She opened it when she was in the train.

I have been thinking over our conversation and have come to the conclusion that it will be better if my daughter receives no further communications from your son. As the whole matter is to end, I see no reason why I should not intercept any letters. Perhaps you might do what is possible at your end. I strongly advise it.

The letter was typed and unsigned. Monica tore it into minute fragments and flung the pieces out of the carriage window. Intercept letters which this girl might—probably would—send to Wilfred: the thought was distasteful to her; it seemed that never was she to be spared from this continual succession of unsavoury and discreditable things. True, it might be wise for the sake of both the girl and her son, it might help to soften the blow if he imagined that he was receiving no replies to his letters; the girl would imagine that he had not written to her. Each would believe that the other had been indulging in a "sea voyage" flirtation. Monica sighed. She had plunged through so much dirt she felt saturated with it, felt that it would take years to become mentally clean again.

At Willingbrough she drove to the office and found Wilfred already installed. He was excited at the prospect of "learning the job". His whole attitude was one of enthusiastic eagerness.

He sat opposite to her at her desk, his hands clasped, his eyes shining, talking rapidly.

"I want to learn everything, Mummy. I'm going to take home price lists, samples of this and that. I want to become completely informed about everything. I want to know all the answers. Do you think that I can do it? I don't mind starting right at the bottom, so long as I can lay a real foundation. You think that I'm right, don't you, darling?"

"Absolutely and completely right. Good luck to you. Never mind *asking* for information, provided you ask from the people who really know."

He nodded, smiling. " 'Lowliness is young ambition's ladder.' I'll be lowly all right."

Monica watched him anxiously as the days passed; she saw his anxious glance towards the hall table where the letters were always left, noticed the sudden frown, as if the absence of one for him both puzzled and disappointed him. Amos noticed it too, and spoke to Monica about it.

"D'you know, I don't believe as that young lady is answering Wilf's letters. It's strange, I never see him pick one up when he comes in, why—good reason for this—there's never one *to* pick up. She doesn't write to the office. I've never seen a sign of anything. D'you think that this father of hers is against it?"

"I've no idea, Amos." Now she must tell more lies, make more concealments. "Perhaps it was just one of those affairs which develop so quickly on board ship. Perhaps she's changed her mind."

"Then it would luke better," Amos snapped suddenly, "if she wrote to the lad and told him, not keep him on tenterhooks like she is now. I've no patience!"

Finally Wilfred came to her room before dinner. "Mummy, may I talk to you about something—well, desperately confidential?"

"Of course. Take a cigarette—there in the silver box."

"It's about Phillida. Do you know, I've only had three letters from her since we got back. I've written and written, sent flowers, books, and she doesn't reply. Do you think that she's ill?" She could catch the tone of anxiety in his voice.

Hating herself, she tried to speak lightly. "My dear, I don't suppose so. Probably after having been away for a long time, there were lots of invitations, lots of things to do—oh, I shouldn't worry."

Wilfred did not speak for a moment, then said, "Mummy, what do you think about my going up there? I mean, you could send me to the Glasgow branch on some pretext, and I could go out to see her."

Conscious of a sense of panic, Monica said, making her voice as light and yet as steady as possible, "I don't think that's a very good idea, darling. After all, her mother liked you, but you don't know what the father's reactions are. I should wait until you get a definite invitation. Otherwise you might—well, jeopardize things. Just be patient—and Wilfred, you are really in love with her?"

He answered readily enough, "Completely, Mummy. She's charming, she's intelligent, kind, very pretty and we've got lots of things in common. She isn't just a doll, not a feather-pate. She can be amusing, but she can be serious. Yes, I'm frightfully in love. That's why it's so worrying not to hear from her. I say, Mummy, what about a telegram? Asking if she's ill, something like that?"

"If you like. Only I shouldn't try to rush things or force the issue."

He smiled. "When you're frightfully in love, you don't think a lot about—forcing issues, darling. Well," he rose and stubbed out his cigarette, "I'll try to be patient. I write every day, and surely—something must happen. Thanks for listening, Mummy. You're a wonderful pal for anyone to have."

Alone she thought, "God, will this account never be paid in full? Must it always hang round my neck like a millstone? The older I grow the more and more people seem to be in-volved, the more lies I have to tell, the more deceptions I must practise. The only scrap of comfort I can find is that—Wilfred is young."

A few days later she saw the announcement in *The Times* that Lady MacPhail and her daughter, Miss Phillida MacPhail, had sailed for New York. They would remain there for some time, visiting relatives of Lady MacPhail. Letters would not be forwarded.

That evening she sent for Wilfred. He came, rather dusty from working in the warehouse, but smiling.

"Hello, darling, anything new?"

Monica said, "Sit down, Wilfred. You don't read *The Times*, do you?"

"Scarcely, sweet. It's too heavy for me. I just skim through the *Daily Mail* and leave it at that. Why?"

She said, "I don't want you to be too hurt, darling. Only —just read that, will you?" She had folded it to show the social news and pointed to the paragraph. "There," she said, "there it is."

He took the folded paper and, standing near her, read the

paragraph which she indicated. To Monica it seemed to take an endless time. Then he laid down the paper.

"I see," he said slowly. "I see. Well, apparently that puts paid to that, eh? Don't worry. Naturally, it's a nasty smack, because I did believe that she was fond of me. Apparently I was wrong. I shan't mope about; in fact, I'm thankful to have some work to do to drive"—this time the pause was longer— "other things out of my mind. Mummy, could you just give Grandfather and Grandmother—well, a hint? Like that song, 'Oh well, it was good while it lasted', eh? Thanks a lot, Mummy. I'll get back to the packing-room. Do you know, I've got some ideas about packing. I want to discuss them with you when we've both got time. Good-bye."

"Good-bye, my dear."

She thought, "If this girl was really fond of him, she's only another person who has to be sacrificed—through me. It may be that she loved Wilfred as I loved Victor. She may have waited day after day for his letters. May have thought, as he did, that she was ill, or that the affair had only been a thing caused by the life of a steamer trip. Poor children. Doing evil that good may come—it may be wise but it isn't easy for the person who has to do the evil. I hate myself, loathe the thought that I've caused pain to the person I love best in all the world —and yet, what was left to me? To have told him the truth, the brutal truth, to have admitted that I deceived the man who he believes was his father, whose memory he venerates, to have shocked dear Amos, the other Wilfred, and to have ruined my son's life . . ." She beat her hands together. "God, what could I have done? God, let this be the end! I have tried to atone. I have worked well and honestly; I've brought happiness to the lives of at least two—elderly—people. Mary Ellen may know, but her life is centred in Amos, and to Amos my son is—the sun, moon and stars. I've never spared myself, and surely if the balance is struck I have done more to bring happiness and content than I have done to break down and destroy. I may be thinking sophistry—the whole thing has gone on for so long. I may have lost all sense of perspective, of right and wrong. Only—God help me—it must end. I can't face any more."

That night, when Wilfred had gone out in his car, she handed the folded *Times* to Amos, saying, "Read that paragraph, will you?"

He read it, slowly, and then handed it to Mary Ellen. She read it and handed it back to Monica.

Amos said, "Does Wilf know?"

"I showed it to him this afternoon."

"How did he take it, poor lad?"

She said almost defiantly, "As I expected him to take it. With his head up."

Mary Ellen spoke. "He's a lot better rid of her. A hussy, if you ask me. Meets a good-luking lad on a steamer and makes a dead set at him, I'd not be surprised. Gets home, and forgets all about him. Nay, I've no time for such."

Monica said, "We don't know. Her parents may have made it difficult for her."

"Nay, that's all my eye and Betty Martin. Girls can fight their parents if they're in love, choose how."

"I don't think," Amos said slowly, "that we'll say anything to Wilf about it. Let it rest, and let's hope as he gets over it. It 'ul hurt the boy, and—why, let him lick his own sores, that's what I think. Aye, it 'ul have hurt him, I doubt."

They never mentioned it to Wilfred. Only when she saw in *The Times* that "a marriage has been arranged, and will shortly take place, between Miss Phillida MacPhail, daughter of Sir Hamish and Lady MacPhail . . ." did she call Wilfred into her office and show him the announcement.

He read it with grave attention, then handed it back to her. He said, "I hope she'll be happy; hope that he's a good fellow."

"The only son of a millionaire, I believe."

"I hope that he's a nice fellow just the same. Thanks for showing the notice to me, Mummy."

He was twenty-one in the Spring of the following year. Amos had been included in the Birthday Honours, and although he shrugged his shoulders and said that they were just "handing them out", it was evident that he was delighted. Again and again Monica heard him, when he entered the house, speaking to the servants. "Is her ladyship in?" or "Do you know if her ladyship will be needing the car?" She thought that the idea of Mary Ellen being "Lady Towers" meant more to him than to be himself "Sir Amos". He had given liberally, and more than liberally, to many effort to improve the conditions of the town; denominations meant nothing to him— the Established Church, the Catholics, the Nonconformists,

were all the same provided they were working to improve the
state of people who were poor or unfortunate.

He insisted on giving a ball, "the biggest and best hall in
the place, wi' supper provided by the finest firm in the North.
Nay, never mind London, what London can do—we can do,
happen better and all."

To celebrate his knighthood and the majority of his grandson, Wilfred, invitations were to be sent to everyone—"aye,
the County, the tradesmen o' Willingbrough, anyone and
everyone who has been a decent friend to me. The County
won't come, Muther? Nay, the County will, I'll lay! If they
don't, all right, it's their loss."

And the County did come, and were astonished at the
enjoyment which they derived. Amos was everywhere; he
beamed, he insisted that everyone must enjoy themselves, and
what was obvious to everyone was that he enjoyed himself.

Lord Stallingford said, " 'Pon my word, Towers, this is a
great evening. That's a good-looking grandson of yours,
dancing with my daughter."

"Wilfred, aye, he's a grand lad. One of my birthday
presents to him is a junior partnership in the firm. He'll do it
credit, and all. Mary Ellen luv, Lord Stallingford is just saying
what a grand lad Wilfred lukes."

She beamed at the tall, angular peer. "Why, we're very
pleased with him, m' lord."

"And you have every right to be. Head boy at Harby,
wasn't he?"

Amos said, "Captain of the School, m' lord."

Monica, watching, dancing at long intervals with her son,
thought, "If this can only be the end of all that terrible business! Wilfred seems happy. Maybe he's forgetting Phillida. I
hope that she's happy too. This is the seal on the success which
Amos has worked for. He's not only made a success in his
business, he's made a success in his life. He and Mary Ellen. . . ."

She watched him, never speaking to anyone of importance
without bringing his wife into the conversation, never failing
to declare that if he had made a success, that success was
largely due to her; Mary Ellen beaming at him, watching him
with love and admiration in her eyes—what a grand pair!
Wilfred standing beside them when he was not actually
dancing, looking handsome, well groomed, his whole attitude
towards them betokening affection.

"Oh, let this be the end of lying," she cried in her heart.

She leaned back in her chair, and watched. Amos was hurrying forward to greet someone—two people, a tall man with fading curly hair, and bright, expressive eyes, eyes that years had taught Monica to recognize as "sailor's eyes", and with him a tall woman.

"Nay, Captain, this is good of you, and of your wife," Amos said, as he wrung the man's hand. "How many years? No, don't tell me! Mrs. Cartwright, your servant. Meet my wife, the woman who's been the 'power behind the throne'."

Cartwright said, "The lady who has really skippered the ship, eh?"

"That's it—the lady who has skippered the ship."

"And brought it into a safe harbour, past all the shoals and shallows. I am delighted to meet you, Lady Towers."

Mary Ellen shook his hand. "Glad to meet you. Now, Amos, have done! Such talk! Mrs. Cartwright, what he's done, he's done by himself, and with the help of our dear daughter, Monica. Monica luv, meet Mrs. Cartwright."

CHAPTER EIGHT

THE years which followed after Wilfred became twenty-one, and was made a junior partner in the firm, seemed to Monica to be the most peaceful and happy she had ever known. Once a year she visited her parents in Switzerland, taking Wilfred with her. They were growing old, and it was obvious that they looked forward to her visits eagerly. They liked and admired Wilfred, and even if they did not give him the whole-hearted admiration offered to him by Amos Towers, their welcome was always warm and kindly.

She liked travelling with her son; he had a "way with him" which made an instant appeal to everyone with whom he came in contact. He was handsome—though he would never be as beautiful as the "Golden Lad", whom he believed to have been his father. He had, Monica thought, forgotten about Phillida MacPhail; not that he took any particular interest in any individual girl—he liked them all, and they liked him. He danced well, played games well, was presentable and well mannered, with nothing of the prig in his composition.

To his grandparents he was devoted, and nothing delighted him more than to persuade Amos and Mary Ellen to go with him to the theatre, or to discover that the local "Empire" had a bill which he felt sure would appeal to them both. Amos had the old-fashioned love of good, healthy, robust Variety, and to visit the music hall in the company of his wife and his grandson made him happy for days.

There were times when he teased Wilfred. "Nay, you're well-nigh twenty-three. Where is this young lady you're going to marry? I don't want another like your Uncle Wilfred, living in a house wih two old, crabby servants—when he's there, which isn't ofteni. One letter says that he's in India, the next that he's going to South America. There'll come a day when our Wilf 'ul be sorry he didn't settle down and have some nice bairns against his old age. There's plenty of nice girls would fancy you, Wilf."

Wilfred would laugh and tell him, "You see, it's your fault."

"My fault! Nay, lad, what's this?"

"How can you expect me to find girls attractive when you snaffled my grandmother, and my father snaffled my mother? I'm looking round for a girl who comes within a hundred miles of either of them. Oh, I shall go on trying to find her, but having been brought up with such a standard—it's disheartening."

Mary Ellen, watching him fondly, would shake her head and say, "Eh, listen to him—a lot of blether."

The world was heading, Monica felt, for disaster. She lay awake wondering what would happen to Wilfred if there was war. It would be such a war as men had never dreamed of. It would mean destruction beyond all human imagination.

Amos shook his head. "Luke, luv, no sense in building bridges before you come to the river."

"Don't worry, darling," Wilfred said, "it may never happen."

She knew, in her heart, that once the machinery was set in the direction of war nothing could stop it. Everyone was heartened and soothed by the result of Munich. Chamberlain was praised extravagantly.

She thought, "And one day all these people who hail him as a saviour now, will blame him for yielding to weakness."

Guarantees given here, given there, recklessly, she felt.

How could we "foot the bill" for all these commitments? Hitler with the assertion that "this is my last demand", grabbing territory, imposing the Nazi regime on all and sundry.

"It's coming nearer and nearer. In my dreams I hear the sound of jack-boots as they march the goose-step."

Then—it came. A quiet Sunday morning, and the Prime Minister telling England that she was at war with Germany; adding that they would be fighting "evil things". They sat very quiet in the peaceful sitting-room, gay with flowers, and bright with chintz, and Monica glanced—as she did so often—at them all, the people she knew and loved best. Mary Ellen, her grave face framed in beautiful white hair, her eyes closed, her lips compressed, her hands lying folded on her lap. Amos—he was over seventy, she remembered—some of his colour faded from his cheeks; his eyes were fixed on Wilfred. They were anxious, troubled; once or twice he sighed gustily. And Wilfred, the son she loved so dearly, he was leaning forward, his hands clasped, his whole face alight and shining. A good face, she thought, with a well-cut mouth and chin, a jaw which betokened determination. Skin which glowed with health, and clear eyes which met those of other people steadily and without wavering. And what was going to happen to him?

"O God, don't let me lose him as I lost Victor!"

Amos said, "Why, now we know, don't we? Turn it off, Wilf."

In silence Wilfred rose and switched off the radio. Then he turned and smiled at them all, an all-embracing smile, a smile which held affection, a wish to comfort, and a determination to put a good face on what was before them.

Monica said, "War—God help us all."

Wilfred answered, "He will, Mummy. This is a righteous war, if ever one was. We've done it before; we shall do it again."

"We—here in this room—paid pretty heavily for the last victory, Wilfred."

He nodded. "I know, but it *was* a victory. They're expensive things."

Amos said, "You'll go?"

"Of course, Grandfather. There isn't anything else to do, is there?"

"As I see it, lad—no."

The young man laughed. "What a grand fellow you are, Grandfather! You—stabilize things somehow. I hope that you'll keep my job open for me, Sir Amos, while I'm away."

The old man's eyes twinkled. "Indeed, Mr. Towers, I shall do that for all my employees, let alone my valued—partner. Noo, Muther, what about having a bottle of fizz and drinking to—England?"

Everything moved so swiftly. Wilfred, as an officer in the Territorials, was given his commission; Wilfred the elder was absorbed into some great ship-building yard on the Tyne. Captain Cartwright came in, his face shining like a schoolboy given a holiday. He was going back to sea; he was to be in charge of a convoy; he was, Monica could see, itching to be off treading his own deck again.

Amos—they had thought that Amos was failing, he had talked himself of the "machinery running down". It seemed that his energy and vitality had been miraculously renewed. Nothing appeared to tire him; he worked long hours and, in addition to his work at Towers', sat on half a dozen committees. He never flagged, never allowed himself to become depressed. Narvik, the re-embarking from Namsos, the invasion by Germany of Holland, Belgium and Luxemburg— nothing shook his invincible optimism. On May 10th, 1940, he rushed into Monica's office, shouting, "It's started, aye, it's started!"

She looked up, startled and disturbed. "What has started?"

"The beginning of the end, the start of the victory. We've gotten Churchill as Prime Minister. Now, my lass, we'll see things! By gum, he'll put some guts into the lot of us, I tell you!"

Even Dunkirk did not shake him. He read everything available about it, wiping the tears from his eyes as he did so.

"By God," he said to Mary Ellen. "Makes you proud, glad that we belong to the same breed! Them little boats! It's glorious. Grandest thing since the Spanish Armada."

She said, "I didn't know as you cared so much, Amos luv."

He smiled at her fondly. "Bless you, I'm not a great talker, but I've always—cared."

He bought a piece of land at the back of Little Manor and had an air-raid shelter built. It was a new source of interest, and in spite of all the work which he was doing it was his toy, his relaxation.

"Ever since I first went on t'Council," he said, "I've been studying the housing problem. I've got a chance now to build summat on my own. Aye, it 'ul take fifty folks. Couple o' bath-rooms, proper sanitation, provisions—that 'ul be your job, Mary Ellen luv."

He had a board painted and set up at the end of the drive. It stated: "Sir Amos and Lady Towers invite you, in case of an air-raid, to make use of their shelter. Fifty people welcome."

Wilfred came home on leave, shabby, thinner, but hard and tough as whipcord. He arrived unexpectedly, and stood knocking at the front door. When it opened he demanded, "Can I use this famous shelter, please?

"I've got ten days, Grannie, ten glorious days," he said.

"Would you like to spend part of them in London, dear?" she asked. "Go with your muther and have a nice time."

He laughed. "I'd like to spend part of the time, and a jolly big part of the time, *in bed*, and another jolly big part of the time *in the bath*. The rest of the time eating your glorious food, Grannie, and talking to you all. Oh, it's grand to be home!"

He was, Monica felt, nearer and dearer than ever. He had grown older, she felt; the last remnants of boyhood had left him. He was a man come to man's estate, capable of bearing responsibility, of making decisions. Amos rushed him off to be measured for new uniforms, positively fatuous concerning the three stars which decorated Wilfred's shoulder-straps.

"Twenty-four—why, barely twenty-four!" Amos boasted. "I'll lay he'll finish up summat really big, will our Wilf."

Then he went off to Egypt, and Monica felt that every-thing had lost its colour. She had gone with him to London and together they had dined and danced, and she had felt that the clock had been put back more than twenty years, and that she was dancing again with Victor. She went back to Willingbrough depressed and unhappy.

Amos was still in the highest spirits. "Nay, we've gotten two grand chaps to help us, this Roosevelt and our own fellow. It 'ul take more'n Hitler to stand up against them two."

Nineteen-forty-two, and the victory of El Alamein came to give heart to a people who had borne many disappointments

and defeats with stoical bravery. It was in the December that
Wilfred was wounded. When the telegram came Monica felt
again the sense of crushing apprehension which she had felt
when Victor was killed. She hesitated to open the telegram,
and Mary Ellen seeing her distress said gently, "Let me have
it, my dear."

She opened it with fingers which were not quite steady,
then looked up and smiled. "God's good," she said. "It just
says that he's wounded, not even gravely or seriously or
dangerously."

Monica drew a deep breath. "Perhaps they'll send him
home. . . ."

Mary Ellen looked at the woman she had known for so
many years. She had watched her change from being young
and, if not beautiful, at least very charming. Well, she was
charming still at fifty. Her hair was shot with silver, but she
had kept her figure, and wore her clothes beautifully.

Very gently she said, "Maybe they will. I mind that they
sent our Vic home, to a hospital in Park Lane. Dada and I
went to see him there. Eh, what a luvely place, and the nurses
—why, Dad said they were like some of these young ladies in
the chorus of theatrical shows."

Impulsively Monica said, "Then—he came on to the
Duchess's hospital and I met him. Mary Ellen, are you sorry
that he met me?"

The older woman met her eyes very steadily. "Nay, I'm
not sorry, my dear. Vic loved you, and you gave him a lot of
happiness . . ." She paused then added, "Same as you've given
Dada and me. Ah, here's Amos."

He entered, smiling and brisk. He had lost a little weight,
but he looked well and full of energy. He went over to his
wife and kissed her, then caught sight of the telegram. The
healthy colour left his face and Mary Ellen laid her hand on
his arm.

"Nay, don't be faint-hearted, Amos. The lad's all right.
He's wounded, not gravely, not seriously, not dangerously.
Read it for yourself."

He took the flimsy sheet. "Aye, that's right. No mention
of it being summat terrible. Praise God."

For the first time since the war began Amos Towers "pulled
strings". Until then he had asked for no preferential treatment
in any form. He had run his business with strict honesty and

impartiality, but now when it was a question of Wilfred, he asked for favours. He wanted the lad in the district, where he might be visited by his family. Lord Stallingford, who admired and liked the energetic Amos, and respected his business ability—a thing which Stallingford himself had never possessed—interested himself. Wilfred was sent to the big hospital only two miles from Willingbrough.

Monica sat by his bed, content and at peace. He was safe; he might have to face a certain amount of pain from his wound, a great jagged wound in the thigh, but he was in no actual danger.

He said that the King had apparently collected more M.C.'s than he knew what to do with, and that someone had suggested that one might be handed to Wilfred Towers. His answers as to how he had won the decoration were evasive and unsatisfactory. He had done nothing; he had managed to obtain a pot of strawberry jam for a General; he had found some nylon stockings for the wife of the Brigadier; it seemed that there was no end to the reasons why he had been honoured.

Mary Ellen said, "I doubt that you tell a lot of lies, our Wilf. Still, it will luke very nice—Captain Wilfred Towers, M.C."

"If you don't mind, Grannie," he told her, "it's Major Towers."

"Well, what do you know about that!"

"Ability rewarded," he smiled.

"I doubt that we must have lost a lot of good men, when they have to make majors of lads like what you are, Wilf."

He was given a reasonably long leave, and they were completely happy. Amos put on a little weight, Mary Ellen lost the expression of anxiety which so often lurked in her eyes, Uncle Wilfred came over from Newcastle to see his nephew, and Monica felt that she was basking in the sunshine of an Indian Summer.

Wilfred returned to Italy, arriving there to take part in the taking of Perugia on July 20th, 1944. He went off very cheerful, saying that he had joined the Army to see the world, and that the end was not only in sight but coming nearer every day. On May 7th, 1945, all the German forces surrendered. The war was over. Monica, Mary Ellen and Amos looked at each other and smiled.

"It's over. . . ."

"Thank God. . . ."

Amos said, "What did I tell you from the start? What did
I tell you that Churchill and Roosevelt would do between
them? It's sad that Roosevelt had to go before he saw
everything finished and tidied up, as you might say, but—
why, maybe he saw the end getting very near before he
went."

Mary Ellen sighed. "What we're thinking is that Wilf 'ul
be coming back. All over the world muthers and grannies and
grand-dads are saying the same thing—'he'll be coming back'.
Aye, and there's plenty of women crying their eyes out, thinking, 'Why couldn't the end have come a bit sooner before he
went?' and they're remembering that they have to bring up
their bairns wi'oot a father."

Her husband nodded. "You mind me of a song that was
sung i' the Boer War—it was called 'The Absentminded
Beggar', by a gentleman called Mr. Kipling. It said, 'We must
help the kids as Tommy's left behind him.' I've been thinking
just the same. As you get older, Monica, you find yourself
luking back a lot, remembering old songs, old sayings and
suchlike.

"So, Mary Ellen, my dear, we're going to 'help the kids as
Tommy'—aye, and Jack an' all—'left behind him'. 'The
Army, the Navy, the Boys in the Air', the chaps as have kept
us safe from that Hitler and his gang." He put his fingers into
a waistcoat pocket and pulled out a folded piece of paper,
handing it to her and saying, "Lady Towers wishes to present
that to the Soldiers 'and Sailors' Family Association, and this
same Lady Towers only hopes that her husband and her
daughter and her grandson made it honestly, but Lady Towers
has her grave doubts—knowing them all as she does."

Mary Ellen opened the cheque. "Amos, it's ten thousand
pounds!"

He laughed. "I've made a mistake; I thought it was only
a hundred! Aye, it's ten thousand, and cheap enough to pay
for the benefits we've received and the lad as has been spared
to us."

"You knew about this, Monica? After all, you're a partner."

"I knew, Mary Ellen, so does Wilfred. He wrote that he
approved, as I do."

Mary Ellen refolded the cheque and wiped her eyes. "I

only hope that God is as pleased about this as what I am,
that's all."

With the return to peace Monica felt that some of the
energy which had stood Amos in such good stead during the
years of war began to diminish a little. He was cheerful; he
enjoyed working; he liked his talks with captains who had
served in the "Wavy Navy" and were slowly returning to
their various steamship companies. She found that he appeared to have more time to sit and chat with them, that he
enjoyed the fact of being able to entertain them in his comfortable office again. More and more work devolved on her,
and she accepted it willingly, content that Amos should be
willing to spare himself a little. He was seventy-three, nearly
seventy-four, his life had been filled with work; he had climbed
from the lowest rungs of the commercial ladder to the top-
most place in his own business. He had known hard work,
and he had savoured the fruits of success.

One evening Mary Ellen came to Monica's room. She said,
"D'you mind if I sit down for a bit of a talk? Monica, has it
struck you that Amos is *tired*?"

"My dear, I think that we're all tired. A war isn't con-
ducive to an easy life. Amos has been quite wonderful. No
wonder that he's glad to rest a little."

Mary Ellen shook her head. "He said a funny thing to me
when he came in tonight. He said, 'It's been a hardish day. I
wish that our Wilf could get home. I'd like to have him here.'
That's not like him, to talk that road. He spoke almost—well,
longingly."

Monica rose and put her arms round the little woman. Her
voice was very gentle, her expression very tender.

"Listen, my dear," she said, "this is where you have to be
very clever"—she smiled—"clever and cunning. He's tired.
We're none of us as young as we were once and Amos has—
never mind what the rest of us may think—borne the burden
and heat of the day. Tell him that *you* are tired, that you need
a rest from the housekeeping, and go down to Torquay or
Bournemouth. Stay at the very nicest hotel, and—take life
very easily. You persuade him to go with you, and I'll make
all arrangements."

Amos was surprisingly ready to fall in with his wife's plans,
and they departed for Bournemouth, leaving Monica in charge.
It was hard work; she often thought that it was more difficult

to run the huge business since the war ended than it had been when England was in a state of war. There were times when she longed to rush out of the office, spring into the car and drive—rapidly, furiously, to some quiet and tranquil place where she could forget orders, counterfoils, invoices, deliveries and the like, and let peace and silence wrap her round. There were days when the whole burden of the vast business seemed too heavy a weight for her to bear, when she was very conscious of the fact that she was over fifty and that for her too—as well as for Amos and Mary Ellen—life was now on the downgrade.

She longed for Wilfred's return, and sought eagerly among her letters each day for word from him telling her that he was on his way home. She longed for the sound of his voice, for his youth, his companionship and his love. Then at last came the telegram for which she had ached.

Leaving Venice today on my way home will telegraph you on arrival London. Demobilization. Love Wilfred.

Immediately Monica felt that her mental skies cleared. He was coming home! He was safe—for as long as he remained on foreign soil she had felt that "something might happen". Perhaps as she sat there he was coming down the Grand Canal, making ready to join the train at Mestre, and to begin his long journey home. For the first time Monica Towers felt that the war had come to an end.

He arrived two days later, tanned with the Italian sun, looking, she thought, taller than ever. The first night they sat talking into the small hours. There was a wonderful friendship and frankness between them, which Monica valued only second to the love which she knew existed between her son and herself.

"And tomorrow Grandfather and Grandmama will be home. They're driving back, eh? That will be nice. I doubt if many men love their grandparents as I love mine. To me they are—something apart. He is such a fine, simple fellow, and yet he's astute and desperately clever. I've never known him unjust, irritable or lacking in the most wonderful kindness and understanding. It's something of a heritage, Mummy, to have to follow a man like Amos Towers! It would be pretty awful if—when I come to be head of the firm—which, please God, won't be for years and years and years—if men said, 'He's all right, this Wilfred, but he doesn't bring to the business what either his grandfather or his mother brought to it.' "

Monica smiled at him. "Do you remember when you first went to school, Grannie quoted something to you out of *David Copperfield* about never being base or mean? You do! Well, *I'll* quote *David Copperfield* to you, darling. When Daniel Peggotty went to see David at school, Steerforth walked in. He talked in his usual charming way to Ham and Mr. Peggotty, and Peggotty—surely one of the most lovable of Dickens's characters—told him that he always did his best. Steerforth laughed, saying, 'And the best of men can do no more.' That's what Amos does—his best, that's what I try to do—my best, and that's what you'll do, my dear, and your best will be very, very good. I have no qualms."

When the Towers arrived home, Monica was shocked to find that Amos had lost weight; his clothes hung on him, he looked older and, she thought, more tired than when he went away. He was completely cheerful; his delight at seeing Wilfred was pathetic.

They sat, that evening, talking intimately as they had always done, and Monica noticed how often Mary Ellen sent anxious, tender glances towards her husband.

"And you had a good holiday, Grandfather?"

"Wilf, I believe that I've got a bit old for holidays, lad. Aye, it was a splendid hotel, people made a lot of fuss over us; you know, being 'Sir Amos and Lady Towers' *does* make a difference, say what you like, but—nay, I'm glad to be back in my own home again. These swagger hotels, with bands and chefs and the like, they're—why, they're impersonal. I was minded of a poem by a gentleman, a clergyman he was, who said, 'When all the world is old, lad, and all the trees are bare . . .' I can't remember the next line, but it goes on, 'Creep home and take your place, lad, the halt and maimed among, God grant you find one face there, you knew when you were young.' If that's not right, it's as right as makes no matter. Why, I'm lucky, there's your grandma—I knew her when I was young, so was she. I knew your muther when we were all a lot younger nor we are now, and"—he leaned towards Wilfred and laid his hand on Wilfred's brown one—"there's you. I've known you for twenty-odd years. Nay, it's a nice thought."

Wilfred laughed. "Grandfather, we're not halt and maimed,

we are all in full possession of our faculties and as strong as horses. I'm afraid I don't think much of your Reverend Kingsley. I like better, 'Grow old along of me, the best is yet to be.' So attention, I've news for you! I'm engaged to be married!" He looked round at them all, his good-looking face alight with happiness, his eyes shining. "Yes, I met her first in North Africa, then again in Naples and then in Rome. She's a nurse; she came out with the grandest old war horse of a Matron you've ever known! A Scotswoman, adored by half the Army—my girl's a Scotswoman." He laughed. "I seem to run to Scotswomen. Do you remember I was crazy about a girl who was a Scot? Dash it, I've forgotten her name— Philomel . . ."

Monica said, "Phillida."

"That's right. MacPhail. I thought it a nice name."

Mary Ellen said, "Nay, luv, get on; tell us about this young lady."

"Her name is Kirsteen——"

Monica said, "Not Kirsteen Fish! Did she work for Towers' in Glasgow?"

"How on earth do you know, Mummy? She did, as a matter of fact. She once worked for you, did some shorthand or typing. Fancy you remembering!"

Monica thought, "I remember everything that happened that day so clearly, so plainly." Aloud she said, "Yes, she's a very nice girl; nice little nose, covered with freckles. Go on, Wilfred."

"I met her Matron first, Janet Orchardson, with more medals and decorations than you could shake a stick at. She asked me to one of the nurses' dances. I met Kirsteen and— there it was."

Amos beamed at them all, then said, "You objected to that verse I quoted some time back. Well, maybe you'll not object to this verse. 'Lord, now lettest thou thy servant depart in peace—for mine eyes have seen thy salvation.' That's how I feel. We've been through wars and rumours of wars, and here we are united and luking forward to the future. Congratulations, Wilf, my dear lad, and bring the young lady to see us as soon as it's possible. I'm a bit wearied, I'll say—Good night, all, and God bless."

From that evening it seemed to Monica that Amos Towers laid down the reins; true, sometimes he drove down to the warehouse in the early afternoon, but he stayed at most for an hour or two, and then returned home. He left all decisions to her and to Wilfred. He was interested in what they told him of new orders here and new contracts made there, but it was an impersonal interest, as if he had no longer any real part in the business.

Mary Ellen was, as she had always been, very calm. She talked to Monica and said that it was just the works running down "like Amos said". She refused to urge him to make efforts, saying, "Nay, if he's tired, he's earned his rest, bless him."

His son came to see him, and told Mary Ellen that he was "shocked at the change in Dad".

"Nothing to be shocked about," she assured him. "Dad's been working longer nor what you've been alive, my dear. Dad's put us all where we are today, single-handed mostly. If he wants a bit of a rest, well—what for not? I'm not going to pester him to make efforts if he doesn't feel like it."

"Has the doctor seen him?"

"Tut, tut. What do you think we all are, Wilfred! Of course the doctor's seen him, even went so far as to bring Sir Martin Fanshaw from Manchester. What d'you think they talked about? Nay, you'd never guess! How to stop the smoke from factory chimneys making places mucky. There's a thing! When he left he told Dr. Mawson that he'd spent a most interesting afternoon. Dad was always clever."

"Then what is it—this weakness?" Wilfred asked, his rather heavy face grave with anxiety. "Did he give it a name?"

She patted his arm. "Lad, don't worrit. Dad's done all the work he needs to do, and if he wants a bit of a rest—he shall have it. Now, Wilf, don't worrit. It only upsets me, and it doesn't do a happorth of good. Everything's all right."

The person who was most unhappy over this gradual fading of Amos Towers was his much-loved Wilfred, Monica's son. The lad brought his girl to see Amos, who took an instant liking to her.

"Yon's all right, Wilf. I don't say that she's beautiful, but she's gotten a kind, healthy, sensible face, and I'll lay as she'll stand by you through thick and thin. Have her over again, lad. I'm right taken with her. You're right in love, eh?"

"Grandfather, I think she's grand—absolutely grand."

Amos chuckled. "Just what I thought about your grandma; what I've gone on thinking about her."

As Summer changed to Autumn and Autumn drifted into Winter, Amos decided that "bed is the best place"; he said that old blood ran thin and that he liked his comfort. "Bed's a grand place. I know where I'm well off."

Wilfred sat with him for hours; whether he was awake or asleep, the lad would sit there, very quiet, reading and glancing from time to time at the bed where Amos lay. Monica thought that she had never seen greater devotion from a young man to an old one. It was to Wilfred that Amos confided that he wished to see his lawyer, that he would like his son to come over from Newcastle, and finally that he felt that his chest was "a bit on the tight side".

His doctor pronounced it a mild attack of bronchitis, and was not unduly concerned, "though how he's managed to get it is a mystery".

Wilfred came from Newcastle, obviously worried and distressed; the lawyer came and was closeted with Amos for a long time. When he left he told Monica that he had rarely met a brain which was more active, more astute.

Dr. Mawson agreed that to have a nurse might be excellent, if only to spare Mary Ellen's strength, and to alleviate the anxiety which Monica and young Wilfred must feel when they were at the warehouse. It was a cold Winter, and the snow fell early. Again and again Amos would chuckle and boast that he knew where he was well off, and that he had no intention of getting up and "paddling about in the snow".

He said to Wilfred, "I'm over-old to find much pleasure in snow—nasty wet stuff. Leave it to the kids to enjoy."

Then one evening, when round the house lay that strange silence which is induced by a heavy fall of snow, the nurse came to Monica's room, where she was changing, and said that she was disturbed.

"His breathing isn't so good, Mrs. Towers. Would you telephone for Dr. Mawson? I want to get back to him."

Monica telephoned to the doctor, then flung on a dressing-gown and went to Amos. Wilfred and Mary Ellen were there, Wilfred with a face from which all vestige of colour was drained; Mary Ellen, looking a little drawn, holding her husband's hand and whispering, "Not in any pain, are you, luv?"

"No, just—a bit—short i' the wind."

There was silence for a few moments, then he asked, "Monica there?"

"I'm here, Amos dear."

"Aye, I'm short-sighted—without my glasses. You're a grand lass. I don't know what Muther and me'd have done without you. Where's Wilf?"

"Here, Grandfather, here." Amos moved his hand uncertainly, and Wilfred took it, holding it very gently. "There."

"Nice—warm hand. Be a good lad—to your muther and Grannie. Nay, I know you will be. Eh, I luv you—Wilf. It's been grand having you. Muther, hold my hand—bless you—what a grand woman. . . ."

He closed his eyes, and opened them again, to say, uncertainly, "No man has ever been so—so—blessed." His lids fell and did not rise again. A few moments later he stopped breathing.

Wilfred, tears pouring down his cheeks, said, "It's the end——"

His grandmother turned to him and said gently, "Not the end, luv, just the start somewhere else."

CHAPTER NINE

THEY sat together, Monica and Mary Ellen. The tumult and the shouting had died, the long procession—complete with two brass bands—had wound its way to and from the cemetery. Amos Towers had finished his last journey.

As a funeral it had been stupendous, and Monica knew that Amos would have given all the arrangements his whole-hearted approval. The skies had been grey and lowering as the monotonous strains of the Dead March—"in Saul"—had hung heavily on the air. The band which ended the procession had played "Will Ye No Come Back Again?", and the Scottish lament had sounded strange and weird in those surroundings, and at the funeral of a man who had no Scottish blood in his veins.

When the procession had returned to Little Manor, Monica had thanked the conductors of both bands, saying to the final band's director, "It was splendid. Sir Amos would have been most touched. But what made you choose that particular piece of music?"

The little man smoothed his rather thin, straggly moustache.

"Well, Mrs. Victor, I wanted the Dead March of Chopang, but it's a bit difficult. We only get one band practice a week, and—that Scotch piece always goes very well."

She had moved about in the crowd of people who came back to the house. They had eaten the food and drunk the drinks which were provided so lavishly, because Mary Ellen said, "Nay, nothing would have put Amos out more'n to have a poor do." They had partaken of everything with a kind of melancholy satisfaction, and yet, from time to time, the North Country humour insisted upon breaking through, and the guests slipped back into recounting reminiscences of Amos Towers which would have delighted no one more than Amos himself.

Wilfred, white-faced and heavy-eyed, seemed to Monica to have taken Amos Towers' death more to heart than anyone. He was assiduous in attending to everyone's wants; he was charming, deferential, kindly to each one irrespective of their class or importance in the social world of Willingbrough, but Monica, watching him, knew that he was suffering grimly and acutely.

Once in passing she caught his hand and pressed it. He turned and smiled.

"Am I doing all right, Mummy?" he whispered.

"Splendidly, darling."

"Is Grannie all right?"

"Uncle Wilfred is with her, in the drawing-room."

"Oh, good!" and he continued his patient round of the room.

Monica found an old man sitting in a corner eating sandwiches. He was so old that she wondered how he had managed to get to the funeral.

He said, "Let me make myself known, Mrs. Towers. My name is Clutterbuck. Councillor Clutterbuck, I was. I was present at the wedding of the late departed and his wife. I knew Mrs. Towers the elder very well. My dear wife passed away many years ago. Both Sir Amos and—ah, I referred to her as 'Mrs. Towers', I should have said Lady Towers—came to the funeral. I felt it only right to make an effort, and it *has* been an effort, to be present this afternoon."

Impulsively Monica said, "Would you like to speak to Lady Towers? Then the car shall take you home. I think that she would appreciate a little talk with you."

The old man nodded. "It would be a great pleasure, a great pleasure." She slipped her hand under his elbow, and they went out to the drawing-room. He said, "Wonderful the way that Sir Amos went from strength to strength. Wonderful man. This beautiful home!"

Monica opened the door of the drawing-room and said, "Mary Ellen, dear, here is someone who just wants a few words with you, then he's going home. Councillor Clutterbuck."

The little old man tottered forward. Monica thought, "He must be nearly ninety, bless him."

Mary Ellen rose and came towards him, her face shining. She was pale, but her bright eyes showed her pleasure. She might be "Lady Towers", but this man had been "the Master" when she was "in service" and she had not forgotten it.

She took his hand. "Why, now, sir, I do call this kind. To visit me in my trouble, and you not so young as you once were."

"Eighty-seven, Lady Towers. Eighty-seven."

"Nay, if you please, not so much of the 'Lady Towers', sir. Aye. Amos would be right pleased about this visit. I mind my wedding—oh, sit down, please sit down—when you made a most beautiful speech. And your dear wife, sir. Oh, what a *kind* lady she was! She was one as knew how to treat servants. If there'd been more like her there'd be no talk of 'servant shortage' today. I had the same to eat as what you had—oh, it brings back old times—times when Amos and me were courting."

Clutterbuck nodded. "That's right—happy days, happy days."

Tears were running down his cheeks, and Monica thought it wise to put an end to the conversation. She told him that the car was waiting. He shook hands warmly with Mary Ellen, and Monica piloted him out. As the door closed she heard Mary Ellen saying to her son, "Now that was kind, wasn't it? I did think a lot of that."

Slowly everyone dispersed. Wilfred was catching a train

back to Newcastle, and young Wilfred went to his room to write letters. Monica and Mary Ellen were left alone.

Mary Ellen sighed. "It's been a long day. Still, I'd not have had it different. It was all as he'd have liked it." She sighed again.

"Aye, we'll miss him. Monica, the one I'm sorriest for is young Wilf. He's broken-hearted. That lad loved Amos, same as Amos loved him. It's—it's queer."

The room was very quiet, the fire burnt steadily, there was an intimacy which brooded over everything, Monica felt, as if this was the time to make admissions, to ask questions. She leaned forward, and asked, "You know, Mary Ellen, don't you?"

The old eyes met hers, eyes which had once held the colour of gentians and now looked like forget-me-nots.

Mary Ellen nodded. "Yes, luv, I've known all along."

Rather breathlessly Monica said, "And you said—nothing."

Very quietly Mary Ellen replied, "No, and I'll tell you for why. My Amos maybe seemed to you just an ordinary, successful tradesman. To me—well, he was a god. I worshipped him, right from the time when he got back my shoe for me—I've told you that story—'til the other day when . . ." her voice shook for a second, "he left us. He was my sun, moon and stars, was Amos. Our Vic was the light of his eyes. When you told us that you were carrying Vic's bairn, I saw his face. It fair—lit up. Mind, then, I didn't know. Then as time went on, I understood what this bairn meant to Amos. To him it was like Vic being born again.

"Mind you, don't think as we ever made any difference between Wilf and Vic—they both had our love; they had the same chances, but there was something about Vic . . . Nay, I don't know. Amos used to call him—our 'Golden Lad'."

Monica said very softly, "You, too . . ."

"Then when you came and told us as you'd slipped, I felt uneasy. Then when the bairn was born and I held him while you came properly round, I looked at him. He wasn't any seven-months' baby! I knew our Vic too well to think that he'd—well, as they say—take his fun where he found it. Not our Vic! I'd heard him talk about you, and I knew that to him you were something—why, almost sacred.

"For a moment I felt black hatred in my heart. I could have killed you—aye, and the bairn, poor little thing. Then, when you were holding it, I went down to Amos. My dear, it was the biggest struggle I've ever been through in my life. There was my Amos, his eyes shining, luking like a young fellow. Crying, 'Muther, it's all right, eh? Tell me, is he'—the doctor had told him it was a little lad—'is he all right? Straight, nicely made?' Then his voice dropped a bit; he said, 'And Monica? Is she comfortable? Muther,' he said, 'that girl is all right, and we must luke after her. Her and the lad.' After that, I gave in. The boy meant happiness for my Amos, and you . . . you've turned out to be a God's blessing. I could no more have shattered his faith, broken his happiness, made him lose his faith in you, than I could have flown. Mind you, I didn't care tuppence about you—then. It was all Amos. I couldn't bear for him to be disappointed. If our Wilf had married, had bairns, I'd have been in a nice pickle, but he didn't, and gradually I began to think that it was all—God's will."

Monica said, "And you never told anyone?"

"My dear, I've learnt what it would do a lot of women good to learn—to keep my tongue still. I watched Amos luking at Wilf. I heard him talking about him—oft-times he'd talk to me when we went to bed. It was all 'the boy' this and 'the boy' that. Slowly, he began to talk about you, how he admired your pluck, how well you understood the business—and I knew that both you and Wilf were precious to him."

She leaned forward and laid her hand on Monica's knee.

"By then, I'd begun to feel that I couldn't bear to lose either of you—and that feeling has grown with the years, my dear."

"I'm not worthy of your love, nor of the love that Amos gave me. Wilfred—I hope he'll always be worthy of it. I think he will. You've given him wonderful examples. But I lied, deceived, cheated. I did everything that was mean and ignoble."

"Don't be over-hard on yourself. You've worked out your own salvation if anyone ever did."

Monica rose and stood with her arm resting on the mantel-shelf. She spoke as if she uttered her thoughts aloud.

"At first it was—I might as well admit it—just a physical attraction. I was young, and he fascinated me. Then Victor came, and I think Victor loved me almost at once," she laughed, "heaven only knows why. When it was too late—I fell in love with Victor. I knew that I had never loved the other man, never. What I felt for Victor was something almost frightening, it was so immense. I didn't marry Victor because I wanted to foist my child on to him. I married him because I was so desperately in love with him. He was going back to France. Do you remember that people said, during the '14-'18 war, that the life of a subaltern was six weeks at the Front? I couldn't bear to think that Victor might be killed and that . . . he'd never know how much I loved him.

"It must all sound strange, improbable, Mary Ellen, but I swear that I am speaking the truth."

"Aye, I know it's the truth—go on."

"We weren't given very long, but we crammed that time with happiness. I have never known such happiness. It's lasted me all my life, and it will be something I shall cherish for the rest of my life. Amos used to ask me why I didn't marry again. How could I marry any man—after Victor? Then again, I knew that marriage would mean more lies, more people to be deceived. Oh, I got so tired of lies and pretences. I felt that I was always standing with my back to the wall, watching, watching, watching, keeping alert so that I never made mistakes. It was ghastly sometimes.

"You and dear Amos, Wilfred and my own boy didn't make it any easier. You were all so kind and good to me, so generous with your praise, affection, and evidences of the trust you placed in me.

"Years went on, and I began to believe that I had finished with being forced to lie—although I realized that my whole life with you here was founded on lies—when another blow came. Wilfred met and fell in love with Phillida MacPhail."

"I mind how queer you went when Wilf told us——"

"Her father—was Wilfred's father. I had to begin lying again. I had to face hurting my son, but—I had to do it. I don't mind your knowing now. MacPhail died about a month ago. I saw it in *The Times*. The girl married an American millionaire. Wilfred's safe."

She sighed, then said, "There's my full confession, Mary Ellen."

"Aye, Catholics say that after confession you can get absolution. Not being a Catholic I don't rightly understand that, but maybe there's a lot in it. I used to say to my lads—Vic and Wilf—'Now, whatever you do as is naughty—come and tell me, and I'll forgive you. Come and say that you're sorry, tell me—truthfully—what you've done, and everything will be all right.' Happen that's the same idea. They were my bairns, and we're all God's bairns. I'm not all that religious, Monica, but I like to read a bit of my Bible every night. There were times when Amos would ask me to read it aloud. He was always very quick in getting to bed. He'd sit there luking at me with his kind, understanding eyes, and if it was a bit he liked, he'd say, 'Aye, it's a grand buke, choose how.' I mind one bit he always liked, same as I do, 'Much is forgiven her because she greatly loved.' To you, my dear, I don't say 'much'—I say, 'Everything is forgiven because you greatly loved.' "

"Then you want me to stay here, to go on—just as we are?"

Monica wiped her eyes, her tears had come while Mary Ellen spoke in her soft, North Country accent, speaking of simple yet profound things in her own simple fashion. Monica felt that for the first time since she married she could "lay down her arms".

When she spoke, Monica heard the return of her brisk, sensible tones. "Stay here? What else would you do? Wilf's good, hard-working, but he's over-young to carry the whole responsibility of a great business like what ours is. My Amos had laid away sufficient for me; without my touching the business, I shall be living in comfort for the rest of my life. He's left you the same share as he's left my Wilfred and your lad. He built that business, did Amos. It was his pride. He started pretty well from nothing. I'd think poorly of you—much as I love you, or of young Wilf—much as I love him—if you didn't do your duty to the business same as Amos did. Stay here! Nay, I never thought as you'd imagine you could do anything else. Besides," she smiled, "I'm a masterful woman, and I like my own road—and I want you here. I'm not a kissing body, but come here and give your muther a right loving kiss."

Monica knelt beside her, and Mary Ellen took her in her arms. The caress was so gentle, so reassuring, that Monica Towers, despite her fifty years, sobbed without restraint.

"Nay, nay, now," Mary Ellen chided her gently. "This 'ul never do. There, honey, that's better. Dry your eyes, and you can just slip up and bathe your face and put on some of that powder that smells so nice. Then go and tell Wilf to leave them letters, and to come down, and we'll all have a nice cup o' tea. There's nothing like tea for making you feel better."

As she spoke the door opened and Wilfred came in. He was pale and looked unhappy. When he saw that his mother had been crying he took a quick step towards her, holding out his hands.

"Mummy dear——"

Mary Ellen said, "Now, Wilf, don't set her off again. We've had a luvely talk, and a few tears never hurt anyone. Nothing your grandpa, bless him, hated more than to see folks miserable. Have you finished your letters, though I doubt you only wrote one to this young lady of yours, with the funny name? I reckon the sooner as she changes it to Towers, the better for everyone. Now, Monica luv, let's have that tea."

Gardone Riviera.
  March, 1953.